FAST RECIPE FOR DOOM

"Ho!" cried the enchanter. "You two claim to be magicians? How do I know you speak sooth?"

"Work a spell for him, Doc," said Shea.

Chalmers, with a look of baffled and apprehensive resignation, began to make a list of the properties needed. After he'd gathered them together he lit a fire and began an incantation.

Suddenly the oyster-colored smoke of the fire thickened and darkened. Chalmers bit off his chant in midstanza and scrambled back. A reptilian head a yard long was poking toward them out of the smoke . . . then another . . . and another.

"God bless my soul!" said Chalmers.

"He'd better," replied Shea.

Crawling from nothingness, complete with yellow cat's eyes and stinger-tipped tails, a seemingly endless stream of giant dragons began to lurch forward . . .

By L. Sprague de Camp
Published by Ballantine Books:

THE RELUCTANT KING
Volume One: THE GOBLIN TOWER
Volume Two: THE CLOCKS OF IRAZ
Volume Three: THE UNBEHEADED KING

THE ANCIENT ENGINEERS

THE TRITONIAN RING

THE FALLIBLE FIEND

LEST DARKNESS FALL

LOVECRAFT: A BIOGRAPHY

THE BEST OF L. SPRAGUE DE CAMP

THE COMPLEAT ENCHANTER
(with Fletcher Pratt)

The Compleat Enchanter:

The Magical Misadventures of Harold Shea

L. Sprague de Camp and Fletcher Pratt

A Del Rey Book

BALLANTINE BOOKS • NEW YORK

A Del Rey Book
Published by Ballantine Books

ACKNOWLEDGMENTS:
THE INCOMPLETE ENCHANTER (Including "The Roaring Trumpet" and "The Mathematics of Magic") copyright ©
1941 by Henry Holt and Company. A somewhat different
form of this novel appeared in the May and August 1940
issues of *Unknown*, copyright © by Street & Smith, Inc.

THE CASTLE OF IRON
Copyright © 1941 by Street & Smith, Inc., for *Unknown*,
April 1941.

ISBN 0-345-31435-2

Manufactured in the United States of America

Book Club Edition: December 1975

First Ballantine Books Edition: April 1976
Fifth Printing: August 1984

First Canadian Printing: May 1976

Cover art by The Brothers Hildebrandt

To
JOHN W. CAMPBELL, JR.,
of
gyronny, argent, and sable

CONTENTS

I write of things which I have neither seen nor learned from another, things which are not and never could have been, and therefore my readers should by no means believe them.

Lucian of Samosata

BOOK ONE

The Roaring Trumpet

1

THERE WERE THREE MEN AND A WOMAN IN THE room. The men were commonplace as to face, and two of them were commonplace as to clothes. The third wore riding breeches, semi-field boots, and a suède jacket with a tartan lining. The extra-fuzzy polo coat and the sporty tan felt with the green feather which lay on a chair belonged to him also.

The owner of this theatrical outfit was neither a movie actor nor a rich young idler. He was a psychologist, and his name was Harold Shea. Dark; a trifle taller, a little thinner than the average, he would have been handsome if his nose were shorter and his eyes farther apart.

The woman—girl—was a tawny blonde. She was the chief nurse at the Garaden Hospital. She possessed—but did not rejoice in—the name of Gertrude Mugler.

The other two men were psychologists like Shea and members of the same group. The oldest, the director of the others' activities, was bushy-haired, and named Reed Chalmers. He had just been asking Shea what the devil he meant by coming to work in such conspicuous garb.

Shea said, defensively: "I'm going to ride a horse when I leave this afternoon. Honest."

"Ever ridden a horse?" asked the remaining member of the group, a large, sleepy-looking young man named Walter Bayard.

"No," replied Shea, "but it's about time I learned."

Walter Bayard snorkled. "What you ought to say is that you're going to ride a horse so as to have an excuse for looking like something out of *Esquire*. First there was that phony English accent you put on

3

for a while. Then you took up fencing. Then last winter you smeared the place with patent Norwegian ski-grease, and went skiing just twice."

"So what?" demanded Shea.

Gertrude Mugler spoke up: "Don't let them kid you about your clothes, Harold."

"Thanks, Gert."

"Personally I think you look sweet in them."

"Unh." Shea's expression was less grateful.

"But you're foolish to go horseback riding. It's a useless accomplishment anyway, with automobiles—"

Shea held up a hand. "I've got my own reasons, Gert."

Gertrude looked at her wrist watch. She rose. "I have to go on duty. Don't do anything foolish, Harold. Remember, you're taking me to dinner tonight."

"Uh-huh."

"Dutch."

Shea winced. "Gert!"

"So long, everybody," said Gertrude. She departed in a rustle of starched cotton.

Walter Bayard snickered. "Big he-man. Dutch!"

Shea tried to laugh it off. "I've tried to train her not to pull those in public. Anyway she makes more money than I do, and if she'd rather have four dates a week Dutch than two on my budget, why not? She's a good kid."

Bayard said: "She thinks you're the wistful type, Harold. She told the super—"

"She did? Goddamn it. . . ."

Chalmers said: "I cannot see, Harold, why you continue to—uh—keep company with a young woman who irritates you so."

Shea shrugged. "I suppose it's because she's the one not impossible on the staff with whom I'm sure I'll never do anything irrevocable."

"While waiting for the dream-girl?" grinned Bayard. Shea simply shrugged again.

"That's not it," said Bayard. "The real reason, Doctor, is that she got the psychological jump on him the first time he took her out. Now he's afraid to quit."

"It's not a matter of being afraid," snapped Shea. He stood up and his voice rose to a roar of surprising

4

volume: "And furthermore, Walter, I don't see that it's any damn business of yours. . . ."

"Now, now, Harold," said Chalmers. "There's nothing to be gained by these outbursts. Aren't you satisfied with your work here?" he asked worriedly.

Shea relaxed. "Why shouldn't I be? We do about as we damn please, thanks to old man Garaden's putting that requirement for a psychology institute into his bequest to the hospital. I could use more money, but so could everybody."

"That's not the point," said Chalmers. "These poses of yours and these outbreaks of temper point to an inner conflict, a maladjustment with your environment."

Shea grinned. "Call it a little suppressed romanticism. I figured it out myself long ago. Look. Walt here spends his time trying to become midwestern tennis champ. What good'll it do him? And Gert spends hours at the beauty parlor trying to look like a fallen Russian countess, which she's not built for. Another fixation on the distant romantic. *I* like to dress up. So what?"

"That's all right," Chalmers admitted, "if you don't start taking your imaginings seriously."

Bayard put in: "Like thinking dream-girls exist." Shea gave him a quick glare.

Chalmers continued: "Oh, well, if you start suffering from—uh—depressions, let me know. Let's get down to business now."

Shea asked: "More tests on hopheads?"

"No," said Chalmers. "We will discuss the latest hypotheses in what we hope will be our new science of paraphysics, and see whether we have not reached the stage where more experimental corroboration is possible.

"I've told you how I checked my premise, that the world we live in is composed of impressions received through the senses. But there is an infinity of possible worlds, and if the senses can be attuned to receive a different series of impressions, we should infallibly find ourselves living in a different world. That's where I got my second check, here at the hospital, in the examination of—uh—dements, mainly para-

5

noiacs. You"—he nodded at Bayard—"set me on the right track with that report on the patient with Korsakov's psychosis.

"The next step would be to translate this theoretical data into experiment: that is, to determine how to transfer persons and objects from one world into another. Among the dements, the shift is partial and involuntary, with disastrous results to the psyche. When—"

"Just a minute," interrupted Shea. "Do you mean that a complete shift would actually transfer a man's body into one of these other worlds?"

"Very likely," agreed Chalmers, "since the body records whatever sensations the mind permits. For complete demonstration it would be necessary to try it, and I don't know that the risk would be worth it. The other world might have such different laws that it would be impossible to return."

Shea asked: "You mean, if the world were that of classical mythology, for instance, the laws would be those of Greek magic instead of modern physics?"

"Precisely. But—"

"Hey!" said Shea. "Then this new science of paraphysics is going to include the natural laws of all these different worlds, and what we call physics is just a special case of paraphysics—"

"Not so fast, young man," said Chalmers. "For the present, I think it wise to restrict the meaning of our term 'paraphysics' to the branch of knowledge that concerns the relationship of these multiple universes to each other, assuming that they actually exist. You will recall that careless use of the analogous term 'metaphysics' has resulted in its becoming practically synonymous with 'philosophy.' "

"Which," said Shea, "is regarded by some as a kind of scientific knowledge; by others as a kind of knowledge outside of science; and by still others as unscientific and therefore not knowledge of any kind."

"My, my, very neatly put," said Chalmers, fishing out a little black notebook. "E. T. Bell could not have said it more trenchantly. I shall include that

6

statement of the status of philosophy in my next book."

"Hey," said Shea, sitting up sharply, "don't I even get a commission?"

Chalmers smiled blandly. "My dear Harold, you're at perfect liberty to write a book of your own; in fact I encourage you."

Bayard grinned: "Harold would rather play cowboy. When I think of a verbal pearl, I don't go around casting it promiscuously. I wait till I can use it in print and get paid for it. But to get back to our subject, how would you go about working the shift?"

Chalmers frowned. "I'll get to that, if you give me time. As I see it, the method consists of filling your mind with the fundamental assumptions of the world in question. Now, what are the fundamental assumptions of our world? Obviously, those of scientific logic."

"Such as—" said Shea.

"Oh, the principle of dependence, for instance. 'Any circumstance in which alone a case of the presence of a given phenomenon differs from the case of its absence is casually relevant to that phenomenon.'"

"Ouch!" said Shea. "That's almost as bad as Frege's definition of number."

Bayard droned: "'The number of things in a given class—'"

"Stop it, Walter! It drives me nuts!"

"'—is the class of all classes that are similar to the given class.'"

"Hrrm," remarked Chalmers. "If you gentlemen are through with your joke, I'll go on. If one of these infinite other worlds—which up to now may be said to exist in a logical but not in an empirical sense—is governed by magic, you might expect to find a principle like that of dependence invalid, but principles of magic, such as the Law of Similarity, valid."

"What's the Law of Similarity?" asked Bayard sharply.

"The Law of Similarity may be stated thus: Effects resemble causes. It's not valid for us, but primitive peoples firmly believe it. For instance, they think you can make it rain by pouring water on the ground with appropriate mumbo jumbo."

7

"I didn't know you could have fixed principles of magic," commented Shea.

"Certainly," replied Chalmers solemnly. "Medicine men don't merely go through hocus-pocus. They believe they are working through natural laws. In a world where everyone firmly believed in these laws, that is, in one where all minds were attuned to receive the proper impressions, the laws of magic would conceivably work, as one hears of witch-doctors' spells working in Africa today. Frazer and Seabrook have worked out some of these magical laws. Another is the Law of Contagion: Things once in contact continue to interact from a distance after separation. As you—"

Shea snapped his fingers for attention. "Just a second, Doctor. In a world such as you're conceiving, would the laws of magic work because people believed in them, or would people believe in them because they worked?"

Chalmers put on the smile that always accompanied his intellectual rabbit-punches. "That question, Harold, is, in Russell's immortal phrase, a meaningless noise."

"No, you don't," said Shea. "That's the favorite dodge of modern epistemologists: every time you ask them a question they can't answer, they smile and say you're making a meaningless noise. I still think it's a sensible question, and as such deserves a sensible answer."

"Oh, but it is meaningless," said Chalmers. "As I can very easily demonstrate, it arises from your attempt to build your—uh—conceptualistic structure on an absolutistic rather than a relativistic basis. But I'll come back to that later. Allow me to continue my exposition.

"As you know, you can build up a self-consistent logic on almost any set of assumptions—"

Bayard opened his half-closed eyes and injected another sharp observation: "Isn't there a flaw in the structure there, Doctor? Seems to me your hypothesis makes transference to the future possible. We should then become aware of natural laws not yet discovered and inventions not yet made. But the future naturally

8

won't be ignorant of our method of transference. Therefore we could return to the present with a whole list of new inventions. These inventions, launched into the present, would anticipate the future, and, by anticipating, change it."

"Very ingenious, Walter," said Chalmers. "But I'm afraid you overlook something. You might indeed secure transference to *a* future, but it would not necessarily be *the* future, the actual future of our own empirico-positivist world. A mental frame of reference is required. That is, we need a complete set of concepts of the physical world, which concepts condition the impressions received by the mind. The concepts of the future will be the product of numerous factors not now known to us. That is—"

"I see," said Shea. "The frame of reference for the actual future is not yet formed, whereas the frames of reference for all past worlds are fixed."

"Precisely. I would go beyond that. Transference to any world exhibiting such a fixed pattern is possible, but to such worlds only. That is, one could secure admission to any of H. G. Wells' numerous futures. We merely choose a series of basic assumptions. In the case of the actual future we are ignorant of the assumptions.

"But speculative extrapolation from our scanty supply of facts has already carried us—uh—halfway to Cloud-Cuckoo land. So let us return to our own time and place and devote ourselves to the development of an experimental technique wherewith to attack the problems of paraphysics.

"To contrive a vehicle for transposition from one world to another, we face the arduous task of extracting from the picture of such a world as that of the *Iliad* its basic assumptions, and expressing these in logical form—"

Shea interrupted: "In other words, building us a syllogismobile?"

Chalmers looked vexed for an instant, then laughed. "A very pithy way of expressing it, Harold. You are wasting your talents, as I have repeatedly pointed out, by not publishing more. I suggest, however, that the term 'syllogismobile' be confined for the present to discussions among us members of the Garaden Institute. When the time comes to try to impress our psychological colleagues with the importance of paraphysics, a somewhat more dignified mode of expression will be desirable."

Harold Shea lay on his bed, smoked, and thought. He smoked expensive English cigarettes, not because he liked them especially, but because it was part of his pattern of affectation to smoke something unusual. He thought about Chalmers' lecture.

It would no doubt be dangerous, as Chalmers had warned. But Shea was getting unutterably bored with life. Chalmers was able but stuffy; if brilliance and dullness could be combined in one personality, Reed Chalmers combined them. While in theory all three members of the Institute were researchers, in practice the two subordinates merely collected facts and left to the erudite Doctor the fun of assembling them and generalizing from them.

Of course, thought Shea, he did get some fun out of his little poses, but they were a poor substitute for real excitements. He liked wearing his new breeches and boots, but riding a horse had been an excruciating experience. It also had none of the imaginary thrill of swinging along in a cavalry charge, which he had half-unconsciously promised himself. All he got was the fact that his acquaintances thought him a nut. Let 'em; he didn't care.

But he was too good a psychologist to deceive himself long or completely. He did care. He wanted to make a big impression, but he was one of those unfortunates who adopt a method that produces the effect opposite to the one they want.

Hell, he thought, no use introspecting myself into the dumps. Chalmers says it'll work. The old bore misses fire once in a while, like the time he tried to psychoanalyze the cleaning woman and she thought he was proposing marriage. But that was an error of technique, not of general theory. Chalmers was sound enough on theory, and he had already warned of dangers in the practical application in this case.

10

Yes. If he said that one could transport oneself to a different place and time by formula, it could be done. The complete escape from—well, from insignificance, Shea confessed to himself. He would be the Columbus of a new kind of journey!

Harold Shea got up and began to pace the floor, excited by the trend of his own thoughts. To explore —say the world of the *Iliad*. Danger: one might not be able to get back. Especially not, Shea told himself grimly, if one turned out to be one of those serf soldiers who died by thousands under the gleaming walls of Troy.

Not the *Iliad*. The Slavic twilight? No; too full of man-eating witches and werewolves. Ireland! That was it—the Ireland of Cuchulinn and Queen Maev. Blood there, too, but what the hell, you can't have adventure without some danger. At least, the dangers were reasonable open-eye stuff you could handle. And the girls of that world—they were something pretty slick by all description.

It is doubtful whether Shea's colleagues noticed any change in his somewhat irregular methods of working. They would hardly have suspected him of dropping Havelock Ellis for the Ulster and Fenian legendary cycles with which he was conditioning his mind for the attempted "trip." If any of them, entering his room suddenly, had come on a list with many erasures, which included a flashlight, a gun, and mercurochrome, they would merely have supposed that Shea intended to make a rather queer sort of camping expedition.

And Shea was too secretive about his intentions to let anyone see the equipment he selected: A Colt .38 revolver with plenty of ammunition, a stainless-steel hunting knife—they ought to be able to appreciate metal like that, he told himself—a flashlight, a box of matches to give him a reputation as a wonder worker, a notebook, a Gaelic dictionary, and, finally, the *Boy Scout Handbook,* edition of 1926, as the easiest source of ready reference for one who expected to live in the open air and in primitive society.

11

Shea went home after a weary day of asking questions of neurotics, and had a good dinner. He put on the almost-new riding clothes and strapped over his polo coat a shoulder pack to hold his kit. He put on the hat with the green feather, and sat down at his desk. There, on sheets of paper spread before him, were the logical equations, with their little horseshoes, upside-down T's, and identity signs.

His scalp prickled a trifle as he gazed at them. But what the hell! Stand by for adventure and romance! He bent over, giving his whole attention to the formulas, trying not to focus on one spot, but to apprehend the whole:

"If P equals not-Q, Q implies not-P, which is equivalent to saying either P or Q or neither, but not both. *But* if not-P is not implied by not-Q, the counter-implicative form of the proposition—"

There was nothing but six sheets of paper. Just that, lying in two neat rows of three sheets, with perhaps half an inch between them. There should be strips of table showing between them. But there was nothing—nothing.

"The full argument thus consists in an epicheirematic syllogism in Barbara, the major premise of which is *not* the conclusion of an enthymeme, though the minor premise of which may or may not be the conclusion of a non-Aristotelian sorites—"

The papers were still there, but overlaying the picture of those six white rectangles was a whirl of faint spots of color. All the colors of the spectrum were represented, he noted with the back of his mind, but there was a strong tendency toward violet. Round and round they went—round—and round—

"If either P or Q is true or (Q or R) is true then either Q is true or (P or R) is false—"

Round and round— He could hear nothing at all. He had no sense of heat or cold, or of the pressure of the chair seat against him. There was nothing but millions of whirling spots of color.

Yes, he could feel temperature now. He was cold. There was sound, too, a distant whistling sound, like that of a wind in a chimney. The spots were fading into a general grayness. There was a sense of pres-

12

sure, also, on the soles of his feet. He straightened his legs—yes, standing on something. But everything around him was gray—and bitter cold, with a wind whipping the skirts of his coat around him.

He looked down. His feet were there all right— hello, feet, pleased to meet you. But they were fixed in grayish-yellow mud which had squilched up in little ridges around them. The mud belonged to a track, only two feet wide. On both sides of it the gray-green of dying grass began. On the grass large flakes of snow were scattered, dandruffwise. More were coming, visible as dots of darker gray against the background of whirling mist, swooping down long parallel inclines, growing and striking the path with the tiniest *ts*. Now and then one spattered against Shea's face.

He had done it. The formula worked!

2

"WELCOME TO IRELAND!" HAROLD SHEA MURMURED to himself. He thanked heaven that his syllogismobile had brought his clothes and equipment along with his person. It would never have done to have been dumped naked onto this freezing landscape. The snow was not alone responsible for the grayness. There was also a cold, clinging mist that cut off vision at a hundred yards or so. Ahead of him the track edged leftward around a little mammary of a hill, on whose flank a tree rocked under the melancholy wind. The tree's arms all reached one direction, as though the wind were habitual; its branches bore a few leaves as gray and discouraged as the landscape itself. The tree was the only object visible in that wilderness of mud, grass and fog. Shea stepped toward it. The serrated leaves bore the indentations of the Northern scrub oak.

But that grows only in the Arctic Circle, he thought. He was bending closer for another look when he heard the *clop-squash* of a horse's hoofs on the muddy track behind him.

He turned. The horse was very small, hardly more than a pony, and shaggy, with a luxuriant tail blowing round its withers. On its back sat a man who might have been tall had he been upright, for his feet nearly touched the ground. But he was hunched before the icy wind driving in behind. From saddle to eyes he was enveloped in a faded blue cloak. A formless slouch hat was pulled tight over his face, yet not so tight as to conceal the fact that he was full-bearded and gray.

Shea took half a dozen quick steps to the roadside. He addressed the man with the phrase he had composed in advance for his first human contact in the world of Irish myth:

"The top of the morning to you, my good man, and would it be far to the nearest hostel?"

He had meant to say more, but paused uncertainly as the man on the horse lifted his head to reveal a proud, unsmiling face in which the left eye socket was unpleasantly vacant. Shea smiled weakly, then gathered his courage and plunged on: "It's a rare bitter December you do be having in Ireland."

The stranger looked at him with much of the same clinical detachment he himself would have given to an interesting case of schizophrenia, and spoke in slow, deep tones: "I have no knowledge of hostels, nor of Ireland; but the month is not December. We are in May, and this is the Fimbulwinter."

A little prickle of horror filled Harold Shea, though the last word was meaningless to him. Faint and far, his ear caught a sound that might be the howling of a dog—or a wolf. As he sought for words there was a flutter of movement. Two big black birds, like oversize crows, slid down the wind past him and came to rest on the dry grass, looked at him for a second or two with bright, intelligent eyes, then took the air again.

"Well, where *am* I?"

14

"At the wings of the world, by Midgard's border."

"Where in hell is that?"

The deep voice took on an edge of annoyance. "For all things there is a time, a place, and a person. There is none of the three for ill-judged questions and empty jokes." He showed Shea a blue-clad shoulder, clucked to his pony and began to move wearily ahead.

"Hey!" cried Shea. He was feeling good and sore. The wind made his fingers and jaw muscles ache. He was lost in this arctic wasteland, and this old goat was about to trot off and leave him stranded. He leaned forward, planting himself squarely in front of the pony. "What kind of a runaround is this, anyway? When I ask someone a civil question—"

The pony had halted, its muzzle almost touching Shea's coat. The man on the animal's back straightened suddenly so that Shea could see he was very tall indeed, a perfect giant. But before he had time to note anything more he felt himself caught and held with an almost physical force by that single eye. A stab of intense, burning cold seemed to run through him, inside his head, as though his brain had been pierced by an icicle. He felt rather than heard a voice which demanded, "Are you trying to stop *me*, niggeling?"

For his life, Shea could not have moved anything but his lips. "N-no," he stammered. "That is, I just wondered if you could tell me how I could get somewhere where it's warm—"

The single eye held him unblinkingly for a few seconds. Shea felt that it was examining his inmost thoughts. Then the man slumped a trifle so that the brim of his hat shut out the glare and the deep voice was muffled. "I shall be tonight at the house of the bonder Sverre, which is the Crossroads of the World. You may follow." The wind whipped a fold of his blue cloak, and as it did so there came, apparently from within the cloak itself, a little swirl of leaves. One clung for a moment to the front of Shea's coat. He caught it with numbed fingers, and saw it was an ash leaf, fresh and tender with the bright green of spring—in the midst of this howling wilderness, where only arctic scrub oak grew!

15

Shea let the pony pass and fell in behind, head down, collar up, hands deep in pockets, squinting against the snowflakes. He was too frozen to think clearly, but he tried. The logical formulas had certainly thrown him into another world. But he hardly needed the word of Old Whiskers that it was not Ireland. Something must have gone haywire in his calculations. Could he go back and recheck them? No—he had not the slightest idea at present what might have been on those six sheets of paper. He would have to make the best of his situation.

But what world had he tumbled into? A cold, bleak one, inhabited by small, shaggy ponies and grim old blue-clad men with remarkable eyes. It might be the world of Scandinavian mythology. Shea knew very little about such a world, except that its No. 1 guy was someone named Odinn, or Woden, or Wotan, and there was another god named Thor who threw a sledge hammer at people he disliked.

Shea's scientific training made him doubt whether he would actually find these gods operating as gods, with more-than-human powers; or, for that matter, whether he would see any fabulous monsters. Still, that stab of cold through his head and that handful of ash leaves needed explaining. Of course, the pain in his head might be an indication of incipient pneumonia, and Old Whiskers might make a habit of carrying ash leaves in his pockets. But still—

The big black birds were keeping up with them. They didn't seem afraid, nor did they seem to mind the ghastly weather

It was getting darker, though in this landscape of damp blotting paper Shea could not tell whether the sun had set. The wind pushed at him violently, forcing him to lean into it; the mud on the path was freezing, but not quite gelid. It had collected in yellow gobs on his boots. He could have sworn the boots weighed thirty pounds apiece, and they had taken in water around the seams, adding clammy socks to his discomfort. A clicking sound, like a long roll of castanets, made him wonder until he realized it was caused by his own teeth.

He seemed to have been walking for days, though he knew it could hardly be a matter of hours. Reluctantly he took one hand from his pocket and gazed at his wrist watch. It read 9:56; certainly wrong. When he held the watch to a numbed ear he discovered it had stopped. Neither shaking nor winding could make it start.

He thought of asking his companion the time, but realized that the rider would have no more accurate idea than himself. He thought of asking how much farther they had to go. But he would have to make himself heard over the wind, and the old boy's manner did not encourage questions.

They plodded on. The snow was coming thickly through the murky twilight. Shea could barely make out the figure before him. The path had become the same neutral gray as everything else. The weather was turning colder. The snowflakes were dry and hard, stinging and bouncing where they struck. Now and then an extra puff of wind would snatch a cloud of them from the moor, whirling it into Shea's face. He would shut his eyes to the impact, and when he opened them find he had blundered off the path and have to scurry after his guide.

Light. He pulled the pack around in front of him and fumbled in it till he felt the icy touch of the flashlight's metal. He pulled it out from under the other articles and pressed the switch button. Nothing happened, nor would shaking, slapping, or repeated snappings of the switch produce any result.

In a few minutes it would be too dark for him to follow the man on the pony by sight alone. Whether the old boy liked it or not, Shea would have to ask the privilege of holding a corner of his cloak as a guide.

It was just as he reached this determination that something in the gait of the pony conveyed a sense of arrival. A moment more and the little animal was trotting, with Shea stumbling and skidding along the fresh snow behind as he strove to keep pace. The pack weighed tons, and he found himself gasping for breath as though he were running up a forty-five-degree angle instead of on an almost level path.

Then there was a darker patch in the dark-gray universe. Shea's companion halted the pony and slid off. A rough-hewn timber door loomed through the storm, and the old man banged against it with his fist. It opened, flinging a flood of yellow light out across the snow. The old man stepped into the gap, his cloak vividly blue in the fresh illumination.

Shea, left behind, croaked a feeble "Hey!" just managing to get his foot in the gap of the closing door. It opened full out and a man in a baggy homespun tunic peered out at him, his face rimmed with drooping whiskers. "Well?"

"May I c-c-come in?"

"Umph," said the man. "Come on, come on. Don't stand there letting the cold in!"

3

SHEA STOOD IN A KIND OF ENTRYHALL, SOAKING IN the delicious warmth. The vestibule was perhaps six feet deep. At its far end a curtain of skins had been parted to permit the passage of the old man who preceded him. The bonder Sverre—Shea supposed this would be his host—pulled them still wider. "Lord, use this as your own house, now and forever," he murmured with the perfunctory hurry of a man repeating a formula like "Pleased to meet you."

The explorer of universes ducked under the skins and into a long hall paneled in dark wood. At one end a fire blazed, apparently in the center of the floor, though bricked round to knee height. Around it were a number of benches and tables. Shea caught a glimpse of walls hung with weapons—a huge sword, nearly as tall as he was, half a dozen small spears or javelins, their delicate steel points catching ruddy high lights from the torches in brackets; a kite-shaped shield with metal overlay in an intricate pattern—

No more than a glimpse. Sverre had taken him by the arm and conducted him through another door, shouting: "Aud! Hallgerda! This stranger's half frozen. Get the steam room ready. Now, stranger, you come with me."

Down a passage to a smaller room, where the whiskered man ordered him: "Get off those wet clothes. Strange garments you have. I've never seen so many buttons and clasps in all my days. If you're one of the Sons of Muspellheim, I'll give you guesting for the night. But I warn you for tomorrow there be men not far from here who would liefer meet you with a sword than a handclasp." He eyed Shea narrowly a moment. "Be you of Muspellheim?"

Shea fenced: "What makes you think that?"

"Traveling in those light clothes this far north. Those that hunt the red bear"—he made a curious motion of his hand as though tracing the outline of an eyebolt in the air—"need warm hides as well as stout hearts." Again he gave Shea that curiously intent glance, as though trying to ravel some secret out of him.

Shea asked: "This is May, isn't it? I understand you're pretty far north, but you ought to get over this cold snap soon."

The man Sverre moved his shoulders in a gesture of bafflement. "Mought, and then mought not. Men say this would be the Fimbulwinter. If that's so, there'll be little enough of warm till the roaring trumpet blows and the Sons of the Wolf ride from the East, at the *Time*."

Shea would have put a question of his own, but Sverre had turned away grumpily. He got rid of his clammy shorts instead, turning to note that Sverre had picked up his wrist watch.

"That's a watch," he offered in a friendly voice.

"A thing of power?" Sverre looked at him again, and then a smile of comprehension distended the wide beard as he slapped his knee. "Of course. Mought have known. You came in with the Wanderer. You're all right. One of those southern warlocks."

From somewhere he produced a blanket and whisked it around Shea's nude form. "This way now," he ordered. Shea followed through a couple of doors to another small room, so full of wood smoke that it made him cough. He started to rub his eyes, then just in time caught at the edge of his blanket. There were two girls standing by the door, neither of them in the least like the Irish colleens he had expected to find. Both were blonde, apple-cheeked, and rather beamy. They reminded him disagreeably of Gertrude Mugler.

Sverre introduced them: "This here's my daughter Aud. She's a shield girl; can lick her weight in polar bears." Shea, observing the brawny miss, silently agreed. "And this is Hallgerda. All right, you go on in. The water's ready to pour."

In the center of the small room was a sunken hearth full of fire. On top of the fire had been laid a lot of stones about the size of potatoes. Two wooden buckets full of water sat by the hearth.

The girls went out, closing the door. Shea, with the odd sensation that he had experienced all this at some previous time—"It must be part of the automatic adjustment one's mind makes to the pattern of this world," he told himself—picked up one of the buckets. He threw it rapidly on the fire, then followed it with the other. With a hiss, the room filled with water vapor.

Shea stood it as long as he could, which was about a minute, then groped blindly for the door and gasped out. Instantly a bucketful of ice water hit him in the face. As he stood pawing the air and making strangled noises a second bucketful caught him in the chest. He yelped, managing to choke out, *"Glup . . . stop . . . that's enough!"*

Somewhere in the watery world a couple of girls were giggling. It was not till his eyes cleared that he realized it was they who had drenched him, and that he was standing between them without his protecting blanket.

His first impulse was to dash back into the steam room. But one of the pair was holding out a towel which it seemed only courtesy to accept. Sverre was approaching unconcernedly with a mug of something. Well, he thought, if they can take it, I can. He discovered that after the first horrible moment his embarrassment had vanished. He dried himself calmly while Sverre held out the mug. The girls' clinical indifference to the physical Shea was more than ever like Gertrude.

"Hot mead," Sverre explained. "Something you don't get down south. Aud, get the stranger's blanket. We don't want him catching cold."

Shea took a gulp of the mead, to discover that it tasted something like ale and something like honey. The sticky sweetness of the stuff caught him in the throat at first, but he was more afraid of losing face before these people than of being sick. Down it went, and after the first gulp it wasn't so bad. He began to feel almost human.

"What's your name, stranger?" inquired Sverre.

Shea thought a minute. These people probably didn't use family names. So he said simply, "Harold."

"Hungh?"

Shea repeated, more distinctly. "Oh," said Sverre. "Harald." He made it rhyme with "dolled."

Dressed, except for his boots, Shea took the place on the bench that Sverre indicated. As he waited for food he glanced round the hall. Nearest him was a huge middle-aged man with red hair and beard, whose appearance made Shea's mind leap to Sverre's phrase about "the red bear." His dark-red cloak fell back to show a belt with carved gold work on it. Next to him sat another redhead, more on the sandy order, small-boned and foxy-faced, with quick, shifty eyes. Beyond Foxy-face was a blond young man of about Shea's size and build, with a little golden fuzz on his face.

At the middle of the bench two pillars of black wood rose from floor to ceiling, heavily carved, and so near the table that they almost cut off one seat. It was now occupied by the gray-bearded, one-eyed man Shea had followed in from the road. His floppy hat was on the table before him, and he was half leaning around one of the pillars to talk to another big blond man—a stout chap whose face bore an expression of permanent good nature, overlaid with worry. Leaning against the table at his side was an empty scabbard that could have held a sword as large as the one Shea had noticed on the wall.

The explorer's eye, roving along the table, caught and was held by that of the slim young man. The latter nodded, then rose and came round the table, grinning bashfully.

"Would ye like a seat companion?" he asked. "You know how it is, as Hávamál says:

Care eats the heart   If you cannot speak
        To another all your thought."

He half-chanted the lines, accenting the alliteration in a way that made the rhymeless verse curiously attractive. He went on: "It would help me a lot with the *Time* coming, to talk to a plain human being. I don't mind saying I'm scared. My name's Thjalfi."

"Mine's Harald," said Shea, pronouncing it as Sverre had done.

"You came with the Wanderer, didn't ye? Are ye one of those outland warlocks?"

It was the second time Shea had been accused of that. "I don't know what a warlock is, honest," said he, "and I didn't come with the Wanderer. I just got lost and followed him here, and ever since I've been trying to find out where I am."

Thjalfi laughed, then took a long drink of mead. As Shea wondered what there was to laugh at, the young man said: "No offense, friend Harald. Only it does seem mighty funny for a man to say he's lost at Crossroads of the World. Ha, ha, I never did hear the like."

"The where did you say?"

"Sure, the Crossroads of the World! You must come from seven miles beyond the moon not to know that. Hai! You picked a queer time to come, with all of *Them* here"—he jerked his finger toward the four

22

bearded men. "Well, I'd keep quiet about not having the power, if I was you. Ye know what the Háva-mál says:

> To the silent and sage   Does care seldom come
>   When he goes to a house as guest.

Ye're likely to be in a jam when the trouble starts if ye don't have protection from one of *Them,* but as long as *They* think ye're a warlock, Uncle Fox will help you out."

He jabbed a finger to indicate the small, sharp-featured man among the four, then went on quickly: "Or are ye a hero? If ye are, I can get Redbeard to take ye into his service when the *Time* comes."

"What time? Tell me what this is all—" began Shea, but at that moment Aud and another girl appeared with wooden platters loaded with food.

"Hai, sis!" called Thjalfi cheerfully, and tried to grab a chop from the platter carried by the second, a girl Shea had not previously seen. The girl kicked him neatly on the shin and set it before the late-comer.

The meal consisted of various meats, with beside them a big slab of bread, looking as though it had been cut from a quilt. There was no sign of knife, fork, or any vegetable element. Of course, they would not have table silver, Shea assured himself. He broke off a piece of the bread and bit into it. It was better than it looked. The meat that he picked up rather gingerly was apparently a boiled pork chop, well-cooked and well-seasoned. But as he was taking the second bite, he noted that the shield girl, Aud, was still standing beside him.

As he looked round Aud made a curtsy and said rapidly: "Lord, with this meal as with all things, your wishes are our law. Is there aught else that you desire?"

Shea hesitated for a moment, realizing it was a formula required by politeness and that he should make some remark praising the food. But he had had a long drink of potent mead on an empty stomach.

23

The normal food habits of an American urged him to action.

"Would it be too much to ask whether you have any vegetables?" he said.

For one brief second both the girl and Thjalfi stared at him. Then both burst into shrieks of laughter, Aud staggering back toward the wall, Thjalfi rolling his head forward on his arms. Shea sat staring, red with embarrassment, the half-eaten chop in his hand. He hardly noticed that the four men at the other side of the table were looking at him till the big red-headed man boomed out:

"Good is the wit when men's children laugh before the Æsir! Now, Thjalfi, you shall tell us what brings this lightness of heart."

Thjalfi, making no effort to control himself, managed to gasp out: "The . . . the warlock Harald wants to eat a turnip!" His renewed burst of laughter was drowned in the roar from Redbeard, who leaned back, bellowing: "Oh, ho, ho, ho, ho! Turnip Harald, ha, ha ha!" His merriment was like a gale with the other three adding their part, even the blue-cloaked Wanderer.

When they had quieted down a little Shea turned to Thjalfi. "What did I do?" he asked. "After all—"

"Ye named yourself Turnip Harald! I'm afeared ye spoiled your chance of standing under Redbeard's banner at the *Time*. Who'd want a hero that ate turnips? In Asgard we use them to fatten hogs."

"But—"

"Ye didn't know better. Well, now your only chance is Uncle Fox. Ye can thank me for saying ye're a warlock. Besides, he loves a good joke; the only humorist in the lot of them, I always say. But eating turnips—ha, ha, that's the funniest thing I've heard since the giant tried to marry the Hammer Thrower!"

Shea, a trifle angry and now completely mystified, turned to ask explanations. Before he could frame the words there was a pounding at the door. Sverre admitted a tall man, pale, blond and beardless, with a proud, stately face and a huge golden horn slung over his back. "There's another of *Them*," whispered

Thjalfi. "That's Heimdall. I wonder if all twelve of *Them* are meeting here."

"Who the devil are *They?*"

"*Sh!*"

The four bearded men nodded welcome to the newcomer. He took his place beside the Wanderer with lithe grace and immediately began to say something to the older man, who nodded in rapt attention. Shea caught a few of the words: "—fire horses, but no use telling you with the Bearer of Bad Tidings present." He nodded contemptuously toward Uncle Fox.

"It is often seen," said the latter, raising his voice a trifle but addressing the red-bearded man as though continuing a conversation begun before, "that liars tell few lies when those are present who can see the truth."

"Or it may be that I have that to tell which I do not wish to have repeated to our enemies by the Evil Companion," said Heimdall, looking straight at Uncle Fox.

"There are even those," continued the latter evenly, still paying Heimdall no attention, "who, having no character of their own, wish to destroy all character by assassinating the reputations of others."

"Liar and thief!" cried Heimdall angrily, bringing his fist down on the table and almost snarling. Shea saw that his front teeth were, surprisingly, of gold.

"Here," rumbled the large redhead, judicially. "Let there be an allaying of the anger of the Æsir in the presence of mortals."

"Let there also," snapped the small man, "be an allaying of insults in the mouth of—"

"All insults are untrue," said Heimdall. "I state facts."

"Facts! Few are the facts that come from that long wagging chin. Facts like the tale of having nine mothers, or the boast of that horn and the great noise it will make— Beware lest mice nest in it and it fail to give a squeak."

25

"You shall hear my trumpet at the *Time,* Father of Lies. And you will not like the sound."

"Some would say that called for the sword."

"Try it. Here is the blade that will carve your stinking carcass."

"Why, you—" Foxy-face and Heimdall were on their feet and bellowing at each other. Their voices had a volume that made Shea wince. The other three bearded men rose and began shouting also. Above their heads the two black birds who had been the Wanderer's companions fled round and round with excited cries.

Just as it looked as though the two original disputants were certain to fling themselves at each other's throat, the bigger redhead grabbed the smaller one by the shoulders and forced him down. "Sit down!" he thundered. The Wanderer, his sonorous voice full of outraged dignity, shouted: "This is disgraceful! We shall have no respect left. I command you to be quiet, both of you!"

"But—" yelled Heimdall.

The Wanderer silenced him with a gesture. "Nothing you can say will be heard. If either of you speaks to the other before bedtime, he shall have nothing less than my gravest displeasure."

Heimdall subsided and went over to a far corner to sit and glare at Fox-face, who returned the glare. Thjalfi whispered to the awed Shea: "It's like this every time three or four of *Them* get together. They're supposed to set us a good example, but the first thing ye know they're at it like a gang of drunken berserks."

"I'd still like to know who *They* are," said Shea.

"Do you mean ye really don't know?" Thjalfi stared at him with eyes full of honest rustic perplexity. "Don't that beat all, now? I wouldn't have believed it if ye hadn't asked for those turnips. Well, the one that was scrapping with Heimdall is Loki. The big red-bearded one next to him is Thor. The old man, the Wanderer, is Odinn, and the fat one is Frey. Have ye got them straight now?"

Shea looked hard at Thjalfi, but there was nothing in the latter's face but the most transparent serious-

26

ness. Either he had stepped through the formula into some downright dream, or he was being kidded, or the five were local Scandinavian chieftains who for some reason had named themselves after the gods of the old Norse pantheon. The remaining possibility—that these were actually gods—was too wildly improbable for consideration. Yet, those birds—the glance he had received from Odinn—and he knew that Odinn was always represented as one-eyed—

The big redhead called Thor got up and went over to the pair whom Thjalfi had identified as Odinn and Frey. For a few minutes they muttered, heads together. At the conclusion of the conference Odinn got up, clapped his floppy hat on his head, whirled his blue cloak around him, took a last gulp of mead and strode out the door.

As the door banged behind him, Loki and Heimdall half rose to their feet. Immediately Thor and Frey jumped up, with the former rumbling: "No more! Save your blows, sons of Asgard, for the *Time*. Or if you must deal buffets, exchange them with me." He lifted a fist the size of a small ham, and both subsided. "It is time for bed, in any case. Come along, Loki. You, too, Thjalfi."

Thjalfi rose reluctantly. "I'll speak a word for ye to Uncle Fox in the morning," he murmured in farewell. "Working for these Æsir is no fun. They're an ornery lot, but I suppose we're better off with 'em than without 'em, what with the *Time* coming. Ye know what Ulf, the poet says:

Bare is the breast   Without banner before it
When heroes bear weapons To the wrack of the world.

Good night."

Shea was not at all sure he wanted to work for Loki as a warlock, whatever that was. There was something sly about the man, uncomfortable. The graceful and forthright Heimdall had impressed him

27

more in spite of the latter's lack of a sense of humor, he mused.

A small noise at the door was Sverre, putting his head in for a look around and then vanishing again. Of the buxom young women nothing had been seen since they took up the wooden platters. Though the house was obviously going to bed, Shea found himself not in the least sleepy. It could hardly be much after nine o'clock. But in a world without artificial light other than that of torches, people would rise and set with the sun. Shea wondered whether he, too, would come around to that dismal habit. Probably, unless he succeeded in getting back to his own world. That was a rather upsetting thought. But, hell, he had taken the risk with his eyes open. Even if this was not the world he had expected to land in, it was still one in which his twentieth-century appliances should give him certain advantages. It would be time enough to worry when—

"Hai, turnip man," said Heimdall suddenly from his corner. "Fill a couple of mugs and bring them hither, will you?"

Shea felt his temper rise at this dictatorial manner. But whatever or whoever Heimdall was, he looked fully capable of enforcing authority. And though the words were peremptory, the tone of voice was evidently meant for kindness. He obeyed.

"Sit down," said Heimdall. "You have been called Harald. Is that correct?"

"Yes, I was told you are Heimdall."

"Nothing less than the truth. I am also known as the Watcher, the Son of Nine Mothers, the Child of Fury, and the Golden. I prefer the titles."

"Well, look here, Heimdall, what's all this—"

"Children of men use the titles or call me sir," said Heimdall severely and rather pompously.

"Sorry, sir."

Heimdall looked down his long nose and condescended a smile that showed the gold teeth. "To me this familiarity is not unpleasant, for I have also been called the Friend of Men. But the Lord of Asgard disapproves."

"You mean Odinn?"

28

"None other."

"The old guy—pardon me, I mean the elderly one-eyed gentleman?"

"You are a well of knowledge."

"I ran into him out on the moor yesterday and followed him here."

"That is not hidden. I saw you."

"You did? Where were you?"

"Many miles eastaway. I also heard your remarks to him. Lucky you were not to have been struck dead."

Shea almost said, "Aw, don't try to kid me." Just in time he remembered the piercing, icy glance Odinn had given him and held his tongue. It wouldn't do to take chances till he knew more about what chances he was taking, what system of natural laws governed this world into which he had fallen. Heimdall was watching him with a slightly amused smile.

"I also heard you tell Thjalfi that you are no warlock, but you know not what it means. You must be from far. However"—he smiled again at Shea's expression of consternation—"few are sorry for that. I'll keep your secret. A joke on the Master of Deception—ho, ho, ho!"

He drank. "And now, child of an ignorant mother," he went on, "it is yet to be seen that you have knowledge of strange things. I propose that we amuse ourselves with the game of questions. Each shall ask of the other seven questions, and he who answers best shall be adjudged the winner. Ask, mortal!"

Seven questions. Shea considered a moment how he could make them yield him the most information. "Where has Odinn gone?" he asked finally.

"One," said Heimdall. "He has gone to the gates of Hell to summon from her grave a woman centuries dead."

"Did you say Hell, honest?" asked Shea.

"It is not to be doubted."

"Well, well, you don't say so." Shea was covering his own incredulity and confusion. This man—god—individual was more difficult than any psychopathic he had ever questioned. He gathered his mental forces for the next try.

"What is Odinn doing that for?"

"Two," replied Heimdall. "The *Time* is coming. Balder dies, and the Æsir need advice. The Wanderer believes that the spae-wife buried at the gates of Hell can tell us what we need to know."

The vaguely ominous statements about the *Time* were beginning to get on Shea's nerves. He asked, "What is meant by the statement, 'the *Time* is coming'?"

"Three. Ragnarök, as all men know. All men but you alone, dewy-eyed innocent."

"What's Ragnarök?"

"Four. The end of the world, babe in a man's body."

Shea's temper stirred. He didn't like this elaborate ridicule, and he didn't think it fair of Heimdall to count his last question, which had been merely a request to explain an unfamiliar word in the previous answer. But he had met irritatingly irrelevant replies at the Garaden Institute and managed to keep himself under control.

"When will all this happen?"

"Five. Not men, or gods, or Vanir, or even the dwarfs know, but it will be soon. Already the Fimbulwinter, the winter in summer that precedes Ragnarök, is upon us."

"They all say there's going to be a battle. Who will win?" Shea was proud of himself for that question. It covered both the participants and the result.

"Six. Gods and men were glad to have the answer to that, youngling, since we shall stand together against the giant folk. But for the present there is this to be said: our chances are far from good. There are four weapons of great power among us: Odinn's spear, Gungnir; the Hammer of Thor that is called Mjöllnir; Frey's sword, the magic blade Hundingsbana; and my own good sword which bears the name of Head." He slapped the hilt of the sword that hung by his side. "But some of the giants, we do not know how or who, have stolen both the great Hammer and Frey's sword. Unless they are recovered it may be that gods and men will drink of death together."

Shea realized with panic that the world whose destruction Heimdall was so calmly discussing was the one in which he, Harold Shea, was physically living. He was at the mercy of a system of events he could not escape.

"What can I do to keep from getting caught in the gears?" he demanded, and then, seeing Heimdall look puzzled, "I mean, if the world's going to bust up, how can I keep out of the smash?"

Heimdall's eyebrows went up. "Ragnarök is upon us, that not gods know how to avoid—and you, son of man, think of safety! The answer is nothing. And now this is your seventh question and it is my turn to ask of you."

"But—"

"Child of Earth, you weary me." He stared straight into Shea's eyes, and once more there was that sensation of an icicle piercing his brain. But Heimdall's voice was smooth. "From which of the nine worlds do you come, strangest of strangers, with garments like to none I have seen?"

Shea thought. The question was a little like, "Have you quit beating your wife?" He asked cautiously, "Which nine worlds?"

Heimdall laughed lightly. "Ho—I thought I was to be the questioner here. But there is the abode of the gods that is Asgard, and that is one world; and the homes of the giants, that are Jötunheim, Musspellheim, Niflheim, and Hell, or five worlds in all. There is Alfheim where live the dwarfs; and Svartalfheim and Vanaheim which we do not know well, though it is said the Vanir shall stand with us at the *Time*. Lastly there is Midgard, which is overrun with such worms as you."

Shea yawned. The mead and warmth were beginning to pull up on him. "To tell the truth, I don't come from any of them, but from outside your system of worlds entirely."

"A strange answer is that, yet not so strange, but it could be true," said Heimdall, thoughtfully. "For I can see the nine worlds from where I sit and nowhere such a person as yourself. Say nothing of this to the other Æsir, and above all to the Wanderer. He

31

would take it ill to hear there was a world in which he held no power. Now I will ask my second question. What men or gods rule this world of yours?"

Shea found himself yawning again. He was too tired for explanations and flipped off his answer. "Well, some say one class and some say another, but the real rulers are called traffic cops. They pinch you—"

"Are they then some form of crab-fish?"

"No. They pinch you for moving too fast, wheres a crab pinches you for moving too slowly."

"Still they are sea gods, I perceive, like my brother Ægir. What is their power?"

Shea fought a losing battle against another yawn. "I'm sorry I seem to be sleepy," he said. "Aren't you going to bed soon, Golden?"

"Me? Ho, ho! Seldom has such ignorance been seen at the Crossroads of the World. I am the Watcher of the Gods, and never sleep. Sleepless One is, indeed, another of my titles. But it is to be seen that it is otherwise with you, youngling, and since I have won the game of questions you may go to bed."

An angry retort rose to Shea's lips at this calm assumption of victory, but he remembered that icy glare in time. Heimdall, however, seemed able to read his mind. "What! You would argue with me? Off to bed—and remember our little plot against the Bringer of Discord. Henceforth you are Turnip Harald, the bold and crafty warlock."

Shea risked just one more question. "What is a warlock, please, sir?"

"Ho, ho! Child from another world, your ignorance is higher than a mountain and deeper than a well. A warlock is a wizard, an enchanter, a weaver of spells, a raiser of spirits. Good-night, Turnip Harald."

The bedroom proved to have a sliding door. Shea found it no bigger than a Pullman section and utterly without ventilation. The bed was straw-stuffed and jabbed him. He could not find comfort. After an hour or so of tossing, he had the experience, not uncommon on the heels of a day of excitements, of finding himself more wide-awake than in the beginning.

For a time his thoughts floated aimlessly; then he

told himself that, since this was an experiment, he might as well spend the sleepless hours trying to assemble results. What were they?

Well, firstly, that there had been an error either in the equations or his use of them, and he had been pitched into a world of Scandinavian mythology —or else Scandinavian history. He was almost prepared to accept the former view.

These people talked with great conviction about their Ragnarök. He was enough of a psychologist to recognize their sincerity. And that icy stare he had felt from Odinn and then Heimdall was something, so far as he knew, outside ordinary human experience. It might be a form of hypnosis, but he doubted whether the technique, or even the idea of hypnotism, would be known to ancient viking chiefs. No, there was something definitely more than human about them.

Yet they had human enough attributes as well. It ought not to be beyond the powers of an experimental psychologist to guide his conduct by analyzing them a little and making use of the results. Odinn? Well, he was off to the gates of Hell, whither Shea had no desire to follow him. Not much to be made of him, anyway, save a sense of authority.

What about Loki? A devastatingly sharp tongue that indicated a keen mind at work. Also a certain amount of malice. Uncle Fox, Thjalfi had called him, and said he was fond of jokes. Shea told himself he would not be surprised to find the jokes were often of a painful order. Working for him might be difficult, but Shea smiled to himself as he thought how he could surprise the god with so simple an object as a match.

Frey he had hardly noticed, Thor apparently was no more than a big, good-natured bruiser, and Thjalfi, the kind of rustic one would find in any country town, quoting Eddic lays instead of the Bible.

Heimdall, however, was a more complex character, certainly lacking in Loki's sense of humor. And he quite evidently felt he had a position of dignity to maintain with relation to the common herd—as witness his insistence on titles. But equally evidently, he was prepared to accept the responsibilities of that position, throw himself heart and soul and with quite a good mind into the right side of the scales—as Loki was not. Perhaps that was why he hated Loki. And Heimdall, underneath the shell of dignity, had a streak of genuine kindness. One felt one could count on him—and deciding he liked Heimdall the best of the lot, Shea turned over and went to sleep.

4

SHEA AWOKE WITH A SET OF FUR-BEARING TEETH AND a headache that resembled the establishment of a drop-forging plant inside his brain—whether from the mead or the effect of those two piercing glances he had received from Heimdall and Odinn he could not tell. It was severe enough to stir him to a morning-after resolution to avoid all three in the future.

When the panel of his bedroom slid back he could hear voices from the hall. Thor, Loki, and Thjalfi were at breakfast as he came in, tearing away with knives and fingers at steaks the size of unabridged dictionaries. The foxy-faced Loki greeted him cheerfully: "Hail, hero of the turnip fields! Will your lordship do us the honor of breakfasting with us?"

He shoved a wooden platter with a hunk of meat on it toward Shea and passed along one of a collection of filled mugs. Shea's mouth was dry, but he almost gagged when a pull at the mug showed it contained beer and sour beer at that.

Loki laughed. "Ridiculous it is," he said, "to see the children of men, who have no fixed customs, grow uneasy when customs about them change. Harald of the Turnips, I am told you are a notable warlock."

Shea looked at his plate. "I know one or two tricks," he admitted.

"It was only to be expected that a hero of such

34

unusual powers would be modest. Now there is this to be said: a man fares ill at Ragnarök unless he have his place. Would you be one of my band at the *Time?*"

Shea gulped. He was still unconvinced about this story of a battle and the end of the world, but he might as well ride with the current till he could master it. "Yes, sir, and thank you."

"The worm consents to ride on the eagle's wings. Thank *you,* most gracious worm. Then I will tell you what you must do; you must go with us to Jötunheim, and that will be a hard journey."

Shea remembered his conversation with Heimdall the night before. "Isn't that where some of the giants live?"

"The frost giants to be exact. That lying Sleepless One claims to have heard Thor's hammer humming somewhere in their castle; and for all of us it will be well to find that weapon. But we shall need whatever we possess of strength and magic in the task—unless, Lord Turnip Eater, you think you can recover it without our help."

Shea gulped again. Should he go with them? He had come looking for adventure, but enough was enough. "What is adventure?" he remembered reading somewhere, with the answer, "Somebody else having a hell of a tough time a thousand miles away." Only—

Thjalfi had come round the table, and said in a low voice:

"Look. My sister Röskva is staying here at the Crossroads, because the Giant Killer don't think Jötunheim would be any place for a woman. That leaves me all alone with these Æsir and an awful lot of giants. I'd be mighty obliged if ye could see your way to keep me company."

"I'll do it," said Shea aloud. Then he realized that his impulsiveness had let him in for something. If Loki and Thor were not sure they could recover the hammer without help, it was likely to be an enterprise of some difficulty. Still, neither Æsir nor giants knew about matches—or the revolver. They would do for magic till something better came along.

35

"I've already spoken to the Lord of the Goat Chariot," Thjalfi was saying. "He'd be glad to have ye come, but he says ye mustn't disgrace him by asking to eat turnips. Ye'd best do something about those clothes. They're more than light for this climate. Sverre-bonder will lend you some others."

Sverre was glad to take the inadequate polo coat and riding breeches as security for the loan of some baggy Norse garments. Shea, newly dressed in accordance with his surroundings, went outside. A low, cheerless sun shone on the blinding white of new snow. As the biting cold nipped his nose Shea was thankful for the yards of coarse wool in which he was swathed.

The goat chariot was waiting. It was as big as a Conestoga wagon, notwithstanding that there were only two wheels. A line of incised runic letters was etched in black around the gold rim; the body was boldly painted red and gold. But the goats constituted the most remarkable feature. One was black, the other white, and they were as big as horses.

"This here's Tooth Gnasher," said Thjalfi, indicating the nigh goat, "and that there's Tooth Gritter," waving at the off goat, the black one. "Say, friend Harald, I'd be mighty obliged if ye'd help me tote the stuff out."

Shea, ignorant of what the "stuff" was, followed Thjalfi into the bonder's house, where the latter pointed to a big oak chest. This, he explained, held the Æsir's belongings. Thjalfi hoisted one end by its bronze handle. Shea took hold of the other, expecting it to come up easily. The chest did not move. He looked at Thjalfi, but the latter merely stood, holding his end off the floor without apparent effort. So Shea took his handle in both hands and gave a mighty heave. He got his end up, but the thing seemed packed with ingots of lead. The pair went through the door, Thjalfi leading, Shea staggering and straining along in the rear. He almost yelled to Thjalfi to hurry and ease the horrible strain on his arms, but this would involve so much loss of face that he stuck

36

it out. When they reached the chariot Shea dropped his end into the snow and almost collapsed across the chest. The icy air hurt his lungs as he drew great gasps of breath.

"All right," said Thjalfi calmly, "you catch hold here, and we'll shove her aboard." Shea forced his unwilling body to obey. They manhandled one end of the chest onto the tail of the chariot and somehow got the whole thing aboard. Shea was uncomfortably aware that Thjalfi had done three-quarters of the work, but the rustic seemed not to notice.

With the load in, Shea leaned against one of the shafts, waiting for his heart to slow down and for the aches in his arms and chest to subside. "Now it is to be seen," said a voice, "that Thjalfi has persuaded another mortal to share his labors. Convenient is this for Thjalfi."

It was the foxy-faced Loki, with the usual note of mockery in his voice. Once more Shea's temper began to rise. Thjalfi was all right—but it *did* look as though he had talked Shea into coming along for the dirty work. If—Whoa! Shea suddenly remembered Loki's title—"Bringer of Discord," and Thjalfi's warning about his jokes. Uncle Fox would doubtless think it very funny to get the two mortals into a quarrel, and for the sake of his own credit he didn't dare let the god succeed.

Just then came a tug at his cloak. He whirled round; Tooth Gritter had seized the lower edge of the garment in his teeth and was trying to drag it off him. "Hey!" cried Shea, and dragged back. The giant goat shook its head and held on while Loki stood with hands on hips, laughing a deep, rich belly-laugh. He made not the slightest move to help Shea. Thjalfi came running round and added his strength to Shea's. The cloak came loose with a rip; the two mortals tumbled backward. Tooth Gritter calmly munched the fragment he had torn from the cloak and swallowed it.

Shea got up scowling and faced a Loki purple with amusement. "Say, you," he began belligerently, "what the hell's so damn funny—" At that instant Thjalfi seized him from behind and whirled him away as

37

though he were a child. "Shut up, ye nitwit!" he flung into Shea's ear. "Don't ye know he could burn ye to a cinder just by looking at ye?"

"But—"

"But nothing! Them's gods! No matter what they do ye dassn't say boo, or they'll do something worse. That's how things be!"

"Okay," grumbled Shea, reflecting that rustics the world over were a little too ready to accept "that's how things be," and that when the opportunity came he would get back some of his own from Loki.

"Ye want to be careful around them goats," continued Thjalfi. "They're mean, and they eat most anything. I remember a funny thing as happened a fortnight back. We found five men that had frozen to death on the moor. I says we ought to take them in so their folks could give 'em burial. Thor says all right, take 'em in. When we got to the house we was going to stay at, the bonder didn't see as how there was any point in bringing 'em inside, 'cause when they got thawed out, they'd get kind of strong. So we stacked 'em in the yard, like firewood. Next morning, would ye believe it, those goats had gotten at 'em and et 'em up. Everything but their buckles!" Thjalfi chuckled to himself.

As Shea was digesting this example of Norse humor, there came a shout of "Come on, mortals!" from Thor, who had climbed into the chariot. He clucked to the goats, who leaned forward. The chariot wheels screeched and turned.

"Hurry!" cried Thjalfi and ran for the chariot. He had reached it and jumped aboard with a single huge bound before Shea even started. The latter ran behind the now rapidly moving vehicle and tried to hoist himself up. His fingers, again numbed with cold, slipped, and he went sprawling on his face in the snow. He heard Loki's infuriating laugh. As he pulled himself to his feet he remembered bitterly that he had made this "journey" to escape the feeling of insignificance and maladjustment that his former life had given him.

There was nothing to do but run after the chariot again. Thjalfi pulled him over the tail and slapped the snow from his clothes. "Next time," he advised, "ye better get a good grip before ye try to jump. Ye know what it says in Hávamál:

It is better to live   Than to lie a corpse;
    The quick man catches the cart."

Thor, at the front of the chariot, said something to the goats. They broke from a trot to a gallop. Shea, clutching the side of the vehicle, became aware that it had no springs. He found he could take the jolting best by flexing his legs and yielding to the jerks.

Loki leaned toward him, grinning. "Hai, Turnip Harald! Let us be merry!" Shea smiled uncertainly. Manner and voice were friendly, but might conceal some new malicious trick. Uncle Fox continued airily: "Be merry while you can. These hill giants are uncertain of humor where we go. He, he, I remember a warlock named Birger. He put a spell on one of the hill giants so he married a goat instead of a girl. The giant cut Birger open, tied one end of his entrails to a tree, and chased him around it. He, he!"

The anecdote was not appetizing and the chariot was bounding on at the same furious pace, throwing its passengers into the air every time it hit a bump. Up—down—bang—up—down—bang. Shea began to regret his breakfast.

Thjalfi said: "Ye look poorly, friend Harald; sort of goose-green. Shall I get something to eat?"

Shea had been fighting his stomach in desperate dread of losing further prestige. But the word "eat" ended the battle. He leaned far over the side of the chariot.

Loki laughed. Thor turned at the sound, and drowned Loki's laughter in a roar of his own. "Haw, haw, haw! If you foul up my chariot, Turnip Harald, I'll make you clean it." There was a kind of good-natured contempt in the tone, more galling than Uncle Fox's amusement.

Shea's stomach finally ceased its convulsions and

39

he sat down on the chest, wishing he were dead. Perhaps it was the discomfort of the seat, but he soon stood up again, forcing himself to grin. "I'll be all right now. I'm just not used to such a pace."

Thor turned his head again and rumbled. "You think this fast, springling? You have in no wise any experience of speed. Watch." He whistled to the goats, who stretched their heads forward and really opened out. The chariot seemed to spend most of the time in the air; at intervals, it would hit a ridge in the road with a thunderous bang and then take off again. Shea clung for dear life to the side, estimating their speed at something between sixty and seventy miles an hour. This is not much in a modern automobile on a concrete road, but something quite different in a two-wheeled springless cart on a rutted track.

"Wow! Wow! Wow!" yelled Thor, carried away by his own enjoyment. "Hang on; here's a curve!" Instead of slackening speed the goats fairly leaped, banking inward on the turn. The chariot lurched in the opposite direction. Shea clung with eyes closed and one arm over the side. "Yoooeee!" bellowed Thor.

It went on for ten minutes more before Thjalfi suggested lunch. Shea found himself actually hungry again. But his appetite qualied at the sight of some slabs that looked like scorched leather.

"*Ulp*—what's that?"

"Smoked salmon," said Thjalfi. "Ye put one end in your mouth, like this. Then ye bite. Then ye swallow. Ye have sense enough to swallow, I suppose?"

Shea tried it. He was amazed that any fish could be so tough. But as he gnawed he became aware of a delicious flavor. When I get back, he thought, I must look up some of this stuff. Rather, *if* I get back.

The temperature rose during the afternoon, and toward evening the wheels were throwing out fans of slush. Thor roared "Whoa!" and the goats stopped. They were in a hollow between low hills, gray save where the snow had melted to show dark patches of grass. In the hollow itself a few discouraged-looking spruces showed black in the twilight.

"Here we camp," said Thor. "Goat steak would be our feasting had we but fire."

"What does he mean?" Shea whispered to Thjalfi.

"It's one of the Thunderer's magic tricks. He slaughters Tooth Gnasher or Tooth Gritter and we can eat all but the hide and bones. He magics them back to life."

Loki was saying to Thor: "Uncertain is it, Enemy of the Worm, whether my fire spell will be effective here. In this hill-giant land there are spells against spells. Your lightning flash?"

"It can shiver and slay but not kindle in this damp," growled Thor. "You have a new warlock there. Why not make him work?"

Shea had been feeling for his matches. They were there and dry. This was his chance. "That'll be easy," he said lightly. "I can make your fire as easy as snapping my fingers. Honest."

Thor glared at him with suspicion. "Few are the weaklings equal to any works," he said heavily. "For my part I always hold that strength and courage are the first requirements of a man. But I will not gainsay that occasionally my brothers feel otherwise, and it may be that you can do as you say."

"There is also cleverness, Wielder of Mjöllnir," said Loki. "Even your hammer blows would be worthless if you did not know where to strike; and it may be that this outlander can show us some new thing. Now I propose a contest, we two and the warlock. The first of us to make the fire light shall have a blow at either of the others."

"Hey!" said Shea. "If Thor takes a swat at me, you'll have to get a new warlock."

"That will not be difficult." Loki grinned and rubbed his hands together. Though Shea decided the sly god would find something funny about his mother's funeral, for once he was not caught. He grinned back, and thought he detected a flicker of approval in Uncle Fox's eyes.

Shea and Thjalfi tramped through the slush to the clump of spruces. As he pulled out his supposedly rust-proof knife, Shea was dismayed to observe that the blade had developed a number of dull-red freckles.

41

He worked manfully hacking down a number of trees and branches. They were piled on a spot from which the snow had disappeared, although the ground was still sopping.

"Who's going to try first?" asked Shea.

"Don't be more foolish than ye have to," murmured Thjalfi. "Redbeard, of course."

Thor walked up to the pile of brush and extended his hands. There was a blue glow of corona discharge around them, and a piercing crack as bright electric sparks leaped from his fingertips to the wood. The brush stirred a little and a few puffs of water vapor rose from it. Thor frowned in concentration. Again the sparks crackled, but no fire resulted.

"Too damp is the wood," growled Thor. "Now you shall make the attempt, Sly One."

Loki extended his hands and muttered something too low for Shea to hear. A rosy-violet glow shone from his hands and danced among the brush. In the twilight the strange illumination lit up Loki's sandy red goatee, high cheekbones, and slanting brows with startling effect. His lips moved almost silently. The spruce steamed gently, but did not light.

Loki stepped back. The magenta glow died out. "A night's work," said he. "Let us see what our warlock can do."

Shea had been assembling a few small twigs, rubbing them to dryness on his clothes and arranging them like an Indian tepee. They were still dampish, but he supposed spruce would contain enough resin to light.

"Now," he said with a trace of swagger. "Let everybody watch. This is strong magic."

He felt around in the little container that held his matches until he found some of the nonsafety kitchen type. His three companions held their breaths as he took out a match and struck it against the box.

Nothing happened.

He tried again. Still no result. He threw the match away and essayed another, again without success. He tried another, and another, and another. He tried two at once. He put away the kitchen matches and got out

42

a box of safety matches. The result was no better. There was no visible reason. The matches simply would not light.

He stood up. "I'm sorry," he said, "but something has gone wrong. If you'll just wait a minute, I'll look it up in my book of magic formulas."

There was just enough light left to read by. Shea got out his *Boy Scout Manual*. Surely it would tell him what to do—if not with failing matches, at least it would instruct him in the art of rubbing sticks.

He opened it at random and peered, blinked his eyes, shook his head, and peered again. The light was good enough. But the black marks on the page, which presumably were printed sentences, were utterly meaningless. A few letters looked vaguely familiar, but he could make nothing of the words. He leafed rapidly through the book; it was the same senseless jumble of hen tracks everywhere. Even the few diagrams meant nothing without the text.

Harold Shea stood with his mouth open and not the faintest idea of what to do next. "Well," rumbled Thor, "where is our warlock fire?"

In the background Loki tittered. "He perhaps prefers to eat his turnips uncooked."

"I . . . I'm sorry, sir," babbled Shea. "I'm afraid it won't work."

Thor lifted his massive fist. "It is time," he said, "to put an end to this lying and feeble child of man who raises our hopes and then condemns us to a dinner of cold salmon."

"No, Slayer of Giants," said Loki. "Hold your hand. He furnishes us something to laugh at, which is always good in this melancholy country. I may be able to use him where we are going."

Thor slowly lowered his arm. "Yours be the responsibility. I am not unfriendly to the children of men; but for liars I have no sympathy. What I say I can do, and that will I do."

Thjalfi spoke. "If ye please, sir, there's a dark something up yonder." He pointed toward the head of the valley. "Maybe we can find shelter."

Thor growled an assent; they got back into the chariot and drove up toward the dark mass. Shea was silent, with the blackest of thoughts. He would leave his position as researcher at the Garaden Institute to go after adventure with a capital A, would he? And as an escape from a position where he felt himself inferior and inclosed. Well, he told himself bitterly, he had landed in another still more inclosed and inferior. Yet why was it his preparations had so utterly failed? There was no reason for the matches' not lighting or the book's turning into gibberish—or for that matter the failure of the flashlight on the night before.

Thjalfi was whispering to him. "By the beard of Odinn, I'm ashamed of you, friend Harald. Why did ye promise a fire if you couldn't make it?"

"I thought I could, honest," said Shea morosely.

"Well, maybe so. Ye certainly rubbed the Thunderer the wrong way. Ye'd best be grateful to Uncle Fox. He saved your life for you. He ain't as bad as some people think, I always say. Usually helps you out in a real pinch."

The dark something grew into the form of an oddly shaped house. The top was rounded, the near end completely open. When they went in Shea found to his surprise that the floor was of some linoleumlike material, as were the curving walls and low-arched roof. There seemed only a single broad low room, without furniture or lights. At the far end they could dimly make out five hallways, circular in cross section, leading they knew not where. Nobody cared to explore.

Thjalfi and Shea dragged down the heavy chest and fished out blankets. For supper the four glumly chewed pieces of smoked salmon. Thor's eyebrows worked in a manner that showed he was trying to control justifiable anger.

Finally Loki said: "It is in my mind that our fireless warlock has not heard the story of your fishing, son of Jörd."

"Oh," said Thor, "that story is not unknown. But it is good that men should hear it and learn from it. Let me think—"

"Odinn preserve us!" murmured Thjalfi in Shea's ear. "I've only heard this a million times."

44

Thor rumbled: "I was guesting with the giant Hymir. We rowed far out in the blue sea. I baited my hook with a whole ox-head, for the fish I fish are worthy a man's strength. At the first strike I knew I had the greatest fish of all: to wit, the Midgard Serpent, for his strength was so great. Three whales could not have pulled so hard. For nine hours I played the serpent, thrashing to and fro, before I pulled him in. When his head came over the gunwale, he sprayed venom in futile wrath; it ate holes in my clothes. His eyes were as great as shields, and his teeth *that* long." Thor held up his hands in the gloom to show the length of the teeth. "I pulled and the serpent pulled again. I was braced with my belt of strength; my feet nearly went through the bottom of the boat.

"I had all but landed the monster, when—I speak no untruth—that fool Hymir got scared and cut the line! The biggest thing any fisherman ever caught, and it escaped!" He finished on a mournful note: "I gave Hymir a thumping he will not soon forget. But it did not give me the trophy I wanted to hang on the walls of Thrudvang!"

Thjalfi leaned toward Shea, singing in his ear:

"A man shall not boast   Of the fish that fled
          Or the bear he failed to flay;
Bigger they be   Than those borne back
          To hang their heads in the hall.

At least that's what Atli's Drapar says."

Loki chuckled; he had caught the words. "True, youngling. Had any but our friend and great protector told such a tale, I would doubt it."

"Doubt me?" rumbled Thor. "How would you like one of my buffets?" He drew back his arm. Loki ducked. Thor uttered a huge good-natured laugh. "Two things gods and mortals alike doubt—tales of fishing and the virtue of women."

He lay back among the blankets, took two deep breaths and seemed to be snoring instantly. Loki and Thjalfi also lapsed into silence.

Shea, unable to sleep, let his mind go over the day's doings. He had shown up pretty badly. It annoyed him, for he was beginning to like these people, even the unapproachable and tempestuous Thor. The big fellow was all right: someone you could depend on right up to the hilt, especially in any crisis that required straight-forward courage. He would see right and wrong divided by a line of absolute sharpness, chalk on one side, coal dust on the other. He became annoyed when others proved to lack his own simple strength.

About Loki, Shea was not quite so sure. Uncle Fox had saved his life, all right, but Shea suspected that there had been a touch of self-interest about the act. Loki expected to make some use of him, and not entirely as a butt of jokes, either. That keen mind had doubtless noted the unfamiliar gear Shea had brought from the twentieth century and was speculating on its use.

But why had those gadgets failed to work? Why had he been unable to read simple English print?

Was it English? Shea tried to visualize his name in written form. It was easy enough, and showed him that the transference had not made him illiterate. But wait a minute, what was he visualizing? He concentrated on the row of letters in his mind's eye. What he saw was:

ᚼᛁᚱᛁᛁᛏ ᛒᚱᚨᛁᛏ ᛌᛖᚮᛁ

These letters spelled Harold Bryan Shea to him. At the same time he realized they weren't the letters of the Latin alphabet. He tried some more visualizations. "Man" came out as:

ᛉᛁᚦᛘ

Something was wrong. "Man," he vaguely remembered, ought not to have four letters.

Then, gradually, he realized what had happened. Chalmers had been right and more than right. His mind had been filled with the fundamental assumptions of this new world. When he transferred from his safe, Midwestern institute to this howling wilderness, he had automatically changed languages. If it were otherwise, if the shift were partial, he would be a dement—insane. But the shift was complete. He was speaking and understanding old Norse, touching old Norse gods and eating old Norse food. No wonder he had had no difficulty making himself understood!

But as an inevitable corollary, his knowledge of English had vanished. When he thought of the written form of "man" he could form no concept but that of the four runic characters:

$$ᚢᛁᚦᚼ$$

He couldn't even imagine what the word would look like with the runes put into other characters. And he had failed to read his *Boy Scout Handbook*.

Naturally his gadgets had failed to work. He was in a world not governed by the laws of twentieth-century physics or chemistry. It had a mental pattern which left no room for matches or flashlights, or non-rusting steel. These things were simply inconceivable to anyone around him. Therefore they did not exist save as curiously shaped objects of no value.

Well, anyway, he thought to himself drowsily, at least I won't have to worry about the figure I cut in front of these guys again. I've fallen so low that nothing I could do would make me a bigger fool. Oh, what the hell—

5

SHEA AWOKE BEFORE DAWN, SHIVERING. THE TEM-
perature was still above freezing, but a wind had
come up, and the gray landscape was curtained with
driving rain. He yawned and sat up with his blanket
round him like an Indian. The others were still asleep
and he stared out for a moment, trying to recover the
thread of last night's thoughts.

This world he was in—perhaps permanently—was
governed by laws of its own. What were those laws?
There was one piece of equipment of which the transference had not robbed him; his modern mind, habitu-
ated to studying and analyzing the general rules guiding individual events. He ought to be able to reason
out the rules governing this existence and to use them
—something which the rustic Thjalfi would never think
of doing. So far the only rules he had noticed were
that the gods had unusual powers. But there must be
general laws underlying even these—

Thor's snores died away into a gasping rattle. The
red-bearded god rubbed his eyes, sat up, and spat.

"Up, all Æsir's men!" he said. "Ah, Harald of
the Turnips, you are already awake. Cold salmon will
be our breakfast again since your fire magic failed."
Then, as he saw Shea stiffen: "Nay, take it not
unkindly. We Æsir are not unkind to mortals, and
I've seen more unpromising objects than you turn
out all right. Make a man of you yet, youngling. Just
watch me and imitate what I do." He yawned and
the yawn spread into a bristling grin.

The others bestirred themselves. Thjalfi got out
some smoked salmon. However good the stuff was,
Shea found the third successive meal of it a little
too much.

They were just beginning to gnaw when there was a heavy tramp outside. Through the rain loomed a gray shape whose outline made Shea's scalp tingle. It was mannish, but at least ten feet tall, with massive columnar legs. It was a giant.

The giant stooped and looked into the travelers' refuge. Shea, his heart beating madly, backed up against the curving wall, his hand feeling for his hunting knife. The face that looked in was huge, with bloodshot gray eyes and a scraggly iron-gray beard, and its expression was not encouraging.

"Ungh," snarled the giant, showing yellow snags of teeth. His voice was a couple of octaves beneath the lowest human bass. " 'Scuse me, gents, but I been looking for my glove. How 'bout having a little breakfast together, huh?"

Shea, Thjalfi and Loki all looked at Thor. The Red God stood with feet wide apart, surveying the giant for some minutes. Then he said, "Good is guesting on a journey. We offer some smoked salmon. But what have you?"

"The name's Skrymir, buddy. I got some bread and dried dragon meat. Say, ain't you Thor Odinnsson, the hammer thrower?"

"That is not incorrect."

"Boy, oh, boy, ain't that something?" The giant made a horrible face that was probably intended for a friendly grin. He reached around for a bag that hung at his back and sitting down in front of the shelter, opened it. Shea got a better view of him, though not one that inspired a more favorable impression. The monster's long gray hair was done up in a topknot with bone skewers stuck through it. He was dressed entirely in furs, of which the cloak must have come from the grandfather of all the bears, though it was none too large for him.

Skrymir took from his bag a slab of Norse bread the size of a mattress, and several hunks of leathery gray meat. These he slapped down in front of the travelers. "All right, youse guys help yourselves," he rumbled. "Let's see some of that salmon, huh?"

Thjalfi mutely handed over a piece of the salmon on which the giant set noisily to work. He drooled, now and then wiping his face with the back of his huge paw, and getting himself well smeared with salmon grease.

Shea found he had to break up his portion of the bread with his knife-handle before he could manage it, so hard was the material. The dragon meat was a little easier, but still required some hard chewing, and his jaw muscles were sore from the beating they had taken in the last twenty-four hours. The dragon meat had a pungent, garlicky flavor that he didn't care for.

As Shea gnawed he saw a louse the size of a cockroach crawl out from the upper edge of one of Skrymir's black fur leggings, amble around a bit in the jungle of hair below the giant's knee, and stroll back into its sanctuary. Shea almost gagged. His appetite tapered off, though presently it returned. After what he had been through lately, it would take more than a single louse to spoil his interest in food for any length of time. What the hell?

Loki, grinning slyly, asked: "Are there turnips in your bag, Hairy One?"

Skrymir frowned. "Turnips? Naw. Whatcha want with 'em?"

"Our warlock"—Loki jerked his thumb at Shea—"eats them."

"What-a-at? No kiddin'!" roared the giant. "I heard of guys that eat bugs and drink cow's milk, but I ain't never heard of nobody what eats turnips."

Shea said: "That's how I get some of my magic powers," with a somewhat sickly smile, and felt he had come out of it fairly well.

Skrymir belched. It was not an ordinary run-of-the-mine belch, but something akin to a natural cataclysm. Shea tried to hold his breath until the air cleared. The giant settled himself and inquired: "Say, how come youse is traveling in Jötunheim?"

"The Wing Thor travels where he will," observed Loki loftily, but with a side glance.

"Aw right, aw right, butcha don't have to get snotty about it. I just was thinking there's some relations of Hrungnir and Geirröd that was laying for

Thor. They'd just love to have a chance to get even witcha for bumping off those giants."

Thor rumbled: "Few will be more pleased than I to meet—"

But Loki interrupted: "Thank you for the warning, friend Skrymir. Good is the guesting when men are friendly. We will do as much for you one of these days. Will you have more salmon?"

"Naw, I had all I want."

Loki continued silkily, "Would it be impertinence to ask whither your giantship is bound?"

"Aw, I'm going up to Utgard. Utgardaloki's throwing a big feed for all the giants."

"Great and glorious will be that feasting."

"You're damn right it'll be great. All the hill giants and frost giants and fire giants together at once— say, that's something!"

"It would give us pleasure to see it. If we went as guests of so formidable a giant as yourself, none of Hrungnir's or Geirröd's friends would dare make trouble, would they?"

Skrymir showed his snags in a pleased grin. "Them punks? Haw, they wouldn't do nothing." He picked his teeth thoughtfully with thumb and forefinger. "Yeah, I guess you can come. The big boss, Utgardaloki, is a good guy and a friend of mine. So you won't have no trouble. If youse'll clear outta my glove, we can start right now."

"What?" All four spoke at once.

"Yeah. My glove, that's what you slept in."

The implications of this statement were so alarming that the four travelers picked up their belongings and scrambled out of the shelter with ludicrous haste —the mighty Thor included.

The rain had ceased. Ragged serpents of mist, pearly against the darker gray of the clouds, crawled over the hills. Outside, the travelers looked back at their shelter. There was no question that it was an enormous glove.

Skrymir grasped the upper edge of the opening with his left hand and thrust the right into the erstwhile dwelling. From where he stood, Shea couldn't see whether the big glove had shrunk to fit or whether it had faded out of sight and been replaced by a smaller one. At the same time he became suddenly conscious of the fact that he was wet to the skin.

Before he had a chance to think over the meaning of these facts, Thor was bellowing at him to help get the chariot loaded.

When he was sitting hunched up on the chest and swaying to the movement of the cart, Thjalfi murmured to him: "I knew Loki would get around the Hairy One. When it's something that calls for smartness, ye can depend on Uncle Fox, I always say."

Shea nodded silently and sneezed. He'd be lucky if he didn't come down with a first-class cold, riding in these wet garments. The landscape was wilder and bleaker around them than even on the previous day's journey. Ahead Skrymir tramped along, the bag on his back swaying with his strides, his sour sweat smell wafting back over the chariot.

Wet garments. Why? The rain had stopped when they emerged from that monstrous glove. There was something peculiar about the whole business of that glove. The others, including the two gods, had unhesitatingly accepted its huge size as an indication that Skrymir was even larger and more powerful than he seemed. He was undoubtedly a giant—but hardly that much of a giant. Shea supposed that although the world he was in did not respond to the natural laws of that from which he had come, there was no reason to conceive that the laws of illusion had changed. He had studied psychology enough to know something of the standard methods used by stage magicians. But others, unfamiliar both with such methods and the technique of modern thought, would not think of criticizing observation with pure logic. For that matter, they would not think of questioning the evidence of observation—

"You know," he whispered suddenly to Thjalfi, "I just wonder whether Loki is as clever as he thinks, and whether Skrymir isn't smarter than he pretends."

The servant of gods gave him a startled glance. "A mighty strange word is that. Why?"

"Well, didn't you say the giants would be fighting against the gods when this big smash comes?"

"Truly I did:

> High blows Heimdall.   The horn is aloft;
> The ash shall shake   And the rime-giants ride
> On the roads of Hell—

leastways that's what Völuspa says, the words of the prophetess."

"Then isn't Skrymir a shade too friendly with someone he's going to fight?"

Thjalfi gave a barking laugh. "Ye don't know much about Öku-Thor to say that. This Skrymir may be big, but Redbeard has his strength belt on. He could twist that there giant right up, snip-snap."

Shea sighed. But he tried once more. "Well, look here, did you notice that when Skrymir put his gloves on, your clothes got wet all of a sudden?"

"Why, yes now that I think of it."

"My idea is that there wasn't any giant glove there at all. It was an illusion, a magic, to scare us. We really slept in the open without knowing it, and got soaked. But whoever magicked us did a good job, so we didn't feel the wet till the spell was off and the big glove disappeared."

"Maybe so. But how does it signify?"

"It signified that Skrymir didn't blunder into us by accident. It was a put-up job."

The rustic scratched his head in puzzlement. "Seems to me ye're being a little mite fancy, friend Harald." He looked around. "I wish we had Heimdall along. He can see a hundred leagues in the dark and hear the wool growing on a sheep's back. But 'twouldn't do to have him and Uncle Fox together. Thor's the only one of the Æsir that can stand Uncle Fox."

Shea shivered. "Say, friend Harald," offered Thjalfi, "how would ye like to run a few steps to warm up?"

Shea soon learned that Thjalfi's idea of warming up did not consist merely of dogtrotting behind the chariot. "We'll race to yonder boulder and back to the chariot," he said. "Be ye ready? Get set; go!" Before Shea fairly got into his stride, his woolens flapping around him, Thjalfi was halfway to the boulder, gravel flying under his shoes, and clothes fluttering stiffly behind him like a flag in a gale. Shea had not covered half the distance when Thjalfi passed him, grinning, on the way back. He had always considered himself a good runner, but against this human antelope it was no contest. Wasn't there *anything* in which he could hold his own against these people?

Thjalfi helped pull him over the tail of the chariot. "Ye do a little better than most runners, friend Harald," he said with the cheerfulness of superiority. "But I thought I'd give ye a little surprise, seeing as how maybe ye hadn't heard about my running. But"—he lowered his voice—"don't let Uncle Fox get ye into any contests. He'll make a wager and collect it out of your hide. Ye got to watch him that way."

"What's Loki's game, anyway?" asked Shea. "I heard Heimdall suggesting he might be on the other side at the big fight."

Thjalfi shrugged. "That there Child of Fury gets a little mite hasty about Loki. Guess he'll turn up on the right side all right, but he's a queer one. Always up to something, sometimes good, sometimes bad, and he won't let anyone boss him. There's a lay about him, the Lokasenna, ye know:

I say to the gods   And the sons of gods
          The things that whet my thoughts;
By the wells of the world There is none with the might
          To make me do his will."

That agreed fairly well with the opinion Shea had formed of the enigmatic Uncle Fox. He would have liked to discuss the matter with Thjalfi. But he found that while he could form such concepts as delayed adolescence, superego, and sadism readily enough, he could think of no words to express them.

If he wanted to be a practicing psychologist in this world, he would have to invent a whole terminology for the science.

He sneezed some more. He was catching cold. His nose clogged, and his eyes ran. The temperature was going down, and an icy breeze had risen that did nothing to add to his happiness.

They lunched without stopping, as they had on the previous day. As the puddles of the thaw began to develop crystals and the chariot wheels began to crunch, Shea blew on his mittens and slapped himself. Thjalfi looked sympathetic. "Be ye really cold, friend Harald?" he said. "This is barely freezing. A few years back we had a winter so cold that when we made a fire in the open, flames froze solid. I broke off some pieces, and for the rest of the winter, whenever we wanted a fire, I used one of them pieces to light it with. Would 'a' come in mighty handy this morning. My uncle Einarr traded off some as amber."

It was told with so straight a countenance, that Shea was not quite certain he was being kidded. In this world it *might* happen.

The terrible afternoon finally waned. Skrymir was walking with head up now, looking around him. The giant waved toward a black spot on the side of a hill. "Hey, youse, there's a cave," he said. "Whatcha say we camp in there, huh?"

Thor looked around. "It is not too dark for more of progress."

Loki spoke up. "Not untrue, Powerful One. Yet I fear our warlock must soon freeze to an ice bone. We should have to pack him in boughs lest pieces chip off, ha-ha!'

"Oh, dote bide be," said Shea, "I cad stad it." Perhaps he could; at least if they went on he wouldn't have to manhandle that chest halfway up the hill.

He was overruled, but, after all, did not have to carry the chest. When the chariot had been parked at the edge of a snowdrift, Skrymir took that bulky object under one arm and led the way up the stony slope to the cave mouth.

"Could you get us fire?" Thor asked Skrymir.

"Sure thing, buddy." Skrymir strode down to a

clump of small trees, pulled up a couple by the roots, and breaking them across his knee laid them for burning.

Shea put his head into the cave. At first he was conscious of nothing but the rocky gloom. Then he sniffed. He hadn't been able to smell anything—not even Skrymir—for some hours, but now an odor pricked through the veil of his cold. A familiar odor —chlorine gas! What—

"Hey, you," roared Skrymir behind him. Shea jumped a foot. "Get the hell outta my way."

Shea got. Skrymir put his head down and whistled. At least he did what would have been called a whistle in a human being. From his lips it sounded more like an air-raid warning.

A little man about three feet tall, with a beard that made him look like a miniature Santa Claus, appeared at the mouth of the cave. He had a pointed hood, and the tail of his beard was tucked into his belt.

"Hey, you," said Skrymir. "Let's have some fire. Make it snappy." He pointed to the pile of logs and brush in front of the cave mouth.

"Yes, sir," said the dwarf. He toddled over to the pile and produced a coppery-looking bar out of his jacket. Shea watched the process with interest, but just then Loki tucked an icicle down his back, and when Shea had extracted it the fire was already burning with a hiss of damp wood.

The dwarf spoke up in a little chirping voice. "You are not planning to camp here, are you?"

"Yeah," replied Skrymir. "Now beat it."

"Oh, but you must not—"

"Shut up!" bellowed the giant. "We camp where we damn please."

"Yessir. Thank you, sir. Anything else, sir?"

"Naw. Go on, beat it, before I step on you."

The dwarf vanished into the cave. They got their belongings out and disposed themselves around the fire, which took a long time to grow. The setting sun broke through the clouds for a minute and smeared them with streaks of lurid vermilion. To Shea's imagination, the clouds took on the form of apocalyptic monsters. Far in the distance he heard the cry of a wolf.

Thjalfi looked up suddenly, frowning. "What's that noise?"

"What noise?" said Thor. Then he jumped up—he had been sitting with his back to the cave mouth— and spun around. "Hai, Clever One, our cave is already not untenanted!" He backed away slowly. From the depths of the cave there came a hiss like that of a steam-pipe leak, followed by a harsh, metallic cry.

"A dragon!" cried Thjalfi. A puff of yellow gas from the cave set them all coughing. A scrape of scales, a rattle of loose stones, and in the dark a pair of yellow eyes the size of dinner plates caught the reflection of the fire.

Æsir, giant, and Thjalfi shouted incoherently, grabbing for whatever might serve as a weapon.

"Here, I cad take care of hib!" cried Shea, forgetting his previous reasoning. He pulled out the revolver. As the great snakelike head came into view in the firelight, he aimed at one of the eyes and pulled the trigger.

The hammer clicked harmlessly. He tried again and again, *click, click*. The jaws came open with a reek of chlorine.

Harold Shea stumbled back. There was a flash of movement past his head. The butt end of a young tree, wielded by Skrymir, swished down on the beast's head.

The eyes rolled. The head half turned toward the giant. Thor leaped in with a roaring yell, and let fly a right hook that would have demolished Joe Louis. There was a crunch of snapping bones; the fist sank right into the reptile's face. With a scream like that of a disemboweled horse the head vanished into the cave.

Thjalfi helped Shea up. "Now maybe ye can see," remarked the servant of gods, "why Skrymir would as lief not take chances with the Lord of the Goats." He chuckled. "That there dragon's going to have him

57

a toothache next spring—if there is any spring before the *Time*."

The dwarf popped out again. "Hai, Skrymir!"

"Huh?"

"I tried to warn you that a fire would bring the dragon out of hibernation. But you wouldn't listen. Think you're smart, don't you? Yah! Yah! Yah!" The vest-pocket Santa Claus capered in the cave mouth for an instant, thumbing his nose with both hands. He vanished as Skrymir picked up a stone to throw.

The giant lumbered over to the cave and felt around inside. "Never catch the little totrug now. They have burrows all through these hills," he observed gloomily.

The evening meal was eaten in a silence made more pointed for Shea by the fact that he felt it was mostly directed at himself. He ought to have known better, he told himself bitterly.

In fact, he ought to have known better than to embark on such an expedition at all. Adventure! Romance! Bosh! As for the dream-girl whose fancied image he had once in a rash moment described to Walter Bayard, those he had seen in this miserable dump were like lady wrestlers. If he could have used the formulas to return instantly, he would.

But he could not. That was the point. The formulas didn't exist any more, as far as he was concerned. Nothing existed but the bleak, snowbound hillside, the nauseating giant, the two Æsir and their servant regarding him with aversion. There was nothing he could do—

Whoa, Shea, steady, he remarked to himself. You're talking yourself into a state of melancholy, which is, as Chalmers once remarked, of no philosophical or practical value. Too bad old Doc wasn't along, to furnish a mature intellect and civilized company. The intelligent thing to do, was not to bemoan the past but to live in the present. He lacked the physical equipment to imitate Thor's forthright approach to problems. But he could at least come somewhere near Loki's sardonic and intelligent humor.

And speaking of intelligence, had he not already decided to make use of it in discovering the laws of this world? Laws which these people were not fitted, by their mental habit, to deduce?

He turned suddenly and asked: "Didn't that dwarf say the fire fetched the dragon out of hibernation?"

Skrymir yawned, and spoke. "Yeah. What about it, snotty?"

"The fire's still here. What if he, or another one comes back during the night?"

"Prob'ly eat you, and serve you right." He cackled a laugh.

"The niggeling speaks sooth," said Loki. "It were best to move our camp."

The accent of contempt in the voice made Shea wince. But he went on: "We don't have to do that, do we, sir? It's freezing now and getting colder. If we take some of that snow and stuff it into the cave, it seems to me the dragon would hardly come out across it."

Loki slapped a knee. "Soundly and well said, turnip-man! Now you and Thjalfi shall do it. I perceive you are not altogether without your uses, since there has been a certain gain in wit since you joined our party. Who would have thought of stopping a dragon with snow?"

Thor grunted.

6

WHEN SHEA AWOKE HE WAS STILL SNIFFLING, BUT at least his head was of normal weight. He wondered whether the chlorine he had inhaled the previous evening might not have helped the cold. Or whether the improvement were a general one, based on his determination to accept his surroundings and make the most of them.

After breakfast they set out as before, Skrymir tramping on ahead. The sky was the color of old lead. The wind was keen, rattling the branches of the scrubby trees and whirling an occasional snowflake before it. The goats slipped on patches of frozen slush, plodding uphill most of the time. The hills were all about them now, rising steadily and with more vegetation, mostly pine and spruce.

It must have been around noon—Shea could only guess at the time—when Skrymir turned and waved at the biggest mountain they had yet seen. The wind carried away the giant's words, but Thor seemed to have understood. The goats quickened their pace toward the mountain, whose top hung in cloud.

After a good hour of climbing, Shea began to get glimpses of a shape looming from the bare crest, intermittently blotted out by the eddies of mist. When they were close enough to see it plainly, it became clearly a house, not unlike that of the bonder Sverre. But it was cruder, made of logs with the bark on, and vastly bigger—as big as a metropolitan railroad terminal.

Thjalfi said into his ear: "That will be Utgard Castle. Ye'll need whatever mite of courage ye have here, friend Harald." The young man's teeth were chattering from something other than cold.

Skrymir lurched up to the door and pounded on it with his fist. He stood there for a long minute, the wind flapping his furs. A rectangular hole opened in the door. The door swung open. The chariot riders climbed down, stretching their stiff muscles as they followed their guide.

The door banged shut behind them. They were in a dark vestibule, like that in Sverre's house but larger and foul with the odor of unwashed giant. A huge arm pushed the leather curtain aside, revealing through the triangular opening a view of roaring yellow flame and thronging, shouting giants.

Thjalfi murmured: "Keep your eyes open, Harald. As Thjodolf of Hvin says:

All the gateways   Ere one goes out
        Thoughtfully should a man scan;
    Uncertain it is   Where sits the unfriendly
        Upon the bench before thee."

Within, the place was a disorderly parody of Sverre's. Of the same general form, with the same benches, its tables were all uneven, filthy, and littered with fragments of food. The fire in the center hung a pall of smoke under the rafters. The dirty straw on the floor was thick about the ankles.

The benches and the passageway behind them were filled with giants, drinking, eating, shouting at the tops of their voices. Before him a group of six, with iron-gray topknots and patchy beards like Skrymir's, were wrangling. One drew back his arm in anger. His elbow struck a mug of mead borne by a harassed-looking man who was evidently a thrall. The mead splashed onto another giant, who instantly snatched up a bowl of stew from the table and slammed it on the man's head.

Down went the man with a squeal. Skrymir calmly kicked him from the path of his guests. The six giants burst into bubbling laughter, rolling in their seats and clapping each other on the back, their argument forgotten.

"Hai, Skridbaldnir!" Skrymir was gripping another giant on the bench by the arm. "How's every little thing wit' you? Commere, I wantcha to meet a friend of mine. This here guy's Asa-Thor!"

Skridbaldnir turned. Shea noticed that he was slenderer than Skrymir, with ash-blond hair, the pink eyes of an albino, and a long, red ulcerated nose.

"He's a frost giant," whispered Thjalfi, "and that gang over there are fire giants." He waved a trembling hand toward the other side of the table, where a group of individuals like taller and straighter gorillas were howling at each other. They were shorter than the other giants, not much more than eight feet tall. They had prognathous jaws and coarse black hair where their bodies were exposed. They scratched ceaselessly.

Halfway down the hall, at one side, sat the biggest hill giant of all, in a huge chair with interwoven serpents carved on the legs and arms. His costume was distinguished from those of the other giants in that the bone skewers through his topknot had rough gold knobs on their ends. One of his lower snag teeth projected for several inches beyond his upper lip. He looked at Skrymir and said: "Hai, bud. I see you got some kids witcha. It ain't a good idea to bring kids to these feeds; they learns bad language."

"They ain't kids," said Skrymir. "They're a couple of men and a couple of Æsir. I told 'em they could come wit' me. That okay, boss?"

Utgardaloki picked his nose and wiped his fingers on his greasy leather jacket before replying: "I guess so. But ain't that one with the red whiskers Asa-Thor?"

"You are not mistaken," said Thor.

"Well, well, you don't say so. I always thought Thor was a big husky guy."

Thor stuck out his chest, scowling. "It is ill to jest with the Æsir, giant."

"Ho, ho, ain't he the cutest little fella?" Utgardaloki paused to capture a small creeping thing that had crawled out of his left eyebrow and crack it between his teeth.

"A fair arrangement," murmured Loki in Shea's ear. "They live on him; he lives on them."

Utgardaloki continued ominously: "But whatcha doing here, you? This is a respectable party, see, and I don't want no trouble."

Thor said: "I have come for my hammer, Mjöllnir."

"Huh? What makes ya think we got it?"

"Ask not of the tree where it got its growth or of the gods their wisdom. Will you give it up, or do I have to fight you for it?"

"Aw, don't be like that, Öku-Thor. Sure, I'd give you your piddling nutcracker if I knew where it was."

"Nutcracker! Why you—"

"Easy!" Shea could hear Loki's whisper. "Son of Odinn, with the strong use strength; with the liar, lies." He turned to Utgardaloki and bowed mockingly: "Chief of giants, we thank you for your courtesy and will not trouble you long. Trusting your word, lord, are we to understand that Mjöllnir is not here?"

" 'Tain't here as far as I know," replied Utgardaloki, spitting on the floor and rubbing his bare foot over the spot, with just a hint of uneasiness.

"Might it not have been brought hither without your knowledge?"

Utgardaloki shrugged. "How in hell should I know? I said as far as I knew. This is a hell of a way to come at your host."

"Evidently there is no objection should the desire come upon us to search the place."

"Huh? You're damn right there's objections! This is my joint and I don't let no foreigners go sniffing around."

Loki smiled ingratiatingly. "Greatest of the Jötun, your objection is but natural with one who knows his own value. But the gods do not idly speak; we believe Mjöllnir is here, and have come in peace to ask it, rather than in arms with Odinn and his spear at our head, Heimdall and his great sword and Ullr's deadly bow. Now you shall let us search for the hammer, or we will go away and return with them to make you such a feasting as you will not soon forget. But if we fail to find it we will depart in all peace. This is my word."

"And mine!" cried Thor, his brows knitting. Beside him Shea noticed Thjalfi's face go to the color of skimmed milk and was slightly surprised to find himself unafraid. But that may be because I don't understand the situation, he told himself.

Utgardaloki scratched thoughtfully, his lips working. "Tell you what," he said at last. "You Æsir are sporting gents, ain't you?"

"It is not to be denied," said Loki guardedly, "that we enjoy sports."

"I'll make you a sporting proposition. You think you are great athaletes. Well, we got pretty tough babies here, too. We'll have some games, and if you beat us at even one of 'em, see, I'll let you go ahead and search. If you lose, out you get."

"What manner of games?"

"Hell, sonny, anything youse want."

Thor's face had gone thoughtful. "I am not unknown as a wrestler," he remarked.

"Awright," said Utgardaloki. "We'll find someone to rassle you down. Can you do anything else?"

Loki spoke up. "I will meet your best champion at eating and our man Thjalfi here will run a race with you. Asa-Thor also will undertake any trial of strength you care to hold."

"Swell. Me, I think these games are kid stuff, see? But it ought be fun for some of the gang to see you take your licking. HAI! Bring Elli up here; here's a punk that wants to rassle!"

With a good deal of shouting and confusion a space was cleared near the fire in the center of the hall. Thor stood with fists on hips, waiting the giant's champion. There came forward, not a giant, but a tall old woman. She was at least a hundred, a hunched bag of bones covered by thin, almost transparent skin, as wrinkled as the surface of a file.

Thor shouted: "What manner of jest is this, Utgardaloki? It is not to be said that Asa-Thor wrestles with women."

"Oh, don't worry none, kid. She *likes* it, don'tcha, Elli?"

The crone bared toothless gums. "Yep," she quavered. "And many's the good man I put down, heh, heh."

"But—" began Thor.

"Y'aint scared to work up a reputation, are you?"

"Ha! Thor afraid? Not of aught the giant kindred can do." Thor puffed out his chest.

"I gotta explain the rules." Utgardaloki put a hand on the shoulder of each contestant and muttered at them.

Shea felt his arm pinched and looked into the bright eyes of Loki. "Great and evil is the magic in this place," whispered Uncle Fox, "and I misdoubt me we are to be tricked, for never have I heard of such a wrestling. But it may be that the spells they use are spells against gods alone and not for the eyes of men. Now I have here a spell against spells, and while these contests go forward you shall take it." He handed Shea a piece of very thin parchment, covered with spidery runic writing. "Repeat it forward, then backward, then forward again, looking as you do at the object you suspect of being an illusion. It may be you will see on the wall the hammer we seek."

"Wouldn't the giants hide it away, sir?"

"Not with their boasting and vainglorious habit. It—"

"Awright," said Utgardaloki in a huge voice, "go!"

Thor, roaring like a lion, seized Elli as though he intended to dash her brains out on the floor. But Elli might have been nailed where she was. Her rickety frame did not budge. Thor fell silent, wrenching at the crone's arms and body. He turned purple in the face from the effort: the giants around murmured appreciatively.

Shea glanced at the slip Loki had given him. The words were readable, though they seemed to consist of meaningless strings of syllables—"Nyi-Nidi-Nordri-Sudri, Austri-Vestri-Altjof-Dvalinn." He obediently repeated it according to the directions, looking at a giant's club that hung on the wall. It remained a

65

giant's club. He turned back to the wrestling where Thor was puffing with effort, his forehead beaded with sweat.

"Witch!" Thor shouted at last, and seized her arm to twist it. Elli caught his neck with her free hand. There was a second's scuffle and Thor skidded away, falling to one knee.

"That's enough!" said Utgardaloki, stepping between them. "That counts as a fall; Elli wins. I guess it's a good job you didn't try to rassle with any of the *big* guys here, eh, Thor, old kid?" The other giants roared an approval that drowned Thor's growl.

Utgardaloki continued: "Awright, you, stand back! Get back, I say, or I'll cut the blood-eagle on a couple of you! Next event's an eating contest. Bring Logi up here. We got some eating for him to do."

A fire giant shuffled through the press. His black hair had a reddish tinge, and his movements were quick and animallike. "Is it lunch time yet?" he rasped. "Them three elk I et for breakfast just kinda got my appetite going."

Utgardaloki explained and introduced him to his opponent. "Please to meetcha," said Logi. "I always like to see a guy what appreciates good food. Say, you oughta come down to Muspellheim sometime. We got a cook there what knows how to roast a whale right. He uses charcoal fire and bastes it with bear grease—"

"That'll do, Logi," said Utgardaloki. "You get that guy talking about the meals he's et and he'll talk till the *Time* comes."

Shea was pushed back by giants as they crowded in. An eddy of the crowd carried him still farther away from the scene of action as the giants made way for a little procession of harried-looking slaves. These bore two huge wooden platters, on each of which rested an entire roasted elk haunch. Shea stood on tiptoe and stretched. Between a pair of massive shoulders he glimpsed Utgardaloki taking his place at the middle of a long table, at each end of which sat one of the contestants.

A shoulder moved across Shea's field of vision, and he glanced up at the owner. It was a comparatively short giant, who bulged out in the middle to make up for his lack of stature. A disorderly mop of black-and-white hair covered his head. But the thing that struck Shea was that, as the giant turned profile to watch the eaters, the eye that looked from under the piebald thatch was bright *blue*.

That was wrong. Fire giants, as he had noted, had black eyes, hill giants gray or black eyes, frost giants pink. Of course, this giant might have a trace of some other blood—but there was a familiar angle to that long, high-bridged nose and something phony-looking about the mop of hair. Heimdall!

Shea whispered behind his hand: "How many mothers did you have, giant with the uncombed thatch?"

He heard a low chuckle and the answer came back: "Thrice three, man from an unknown world! But there is no need to shout; I can hear your lightest whisper, even your thoughts half formed."

"I think we're being tricked," continued Shea. He didn't say it even in a whisper this time, merely thought it, moving his lips.

The answer was pat: "That is what was to be expected, and for no other reason did I come hither. Yet I have not solved the nature of the spells."

Shea said: "I have been taught a spell"—and remembered Heimdall's enmity to Loki and all his works, just in time to keep from mentioning Uncle Fox—"which may be of use in such a case."

"Then use it," Heimdall answered, "while you watch the contest."

"Awright, ready, you two?" Utgardaloki shouted. "Go!"

The giants gave a shout. Shea, his eyes fixed on Loki, was repeating: "Nyi—Nidri—Nordri—Sudri." The sly god bounced in his oversize chair as he applied his teeth to the elk haunch. The meat was disappearing in hunks the size of a man's fist at the rate of two hunks per second. Shea had never seen anything like it, and wondered where Loki was putting it all. He heard Thjalfi's voice, thin in the basso-profundo clamor of the giants: "Besit yourself, Son of Laufey!!"

Then the bone, the size of a baseball bat, was clean. Loki dropped it clattering to the platter and sat back with a sigh. A whoop went up from the assembled giants. Shea saw Loki start forward again, the eyes popping from his head. Utgardaloki walked to the opposite end of the table. He bellowed: "Logi wins!"

Shea turned to look at the other contestant. But his head bumped a giant's elbow so violently that he saw stars. His eyes beaded with tears. For one fleeting second he saw no Logi there at all, only a great leaping flame at the opposite end of the table. A flicker—the teardrop was gone, and with it the picture.

Logi sat contentedly at the other end of the table, and Loki was crying: "He finished no sooner than myself!"

"Yeah, sonny boy, but he et the bone and the platter too. I said Logi wins!" boomed Utgardaloki.

"Heimdall!" Shea said it so loud that the god thrust a hand toward him. Fortunately the uproar around drowned his voice. "It *is* a trick, an illusion. Logi is a flame."

"Now, good luck go with your eyes, no-warlock and warlock. Warn Asa-Thor, and use your spell on whatever you can see, for it is more than ever important that the hammer be found. Surely, these tricks and sleights must mean the *Time* is even nearer than we think, and the giants are desirous not to see that weapon in the hands of Redbeard. Go!"

Utgardaloki, posted on the table where the eating contest had been held, was directing the clearing of a section of the hall. "The next event is a footrace," he was shouting. "You, shrimp!"—Utgardaloki pointed at Thjalfi. "You're going to run against my son Hugi. Where is that young half-wit? *Hugi!*"

"Here I am, pop." A gangling, adolescent giant wormed his way to the front. He had little forehead and less chin, and a crop of pimples the size of poker chips. "You want me to run against him? He, he, he!" Hugi drooled down his chin as he laughed.

Shea ducked and dodged, squeezing through toward Thor, who was frowning with concentration as he watched the preparations for the race. Thjalfi and the drooling Hugi placed themselves at one end of the hall. "Go!" cried Utgardaloki, and they raced for the far end of the hall, a good three hundred yards away. Thjalfi went like the wind, but Hugi went like a bullet. By the time Thjalfi had reached the far end his opponent was halfway back.

"Hugi wins first heat!" roared Utgardaloki above a tornado of sound. "It's two outta three."

The crowd loosened a little as the contestants caught their breath. Shea found himself beside Thor and Loki.

"Hai, Turnip Harald," rumbled the Redbeard, "where have you been?"

"It is more like anything else that he has been concealed under a table like a mouse," remarked Loki, but Shea was too full of his news to resent anything.

"They're trying to put over tricks on you—on us," he burst out. "All these contests are illusions."

He could see Thor's lips curl. "Your warlock can see deeper into a millstone than most," growled he angrily to Loki.

"No, but I mean it, really." Hugi had just passed them to take his place for the second heat, the hall's huge central fire on the other side. "Look," said Shea. "That runner of theirs. He casts no shadow!"

Thor glanced and as comprehension spread across his features, turned purple. But just then Utgardaloki cried "Go!" again, and the second race was on. It was a repetition of the first. Utgardaloki announced over a delighted uproar that Hugi was the winner.

"I am to pick up their damned cat next," growled Thor. "If that be another trick of theirs, I'll—"

"Not so loudly," whispered Loki. "Soft and slow is the sly fox taken. Now Thor, you shall try this cat-lifting as though nothing were amiss. But Harald here, who is only half subject to their spells because he is a mortal and without fear, shall search for Mjöllnir. Youngling, you are our hope and stay. Use, use the spell I gave you."

A chorus of yells announced that Utgardaloki's cat had arrived. It was a huge beast, gray, and the size of a puma. But it did not look too big for the burly Thor to lift. It glared suspiciously at Thor and spat a little

Utgardaloki rumbled: "Quiet, you. Ain'tcha got no manners?" The cat subsided and allowed Thor to scratch it behind the ears, though with no appearance of pleasure.

How had he seen through the illusion of the eating contest? Shea asked himself. A teardrop in the eye. Would he have to bang his head again to get another one? He closed his eyes and then opened them again, looking at Thor as he put an arm around the big cat's belly and heaved. No teardrop. The cat's belly came up, but its four big paws remained firmly planted.

How to induce a teardrop? A mug of mead stood on the table. Shea dipped a finger into the liquid and shook a drop into his eye. The alcohol burned and stung, and he could hear Thor's grunt and the whooping of the giants. He shook his head and opened the eye again. Through a film of tears, as he repeated "Sudri—Nordri—Nidi—Nyi—" It was not a cat Thor was lifting, but the middle part of a snake as big around as a barrel. There was no sign of head or tail; the visible section was of uniform thickness, going in one door of the hall and out the other.

"Loki!" he said. "That's not a cat. It's a giant snake that Thor's trying to lift!"

"With a strange shimmering blackish cast over its scales?"

"Yes; and no head or tail in sight."

"Now, right good are your eyes, eater of turnips! That will be nothing less than the Midgard Serpent that curls round the earth! Surely we are surrounded by evil things. Hurry with the finding of the hammer, for this is now our only hope."

Shea turned from the contest, making a desperate effort to concentrate. He looked at the nearest object, an aurochs skull on a pillar, tried another drop of

70

mead in his eye and repeated the spell, forward, backward, and forward. No result. The skull was a skull. Thor was still grunting and heaving. Shea tried once more on a knife hanging at a giant's belt. No result.

He looked at a quiver of arrows on the opposite wall and tried again. The sweet mead was sticking his eyelashes together and he felt sure he would have a headache after this. The quiver blurred as he pronounced the words. He found himself looking at a short-handled sledge hammer hanging by a rawhide loop.

Thor had given up the effort to lift the cat and came over to them, panting. Utgardaloki grinned down at him with the indulgence one might show a child. All around the giants were breaking up into little groups and calling for more drink.

"Want any more, sonny boy?" the giant chieftain sneered. "Guess you ain't so damn good as you thought you was, huh?"

Shea plucked at Thor's sleeve as the latter flushed and started to retort. "Can you call your hammer to you?" he whispered.

The giant's ears caught the words. "Beat it, thrall," he said belligerently. "We got business to settle and I won't have no snotty little mortals butting in. Now, Asa-Thor, do you want any more contests?"

"I—" began Thor again.

Shea clung to his arm. "Can you?" he demanded.

"Aye, if it be in view."

"I said get outta here, punk!" bellowed Utgardaloki, the rough good nature vanishing from his face. He raised an arm like a tree trunk.

"Point at that quiver of arrows and call!" shouted Shea. He dodged behind Thor as the giant's arm descended. The blow missed. He scuttled among the crowding monsters, hitting his head against the pommel of a giant's sword. Utgardaloki was roaring behind him. He ducked under a table and past some foul-smelling fire giants. He heard a clang of metal as Thor pulled on the iron gloves he carried at his belt. Then over all other sounds rose the voice of the

71

red-bearded god, making even Utgardaloki's voice sound like a whisper:

"Mjöllnir the mighty, slayer of miscreants, come to your master, Thor Odinnsson!"

For a few breathless seconds the hall hung in suspended animation. Shea could see a giant just in front of him with mouth wide open, Adam's apple rising and falling. Then there was a rending snap. With a deep humming, the hammer that had seemed a quiver of arrows flew straight through the air into Thor's hands.

There was a deafening yell from the swarms of giants. They swayed back, then forward, squeezing Shea so tightly he could hardly breathe. High over the tumult rose the voice of Thor:

"I am Thor! I am the Thunderer! Ho, ho, hohoho, yoyoho!" The hammer was whirling round his head in a blur, sparks dancing round it. Level flashes of lightning cracked across the hall followed by deafening peals of thunder. There was a shriek from the giants and a rush towards the doors.

Shea shot one glimpse as the hammer flew at Utgardaloki and spattered his brains into pink oatmeal, rebounding back into Thor's gloves. Then he was caught completely in the panic rush and almost squeezed to death. Fortunately for him, the giants on either side wedged him so tightly he couldn't fall to be trampled.

The pressure suddenly gave way in front. Shea caught the giant ahead of him around the waist and hung on. Behind came Thor's battle howl, mingled with constant thunder and the sound of the hammer shattering giant skulls—a noise that in a calmer moment Shea might have compared to that made by dropping a watermelon ten stories. The Wielder of Mjöllnir was thoroughly enjoying himself; his shouts were like the noise of a happy express train.

Shea found himself outside and running across damp moss in the middle of hundreds of galloping giants and thralls. He dared not stop lest he be stepped on. An outcrop of rock made him swerve. As he did so he caught sight of Utgard. There was already a yawning gap at one end of the roof.

The central beam split; a spear of blue-green lightning shot skyward, and the place began to burn brightly around the edges of the rent.

A clump of trees cut off the view. Shea ran downhill with giants still all around him. One of the group just ahead missed his footing and went rolling. Before Shea could stop, he had tripped across the fellow's legs, his face plowing up cold dirt and pine needles. A giant's voice shouted: "Hey, gang! Look at this!"

"Now they've got me," he thought. He rolled over, his head swimming from the jar. But it was not he they were interested in. The giant over whose legs he had fallen was Heimdall, his wig knocked askew to reveal a patch of golden hair. The straw with which he had stuffed his jacket was dribbling out. He was struggling to get up; around him a group of fire giants were gripping his arms and legs, kicking and cuffing at him. There was a babble of rough voices:

"He's one of the Æsir, all right!" "Sock him!" "Let's get out of here!" "Which one is he?" "Get the horses!"

If he could get away, Shea thought, he could at least take news of Heimdall's plight to Thor. He started to crawl behind the projecting root of a tree, but the movement was fatal. One of the fire giants hallooed: "There's another one!"

Shea was caught, jerked upright, and inspected by half a dozen of the filthy gorillalike beings. They took particular delight in pulling his hair and ears.

"Aw," said one of them, "he's no As. Bump him off and let's get t' hell out of here."

One of them loosened a knife at his belt. Shea felt a deadly constriction of fear around the heart. But the largest of the lot—leadership seemed to go with size in giantland—roared: "Lay off! He was with that yellow-headed stumper. Maybe he's one of the Vanir and we can get something for him. Anyway, it's up to Lord Surt. Where the hell are those horses?"

At that moment more fire giants appeared, leading a group of horses. They were glossy black and bigger than the largest Percherons Shea had ever seen. Three hoofs were on each foot, as with the ancestral Miocene

73

horse; their eyes glowed red like live coals and their breath made Shea cough. He remembered the phrase he had heard Heimdall whispering to Odinn in Sverre's house—"fire horses."

One of the giants produced leather cords from a pouch. Shea and Heimdall were bound with brutal efficiency and tossed on the back of one of the horses, one hanging down on either side. The giants clucked to their mounts, which started off at a trot through the gathering dusk among the trees.

Far behind them the thunders of Thor still rolled. From time to time his distant lightnings cast sudden shadows along their path. The redbeard was certainly having fun.

7

THE AGONIZING HOURS THAT FOLLOWED LEFT LITTLE detailed impression on Harold Shea's mind. They would not, he told himself even while experiencing them. The impression was certainly painful while being undergone. There was nothing to see but misty darkness; nothing to feel but breakneck speed and the torment of his bonds. He could twist his head a little, but of their path could obtain no impression but now and then the ghost of a boulder or a clump of trees momentarily lit by the fiery eyes of the horses. Every time he thought of the speed they were making along the rough and winding route his stomach crawled and the muscles of his right leg tensed as he tried to apply an imaginary automobile brake.

When the sky finally turned to its wearisome blotting-paper gray the air was a little warmer, though still raw. A light drizzle was sifting down. They were in a countryside of a type totally unfamiliar to Shea. A boundless plain of tumbled black rock rose here and there to cones of varying size. Some of the cones smoked, and little pennons of steam wafted from cracks in the basalt. The vegetation consisted mostly of clumps of small palmlike tree ferns in the depressions.

They had slowed down to a fast trot, the horses picking their way over the ropy bands of old lava flows. Now and again one or more fire giants would detach themselves from the party and set off on a tangent to the main course.

Finally, a score of the giants clustered around the horse that bore the prisoners, making toward a particularly large cone from whose flanks a number of smoke plumes rose through the drizzle. To Shea the fire giants still looked pretty much alike, but he had no difficulty in picking out the big authoritative one who had directed his capture.

They halted in front of a gash in the rock. The giants dismounted, and one by one led their steeds through the opening. The animals' hoofs rang echoing on the rock floor of the passage, which sprang above their heads in a lofty vault till it suddenly ended with a right-angled turn. The cavalcade halted; Shea heard a banging of metal on metal, the creak of a rusty hinge, and a giant voice that cried: "Whatcha want?"

"It's the gang, back from Jötunheim. We got one of the Æsir and a Van. Tell Lord Surt."

"Howdja make out at Utgard?"

"Lousy. Thor showed up. He spotted the hammer somehow, the scum, and called it to him and busted things wide open. It was that smart-aleck Loki, I think."

"What was the matter with the Sons of the Wolf? They know what to do about old Red Whiskers."

"Didn't show. I suppose we gotta wait for the *Time* for them to come around."

The horses tramped on. As they passed the gate-keeper, Shea noticed that he held a sword along which flickered a yellow flame with thick, curling smoke rising from it, as though burning oil were running down the blade. Ahead and slanting downward, the place they had entered seemed an underground hall of vaguely huge proportions, full of great pillars. Flares

75

of yellow light threw changing shadows as they moved. There was a stench of sulphur and a dull, machine-like banging. As the horses halted behind some pillars that grew together to make another passage, a thin shriek ululated in the distance: "Eee-e-e."

"Bring the prisoners along," said a voice. "Lord Surt wants to judge 'em."

Shea felt himself removed and tucked under a giant's arm like a bundle. It was a method of progress that woke all the agonies in his body. The giant was carrying him face down, so that he could see nothing but the stone floor with its flickering shadows. The place stank.

The door opened and there was a babble of giant voices. Shea was flung upright. He would have fallen if the giant who had been carrying him had not propped him up. He was in a torchlit hall, very hot, with fire giants standing all around, grinning, pointing, and talking, some of them drinking.

But he had no more than a glance for them. Right in front, facing him, flanked by two guards who carried the curious burning swords, sat the biggest giant of all—a giant dwarf. That is, he was a full giant in size, at least eleven feet tall, but with the squat bandy legs, the short arms and huge neckless head of a dwarf. His hair hung lank around the nastiest grin Shea had ever seen. When he spoke, the voice had not the rumble of the other giants, but a reedy, mocking falsetto:

"Welcome, Lord Heimdall, to Muspellheim! We are delighted to have you here." He snickered. "I fear gods and men will be somewhat late in assembling for the battle without their horn blower. Hee, hee, hee. But, at least, we can give you the comforts of one of our best dungeons. If you must have music, we will provide a willow whistle. Hee, hee, hee. Surely so skilled a musician as yourself could make it heard throughout the nine worlds." He ended with another titter at his own humor.

Heimdall kept his air of dignity. "Bold are your words, Surt," he replied, "but it is yet to be seen whether your deeds match them when you stand on Vigrid Plain. It may be that I have small power against you of the Muspellheim blood. Yet I have a brother named Frey, and it is said that if you two come face to face, he will be your master."

Surt sucked two fingers to indicate his contempt. "Hee, hee, hee. It is also said, most stupid of godlings, that Frey is powerless without his sword. Would you like to know where the enchanted blade, Hundings-bana, is? Look behind you, Lord Heimdall!"

Shea followed the direction of Heimdall's eyes. Sure enough, on the wall there hung a great two-handed sword, its blade gleaming brightly in that place of glooms, its hilt all worked with gold up to the jeweled pommel.

"While it hangs up there, most stupid of Æsir, I am safe. Hee, hee, hee. Have you been wondering why that famous eyesight of yours did not light on it before? Now you know, most easily deceived. In Muspellheim, we have found the spells that make Heimdall powerless."

Heimdall was unimpressed. "Thor has his hammer back," he remarked easily. "Not a few of your fire giants' heads will bear witness—if you can find them."

Surt scowled and thrust his jaw forward, but his piping voice was as serene and mocking as before. "Now, that," he said, "really gives me an idea. I thank you, Lord Heimdall. Who would have thought it possible to learn anything from one of the Æsir? Hee, hee, hee. Skoa!"

A lop-eared fire giant shuffled forward. "What-cha want, boss?"

"Ride to the gates of Asgard. Tell them I have their horn tooter here. I will gladly send the nuisance back to his relatives; but in exchange I want that sword of his, the one they call Head. Hee, hee, hee. I am collecting gods' swords, and we shall see, Lord Heimdall, how you fare against the frost giants without yours."

He grimed all around his face and the fire giants in the background slapped their knees and whooped. "Pretty hot stuff boss!" "Ain't he smart," "Two of the four great weapons!" "Boy, will we show em!"

Surt gazed at Shea and Heimdall for a moment,

enjoying to the utmost the roar of appreciation and Heimdall's sudden pallor. Then he made a gesture of dismissal. "Take the animals away and put 'em in a dungeon before I die laughing."

Shea felt himself seized once more and carried off, face downward in the same ignominious position as before.

Down—down—down they went, stumbling through the lurid semidark. At last they came to a passage lined with cells between whose bars the hollow eyes of previous arrivals stared at them. The stench had become overpowering.

The commanding giant thundered: "Stegg!"

There was a stir in an alcove at the far end of the passage, and out came a scaly being about five feet tall, with an oversize head decorated by a snub nose and a pair of long pointed ears. Instead of hair and beard it had wormlike excrescences on its head. They moved. The being squeaked: "Yes, Lord."

The giant said: "Got a couple more prisoners for you. Say, what stinks?"

"Please, lord, mortal him die. Five days gone."

"You lug! And you left him in there?"

"No lord here. Snögg say 'no,' must have lord's orders to do—"

"You damn nitwit! Take him out and give him to the furnace detail! Hai, wait, take care of these prisoners first. Hai, bolt the door, somebody. We don't take no chances with the Æsir."

Stegg set about efficiently stripping Shea and Heimdall. Shea wasn't especially afraid. So many extraordinary things had happened to him lately that the whole proceeding possessed an air of unreality. Besides, even the difficulties of such a place might not be beyond the resources of a well-applied brain.

Stegg said: "Lord, must put in dead mortal's cell. No more. All full."

"Awright, get in there, youse." The giant gave Shea a cuff that almost knocked him flat and set him staggering toward the cell which Stegg had opened. Shea avoided the mass of corruption at one side and looked for a place to sit down. There was none. The only furnishings of any kind consisted of a bucket whose purpose was obvious.

Heimdall followed him in, still wearing his high, imperturbable air. Stegg gathered up the corpse, went out, and slammed the door. The giant took hold of the bars and heaved on them. There was no visible lock or bolt, but the door stayed tight.

"Oh, ho!" roared the giant. "Don't the Sleepless One look cute? When we get through with the other Æsir we'll come back and show you some fun. Have yourselves a time." With this farewell, the giants all tramped out.

Fortunately the air was warm enough so Shea didn't mind the loss of his garments from a thermal point of view. Around them the dungeon was silent, save for a drip of water somewhere and the occasional rustle of a prisoner in his cell. Across from Shea there was a clank of chains. An emaciated figure with a wildly disordered beard shuffled up to the bars and screamed, "Yngvi is a louse!" and shuffled back again.

"What means he?" Heimdall called out.

From the right came a muffled answer: "None knows. He says it every hour. He is mad, as you will be."

"Cheerful place," remarked Shea.

"Is it not?" agreed Heimdall readily. "Worse have I seen, but happily without being confined therein. I will say that for a mortal, you are not without spirit, Turnip Harald. Your demeanor likes me well."

"Thanks." Shea had not entirely forgotten his irritation over Heimdall's patronizing manner, but the Sleepless One held his interest more than the choleric and rather slow-witted Thor or the sneering Loki. "If you don't mind my asking, Golden One, why can't you just use your powers to get out?"

"To all things there is a limit," replied Heimdall, "of size, of power, and of duration. Wide is the lifetime of a god; wider than of a thousand of your feeble species one after the other. Yet even gods grow old and die. Likewise, as to these fire giants and their chief, Surt, that worst of beings. I have not much

79

strength. If my brother Frey were here now, or if we were among the frost giants, I could overcome the magic of that door."

"How do you mean?"

"It has no lock. Yet it will not open save when an authorized person pulls it and with intent to open. Look, now"—Heimdall pushed against the bars without effect—"if you will be quiet for a while, I will try to see my way out of this place."

The Sleepless One leaned back against the wall, his eyes moving restlessly about. His body quivered with energy in spite of his relaxed position.

"Not too well can I see," he announced after a few minutes. "There is so much magic here—fire magic of a kind both evil and difficult—that it hurts my head. Yet this much I see clearly: around us all is rock, with no entrance but the way by which we came. Beyond that there lies a passage with trolls to watch it. *Ugh*, disgusting creatures." The golden-haired god gave a shudder of repugnance.

"Can you see beyond?" asked Shea.

"A little. Beyond the trolls, a ledge sits over a pile of molten slag at the entrance of the hall where the flaming swords are forged, and then—and then"—his forehead contracted, his lips moved a trifle—"a giant sits by the pool of slag. No more can I see."

Heimdall relapsed into gloomy silence. Shea felt considerable respect and some liking for him, but it is hard to be friendly with a god, even in a prison cell. Thjalfi's cheerful human warmth was missing.

Stegg re-entered the cell hall. One of the prisoners called out: "Good Stegg, a little water, please; I die of thirst."

Stegg turned his head a trifle. "Dinner time soon, slave." The prisoner gave a yell of anger and shouted abuse at the troll, who continued down to his alcove in the most perfect indifference. Here he hoisted himself into a broken-down stool, dropped his chin on his chest, and apparently went to sleep.

"Nice guy," said Shea.

The prisoner across the way came to the front of his cell and shrieked, "Yngvi is a louse!" again.

"The troll is not asleep," said Heimdall. "I can hear

his thoughts, for he is of a race that can hardly think at all without moving the lips. But I cannot make them out. Harald, you see a thing that is uncommon; namely, one of the Æsir confessing he is beaten. But there is this to be said: if we are held here it will be the worst of days for gods and men."

"Why would that be?"

"So near is the balance of strength, gods against giants, that the issue of what will happen at the *Time* hangs by a thread. If we come late to the field we shall surely lose; the giants will hold the issues against our mustering. And I am here—here in this cell— with my gift of eyesight that can see them in time to warn. I am here, and the Gjallarhorn, the roaring trumpet that would call gods and heroes to the field, is at Sverre's house."

Shea asked: "Why don't the Æsir *attack* the giants before the giants are ready, if they know there's going to be a war anyway?"

Heimdall stared at him. "You know not the Law of the Nine Worlds, Harald. We Æsir cannot attack the giants all together before the *Time*. Men and gods live by law; else they would be but giants."

He began to pace back and forth with rapid steps, his forehead set in a frown. Shea noted that even at this moment the Sleepless One was careful to place one foot before the other to best display the litheness of his walk.

"Surely they'll miss you," said Shea. "Can't they set other guards to watch the giants get together, or" —he finished lamely at the glint in Heimdall's eye— "something?"

"A mortal's thoughts! Aye!" Heimdall gave a short bark of bitter laughter. "Set other guards, here and there! Listen, Turnip Harald; Harald the fool. Of all us Æsir, Frey is the best, the only one who can stand before Surt with weapons in hand. Yet the worlds are so made, and we cannot change it, that one race Frey fears. Against the frost giants he has no power. Only I, I and my sword Head, can deal with them; and if I am not there to lead my band against the frost giants, we shall live to something less than a ripe old age thereafter."

81

"I'm sorry—sir," said Shea.

"Aye. No matter. Come, let us play the game of questions. Few and ill are the thoughts that rise from brooding."

For hours they plied each other with queries about their respective worlds. In that ominous place, time could be measured only by meals and the periodic shrieks of "Yngvi is a louse!" About the eighth of these cries, Stegg came out of his somnolent state, went out, and returned with a pile of bowls. These he set in front of the cells. Each bowl had a spoon; one was evidently expected to do one's eating through the bars. As the troll put the bowls in front of Shea's cell, he remarked loftily: "King see subjects eat."

The mess he put in them consisted of some kind of porridge with small lumps of fish in it, sour to the taste. Shea did not blame his fellow prisoners when they broke into loud complaints about the quality and quantity of the food. Stegg paid not the slightest attention, relapsing into his chair till they had finished, when he gathered up the bowls and carried them out.

The next time the door opened, it was not Stegg but another troll. In the flickering torchlight this one was, if possible, less handsome than his predecessor. His face was built around a nose of such astonishing proportions that it projected a good eighteen inches, and he moved with a quick, catlike stride. The prisoners, who had been fairly noisy while Stegg was in charge, now fell silent.

The new jailer stepped quickly to Shea's cell. "You new arrivals?" he snapped. "I am Snögg. You be good, nothing hurt you. You be bad, *zzzp*." He made a motion with his finger to indicate the cutting of a throat, and turning his back on them, paced down the row of cells, peering suspiciously into each.

Shea had never in his life slept on a stone floor. So he was surprised, an indefinite time later, to awaken and discover that he had done it for the first time, with the result of being stiff.

He got up, stretching. "How long have I been asleep?" he asked Heimdall.

"I do not know that. Our fellow prisoner, who dislikes someone called Yngvi, ceased his shouting some time since."

The long-nosed jailer was still pacing. Still muzzy with sleep Shea could not remember his name, and called out: "Hey, you with the nose! How long before break—"

The troll had turned on him, shrieking: "What you call me? You stinking worm! I—*zzzp!*" He ran down to the alcove, face distorted with fury, and returned with a bucket of water which he sloshed into Shea's surprised face. "You son of unwed parents!" raged he. "I roast you with slow fire! I am Snögg. I am master! You use right name."

Heimdall was laughing silently at the back of the cell.

Shea murmured: "That's one way of getting a bath at all events. I guess our friend Snögg is sensitive about his nose."

"That is not un-evident," said Heimdall. "Hai! How many troubles the children of men would save themselves, could they but have the skill of the gods for reading the thought that lies behind the lips. Half of all they suffer, I would wager."

"Speaking of wagers, Sleepless One," said Shea, "I see how we can run a race to pass the time."

"This cage is somewhat less than spacious," objected Heimdall. "What are you doing? It is to be trusted that you do not mean an eating race with those cockroaches."

"No. I'm going to race *them*. Here's yours. You can tell him by his broken feeler."

"The steed is not of the breed," observed Heimdall, taking the insect. "Still, I will name him Gold Top, after my horse. What will you call yours, and how shall we race them?"

Shea said: "I shall call mine Man o' War after a famous horse in our world." He smoothed down the dust on the floor, and drew a circle in it with his finger. "Now," he explained, "let us release our racers in the center of the circle, and the one whose roach crossed the rim first shall win."

"A good sport. What shall the wager be? A crown?"

"Seeing that neither of us has any money at all," said Shea, "why don't we shoot the works and make it fifty crowns?"

"Five hundred if you wish."

Man o' War won the first race. Snögg, hearing the activity in the cell, hustled over. "What you do?" he demanded. Shea explained. "Oh," sniffed the troll. "All right, you do. Not too noisy, though. I stop if you do." He stalked away, but was soon back again to watch the sport. Gold Top won the second race— Man o' War the third and fourth. Shea, glancing up, suppressed an impulse to tweak the sesquipedalian nose that the troll had thrust through the bars.

By and by Snögg went out and was replaced by Stegg, who did not even notice the cockroach racing. As he hoisted himself into his chair, Shea asked whether he could get them some sort of small box or basket.

"Why you want?" asked Stegg.

Shea explained he wanted it to keep the cockroaches in.

Stegg raised his eyebrows. "I too big for this things," he said loftily and refused to answer another word.

So they had to let the racers go rather than hold them in their hands all day. But Shea saved a little of his breakfast and later, by using it as bait, they captured two more cockroaches.

This time, after a few victories for Shea, Heimdall's roach began to win consistently. By the time the man across the passage had yelled "Yngvi is a louse!" four times Shea found himself Heimdall's debtor to the extent of something like thirty million crowns. It made him suspicious. He watched the golden god narrowly during the next race, then burst out: "Say, that's not fair! You're fixing my cockroach with your glittering eye and slowing him up!"

"What, mortal! Dare you accuse one of the Æsir?"

"You're damn right, I dare! If you're going to use your special powers, I won't play."

A smile slowly spread across Heimdall's face. "Young Harald, you do not lack for boldness, and I have said before that you show glimmerings of wit.

In truth, I have slowed up your steed; it is not meet that one of the Æsir should be beaten at aught by a mortal. But come, let that one go, and we will begin again with new mounts, for I fear that animal of yours will never again be the same."

It was not difficult to catch more roaches. "Once more I shall name mine Gold Top, after my horse," said Heimdall. "It is a name of good luck. Did you have no favorite horse?"

"No, but I had a car, a four-wheeled chariot, it was called—" began Shea, and then stopped. What was the name of that car? He tried to reproduce the syllables—nyrose, no—neelose, no, not that either—neroses, nerosis—something clicked into place in his brain, a series of somethings, like the fragments of a jigsaw puzzle.

"Heimdall!" he cried suddenly, "I believe I know how we can get out of here!"

"That will be the best of news," said the Sleepless One, doubtfully, "if the deed be equal to the thought. But I have looked, now, deeply into this place, and I do not see how it may be done without outside aid. Nor shall we have help from any giant with the *Time* so near."

"Whose side will the trolls be on?"

"It is thought that the trolls will be neuter. Yet strange it would be if we could beguile one of these surly ones to help us."

"Nevertheless, something you said a little while back gives me an idea. You remember? Something about the skill of the gods at reading the thought that lies behind the lips?"

"Aye."

"I am—I was—of a profession whose business it is to learn people's thoughts by questioning them, and by studying what they think today, predict what they will think tomorrow in other circumstances. Even to provoke them to thinking certain things."

"It could be. It is an unusual art, mortal, and a great skill, but it could be. What then?"

"Well, then, this Stegg, I don't think we can get far with him, I've seen his type before. He's a—a—a something I can't remember, but he lives in a world of his own imaginings, where he's a king and we're all his slaves. I remember, now—a paranoiac. You can't establish contact with a mind like that."

"Most justly and truly reasoned, Harald. From what I am able to catch of his thought this is no more than the truth."

"But Snögg is something else. We can do something with him."

"Much though I regret to say it, you do not drown me in an ocean of hope. Snögg is even more hostile than his unattractive brother."

Shea grinned. At last he was in a position to make use of his specialized knowledge. "That's what one would think. But I have studied many like him. The only thing that's wrong with Snögg is that he has a . . . a feeling of inferiority—a complex we call it—about that nose of his. If somebody could convince him he's handsome—"

"Snögg handsome! Ho, ho! That is a jest for Loki's tongue."

"*Sssh!* Please, Lord Heimdall. As I say, the thing he wants most is probably good looks. If we could . . . if we could pretend to work some sort of spell on his nose, tell him it has shrunk and get the other prisoners to corroborate—"

"A plan of wit! It is now to be seen that you have been associating with Uncle Fox. Yet do not sell your bearskin till you have caught the animal. If you can get Snögg sufficiently friendly to propose your plan, then will it be seen whether confinement has really sharpened your wits or only addled them. But, youngling, what is to prevent Snögg feeling his nose and discovering the beguilement for himself?"

"Oh, we don't have to guarantee to take it all off. He'd be grateful enough for a couple of inches."

8

WHEN SNÖGG CAME ON DUTY AT NIGHTFALL, HE found the dungeon as usual, except that Shea's and Heimdall's cell was noisy with shouts of encouragement to their entries in the great cockroach derby. He went over to the cell to make sure that nothing outside the rules of the prison was going on.

Shea met his suspicious glower with a grin. "Hi, there, friend Snögg! Yesterday I owed Heimdall thirty million crowns, but today my luck has turned and it's down to twenty-three million."

"What do you mean?" snapped the troll.

Shea explained, and went on: "Why don't you get in the game? We'll catch a roach for you. It must be pretty dull, with nothing to do all night but listen to the prisoners snore."

"Hm-m-m," said Snögg, then turned abruptly suspicious again. "You make trick to let other prisoner escape, I—*zzzzp!*" He motioned across his throat again. "Lord Surt, he say."

"No, nothing like that. You can make your inspection any time. *Sssh!* There's one now."

"One what?" asked Snögg, a little of the hostility leaving his voice. Shea was creeping toward the wall of his cell. He pounced like a cat and came up with another cockroach in his hand. "What'll his name be?" he asked Snögg.

Snögg thought, his little troll brain trying to grasp the paradox of a friendly prisoner, his eyes moving suspiciously. "I call him Fjörm, after river. That run fast," he said at last.

"That where you are from?"

"Aye."

Heimdall spoke up. "It is said, friend Snögg, that

87

Fjörm has the finest fish in all the nine worlds, and I believe it, for I have seen them."

The troll looked almost pleased. "True word. Me fish there, early morning. Ho, ho! Me wade—snap! Up come trout. Bite him, flop, flop in face. Me remember big one, chase into shallow."

Shea said: "You and Öku-Thor ought to get together. Fjörm may have the best fish, but he has the biggest fish story in the nine worlds."

Snögg actually emitted a snicker. "Me know that story. Thor no fisher. He use hook and line. Only trolls know how to fish fair. We use hands, like this." He bent over the floor, his face fixed in intense concentration then made a sudden sweeping motion, quick as a rattlesnake's lunge. "Ah!" he cried. "Fish! I love him! Come, we race."

The three cockroaches were tossed into the center of the circle and scuttled away. Snögg's Fjörm was the first to cross the line to the troll's unconcealed delight.

They ran race after race, with halts when one of the roaches escaped and another had to be caught. Snögg's entry showed a tendency to win altogether at variance with the law of probability. The troll did not notice and would hardly have grasped the fact that Heimdall was using his piercing glance on his own and Shea's roaches and slowing them up, though Snögg was not allowed to win often enough to rouse his sleeping suspicions. By the time Stegg relieved him in the morning he was over twenty million crowns ahead. Shea stretched out on the floor to sleep with the consciousness of a job well done.

When he awoke, just before Snögg came on duty the next night, he found Heimdall impatient and uneasy, complaining of the delay while Surt's messenger was riding to demand the sword Head as ransom. Yet it speedily became obvious that the Snögg campaign could not be hurried.

"Don't you ever get homesick for your river Fjörm?" asked Shea, when the troll had joined them.

"Aye," replied Snögg. "Often. Like 'um fish."

"Think you'll be going back?"

"Will not be soon."

"Why not?"

Snögg squirmed a little. "Lord Surt him hard master."

"Oh, he'd let you go. Is that the only reason?"

"N-no. Me like troll girl Elvagevu. Haro! Here, what I do, talk privacy life with prisoner? Stop it. We race."

Shea recognized this as a good place to stop his questioning, but when Snögg was relieved, he remarked to Heimdall: "That's a rich bit of luck. I can't imagine being in love with a female troll, but he evidently is—"

"Man from another world, you observe well. His thoughts were near enough his lips for me to read. This troll-wife, Elvagevu, has refused him because of the size of his nose."

"Ah! Then we really have something. Now, tonight—"

When the cockroach races began that night, Heimdall reversed the usual process sufficiently to allow Snögg to lose several races in succession. The long winning streak he later developed was accordingly appreciated, and it was while Snögg was chuckling over his victories, snapping his finger joints and bouncing in delight that Shea insinuated softly: "Friend Snögg, you have been good to us. Now, if there's something we could do for you, we'd be glad to do it. For instance, we might be able to remove the obstacle that prevents your return to Elvagevu."

Snögg jumped and glared suspiciously. "Not possible," he said thickly.

Heimdall looked at the ceiling. "Great wonders have been accomplished by prisoners," he said, "when there is held out to them the hope of release."

"Lord Surt him very bad man when angry," Snögg countered, his eyes moving restlessly.

"Aye," nodded Heimdall. "Yet not Lord Surt's arm is long enough to reach into the troll country—after one who has gone there to stay with his own troll-wife."

Snögg cocked his head on one side, so that he

looked like some large-beaked bird. "Hard part is," he countered, "to get beyond Lord Surt's arm. Too much danger."

"But," said Shea, falling into the spirit of the discussion, "if one's face were altogether changed by the removal of a feature, it might be much easier and simpler. One would not be recognized."

Snögg caressed his enormous nose. "Too big—You make fun of me!" he snapped with sudden suspicion.

"Not at all," said Shea. "Back in my own country a girl once turned me down because my eyes were too close together. Women always have peculiar taste."

"That's true." Snögg lowered his voice till it was barely audible. "You fix nose, I be your man: I do all for you."

"I don't want to guarantee too much in advance," said Shea. "But I think I can do something for you. I landed here without all my magic apparatus, though."

"All you need I get," said Snögg, eager to go the whole way now that he had committed himself.

"I'll have to think about what I need," said Shea.

The next day, when Stegg had collected the breakfast bowls, Shea and Heimdall lifted their voices and asked the other prisoners whether they would cooperate in the proposed method of escape. They answered readily enough. "Sure, if 'twon't get us into no trouble." "Aye, but will ye try to do something for me, too?" "Mought, if ye can manage it quiet." *"Yngvi is a louse!"*

Shea turned his thoughts to the concoction of a spell that would sound sufficiently convincing, doing his best to recall Chalmers' description of the laws of magic to which he had given so little attention when the psychologist stated them. There was the law of contagion—no, there seemed no application for that. But the law of similarity? That would be it. The troll, himself familiar with spells and wizardry, would recognize an effort to apply that principle as in accordance with the general laws of magic. It remained, then, to surround some application of the law of similarity with sufficient hocus-pocus to make Snögg believe something extra-special in the way of spells was going on. By their exclamation over the diminishing size of Snögg's nose the other prisoners would do the rest.

"Whom should one invoke in working a spell of this kind?" Shea asked Heimdall.

"Small is my knowledge of this petty mortal magic," replied Heimdall. "The Evil Companion would be able to give you all manner of spells and gewgaws. But I would say that the names of the ancestors of wizardry would be not without power in such cases."

"And who are they?"

"There is the ancestor of all witches, by name Witolf; the ancestor of all warlocks, who was called Willharm. Svarthead was the first of the spell singers, and of the giant kindred Ymir. For good luck and the beguiling of Snögg you might add two who yet live—Andvari, king of the dwarfs, and the ruler of all trolls, who is the Old Woman of Ironwood. She is a fearsome creature, but I think not unpleasant to one of her subjects."

When Snögg showed up again Shea had worked out his method for the phony spell. "I shall need a piece of beeswax," he said, "and a charcoal brazier already lit and burning; a piece of driftwood sawn into pieces no bigger than your thumb; a pound of green grass, and a stand on which you can balance a board just over the brazier."

Snögg said: *"Time* comes very near. Giants muster —When you want things?"

Shea heard in the background Heimdall's gasp of dismay at the first sentence. But he said: "As soon as you can possibly get them."

"Maybe tomorrow night. We race?"

"No—yes," said Heimdall. His lean, sharp face looked strained in the dim light. Shea could guess the impatience that was gnawing him, with his exalted sense of personal duty and responsibility. And perhaps with reason, Shea assured himself. The fate of the world, of gods and men, in Heimdall's own words, hung on that trumpet blast. Shea's own fate, too, hung on it—an idea he could never contemplate without a sense of shock and unreality, no matter how frequently he repeated the process of reasoning it all out.

Yet not even the shock of this repeated thought could stir him from the fatalism into which he had fallen. The world he had come from, uninteresting though it was, had at least been something one could grasp, think over as a whole. Here he felt himself a chip on a tossing ocean of strange and terrible events. His early failures on the trip to Jötunheim had left him with a sense of helplessness which had not entirely disappeared even with his success in detecting the illusions in the giants' games and the discovery of Thor's hammer. Loki then, and Heimdall later had praised his fearlessness—ha, he said to himself, if they only knew! It was not true courage that animated him, but a feeling that he was involved in a kind of strange and desperate game, in which the only thing that mattered was to play it as skillfully as possible. He supposed soldiers had something of that feeling in battle. Otherwise, they would all run away and there wouldn't be any battle—

His thoughts strayed again to the episode in the hall of Utgard. Was it Loki's spell or the teardrop in his eye that accounted for his success there? Or merely the trained observation of a modern mind? Some of the last, certainly; the others had been too excited to note such discordant details as the fact that Hugi cast no shadow. At the same time, his modern mind balked over the idea that the spell had been effective. Yet there was something, a residue of phenomenon, not accounted for by physical fact.

That meant that, given the proper spell to work, he could perform as good a bit of magic as the next *man*. Heimdall, Snögg, and Surt all had special powers—built in during construction as it were—but their methods would do him, Shea, no good at all. He was neither god, troll—thank Heaven!—nor giant.

Well, if he couldn't be a genuine warlock, he could at least put on a good show. He thought of the little poses and affectations he had put on during his former life. Now life itself depended on how well he could assume a pose. How would a wizard act? His normal behavior should seem odd enough to Snögg for all practical purposes.

The inevitable night dragged out, and Stegg arrived to take over his duties. Snögg hurried out. Shea managed to choke down what was sardonically described as his breakfast and tried to sleep. The first yell of "Yngvi is a louse!" brought him up all standing. And his fleabites seemed to itch more than usual. He had just gotten himself composed when it was time for dinner again and Snögg.

The troll listened, twitching with impatience, till Stegg's footfall died away. Then he scurried out like a magnified rat and returned with his arms full of the articles Shea had ordered. He dumped them in the middle of the passage and with a few words opened the door of Shea's and Heimdall's cell.

"Put out all but one of the torches," said Shea. While Snögg was doing this the amateur magician went to work. Holding the beeswax over the brazier, he softened it enough to work and pressed it into conical shape, making two deep indentations on one side till it was a crude imitation of Snögg's proboscis.

"Now," he whispered to the popeyed troll, "get the water bucket. When I tell you, pour it into the brazier."

Shea knelt before the brazier and blew into it. The coals brightened. He picked up a fistful of the driftwood chips and began feeding them onto the glowing charcoal. They caught, little varicolored flames dancing across them. Shea, on his haunches and swaying to and fro, began his spell:

> "Witolf and Willharm,
> Stand, my friends!
> Andvari, Ymir,
> Help me to my ends!
> The Hag of the Ironwood
> Shall be my aid;
> By the spirit of Svarthead,
> Let this spell be made!"

The beeswax, on the board above the brazier, was softening. Slowly the cone lost its shape and slumped. Transparent drops trickled over the edge of the board, hung redly in the glow, and dropped with a hiss and spurt of yellow flame into the brazier.

Shea chanted:

> "Let wizards and warlocks
> Combine and conspire
> To make Snögg's nose melt
> Like the wax on this fire!"

The beeswax had become a mere fist-shaped lump. The trickle into the brazier was continuous: little flames rose yellowly and were reflected from the eyes of the breathlessly watching prisoners.

Shea stuffed handfuls of grass into the brazier. Thick rolls of smoke filled the dungeon. He moved his arms through the murk, wriggling the fingers and shouting:

"Hag of the Ironwood, I invoke you in the name of your subject!"

The waxen lump was tiny now. Shea leaned forward into the smoky half-light, his eyes smarting, and rapidly molded it into something resembling the shape of an ordinary nose. "Pour, now!" he cried. *Swoosh!* went the water into the brazier, and everything was blotted from vision by a cloud of vapor.

He struggled away and to an erect position. Sweat was making little furrows in the dirt along his skin, with the sensation of insects crawling. "All right," he said. "You can put the light back on now." The next few seconds would tell whether his deception was going to work. If the other prisoners did not fail him—

Snögg was going along the passage, lighting the extinguished torches from the one that remained. As the light increased and he turned to place one in its bracket on the opposite side of the wall, Shea joined involuntarily in the cry of astonishment that rose from every prisoner in the cells.

94

Snögg's nose was no bigger than that of a normal human being.

Harold Shea *was* a warlock.

"Head feel funny," remarked Snögg in a matter-of-fact tone.

9

THE TROLL PUT THE LAST TORCH IN PLACE AND turned to Shea, caressing the new nose with a scaly hand. "Very good magic, Harald Warlock!" he said, chuckling and dancing a couple of steps. "Hai! Elvagevu, you like me now!"

Shea stood rooted, trying to absorb events that seemed to have rushed past him. The only sound he could utter was *"Guk!"*

He felt Heimdall's hand on his shoulder. "Well and truly was that spell cast," said the Sleepless One. "Much profit may we have from it. Yet I should warn you, warlock, that it is ill to lie to the gods. Why did you tell me, at the Crossroads of the World, that you had no skill in magic?"

"Oh," said Shea, unable to think of anything else, "I guess I'm just naturally modest. I didn't wish to presume before you, sir."

Snögg had gone off into a ludicrous hopping dance around the hall. "Beautiful me!" he squealed. "Beautiful me!"

Shea thought that Snögg, with or without nose, was about the ugliest thing he had ever seen. But there seemed little point in mentioning the fact. Instead, he asked, "How about getting us out of here now, friend Snögg?"

Snögg moderated his delight enough to say: "Will be do. Go your cage now. I come with clothes and weapon."

Shea and Heimdall exchanged glances. It seemed hard to go back into that tiny cell, but they had to trust the troll now, so they went.

"Now it remains to be seen," said Heimdall, "whether that scaly fish-eater has betrayed us. If he has—" He let his voice trail off.

"We might consider what we could do to him if he has," grinned Shea. His astonishing achievement had boosted his morale to the skies.

"Little enough could I accomplish in this place of fire magic," said Heimdall, gloomily, "but such a warlock as yourself could make his legs sprout into serpents."

"Maybe," said Shea. He couldn't get used to the idea that he, of all people, could work magic. It was contrary to the laws of physics, chemistry, and biology. But then, where he was the laws of physics, chemistry and biology had been repealed. He was under the laws of magic. His spell had conformed exactly to those laws, as explained by Dr. Chalmers. This was a world in which those laws were basic. The trick was that he happened to know one of those laws, while the general run of mortals—and trolls and gods, too—didn't know them. Naturally, the spells would seem mysterious to them, just as the changing color of two combined chemicals was mysterious to anyone who didn't know chemistry. If he had only provided himself with a more elaborate knowledge of those laws instead of the useless flashlights, matches, and guns—

A tuneless whistle cut across his thoughts. It was Snögg, still beaming, carrying a great bundle of clothes and something long.

"Here clothes, lords," he grinned, the tendrils on his head writhing in a manner that no doubt indicated well-being, but which made Shea's skin crawl. "Here swords, too. I carry till we outside, yes?" He held up a length of light chain. "You put round wrists, I lead you. Anybody stop, I say going to Lord Surt."

"Hurry, Harald," said Heimdall as Shea struggled into the unfamiliar garments. "There is yet hope, though it grows dim, that we may reach the other Æsir before they give my sword away."

96

Shea was dressed. He and Heimdall took the middle and end of the chain, while Snögg tucked the other end in his belt and strode importantly before them, a huge sword in either hand. They were as big as Hundingsbana, but with plain hilts and rust-spotted blades. The troll carried them without visible effort.

Snögg opened the door at the end of the dungeon. "Now you keep quiet," he said. "I say I take you to Surt. Look down, you much abused."

One of the prisoner called softly. "Good luck go with you, friends, and do not forget us." Then they were outside, shambling along the gloom of the tunnel. Shea hunched his shoulders forward and assumed as discouraged an expression as he could manage.

They passed a recess in the tunnel wall, where sat four trolls. Their tridents leaned beside them, and they were playing the game of odds-and-evens with their fingers. One of the four got up and called out something in troll language. Snögg responded in the same tongue, adding: "Lord Surt want."

The troll looked dubious. "One guard not enough. Maybe they get away."

Snögg rattled the chain. "Not this. Spell on this chain. *Goinn almsorg thjalma.*"

The troll seemed satisfied with the explanation and returned to his sport. The three stumbled on through the dimness past a big room hewn out of the rock, full of murky light and motion. Shea jumped as someone—a man from the voice—screamed, a long, high scream that ended with gasps of "Don't . . . don't . . . don't." There was only a glimpse of what was going on, but enough to turn the stomach.

The passage ended in a ledge below which boiled a lake of molten lava. Beside the ledge sat a giant with one of the flaming swords. As he looked up, his eyes were pits beneath the eyebrow ridges.

Snögg said: "Prisoners go to Lord Surt. Orders."

The giant peered at them. "Say," he said, "ain't you the troll Snögg? What happened to your nose?"

"I pray Old Woman of Ironwood. She shrink him!" Snögg grinned.

"Okay, I guess it's all right." As they passed, the giant thrust a foot in front of Shea, who promptly stumbled over it, in sickening fear of going down into the lava. The giant thundered, "Haw, haw, haw!"

"You be careful," snapped Snögg. "You push prisoners in, Surt push you in, by Ymir."

"Haw, haw, haw! Gawan, Scalyface, before I push you in."

Shea picked himself up, giving the giant a look that should have melted lead at twenty paces. If he could remember that face and sometime—but, no, he was romancing. Careful, Shea, don't let things go to your head.

They turned from the ledge into another tunnel. This sloped up then leveled again where side tunnels branched in from several directions. Snögg picked his way unerringly through the maze. A tremendous banging grew on them, and they were passing the entrance of some kind of armory. The limits of the place were invisible in the flickering red glare, through which scuttled naked black things, like licorice dolls. Heimdall whispered: "These would be dark dwarfs from Svartalfheim, where no man nor As has ever been."

They went on, up, right, left. A sultry glow came down the tunnel ahead, as though a locomotive were approaching around the curve. There was a tramp of giant feet. Around the corner came a file of the monsters, each with a flaming sword, marching and looking straight ahead, like somnambulists. The three flattened themselves against the wall as the file tramped past, their stench filling the passage. The rearmost giant fell out and turned back.

"Prisoners to Lord Surt," said Snögg. The giant nodded, cleared his throat, and spat. Shea got it in the neck. He retched slightly and swabbed with the tail of his cloak as the giant grinned and hurried after the rest.

They were in the upper part of the stronghold now, moving through forests of pillars. Snögg abandoned his bold stride, put a finger to his lips and began to slide softly from pillar to pillar. The tread of a giant resounded somewhere near. All three squeezed themselves into a triangle of shadow behind a pillar. The footsteps waxed, stopping just on the opposite side, and all three held breath. They heard the giant hawk, then spit, and the little *splat!* on the floor. The footsteps moved off.

"Give me chain," whispered Snögg. He rolled it into a tight ball, and led the way, tiptoeing into another maze of passages. "This is way," he whispered, after a few minutes. "We wait till passage clear. Then I go make giant chase. Then you go, run fast. Then— *ssst!* Lie down on floor, quick!"

They fell flat at the word, next to the wall. Shea felt the floor vibrate beneath him to the tread of invisible giants. They were coming nearer, toward them, right over them, and the sound of their feet was almost drowned for Shea in the beating of his own heart. He shut his eyes. One of the giants rumbled heavily: "So I says to him, 'Whassa matter, ain'tcha got no guts?' And he says—" The rest of the remark was carried away.

The three rose and tiptoed. Snögg motioned them to stop, peering around a corner. Shea recognized the passage by which they had entered the place—how long before? Snögg took one more peek, turned and handed Shea one sword, giving the other to Heimdall. "When giant chase me," he whispered, "run; run fast. Dark outside. You hide."

"How will you find us?" asked Shea.

Snögg's grin was visible in the gloom. "Never mind. I find you all right. You bet." He was gone.

Shea and Heimdall waited. They heard a rumbling challenge from the sentry and Snogg's piping reply. A chain clanked, the sound suddenly drowned in a frightful roar. "Why, you snotty little—" Feet pounded into the night, and shoutings.

Shea and Heimdall raced for the entrance and out past the door, which swung ajar. It was blacker than the inside of a cow, except where dull-red glows lit the under sides of smoke plumes from vents in the cones.

They headed straight out and away, Shea, at least, with no knowledge of where they were going. It would be time enough to think of direction later, anyway. They had to walk rather than run, even when their eyes had become accustomed to the gloom, and even so, narrowly missed a couple of bad falls on the fantastically contorted rock.

The huge cone of Surt's stronghold faded into the general blackness behind. Then there was a hiss in the dark and they were aware of Snögg's fishy body smell. The troll moved light and sure, like a cat. He was chuckling. "Hit giant in nose with chain. Should see face. He, he, he!"

"Whither do you lead us, troll?" asked Heimdall.

"Where you want to go?"

Heimdall thought. "The best would be Sverre's house, the Crossroads of the World. Or failing that, the gates of Hell, where one may hope to find even yet the Wanderer at his task. He must know, soon as ever, what we have seen. That were a fortnight's journey afoot. But if I could get to some high cold place, where this fire magic is not, I could call my horse, Gold Top."

"Look out!" said Snögg suddenly. "Giants come!"

A flickering yellow light was showing across the lava beds. Snögg vanished into a patch of shadow, while Shea and Heimdall crouched under the edge of a dyke in the lava flow. They heard the crunch of giant feet on the basalt. The shadows swayed this way and that with the swinging of the fiery swords. A giant voice rumbled. "Hey, you, this is a rough section. There's enough pockets to hide fifty prisoners."

Another voice: "Okay, okay. I suppose we gotta poke around here all night. Me, I don't think they came this way, anyhow."

"You ain't supposed to think," retorted the first voice, nearer. "Hey, Raki!"

"Here," growled a third, more distant, giant.

"Don't get too far away," shouted the first.

"But the other guys are clear outta sight!" complained the distant Raki.

"That don't matter none. We gotta keep close together. Ouch!" The last was a yell, mixed with a thump and a scramble. "If I catch those scum, they'll pay for this."

The light from the nearest giant's sword grew stronger, creeping toward Shea and Heimdall inch by inch. The fugitives pressed themselves right through it. Inch by inch—

The giant was clearly visible around the end of the lava dyke, holding his sword high and moving slowly, peering into every hollow. Nearer came the light. Nearer. It washed over the toes of Shea's boots, then lit up Heimdall's yellow mane.

"Hey!" roared the giant in his foghorn bass. "Raki! Randver! I got 'em! Come, quick!" He rushed at a run. At the same time there was a thumping behind them and the nearest of the other two leaped up out of nowhere, swinging his sword in circles.

"Take that one, warlock!" barked Heimdall, pointing with his sword at the first of the two. He vaulted lightly to the top of the dyke and made for the second giant.

Shea hefted his huge blade with both hands. You simply couldn't fence with a crowbar like this. It was hopeless. But he wasn't afraid—hot dog, he wasn't afraid! What the hell, anyway? The giant gave a roar and a leap, whirling the fiery sword over his head in a figure eight to cut the little man down in one stroke.

Shea swung the ponderous weapon up in an effort to parry that downstroke. He never knew how, but in that instant the sword went as light as an amusement park cane. The blades met. With a tearing scream of metal Shea's sword sheared right through the flaming blade. The tip sailed over his head, landing with a crackle of flame in some brush behind. Almost without Shea's trying, his big blade swept around in a perfect stop-thrust in carte, and through the monster's throat. With a bubbling shriek the giant crashed to earth.

Shea spun around. Beyond the lip of the dyke Heimdall was hotly engaged with his big adversary, their blades flickering, but the third giant was coming up to take a part. Shea scrambled up on the dyke and ran toward him, surprised to discover he was shouting at the top of his voice.

The giant changed course and in no time was towering right over him. Shea easily caught the first slash with a simple parry carte. The giant hesitated, irresolute; Shea saw his chance, whipped both blades around in a bind in octave, and lunged. The giant's flaming sword was pushed back against its owner, and Shea's point took him in the stomach with such a rush that Shea almost fell onto the collapsing monster's body.

"Ho, ho!" cried Heimdall. He was standing over his fallen opponent, terrible bloody slashes in the giant's body showing dim red in the light of the burning swords on the ground. "Through the guts! Never have I seen a man who used a sword as he would a spear, thrust and not strike. By Thor's hammer, Warlock Harald, I had not expected to find you so good a man of your hands! I have seen those do worse who were called berserks and champions." He laughed, and tossed his own sword up to catch it by the hilt. "Surely you shall be of my band at the *Time*. Though in the end it is nothing remarkable, seeing what blade you have there."

The big sword had become heavy again and weighted Shea's arm down. There was a trickle of blood up over the hilt onto his hand. "Looks like a plain sword to me," he said.

"By no means. That is the enchanted sword, Frey's invincible Hundingsbana, that shall one day be Surt's death. Hai! Gods and men will shout for this day; for the last of the war weapons of the Æsir is recovered! But we must hurry. Snögg!"

"Here," said the troll, emerging from a clump of tree ferns. "Forgot to say. I put troll spell on sword so light from blade don't show giants where we go. It wear off in a day or two."

"Can you tell us where there is a mountain tall and cold near here?" asked Heimdall.

"Is one—oh, many miles north. Called Steinnbjörg. Walk three days."

"That is something less than good news," said Heimdall. "Already we have reached the seventh night since Thor's play with the giants of Jötunheim. By the length of his journey the Wanderer should tomorrow be at the gates of Hell. We must seek him there; much depends on it."

Shea had been thinking furiously. If he knew enough to be a warlock, why not use the knowledge?

"Can I get hold of a few brooms?" he demanded.

"Brooms? Strange are your desires, warlock of another world," said Heimdall.

"What you want him for?" asked Snögg.

"I may be able to work a magic trick."

Snögg thought. "In thrall's house, two mile east, maybe brooms. Thrall he get sick, die."

"Lead on," said Shea.

They were off again through the darkness. Now and then they glimpsed a pinpoint of light in the distance, as some one of the other giant search parties moved about, but none approached them.

10

THE THRALL'S HUT PROVED A CRAZY PILE OF BASALT blocks chinked with moss. The door sagged ajar. Inside it was too black to see anything.

"Snögg," asked Shea, "can you take a little of the spell off this sword so we can have some light?"

He held it out. Snögg ran his hands up and down the blade, muttering. A faint golden gleam came from it, revealing a pair of brooms in one corner of the single-room hut. One was fairly new, the other an ancient wreck with most of the willow twigs that had composed it broken or missing.

"Now," he said, "I need the feathers of a bird. Preferably a swift, as that's about the fastest flier. There ought to be some around."

"On roof, I think," said Snögg. "You wait; I get." He slid out, and they heard him grunting and scram-

103

bling up the hut. Presently he was back with a puff of feathers in his scaly hand.

Shea had been working out the proper spell in his head, applying both the Law of Contagion and the Law of Similarity. Now he laid the brooms on the floor and brushed them gently with the feathers, chanting:

"Bird of the south, swift bird of the south,
    Lend us your wings for a night.
Stir these brooms to movement, O bird of the south
    As swift as your own and as light."

He tossed one of the feathers into the air and blew at it, so that it bobbed about without falling.

"Verdfölnir, greatest of hawks, I invoke you!" he cried. Catching the feather, he stooped, picking at the strings that held the broom till they were loosened, inserted the feathers in the broom, and made all tight again. Kneeling, he made what he hoped were mystic passes over the brooms, declaiming:

"Up, up, arise!
    Bear us away;
We must be in the mountains
    Before the new day."

"Now," he said, "I think we can get to your Steinnbjörg soon enough."

Snögg pointed to the brooms, which in that pale light seemed to be stirring with a motion of their own. "You fly through air?" he inquired.

"With the greatest of ease. If you want to come, I guess that new broom will carry two of us."

"Oh, no!" said Snögg, backing away. "No thank, by Ymir! I stay on ground, you bet. I go to Elvagevu on foot. Not break beautiful me. You not worry. I know way."

Snögg made a vague gesture of farewell and slipped out the door. Heimdall and Shea followed him, the latter with the brooms. The sky was beginning to show its first touch of dawn. "Now, let's see how these broomsticks of ours work," said Shea.

"What is the art of their use?" asked Heimdall.

Shea hadn't the least idea. But he answered boldly. "Just watch me and imitate me," he said, and squatting over his broom, with the stick between his legs and Hundingsbana stuck through his belt, said:

"By oak, ash, and broom
Before the night's gloom,
We soar to Steinnbjörgen
To stay the world's doom."

The broom leaped up under him with a jerk that almost left its rider behind.

Shea gripped the stick till his knuckles were white. Up—up—up he went, till everything was blotted out in the damp opaqueness of cloud. The broom rushed on at a steeper and steeper angle, till Shea found to his horror that it was rearing over backward. He wound his legs around the stick and clung, while the broom hung for a second suspended at the top of its loop with Shea dangling beneath. It dived, then fell over sidewise, spun this way and that, with its passenger flopping like a bell clapper.

The dark earth popped out from beneath the clouds and rushed up at him. Just as he was sure he was about to crash, he managed to swing himself around the stick. The broom darted straight ahead at frightening speed, then started to nose up again. Shea inched forward to shift his weight. The broom slowed up, teetered to a forty-five degree angle and fell off into a spin. The black rock of Muspellheim whirled madly beneath. Shea leaned back, tugging up on the stick. The broom came out of it and promptly fell into another spin on the opposite side. Shea pulled it out of that, too, being careful not to give so much pressure this time. By now he was so dizzy he couldn't tell whether he was spinning or not.

For a few seconds the broom scudded along with a pitching motion like a porpoise with the itch. This was worse than Thor's chariot. Shea's stomach, always sensitive to such movements, failed him abruptly and he strewed Muspellheim with the remains of his last meal. Having accomplished this, he set himself grimly to the task of mastering his steed. He discovered that it had the characteristics of an airplane both longitudinally and laterally unstable. The moment it began to nose up, down, or sidewise the movement had to be corrected instantly and to just the right degree. But it could be managed.

A thin, drawn-out cry of "Haaar-aaald!" came to him. He had been so busy that he had had no time to look for Heimdall. A quarter mile to his right, the Sleepless One clung desperately to his broom, which was doing an endless series of loops, like an amusement park proprietor's dream of heaven.

Shea inched his own broom around a wide circuit. A hundred yards from Heimdall, the latter's mount suddenly stopped looping and veered straight at him. Heimdall seemed helpless to avoid the collision, but Shea managed to pull up at the last minute, and Heimdall, yellow hair streaming, shot past underneath. Shea brought his own broom around, to discover that Heimdall was in a flat spin.

As his face came toward Shea, the latter noted it looked paler than he had ever seen it. Then As called: "How to control this thing, oh very fiend among warlocks?"

"Lean to your left!" shouted Shea. "When she dives, lean back far enough to level her out!" Heimdall obeyed, but overdid the lean-back and went into another series of loops. Shea yelled to shift his weight forward when the broom reached the bottom of the loop.

Heimdall overdid it again and took a wild downward plunge, but was grasping the principle of the thing and pulled out again. "Never shall we reach Odinn in time!" he shouted, pointing down. "Look, how already the hosts of Surt move toward Ragnarök!"

106

Shea glanced down at the tumbled plain. Sure enough, down there long files of giants were crawling over it, the flaming swords standing out like fiery particles against the black earth.

"Which way is this mountain?" he called back.

Heimdall pointed toward the left. "There is a high berg in that direction, I think; though still too strong is the fire magic for me to see clearly."

"Let's get above the clouds then. Ready?" Shea shifted back a little and they soared. Dark grayness gripped them, and he hoped he was keeping the correct angle. Then the gray paled to pearl, and they were out above an infinite sea of cloud, touched yellow by a rising sun.

Heimdall pointed. "Unquestionably the Steinnbjörg lies yonder. Let us speed!"

Shea looked. He could make out nothing but one more roll of cloud, perhaps a little more solid than the others. They streaked toward it.

"There must be an arresting!" cried Heimdall. "How do you stop this thing?" They had tried three times to land on the peak; each time the brooms had skimmed over the rocks at breathless speed.

"I'll have to use a spell," replied Shea. He swung back, chanting:

> "By oak, ash, and yew
> And heavenly dew,
> We've come to Steinnbjörgen;
> Land softly and true!"

The broomstick slowed down, and Shea fishtailed it into an easy landing. Heimdall followed, but plowed deep into a snowdrift. He struggled out with hair and eyebrows all white, but with a literally flashing smile on his face. "Warlocks there have been, Harald, but never like you. I find your methods somewhat drastic."

"If you don't want that broom any more," Shea

retorted, "I'll take it and leave this old one. I can use it."

"Take it, if it pleases your fancy. But now you, too, shall see a thing." He put both hands to his mouth and shouted. "Yo hoooo! Gulltop! Yo hooooo, Gulltop! Your master, Heimdall Odinnsson, calls!"

For a while nothing happened. Then Shea became aware of a shimmering, polychromatic radiance in the air about him. A rainbow was forming and he in the center of it. But unlike most rainbows, this one was end-on. It extended slowly down to the very snow at their feet; the colors thickened and grew solid till they blotted out the snow and clouds and crags behind them. Down the rainbow came trotting a gigantic white horse with a mane of bright metallic yellow. The animal stepped off the rainbow and nuzzled Heimdall's chest.

"Come," said Heimdall. "I grant you permission to ride with me, though you will have to sit behind. Mind you do not prick him with Hundingsbana."

Shea climbed aboard with his baggage of sword and broom. The horse whirled around and bounded onto the rainbow. It galloped fast, with a long reaching stride, but almost no sound, as though it were running across an endless feather bed. The wind whistled past Shea's ears with a speed he could only guess.

After an hour or two Heimdall turned his head. "Sverre's house lies below the clouds; I can see it."

The rainbow inclined downward, disappearing through the gray. For a moment they were wrapped in mist again, then out, and the rainbow, less vivid but still substantial enough to bear them, curved direct to the bonder's gate.

Gold Top stamped to a halt in the yard, slushy with melting snow. Heimdall leaped off and toward the door, where a couple of stalwart blonds stood on guard.

"Hey," called Shea after him. "Can't I get something to eat?"

"Time is wanting," shouted the Sleepless One over his shoulder, disappearing through the door, to return in a moment with horn and sword. He spoke a word or two to the men at the door, who ran around the house, and presently were visible leading out horses of their own.

"Heroes from Valhall," explained Heimdall, buckling on his baldric, "set to guard the Gjallarhorn while the negotiations for my release were going on." He snatched up the horn and vaulted to the saddle. The rainbow had changed direction, but lay straight away before them as Gold Top sprang into his stride again.

Shea asked: "Couldn't you just blow your horn now without waiting to see Odinn?"

"Not so, Warlock Harald. The Wanderer is lord of gods and men. None act without his permission. But I fear me it will come late—late." He turned his head. "Hark! Do you hear—Nay, you cannot. But my ears catch a sound which tells me the dog Garm is loose, that great monster."

"Why does it take Odinn so long to get to Hell?" said Shea, puzzled.

"He goes in disguise, as you saw him on the moor, riding a common pony. The spae-wife Grua is of the giant brood. Be sure she would refuse to advise him, or give him ill adivce, did she recognize him as one of the Æsir."

Gold Top was up out of the clouds, riding the rainbow that seemed to stretch endlessly before. Shea could think only how many steaks one could get from the huge animal. He had never eaten horseflesh, but in his present mood was willing to try.

The sun was already low when they pierced the cloud-banks again. This time they dropped straight into swirls of snow. Beneath and then around them Shea could make out a ragged, gloomy landscape of sharp black pinnacles, too steep to gather drifts.

The rainbow ended abruptly, and they were on a rough road that wound among the rock towers. Gold Top's hoofs clop-clopped sharply on frozen mud. The road wound tortuously, always downward into a great gorge, which reared up pillars and buttresses on either side. Snowflakes sank vertically through the still air around them, feathering the forlorn little patches of moss that constituted the only vegetation. Cold tore at them like a knife. Enormous icicles, like the trunks of elephants, were suspended all around. There was no sound but the tread of the horse and his quick breathing, which condensed in little vapor plumes around his nostrils.

Darker and darker it grew, colder and colder. Shea whispered—he did not know why, except that it seemed appropriate—"Is this Hell of yours a cold place?"

"The coldest in the nine worlds," said Heimdall. "Now you shall pass me up the great sword, that I may light our way with it."

Shea did so. Ahead, all he could see over Heimdall's shoulder now was blackness, as though the walls of the gorge had shut them in above. Shea put out one hand as they scraped one wall of the chasm, then jerked it back. The cold of the rock bit through his mitten into his fingers like fire.

Gold Top's ears pricked forward in the light from the sword. They rounded a corner, and came suddenly on a spark of life in that gloomy place, lit by an eerie blue-green phosphorescence. Shea could make out in that half-light the tall, slouch-hatted figure of the Wanderer, and his pony beside him. There was a third figure, cloaked and hooded in black, its face invisible.

Odinn looked toward them as they approached. "Hai, Muginn brought me tidings of your captivity and your escape. The second was the better news," said the sonorous voice.

Heimdall and Shea dismounted. The Wanderer looked sharply at Shea. "Are you not that lost one I met near the crossroads?" he asked.

"It is none other," put in Heimdall, "and a warlock of power is he, as well as the briskest man with sword that ever I saw. He is to be of my band. We have Hundingsbana and Head. Have you won that for which you came?"

"Enough, or near enough. Myself and Vidarr are to stand before the Sons of the Wolf, those dreadful monsters. Thor shall fight the Worm; Frey, Surt. Ullr and his men are to match the hill giants and you the frost giants, as already I knew."

110

"Allfather, you are needed. The dog Garm is loose and Surt is bearing the flaming sword from the south with the frost giants at his back. The *Time* is here."

"Aieeee!" screeched the black-shrouded figure. "I know ye now, Odinn! Woe the day that my tongue—"

"Silence, hag!" The deep voice seemed to fill that desolate place with thunder. "Blow, son of mine, then. Rouse our bands, for it is *Time*."

"Aieeee!" screeched the figure again. "Begone, accursed ones, to whatever place from whence ye came!" A hand shot out, and Shea noticed with a prickling of the scalp that it was fleshless. The hand seized a sprinkle of snow and threw it at Odinn. He laughed.

"Begone!" shrieked the spae-wife, throwing another handful of snow, this time at Heimdall. His only reply was to set the great horn to his lips and take a deep breath.

"Begone, I say!" she screamed again. Shea had a bloodcurdling glimpse of a skull under the hood as she scooped up the third handful of snow. "To whatever misbegotten place ye came from!" The first notes of the roaring trumpet sang and swelled and filled all space in a tremendous peal of martial, triumphant music. The rocks shook, and the icicles cracked, and Harold Shea saw the third handful of snow, a harmless little damp clot, flying at him from Grua's bony fingers. . . .

"Well," said the detective, "I'm sorry you can't help me out no more than that, Dr. Chalmers. We gotta notify his folks in St. Louis. We get these missing-person cases now and then, but we usually find 'em. You'll get his things together, will you?"

"Certainly, certainly," said Reed Chalmers. "I thought I'd go over the papers now."

"Okay. Thanks. Miss Mugler, I'll send you a report with my bill."

"But," said Gertrude Mugler, "I don't want a report! I want Mr. Shea!"

The detective grinned. "You paid for a report, whether you want it or not. You can throw it away.

So long. 'By, Dr. Chalmers. 'By, Mr. Bayard. Be seein' you." The door of the room closed.

Walter Bayard, lounging in Harold Shea's one good armchair, asked: "Why didn't you tell him what you think really happened?"

Chalmers replied: "Because it would be—shall I say—somewhat difficult to prove. I do not propose to make myself a subject of public ridicule."

Gertrude said: "That wasn't honest of you, Doctor. Even if you won't tell me, you might at least—"

Bayard wiggled an eyebrow at the worried girl. "Heh, heh. Who was indignantly denying that Harold might have run away from her maternal envelopment, when the detective asked her just now?"

Gertrude snapped: "In the first place it wasn't so, and in the second it was none of his damn business, and in the third I think you two might at least co-operate instead of obstructing, especially since I'm paying for Mr. Johnson's services!"

"My dear Gertrude," said Chalmers, "if I thought it had the slightest chance of doing any good, I should certainly acquaint your Mr. Johnson with my hypothesis. But I assure you that he would decline to credit it, and even if he did, the theory would present no—uh—point of application for his investigatory methods."

"Something in that, Gert," said Bayard. "You can prove the thing in one direction, but not the reverse. If Shea can't get back from where we think he's gone, it's a cinch that Johnson couldn't. So why send Johnson after him?" He sighed. "It'll be a little queer without Harold, for all his—"

Wham! The outward rush of displaced air bowled Chalmers over, whipped a picture from the wall with a crash of glass, and sent the pile of Shea's papers flying. There may have been minor damage as well.

If there was, neither Gertrude nor Chalmers nor Bayard noticed it. In the middle of the room stood the subject of their talk, swathed in countless yards of blanket-like woolen garments. His face was tanned and slightly chapped. In his left hand he held a clumsy broom of willow twigs.

"Hiya," said Shea, grinning at their expressions.

"You three had dinner yet? Yeah? Well, you can come along and watch me eat." He tossed the broom in a corner. "Souvenir to go with my story. Useful while it lasted, but I'm afraid it won't work here."

"B-but," stammered Chalmers, "you aren't going out to a restaurant in those garments?"

"Hell, yes? I'm hungry."

"What will people think?"

"What do I care?"

"God bless my soul," exclaimed Chalmers, and followed Shea out.

BOOK TWO

The Mathematics of Magic

"STEAK," SAID HAROLD SHEA.

"Porterhouse, sirloin—?" asked the waitress.

"Both, so long as they're big and rare."

"Harold," said Gertrude Mugler, "whatever this is all about, please be careful of your diet. A large protein intake for a man who doesn't do physical labor—"

"Physical labor!" barked Shea. "The last meal I had was twenty-four hours ago, and it was a little dish of oatmeal mush. Sour, too. Since then I've fought a duel with a couple of giants, done acrobatics on a magic broomstick, had a ride on a god's enchanted brewery-horse— Well, anyway, I've been roasted and frozen and shaken and nearly scared to death, and by Thor's hammer I want food!"

"Harold, are you—are you feeling well?"

"Fine, toots. Or I will be when I surround some grub." He turned to the waitress again: "Steak!"

"Listen, Harold," persisted Gertrude. "Don't! You pop out of nowhere in that crazy costume; you talk wildly about things you couldn't expect anyone to believe—"

"You don't have to believe I popped out of nowhere, either," said Shea.

"Then can't you tell me what's wrong?"

"Nothing's wrong, and I'm not going to talk about it until I've consulted Dr. Chalmers."

"Well," said Gertrude, "if that's your attitude— come on, Walter, let's go to a movie."

"But," bleated Walter Bayard, "I want to listen—"

"Oh, be a gentleman for once in your life!"

"Oh, all right, Gert." He leered back at Shea as

he went. "Anyway you didn't bring back any dream-girls."

Shea grinned after them. "There goes the guy who used to kid me about how Gert had gotten the psychological jump on me," he said to Chalmers. "I hope she rides herd on him."

Reed Chalmers smiled faintly. "You forget—uh—Walter's infallible defense mechanism."

"What's that?"

"When the pressure becomes too great, he can simply go to sleep on her."

Shea gave a suppressed snort. "You know not what you—ah, food!" He attacked his plate, working his mouth around a piece of steak big enough to choke a horse; with effort, like a snake engulfing a toad. An expression of pure bliss spread over his face as he chewed. Chalmers noted that his colleague ignored the fact that half the restaurant was staring at the tableux of a long-faced young man in baggy Norse woolens.

"A—uh—somewhat less rapid rate of ingestion—" Chalmers began.

Shea shook a finger, gulped down his mouthful, and spoke: "Don't worry about me." Between mouthfuls he told his story.

Reed Chalmers' mild eyes bugged as he watched and listened to his young friend. "Good gracious! That's the third of those steaks, somewhat inadequately called small. You'll—uh—render yourself ill."

"This is the last one. Hey, waitress! May I please have an apple pie? Not just a segment; I want a whole pie." He turned back to Chalmers. "So the spook said, 'Go on back to where you came from,' and here I am!"

Chalmers mused: "While I have known you, Harold, to commit venial sins of rhetorical exaggeration incompatible with true scientific accuracy, I have never known you to engage in deliberate fabrication. So I believe you. The general alteration in your appearance and bearing furnishes persuasive corroboration."

"Have I changed?" asked Shea.

"You show the effects of physical hardship, as well as exposure to the sun and wind."

"That all?"

Chalmers pondered: "You would like me to say, would you not, that your air of self-conscious brashness has been replaced by one of legitimate self-confidence?"

"Well—uh . . ."

Chalmers continued: "Those conscious of shortcomings are always eager to be informed of radical improvement. Actually such improvements, when they occur at all in an adult, take place slowly. No miraculous change is to be expected in a couple of weeks." He twinkled at Shea's discomfort, and added: "I will admit that you seem to show some alteration of personality, and I think in the right direction."

Shea laughed. "At least I learned to appreciate the value of theory. If you'd been along we'd really have gotten somewhere in applying the screwy laws of the world of Scandinavian myth."

"I—" Chalmers stopped.

"What?"

"Nothing."

"Of course," said Shea, "you'd never have stood the physical end of it."

Chalmers sighed. "I suppose not."

Shea went on: "It checked your theory of paraphysics all right. In that universe the laws of similarity and contagion held good—at least, the magic spells I figured out with their help worked."

Chalmers brushed his gray mop out of his eyes. "Amazing! I asserted that the transfer of the physical body, to another spacetime frame by symbolic logic —what did you call it? A syllogismobile!—was possible. But it is a shock to have so—uh—far-fetched a deduction confirmed by experimental proof."

Shea said: "Sure, we've got something all right. But what are we going to do with it?"

Chalmers frowned. "It is rather obscure. Presents a whole new world-picture, unlike anything but some

119

of the Oriental religions. An infinity of universes, moving along parallel but distinct space-time vectors. But, as you put it, what can be done with it? If I publish the results of your experiment they'll simply say poor old Chalmers has . . . uh . . . a tile loose, and in any case an experimental psychologist has no business venturing into physics. Think of Oliver Lodge!" He shuddered. "The only satisfactory proof would be to send some of the doubters to another universe. Unfortunately, we could hardly count on their encountering Grua with a handful of enchanted snow. They would be unable to return, and the doubters left behind would be doubters still. You perceive the difficulty."

"Huh-uh. Wonder how the fight came out? It might be worth while going back to see."

"It would be inadvisable. The Ragnarök was only beginning when you left. You might return to find the giants had won and were in charge. If you wish adventure, there are plenty of other and less—" The voice trailed off.

"Other what?"

"Well, perhaps nothing of importance. I was about to say—systematic attainable universes. Since you left I have been engaged in the development of the structural theory of a multiple-universe cosmology, and—"

Shea interrupted. "Listen, Dr. Chalmers. We both know too much psychology to kid each other. Something's eating you besides paraphysical mathematics."

"Harold"—Chalmers gave a sigh—"I've always maintained that you'd make a better . . . uh . . . salesman or politician than psychologist. You're weak on theory, but in offhand, rule-of-thumb diagnosis of behavior patterns, you are incomparable."

"Don't evade, Doctor."

"Very well. Were you perhaps thinking of making another journey soon?"

"Why, I just got back and haven't had time to think. Say! You aren't suggesting you'd like to go along, are you?"

Reed Chalmers rolled a fragment of bread into a precise gray pill. "As a matter of fact that's what

I was suggesting, Harold. Here I am, fifty-six years old, without family or intimate friends—except you young men of the Garaden Institute. I have made—or believe I have—the greatest cosmological discovery since Copernicus, yet its nature is such that it cannot be proved, and no one will credit it without the most exhaustive proof." He shrugged slightly. "My work is done, but to a result that will afford me no appreciation in this world. May I not . . . uh . . . be permitted the foible of seeking a fuller life elsewhere?"

Back in Shea's room and seated in the best armchair, Chalmers stretched his legs and meditatively sipped a highball. "I'm afraid your suggestion of Cuchulainn's Ireland does not meet with my approval. An adventurous life, no doubt—but culturally a barbarism, with an elaborate system of taboos, violations of which are punished by the removal of heads."

"But the girls—" protested Shea. "Those piano-legged Scowegian blondes—they all reminded me of Gertrude—"

"For a person of my age amorous adventure has few attractions. And as my partner in this enterprise I must ask you to remember that while you have . . . uh . . . certain physical skills that would be useful anywhere, I am limited to fields where intellectual attainments would be of more value than in ancient Ireland. The only non-warriors who got anywhere in those days were minstrels—and I can neither compose lays nor play the harp."

Shea grinned maliciously. "All right, you leave the girls to me, then. But I guess you're right; we'll have to drop Queen Maev and Ossian." He peered around the bookshelves. "How about this?"

Chalmers examined the volume he handed down. "Spenser's *Faerie Queene*. Mm-m-m—'vision unrolled after vision to the sound of varying music,' as Dr. Johnson said. Certainly a brilliant and interesting world, and one in which I personally might have some place. But I am afraid we should find it uncomfortable if we landed in the latter half of the story, where Queen Gloriana's knights are having a harder time, as though Spenser were growing discouraged, or the narrative for some reason were escaping from his hands, taking on a life of its own. I'm not sure we could exercise the degree of selectivity needed to get into the story at the right point. After all, in your last experience, you attempted Ireland and arrived in Scandinavian myth."

"But," protested Shea, "if you're going adventuring you can't avoid—" and then stopped, his mouth open.

"You were about to say 'danger,' were you not?" said Chalmers, with a smile. "I confess—"

Shea got to his feet. "Doctor . . . Doc—" he burst out. "Listen: why shouldn't we jump right into that last part of the *Faerie Queene* and help Gloriana's knights straighten things out? You said you had worked out some new angles. We ought to be better than anyone else in the place. Look what I was able to do in the Ragnarök with the little I know!"

"You are immodest, Harold," replied Chalmers, but he was leaning forward. "Still, it is an . . . uh . . . attractive plan; to look in another world for the achievement denied in this. Suppose you fill my glass again while we consider details."

"Well, the first detail I'd like to know something about is what new wrinkles in theory you have in mind."

Chalmers settled himself and took on his lecture-room manner. "As I see it, our universes have a relation analogous to that of a pencil of parallel vectors," said he. "The vectors themselves represent time, of course. That gives us a six-dimensional cosmos —three in space, one in time, and two which define the relationships of one universe of the cosmos to another.

"You know enough mathematics to be aware that the 'fourth dimension,' so called, is only a dimension in the sense of a measurable quality, like color or density. The same applies for the interuniversal dimensions. I maintain—"

"Whoa!" said Shea. "Is there an infinite number of universes?"

"Ahem—I wish you would learn to avoid interruptions, Harold. I used to believe so. But now I consider the number finite, though very large.

"Let me continue. I maintain that what we call 'magic' is merely . . . the physics of some of these other universes. This physics is capable of operating along the interuniversal dimensions—"

"I see," Shea interrupted again. "Just as light can operate through interplanetary space, but sound requires some such conducting medium as air or water."

"The analogy is not perfect. Let me continue. You know how the theme of conjuring things up and making them disappear constantly recurs in fairy tales. These phenomena become plausible if we assume the enchanter is snatching things from another universe or banishing them to one."

Shea said: "I see an objection. If the laws of magic don't operate in the conducting medium of our universe, how's it possible to learn about them? I mean, how did they get into fairy stories?"

"The question is somewhat obvious. You remember my remarking that dements suffered hallucinations because their personalities were split between this universe and another? The same applies to the composers of fairy stories, though to a lesser degree. Naturally, it would apply to any writer of fantasy, such as Dunsany or Hubbard. When he describes some strange world, he is offering a somewhat garbled version of a real one, having its own set of dimensions quite independent of ours."

Shea sipped his highball in silence. Then he asked: "Why can't we conjure things into and out of this universe?"

"We can. You successfully conjured yourself out of this one. But it is probable that certain of these parallel universes are easier of access than others. Ours—"

"Would be one of the hard kind?"

"Ahem. Don't interrupt, please. Yes. Now as to the time dimension, I'm inclined to think we can travel among universes only at right angles to the pencil of space-time vectors, if you follow my use of a . . . a somewhat misleading analogy.

"However, it appears likely that our vectors are

123

curved. A lapse of time, along the inner side of the curve would correspond to a greater lapse of time along the outer. You know the theme in certain fairy tales— the hero comes to fairyland, spends three days, and returns to find he has been gone three minutes or three years.

"The same feature would account for the possibility of landing in someone's imagined idea of the future. This is clearly a case where a mind has been running along one of the outer curved vectors at a speed which has outstripped the passage of time along our own inner side of the curve. The result— Harold, are you following me?"

Shea's highball glass had rolled onto the rug with a gentle *plunk,* and the suspicion of a snore came from his chair. Fatigue had caught up with him at last.

Next week-end, Harold Shea went up to Cleveland. He was approaching this second time-journey with some misgivings. Chalmers was an astute old bird— no doubt about that. A good theorist. But it was the pursuit of the theory rather than its result that interested the old boy. How would he work out as a companion in a life of arduous adventure—a man of fifty-six, who had always led a sedentary life, and for that matter, who always seemed to prefer discussion to experience—

Well, too late to pull out now, Shea told himself, as he entered the shop of the Montrose Costume Co. He asked to see medieval stuff. A clerk, who seemed to think that the word "medieval" had something to do with pirates, finally produced an assortment of doublets and hose, feathered hats, and floppy boots of thin yellow leather. Shea selected a costume that had once been worn by the leading man in De Koven's *Robin Hood.* It had no pockets, but a tailor could be found to remedy that. For Chalmers, he bought a similar but plainer outfit, with a monkish robe and attached hood. Chalmers was to go as a palmer, or pilgrim, a character which both felt would give him some standing.

The costume company's assortment of arms and armor proved not only phony but impractical. The chain mail was knitted woolens dipped in aluminum paint. The plate was sheets of tin-can thinness. The swords had neither edge, balance, nor temper. The antique shops had nothing better; their antique weapons were mostly Civil War cavalry sabers. Shea decided to use his own fencing épée. It had a rather stiff blade, and if he unscrewed the point d'arrêt, ground the end down to a sharp point, and contrived some kind of sheath, the weapon would do till he got something better.

The most serious question, as he explained to Chalmers on his return, was concern with the formulas of the magic they intended to use on their arrival. "How do you expect to read English in the land of Faerie when I couldn't in Scandinavia?" he demanded.

"I've allowed for that," Chalmers replied. "You forget that mathematics is a . . . a universal language, independent of words."

"All right. But will your mathematical symbols mean the same things?"

"Glance at this sheet, Harold. Knowing the principles of symbolic logic to begin with, I can look over this pictured equation with an apple at the left and a great many apples at the right, and thus realize it means that an apple belongs to the class of apples. From that I shall infer that the horseshoe-shaped symbol in the center means 'is a member of the class of.' "

"You think that'll work, honest? But, say, how do we know that you and I will land in the same part of the Faerie world?"

Chalmers shrugged. "For that matter, how do we know we shan't land in Greek mythology? There are still laws of this method of transference to be worked out. We can only hold on to each other, read the formulas in chorus, and hope for the best."

Shea grinned. "And if it doesn't work, what the hell? Well, I guess we're ready." He inhaled deeply. "If P equals not-Q, Q implies not-P, which is equivalent to saying either P or Q but not both. But if not-P is not implied by not-Q—Come in, Mrs. Ladd."

Shea's landlady opened the door, and opened her mouth to say something. But the something failed to come forth. She stared agape at a pair of respectable psychologists, standing side by side in medieval costumes, with rucksacks on their shoulders. They were holding hands and with their free hands holding sheets of paper. Chalmers purpled with embarrassment.

Shea bowed easily. "We're doing an experiment, Mrs. Ladd. We may be away for some time. If Mr. Bayard asks for us, let him in and tell him he can look at the papers in the top right-hand drawer. And you might mail this letter. Thanks." He explained to Chalmers: "It's to Gert; to tell her not to waste her money by setting Johnson after us."

"But, Mr. Shea—" said the landlady.

"Please, Mrs. Ladd. You can sit down and watch if you like. Let's go, Doctor—a conclusion can be drawn concerning the relation between two classes even if the evidence refers only to a part of some third class to which both are related. Whatever is predicated affirmatively or negatively of a class may be predicated in like manner of everything asserted to be contained in that class—"

Mrs. Ladd watched, ample bosom heaving. Her eyes bulged from her head; she'd have material for backfence conversation for months to come.

Pfmp! There was a movement of air, muttering the papers on the table and whirling ashes from the ash trays. Mrs. Ladd, pulling herself together, moved a trembling hand through the space where her strangely dressed lodgers had stood.

It met no resistance.

2

Chalmers spoke first. "Astounding! I should have thought the passage more difficult."

"Uh-huh." Shea looked around, sniffing the air with his head up. "Looks like a plain forest to me. Not as cold as the last one, thank God."

"I . . . I suppose so. Though I'm sure I don't know what type of tree that is."

"I'd say some kind of eucalyptus," replied Shea. "That would mean a warm, dry climate. But look where the sun is. That means late afternoon, so we better get started."

"Dear me, I suppose so. Which direction would you suggest?"

"Dunno, but I can find out." Shea dropped his rucksack and swarmed up the nearest tree. He called down: "Can't see much. No, wait, there's a slope off that direction." He waved an arm, almost lost his footing, and slid down again in a small torrent of bark and leaves.

They started toward the slope in the hope that it represented a river valley, where they could expect to find human habitations. After half a mile a scraping sound halted him wordlessly. They crept forward, peering. A tall, spotted buck was rubbing its horns against a tree. It flung up its head as it heard them, gave a sneezelike snort, and leaped gracefully away.

Shea said: "If he's just getting rid of his velvet, it ought to be late summer or early fall."

"I wasn't aware you were so much of a woodsman, Harold."

"What the hell, Doc . . . Doctor, I've been having practice. What's that?"

Something far off had gone *"Ow-ooh,"* a sort of

musical grunt, as though somebody had casually scraped the C string of a cello.

Chalmers fingered his chin. "It sounds remarkably like a lion. I trust we need not expect to encounter lions in this country."

The noise came again, louder. "Don't bet on it, Doctor," said Shea. "If you remember your Spenser, there were plenty of lions around; also camels, bears, wolves, leopards, and aurochs, as well as human fauna like giants and Saracens. Not to mention the Blatant Beast, which had the worst qualities of all and slandered people besides. What worries me is whether lions can climb trees."

"Merciful Heavens! I don't know about lions, but I'm afraid I shouldn't be equal to much climbing. Let's hurry."

They strode on through the wood, a wood of open glades with little underbrush and no recognizable paths. A little breeze came up to make the leaves whisper overhead. The coughing roar of the lion came again, and Shea and Chalmers, without realizing, stepped up their pace to a trot. They glanced at each other and slowed down again.

Chalmers puffed: "It's good for a man of my age to have a little . . . uh . . . exercise like this."

Shea grinned with one side of his mouth. They came out onto the edge of a meadow that stretched a couple of hundred yards downhill. At the bottom of the valley, more trees evidently concealed a stream. Shea scrambled up another tree for a look. Beyond the stream and its wide, shallow vale stood a castle, small in the distance and yellow in the low sun, with pennants writhing lazily from its turrets. He called down the news.

"Can you make out the devices on any of the pennants?" Chalmers answered. "I was . . . I am . . . not altogether inexpert in matters of heraldry. It might be wise to learn something of the character of the institution."

"Not a damn thing," said Shea, and swung himself down. "Air's too quiet and she's too far away. Anyhow, I'd rather take a chance on the castle than on being part of a lion's breakfast. Let's go."

In the tone of an announcer offering the express for East Chicago, Laporte, and South Bend on Track 18, a voice cried at them: "Who would enter Castle Caultrock?"

There was nobody in sight, but the travelers' eyes caught a flash of metal on one of the projecting balconies where the drawbridge chains entered the wall. Shea shouted back the rehearsed answer: "Travelers, to wit, Harold Shea, gentleman and squire, and Reed Chalmers, palmer!" Wonder what they'd say about the "gentleman," thought Shea, if they knew my father was head bookkeeper of a meat-packing concern?

The answer floated back: "This is a castle of deeds and ladies. The holy palmer may enter in the name of God, but no gentleman unless he be accompanied by his fair dame, for such is the custom of this place."

Shea and Chalmers looked at each other. The latter was smiling happily. "Perfect selectivity!" he murmured. "This is exactly right; right at the beginning of Spenser's fourth book—" His voice trailed off and his face fell. "I don't quite know what to do about your being left out—"

"Go ahead in. I've slept in the open before."

"But—" Just then a movable section in the bars of the portcullis creaked outward, and a man in armor stumbled through, apparently pushed from behind. There was a shout of derisive laughter. A horse was squeezed through the opening behind. The man took the reins and came toward them. He was a small man with close-cropped hair. A scar intersected one corner of a mouth drawn into a doleful expression.

"Hi," said Shea. "Did they throw you out?"

"I hight Hardimour. Aye; it is even the hour of vespers, and being ladyless I am put forth from the fair entertainment within." He smiled wryly. "And what hight you? Nay, tell me not now; for I see my dinner and bed approach, mounted on the back of a jennet."

The travelers turned to follow Hardimour's eyes behind them. Across the even meadow came a pair of horses, bearing an armored knight and his lady. The latter rode sidesaddle, clad in rich garments of a trailing, impractical kind.

The little knight vaulted to his saddle with a lightness that was surprising, considering the weight of his hardware. He shouted, "Defend yourself, knight, or yield me your lady!" and snapped down his visor with a clang.

The smaller horse, with the woman, swung to one side. Shea gave a low whistle as he got a look at her: a slim, pale girl, with features as perfect as a cameo, and delicately rounded eyebrows. The other rider, without a word, whipped a cloth covering from his shield, revealing a black field on which broken spear points were picked out with silver. He swung a big black lance into position.

Heads appeared along the battlements of the castle. Shea felt Chalmers pluck at his sleeve. "That Sir Hardimour is in for trouble," said the older psychologist. "Sable, semé of broken spears is the bearing of Britomart."

Shea was watching the knights, who had spurred their horses to a heavy gallop. *Wham!* went lances against shields, and there were sparks in the fading light. The head of the little knight from the castle went back, his feet came up, and he turned a somersault through the air. He landed on his head with the sound of thirty feet of chain being dropped on a manhole cover.

The stranger knight reined in and brought his horse back at a walk. Shea, followed by Chalmers, ran to where Sir Hardimour sprawled. The little knight seemed to be out cold. As Shea fumbled with unfamiliar fingers at his helmet fastenings, he sat up groggily and helped get it off. He drew in a long breath.

"By'r Lady," he remarked with a rueful grin, "I have stood before Blandamour of the Iron Arm, but that was as rude a dint as ever I took." He looked up as the knight who had overthrown him approached. "It seems I was too ambitious. To whom do I owe the pleasure of a night with the crickets?"

The other pulled up his visor to reveal a fresh young face. "Certes," he said in a light, high-pitched voice, "you are a very gentle person, young sir, and shall not spend a night with the crickets and bugbears if I can help it. Ho, warder!"

The castle guard's head came through the gate in the portcullis. "Your worship," he said.

"Have I fairly gained admittance to Castle Caultrock as the knight of this lady?"

"That is most true."

The knight of the shivered spears on their field of black put both hands up to his own helmet and lifted it off. A sunburst of golden hair burst forth and flowed down to his—her—waist. Behind him Shea heard Chalmers chuckle, "I told you it was Britomart." He remembered that Britomart was the warrior girl who could beat most of the men in the *Faerie Queene*.

She was speaking: "Then I declare I am the lady of this good knight who has been overthrown, and since he has a lady he may enter."

The warder looked worried and scratched his chin. "The point is certainly very delicate. If you are her knight—and yet his lady—how can she be your lady and he your knight? Marry I warrant me this is a case Sir Artegall himself could not unravel. Enter, all three!"

Shea spoke up: "Beg pardon, miss, but I wonder if I could arrange to go in as your friend's man?"

"That you may not, sir," she replied haughtily. "She shall be no man's lady till I restore her to her husband; for this is that Lady Amoret who was foully stolen from her spouse's arms by Busyrane, the enchanter. If you wish to be her knight, you must even try Sir Hardimour's fate against me."

"Hm-m-m," said Shea. "But you're going in as Sir Hardimour's lady?" They nodded. He turned to the latter. "If I had a horse and all the fixings, Sir Knight, I'd fight you for the privilege of being Miss Britomart's man. But as it is I'll challenge you to a round on foot with swords and without armor."

Hardimour's scarred face registered an astonishment that changed to something like pleasure. "Now, that is a strange sort of challenge—" he began.

"Yet not unheard of," interrupted the statuesque Britomart. "I mind me that Sir Artegall fought thus against three brothers at the Ford of Thrack."

Chalmers was plucking at Shea's sleeve again. "Harold, I consider it most unwise—"

"*Shh!* I know what I'm doing. Well, Sir Knight, how about it?"

"Done." Sir Hardimour unbuckled himself from his chrysalis of steel. He stepped forward, his feet feeling uncertainly on the smooth grass which he was used to crossing in metal shoes.

Hardimour stamped and swung his sword a couple of times in both hands. He shifted it to one and moved toward Shea. Shea waited quietly, balancing the épée. Hardimour made a couple of tentative cuts at Shea, who parried easily. Then, feeling surer of his footing, Hardimour stepped forward nimbly, swinging his sword up for a real clash. Shea straightened his arm and lunged, aiming for Hardimour's exposed forearm. He missed, and jumped back before the knight's sword came down, gleaming red in the setting sun.

As the blade descended, Shea flipped it aside with a parry in carte, being careful not to let the heavy blade meet his thin épée squarely. Hardimour tried again, a forehand cut at Shea's head. Shea ducked under it and pricked Hardimour's arm before he could recover. Shea heard Chalmers' quick intake of breath and an encouraging word from Britomart, "Bravely done, oh, bravely!"

Hardimour came on again, swinging. Shea parried, lunged, missed again, but held his lunge and drilled the knight's arm properly with a remise. The slim steel needle went through the muscles like butter. Britomart clapped her hands.

Shea withdrew his blade and recovered, keeping the épée flickering between them. "Had enough?" he asked.

"By God's wounds, no!" gritted Hardimour. The sleeve of his shirt was turning dark red, and he was sweating, but he looked thoroughly grim. He swung the sword up in both hands, wincing slightly. The épée flickered out and ripped his now-dripping shirt-sleeve. He checked, and held his sword out in front of him, trying to imitate Shea's fencing position. Shea tapped it ringingly a couple of times, gathered it up in a bind in octave, and lunged. Hardimour saved himself by stumbling backward. Shea followed him. *Flick, flick, flick* went the thin blade, Hardimour's eyes following it in fearful fascination. He tried to parry the repeated thrust, but could no longer control his big blade. Shea forced him back zigzag, got him into the position he wanted, feinted, and lunged. He stopped his point just as it touched the smaller man's chest. Hardimour put a foot back, but found no support. His arms went up, his sword whirling over and over, till it went *plunk* into the moat. Sir Hardimour followed it with a great splash.

When he came up with a green water plant plastered on his forehead, Shea was kneeling at the edge. Hardimour cried: *"Gulp . . . pffth . . . ugh! . . .* help! I can't swim!"

Shea extended Chalmers' staff. Hardimour caught it and pulled himself up. As he scrambled to his feet, he found that villainous épée blade flickering in his face.

"Give up?" demanded Shea.

Hardimour blinked, coughed up some more water, and sank to his knees. "I cry craven," he said grudgingly. Then: "Curse it! In another bout I'll beat you, Master Harold!"

"But I won this one," said Shea. "After all, I didn't want to sleep with the crickets, either."

"Right glad am I that you shall not," said Hardimour honestly, feeling of his arm. "What galls me is that twice I've been put to shame before all these noble lords and ladies of Castle Caultrock. And after all, I must stay without."

Chalmers spoke up. "Hasn't the castle some rule about admitting persons in distress?"

"I bethink me this is even the case. Sick or wounded knights may enter till they are well."

"Well," said Shea, "that arm won't be well for a couple of months."

"Perhaps you caught a cold from your ducking," advised Chalmers.

"I thank you, reverend palmer. Perhaps I did."
Hardimour sneezed experimentally.

"Put more feeling into it," said Shea.

Hardimour did so, adding a racking cough. "Ah me,
I burn with ague!" he cried, winking. "Good people
of the castle, throw me at least a cloak to wrap myself in, ere I perish! Oooo-ah!" He sank realistically
to the ground. They got him up, and supported him,
staggering, across the drawbridge. Britomart and
Amoret followed, the former leading the three horses.
This time the warder made no objection.

3

A TRUMPET BLEW THREE NOTES AS THEY PASSED
through the gate in the portcullis. The last note was
sour. As the travelers entered a paved courtyard littered by heaps of dirty straw, they were surrounded
by a swarm of little page boys in bright-colored
costumes. All were chattering, but they seemed to
know what to do. They attached themselves two by
two to each of the new arrivals and led them toward
the door of a tall, graystone building that rose from
the opposite side of the court.

Shea was taken in tow by a pair of youths who
gazed at him admiringly. Each wore medieval hose,
with one leg red and the other white. As he mounted
a winding stair under their guidance, one of them
piped: "Are you only a squire, sir?"

"Shh!" said the other. "Have you no manners,
Bevis? The lord hasn't spoken."

"Oh, that's all right," said Shea. "Yes, I'm only a
squire. Why?"

"Because you're such a good swordsman, worshipful sir. Sir Hardimour is a right good knight." He

looked wistful. "Will you show me that trick of catching an enemy's blade sometime, worshipful sir? I want to slay an enchanter."

They had arrived at the entrance of a long, high room, with a huge four-poster bed in one corner. One of the pages ran ahead and, kneeling before a cross-legged chair, brushed it off for Shea to sit on. As he did so, the other reached around him and unbuckled his sword belt, while the first ran out of the room. A moment later he was back, carrying a big copper basin of steaming water, a towel over his arm.

Shea gathered he was expected to wash his hands. They needed it.

"In the name of Castle Caultrock," said the little Bevis, "I crave your lordship's pardon for not offering him a bath. But the hour of dinner is now so near—"

He was interrupted by a terrific blowing of trumpets, mostly out of tune and all playing different things, that might have heralded the arrival of the new year.

"The trumpets for dinner!" said the page who was wiping Shea's hands for him, somewhat to his embarrassment. "Come."

It had fallen dusk outside. The winding stair up which they had come was black as a boot. Shea was glad of the page's guiding hand. The boy surefootedly led the way to the bottom, across a little entry hall where a single torch hung in a wall bracket. He threw open a door, announcing in his thin voice, "Master Harold de Shea!"

The room beyond was large—at least fifty feet long and nearly as wide, wretchedly lighted—according to American standards—by alternate torches and tapers along the wall. Shea, who had recently been in the even dimmer illumination of Bonder Sverre's house, found the light good enough to see that the place was filled with men and ladies, gabbing as they moved through an arch at the far end into the dining hall.

Chalmers was not to be seen. Britomart was visible a few feet away. She was the tallest person in the room

135

with the exception of himself, and fully equal to his own five feet eleven.

He made his way toward her. "Well, Master Squire," she greeted him unsmilingly, "it seems that since I have become your lady you are to take me to dinner. You may give the kiss of grace, but no liberties, you understand?" She pushed her cheek toward him, and since he was apparently expected to do so, he kissed it. That was easy enough. With a little make-up she might have been drawn by George Petty.

Preceded by the little Bevis they entered into the tall dining hall. They were led to the raised central part of the U-shaped table. Shea was glad to see that Chalmers had already been seated, two places away from him. The intervening space was already occupied by the cameolike Amoret. To the evident discomfort of Chalmers, she was pouring the tale of her woes into his ear with machine-gun speed.

"—and, oh, the tortures that foul fiend Busyrane put me to!" she was saying. "With foul shows and fantastic images on the walls of the cell where I was held. Now he'd declare how my own Scudamour was unfaithful to me; now offer me great price for my virtue—"

"How many times a day did he demand it?" inquired a knight beyond, leaning down the table.

"Never less than six," said Amoret, "and oft as many as twenty. When I refused—as ever I must—the thing's past understanding—"

Shea heard Chalmers murmur: "What, never? No never. What, *never*—"

The knight said: "Sir Scudamour may well take pride in such a wife, gentle lady, who has borne so much for his sake."

"What else could she do?" asked Britomart coldly.

Shea spoke up: "I could think of one or two things."

The Petty girl turned on him, blue eyes flashing. "Master Squire, your insinuations are vile, and unworthy the honor of knighthood! Had you made them beyond that gate, I would prove them so on your body, with spear and sword."

She was, he observed with some astonishment, genuinely angry. "Sorry; I was joking," he offered.

"Chastity, sir, is no subject for jest!" she snapped.

Before the conversation could be carried further, Shea jumped at another tremendous blast of trumpets. A file of pages pranced in with silver plates. Shea noted, there was only one plate for him and Britomart together. Looking down the table, he saw that each pair, knight and lady, had been similarly served. This was apparently one of the implications of being a knight's "lady." Shea would have liked to inquire whether there were any others; but in view of Britomart's rebuff at his mild joke at Amoret, he didn't quite dare.

The trumpets blew again, this time to usher in a file of serving men bearing trays of food. That set before Shea and Britomart was a huge pastry, elaborately made in the form of a potbellied medieval ship, upon which the page Bevis fell with a carving knife. As he worked at it, Chalmers leaned around Amoret's back, and touching Shea's sleeve, remarked: "Everything's going according to plan."

"How do you mean?"

"The logical equations. I looked at them in my room. They puzzled me a bit at first, but I checked them against that key I made up, and everything fitted into place."

"Then you can really work magic?"

"I'm pretty sure. I tried a little enchantment on a cat that was strolling around. Worked a spell on some feathers and gave it wings." He chuckled. "I daresay there will be some astonishment among the birds in the forest tonight. It flew out the window."

Shea felt a nudge at his other side, and turned to face Britomart. "Will my lord, as is his right, help himself first?" she said. She indicated the plate. Her expression plainly said she hoped any man who helped himself before her would choke on what he got. Shea surveyed her for a second.

"Not at all," he answered. "You go first. After all, you're a better knight than I am. You pitched Hardimour down with a spear. If you hadn't softened him up, I couldn't have done a thing."

137

Her smile told him he had gauged her psychology correctly. "Grace," said she. She plunged her hand into the pile of meat that had come out of the pastry ship, put a good-sized lump into her mouth. Shea followed her example. He nearly jumped out of his chair, and snatched for the wine cup in front of him.

The meat tasted like nothing on earth. It was heavily salted, and sweet, and almost all other flavors were drowned in a terrific taste of cloves. Two big tears of agony came into Shea's eyes as he took a long pull at the wine cup.

The wine reeked of cinnamon. The tears ran down his cheek.

"Ah, good Squire Harold," came Amoret's voice, "I don't wonder that you weep at the tale of the agonies through which I have passed. Was ever faithful lady so foully put upon?"

"For my part," said the knight farther down the table, "I think this Busyrane is a vile, caitiff rogue, and willingly would I take the adventure of putting an end to him."

Britomart gave a hard little laugh. "You won't find that so easy, Sir Erivan. Firstly, you shall know that Busyrane dwells in the woods where the Losels breed, those most hideous creatures that are half-human in form, yet eat of human flesh. They are ill to overcome. Secondly, this Busyrane conceals his castle by arts magical, so it is hard to find. And thirdly, having found it and Busyrane himself, he is a very stout and powerful fighter, whom few can match. In all Faerie, I know of only two that might overthrow him."

"And who are they?" asked Erivan.

"This one is Sir Cambell, who is a knight of great prowess. Moreover, he has to wife Cambina, who is much skilled in the white magic that might pass both through the Losels and Busyrane's enchantments. The other is my own dear lord and affianced husband, Sir Artegall, justiciar to our queen."

"There you see!" cried Amoret. "That's the kind of person who was after me. Oh, what sufferings! Oh, how I ever——"

"*Ssst,* Amoret!" interrupted Chalmers. "Your food's getting cold, child."

"How true, good palmer." A tear trickled down Amoret's lovely pale cheek as she rolled a huge ball of food between her fingers and thrust it into her mouth. As she chewed she managed to exclaim: "Oh, what would I do without the good friends who aid me!" There was certainly nothing weak about the frail-looking lady's appetite.

Trumpets sounded the end of the course, and as one set of serving men took away the plates, another emerged with more dishes. Pages came running to each couple with metal bowls of water and towels. Sir Erivan, beyond Chalmers, lifted his wine cup and then set it down again.

"Ho, varlet!" he cried. "My wine cup is empty. Is it the custom of Caultrock to let the guests perish of thirst?"

The servitor signaled another, and a small wizened man in a fur-lined jacket hurried up and bowed to Sir Erivan.

"My very gracious lord," he said, "I crave your pardon. But a most strange malady has befallen the wine, and it's turned sour. All the wine in Castle Caultrock. The good Fray Montelius has pronounced an exorcism over it, but to no purpose. There must be a powerful enchantment on it."

"What?" shouted Sir Erivan. "By the seven thousand demons of Gehenna, do you expect us to drink *water?*" And then, shrugging his shoulders, he turned toward Chalmers. "You see how it is, reverend sir. Daily we knights of Faerie are compassed closer about by these evil spells till we know not what to do. I misdoubt me they will make trouble at the tournament."

"What tournament?" asked Shea.

"The tournament of Satyrane, the woodland knight, at his forest castle, three days hence. It will be a most proud and joyous occasion. There's to be jousting, ending with a mêlée, for the prize among knights, and also a tourney of beauty for the ladies after. I've heard that the prize of beauty is to be that famous girdle of the Lady Florimel, which none but the most chaste may bind on."

"Oh, how you frighten me!" said Amoret. "I was kidnaped from a tournament, you know. Now I shall hardly dare attend this one, if there will be enchanters present. Just think, one might win the prize of valor and I be awarded to him of right!"

"*I* shall be in the lists for you," said Britomart, a trifle haughtily.

Shea asked: "Does the winner of the men's prize get the winner of the prize of beauty?"

Sir Erivan looked at him in some astonishment. "You are pleased to jest— No, I see you are really a foreigner and don't know. Well, then, such is the custom of Faerie. But I misdoubt me these enchanters and their spells." He shook his head gloomily.

Shea said: "Say, my friend Chalmers and I might be able to help you out a little."

"In what manner?"

Chalmers was making frantic efforts to signal him to silence, but Shea ignored them. "We know a little magic of our own. Pure white magic, like that Lady Cambina you spoke of. For instance— Doc, think you could do something about the wine situation?"

"Why . . . ahem . . . that is . . . I suppose I might, Harold. But don't you think—"

Shea did not wait for the objection. "If you'll be patient," he said, "my friend the palmer will work some of his magic. What'll you need, Doc?"

Chalmers' brow furrowed. "A gallon or so of water, yes. Perhaps a few drops of good wine. Some grapes and bay leaves—"

Somebody interrupted: "As well ask for the moon in a basket as grapes at Caultrock. Last week came a swarm of birds and stripped the vines bare. Enchanter's work, by hap; they do not love us here."

"Dear me! Would there be a cask?"

"Aye, marry, a mort o' 'em. Rudiger, an empty cask!"

The cask was rolled down the center of the tables. The guests buzzed as they saw the preparations. Other articles were asked and refused till there was produced a stock of cubes of crystallized honey, crude and unstandardized in shape, "—but they'll do as sugar cubes, lacking anything better," Chalmers told Shea.

A piece of charcoal served Chalmers for a pencil. On each of the lumps of crystallized honey he marked a letter, O, C, or H. A little fire was got going on the stone floor in the center of the tables. Chalmers dissolved some of the honey in some of the water, put the water in the cask and some of straw in the water. The remaining lumps of honey he stirred about the table top with his fingers, as though playing some private game of anagrams, reciting meanwhile:

"So oft as I with state of present time
    The image of our . . . uh . . . happiness compare,
So oft I find how less we are than prime,
    How less our joy than that we once did share:
Thus do I ask those things that once we had
    To make an evening run its wonted course,
And banish from this company the sad
    Thoughts that in utter abstinence have their source:
    Change then! For, being water, you cannot be worse!"

As he spoke, he withdrew a few of the lumps, arranging them thus:

$$H \quad H$$

$$H \quad C \quad O \quad O \quad H$$

$$H \quad H$$

"By the splendor of Heaven!" cried a knight with a short beard, who had risen and was peering into the cask. "The palmer's done it!"

Chalmers reached over and pulled the straw from

141

the top of the cask, dipped some of the liquid into his goblet and sipped. "God bless my soul!" he murmured.

"What is it, Doc?" asked Shea.

"Try it," said Chalmers, passing him the goblet.

Shea tried it and for the second time that evening almost upset the table.

The liquid was the best Scotch whiskey he had ever tasted.

The thirsty Sir Erivan spoke up: "Is aught amiss with your spell-wrought wine?"

"Nothing," said Chalmers, "except that it's rather . . . uh . . . potent."

"May one sample it, Sir Palmer?"

"Go easy on it," said Shea, passing down the goblet.

Sir Erivan went easy, but nevertheless exploded into a series of coughs. *Whee!* A beverage for the gods on Olympus! None but they would have gullets of the proper temper. Yet methinks I should like more."

Shea diluted the next slug of whiskey with water before giving it to the serving man to pass down the table. The knight with the short beard made a face at the flavor. "This tastes like no wine I wot of," said he.

"Most true," said Erivan, "but 'tis proper nectar, and makes one feel wonnnnnnderful! More, I pray you!"

"May I have some, please?" asked Amoret, timidly.

Chalmers looked unhappy. Britomart intervened: "Before you sample strange waters I myself will try." She picked up the goblet she was sharing with Shea, took a long, quick drink.

Her eyes goggled and watered, but she held it well. "Too . . . strong for my little charge," said she when she got her breath back.

"But, Lady Britomart—"

"Nay. It would not— Nay, I say."

The servitors were busy handing out the Scotch, which left a trail of louder talk and funnier jokes in its wake. Down the table some of the people were dancing; the kind of dance wherein you spend your time holding up your partner's hand and bowing. Shea had just enough whiskey in him to uncork his natural recklessness. He bowed half-mockingly to Britomart. "Would my lady care to dance?"

"No," she said solemnly. "I do it not. So many responsibilities have I had that I've never learned. Another drink, please."

"Oh, come on! I don't, either, the way they do here. But we can try."

"No," she said. "Poor Britomart never indulges in the lighter pleasures. Always busy, righting wrongs and setting a good example of chastity. Not that anyone heeds it."

Shea saw Chalmers slip Amoret a shot of whiskey. The perfect beauty coughed it down. Then she began talking very fast about the sacrifices she had made to keep herself pure for her husband. Chalmers began looking around for help. Serves the Doc right, thought Shea. Britomart was pulling his sleeve.

"It's a shame," she sighed. "They all say Britomart needs no man's sympathy. She's the girl who can take care of herself."

"Is it as bad as all that?"

"Mush worst. I mean much worse. They all say Britomart has no sense of humor. That's because I do my duty. Conscientious. That's the trouble. *You* think I have a sense of humor, don't you, Master Harold de Shea?" She looked at him accusingly.

Shea privately thought that "they all" were right. But he answered: "Of course I do."

"That's splendid. It gladdens my heart to find someone who understands. I like you, Master Harold. You're tall, not like these little pigs of men around here. Tell me, *you* don't think I'm too tall, do you? You wouldn't say I was just a big blond horse?"

"Perish the thought!"

"Would you even say I was good-looking?"

"And how!" Shea wondered how this was going to end.

"Really, truly good-looking, even if I am tall?"

"Sure, you bet, honest." Shea saw that Britomart

143

was on the verge of tears. Chalmers was busy trying to stanch Amoret's verbal hemorrhage, and couldn't help.

"Thass glorious. I'm so glad to find somebody who likes me as a woman. They all admire me, but nobody cares for me as a woman. Have to set a good example. Tell you a secret." She leaned toward him in such a marked manner that Shea glanced around to see whether they were attracting attention.

They were not. Sir Erivan, with a Harpo Marx expression, was chasing a plump, squeaking lady from pillar to pillar. The dancers were doing a snake dance. From one corner came a roar where knights were betting their shirts at knucklebones.

"Tell you shecret," she went on, raising her voice. "I get tired of being a good example. Like to be really human. Just once. Like this." She grabbed Shea out of his seat as if he had been a puppy dog, slammed him down on her lap, and kissed him with all the gentleness of an affectionate tornado.

Then she heaved him out of her lap with the same amazing strength and pushed him back into his place. "No," she said gloomily. "No. My responsibilities. Must think on them." A big tear rolled down her cheek. "Come, Amoret. We must to bed."

The early sun had not yet reached the floor of the courtyards when Shea came back, grinning. He told Chalmers: "Say, Doc, silver has all kinds of value here! The horse and ass together only cost $4.60."

"Capital! I feared some other metal would pass current, or that they might have no money at all. Is the . . . uh . . . donkey domesticated?"

"Tamest I ever saw. Hello, there, girls!" This was to Britomart and Amoret, who had just come out. Britomart had her armor on, and a stern, martial face glowered at Shea out of the helmet.

"How are you this morning?" asked that young man, unabashed.

"My head beats with the cruel beat of an anvil, as you must know." She turned her back. "Come,

144

Amoret, there is no salve like air, and if we start now we shall be at Satyrane's castle as early as those who ride late and fast with more pain."

"We're going that way, too," said Shea. "Hadn't we better ride along with you?"

"For protection's sake, mean you? Hah! Little enough use that overgrown bodkin you bear would be if we came to real combat. Or is it that you wish to ride under the guard of my arm?" She shook it with a clang of metal.

Shea grinned. "After all, you *are* technically my ladylove—" He ducked as she swung at him, and hopped back out of reach.

Amoret spoke up: "Ah, Britomart, but do me the favor of letting them ride with us! The old magician is so sympathetic."

Shea saw Chalmers start in dismay. But it was too late to back out now. When the women had mounted they rode through the gate together. Shea took the lead with the grumpily silent Britomart. Behind him, he could hear Amoret prattling cheerfully at Chalmers, who answered in monosyllables.

The road, no more than a bridle path without marks of wheeled traffic, paralleled the stream. The occasional glades that had been visible near Castle Caultrock disappeared. The trees drew in on them and grew taller till they were riding through a perpetual twilight, only here and there touched with a bright fleck of sunlight.

After two hours Britomart drew rein. As Amoret came up, the warrior girl announced: "I'm for a bath. Join me, Amoret?"

The girl blushed and simpered. "These gentlemen—"

"Are gentlemen," said Britomart, with a glare at Shea that implied he had jolly well better be a gentleman, or else. "We will halloo." She led the way down the slope and between a pair of mossy trunks.

The two men strolled off a way and sat. Shea turned to Chalmers. "How's the magic going?"

"Ahem," said the professor. "We were right about the general worsening of conditions here. Everyone

145

seems aware of it, but they don't quite know what causes it or what to do about it."

"Do you?"

Chalmers pinched his chin. "It would seem—uh —reasonable to suspect the operations of a kind of guild of evil, of which various enchanters, like this Busyrane mentioned last night, form a prominent part. I indicate the souring of the wine and the loss of the grapes as suggestive examples. It would not even surprise me to discover that a well-organized revolutionary conspiracy is afoot. The question of whether such a subversive enterprise is justified is of course a moral one, resting on that complex of sentiments which the German philosophers call by the characteristically formidable name of *Weltansicht*. It therefore cannot be settled by scientific—"

Shea said: "Yeah. But what can we do about it?"

"I'm not quite certain. The obvious step would be to observe some of these people in operation and learn something of their technique. This tournament— Good gracious, what's that?"

From the river came a shriek. Shea stared at Chalmers for three seconds. Then he jumped up and ran toward the sound.

As he burst through the screen of brush, he saw the two women up to their necks in a little pool out near the middle of the river. Wading toward them, their backs to Shea, were two wild-looking, half-naked men in tartan kilts. They were shouting with laughter.

Shea did a foolish thing. He drew his épée, slid down the six-foot bank, and plowed into the water after the men, yelling. They whirled about, whipped out broadswords from rawhide slings, and splashed toward him. He realized his folly: knee-deep in water he would be unable to use his footwork. At best his chances were no more than even against one of these men. Two . . .

The bell-guard of the épée gave a clear ringing note as he parried the first cut. His riposte missed, but the kilted man gave a little. Shea out of the tail of his eye saw the other working around to get behind him. He parried, thrust, parried.

"Wurroo!" yelled the wild man, and swung again. Shea backed a step to bring the other into his field of vision. Cold fear gripped him lest his foot slip on an unseen rock. The other man was upon him, swinging his sword up with both hands for the kill. "Wurroo!" he yelled like the other. Shea knew sickeningly that he couldn't get his guard around in time. . . .

Thump! A rock bounced off the man's head. The man sat down. Shea turned back to the first and just parried a cut at his head. The first kiltie was really boring in now. Shea backed another step, slipped, recovered, parried, and backed. The water tugged at his legs. He couldn't meet the furious swings squarely for fear of snapping his light blade. Another step back, and another, and the water was only inches deep. Now! Disengage, double, one-two, *lunge*—and the needle-point slid through skin and lungs and skin again. Shea recovered and watched the man's knees sag. Down he went.

The other was picking himself out of the water some distance down. When Shea took a few steps toward him, he scrambled up the bank and ran like a deer, his empty swordsling banging against his back.

Amoret's voice announced: "You may come now, gentlemen." Shea and Chalmers went back to the river to find the girls dressed and drying their hair by spreading it to the sun on their hands.

Shea asked Britomart: "You threw that rock, didn't you?"

"Aye. Thanks and more than thanks, Squire Harold. I cry your grace for having thought that slaughtering blade of yours a toy."

"Don't mention it. That second bird would have nailed me if you hadn't beaned him with a rock. But say, why did you just sit there in the pool? A couple of steps would have taken you to the deep water. Or can't you swim?"

"We can swim," she replied. "But it would not be

meet to expose our modesty by leaving the pool, least of all to the wild Da Derga."

Shea forebore to argue about the folly of modesty that exposed one to death or to a fate that Britomart would undoubtedly consider worse. The blonde beauty was showing a much friendlier disposition toward him, and he did not wish to jeopardize it by argument over undebatable questions.

When they rode on, Britomart left Amoret to inflict her endless tale of woe on Chalmers, while she rode with Shea. Shea asked leading questions, trying not to reveal his own ignorance too much.

Britomart was, it transpired, one of Queen Gloriana's "Companions" or officers—a "count" in the old Frankish sense of the term. There were twelve of them, each charged with the righting of wrongs in some special field of the land of Faerie.

Ye olde tyme policewoman, thought Shea. He asked whether there were grades of authority among the Companions.

Britomart told him: "That hangs by what matter is under consideration. In questions involving the relations of man to man, I am less than those gallant knights, Sir Cambell and Sir Triamond. Again, should it be a point of justice, the last authority rests with Sir Artegall."

Her voice changed a trifle on the last word. Shea remembered how she had mentioned Artegall the evening before. "What's he like?"

"Oh, a most gallant princely rogue, I warrant you!" She touched her horse with the spurs so that he pranced, and she had to soothe him with: "Quiet, Beltran!"

"Yes?" Shea encouraged.

"Well, for the physical side of him, somewhat dark of hair and countenance; tall, and so strong with lance that not Redcross or Prince Arthur himself can bear the shock of his charge. That was how I came to know him. We fought; I was the better with the spear, but at swords he overthrew me and was like to have killed me before he found I was a woman. I fell in love with him forthwith," she finished simply.

148

Singular sort of courtship, thought Shea, but even in the world I came from there are girls who fall for that kind of treatment. Aloud he said: "I hope he fell for you, too."

Britomart surprised him by heaving a sigh. "Alas, fair squire, that I must confess I do not know. 'Tis true he plighted himself to marry me, but he's ever off to some tournament, or riding to some quest that I know not the end or hour of. We'll be married when he gets back, quotha, but when he does return, it's to praise my courage or strength, and never a word to show he thinks of me as a woman. He'll clap me on the back and say: 'Good old Britomart, I knew I could depend on you. And now I have another task for you; a dragon this time.' "

"Hm-m-m," said Shea. "Don't suppose you ever heard of psychology?"

"Nay, not I."

"Do you ever dress up? I mean, like some of those ladies at Castle Caultrock."

"Of what use to me such foibles? Could I pursue my tasks as Companion in such garb?"

"Do you ever roll your eyes up at Artegall and tell him how wonderful he is?"

"Nay, marry beshrew me! What would he think of so unmaidenly conduct?"

"That's just the point; just what he's waiting for! Look here, in my country the girls are pretty good at that sort of thing, and I've learned most of the tricks. I'll show you a few, and you can practice on me. I don't mind."

They dined rather thinly that night, on coarse brown bread and cheese which Britomart produced from a pack at the back of her saddle. They slept in cushiony beds of fern, three inches deep. The next day they rode in the same arrangement. Chalmers rather surprisingly consented. He explained: "The young lady is certainly very . . . uh . . . verbose, but she has a good deal of information to offer with regard to the methods of this Busyrane. I should prefer to continue the conversation."

As soon as they were on the road Britomart pulled up her visor and, leaning toward Shea, rolled her eyes. "You must be weary, my most dear lord," she said, "after your struggle with those giants. Come sit and talk. I love to hear—"

Shea grinned. "Overdoing it a little, old girl. Better start again."

"You must be weary— Hola, what have we here?"

The track had turned and mounted to a plateaulike meadow. As they emerged into the bright sun, a trumpet sounded two sharp notes. There was a gleam of metal from the other side. Shea saw a knight with a shield marked in wavy stripes of green drop his lance into place and start toward him.

"Sir Paridell, as I live!" snapped Britomart, in her policewoman's voice. "Oft an illdoer and always a lecher. Ha! Well met! Gloriana!" The last shouted word was muffled in her helmet as the visor snapped shut. Her big black horse bounded toward this sudden opponent, the ebony lance sticking out past his head. They met with a crash. Paridell held the saddle, but his horse's legs flew out from under. Man and animal came down together in a whirlwind of dust—

Shea and Chalmers reached him together and managed to pull the horse clear. When they got Paridell's helmet off he was breathing, but there was a thin trickle of blood at his lips. He was unconscious.

Shea gazed at him a moment, then had an inspiration. "Say, Britomart," he asked, "what are the rules about taking the arms of a guy like that?"

Britomart looked at her late opponent without pity. "Since the false knave attacked us, I suppose they belong to me."

"He must have heard I was traveling in your company," piped Amoret. "Oh, the perils I go through!"

Shea was not to be put off. "I was wondering if maybe I couldn't use that outfit."

Paridell's squire, a youth with a thin fuzz of beard on his chin and the trumpet over his shoulder, had joined them. He was bending over his master, trying to revive him by forcing the contents of a little flask between his lips. Now he looked up. "Nay, good sir," he said to Britomart, "punish him not so. He did but catch a glimpse of you as you rode up, and mistook this dame for the Lady Florimel."

A flush of anger went up Britomart's face. "In very truth!" she cried. "Now if I had no thought before of penalties, this would be more than I needed. Sir, I am Britomart of the Companions, and this Paridell of yours is a most foul scoundrel. Strip him of his arms!"

"What about me?" asked Shea insistently. "That tournament—"

"You could not ride in the tournament in a knight's arms without being yourself knight, fair squire."

"Ahem!" said Chalmers. "I think my young friend would make a very good addition to the knights of your Queen Gloriana's court."

"True, reverend sir," said Britomart, "but the obligation of knighthood is not lightly undertaken. He must either watch by his arms in a chapel all night, and have two proved knights to vouch him; or he must perform some great deed on the battlefield. Here we have neither the one nor the other."

"I remember how my Scudamour—" began Amoret.

But Chalmers broke in, "Couldn't you swear him in as a kind of deputy?"

"There is no—" began Britomart, and then checked herself. " 'Tis true, I have no squire at present. If you, Master Harold, will take the oaths and ride as my squire, that is, without a crest to your helmet, it might be managed."

The oath was simple enough, about allegiance to Queen Gloriana and Britomart in her name, a promise to suppress malefactors, protect the weak, and so on.

Shea and Chalmers pulled off Sir Paridell's armor together. His squire clucked distractedly through the process. Paridell came to in the middle of it, and Chalmers had to sit on his head until it was finished.

Shea learned that a suit of armor was heavier than it looked. It was also a trifle small in the breastplate. Fortunately Paridell—a plump young man with bags under his eyes—had a large head. So there was no

trouble with the well-padded helmet, from which Britomart knocked off the crest with the handle of her
sword.

She also lent Shea her own shield cover. She explained that Paridell's engrailed green bars would
cause any of half a dozen knights to challenge him
to a death duel on sight.

They had eaten the last of their provisions at lunch.
Shea had remarked to Chalmers on the difficulty of
getting a bellyful of adventure and one of food on
the same day. So the sight of Satyrane's castle, all
rough and craggy and set amid trees, held a welcome promise of food and entertainment. Unlike that
of Caultrock, it had portcullis and gate open onto the
immense courtyard. Here workmen were hammering at temporary stands at one side.

The place was filled with knights and ladies, most
of them familiar to Britomart and Amoret. Shea quite
lost track of the number he was introduced to. In
the hall before the dinner trumpet he met one he'd
remember: Satyrane himself, a thick bear of a man,
with a spade beard and huge voice.

"All Britomart's friends are mine!" he shouted.
"Take a good place at the table, folks. Hungry, not
so? We're all hungry here; like to starve." He
chuckled. "Eat well, good squire; you'll need strength
tomorrow. There will be champions. Blandamour of
the Iron Arm has come, and so have Cambell and
Triamond."

4

AT TEN THE NEXT MORNING, SHEA CAME OUT OF
the vaultlike castle and blinked into the morning sun.
Armor pressed his body in unfamiliar places. The
big broadsword at his side was heavier than any he
had ever handled.

The stands were finished and occupied by a vocal swarm of gentlemen and ladies in bright clothes. At their center was a raised booth under a canopy. In it sat an old man with frosty-white hair and beard. He held a bundle of little yellow sticks.

"Who's he?" asked Shea of Britomart, walking just a step ahead of him across the wide courtyard to a row of tents at the opposite side.

"*Sssh!* The honorable judge of the lists. Each time one of the knights scores a brave point he shall notch the stick of that knight, and thus the winner will be chosen."

They had reached the row of tents, behind which grooms held horses. A trumpet blew three clear notes and a mounted herald rode right past them. Behind him came Satyrane on a big white horse. He had his helmet off, and was grinning and bobbing his head like a clumsy, amiable bear. He held a richly carved gold casket. As he reached the front of the stands, he opened it up and took from it a long girdle, intricately worked and flashing with jewels. The trumpeter blew another series of notes, and shouted in a high voice:

"This is that girdle of Florimel which none but the chaste may wear. It shall be the prize of the lady judged most beautiful of all at this tourney; and she shall be lady to that knight who gains the prize of valor and skill. These are the rules."

"Some piece of rubbish, eh, folks?" shouted Satyrane and grinned. Shea heard Britomart, next to him, mutter something about "No manners." The woodland knight completed his circuit and came to a stand near them. A squire passed up his helmet. From the opposite end of the lists a knight came forward, carrying a long slim lance, with which he lightly tapped Satyrane's shield. Then he rode back to his place.

"Do you know him?" asked Shea to make conversation.

"Nay, I ken him not," replied Britomart. "Some Saracen: see how his helmet ends in a spike and crescent peak and his shoulder plates flare outward."

The trumpet sounded again, two warning notes. The antagonists charged. There was a clang like a

153

dozen dropped kettles. Bright splinters of wood flew as both spears broke. Neither man went down, but the Saracen's horse was staggering as he reached Shea's end of the lists and he himself reeling drunkenly in the saddle, clutching for support.

Satyrane was judged winner amid a patter of applause. Shea caught sight of Chalmers in the stands, shouting with the rest. Beside him was a heavily veiled woman, whose slender-bodiced figure in the tight gown implied good looks.

Another knight had taken his place at the opposite end of the lists. The crowd murmured.

"Blandamour of the Iron Arm," remarked Britomart, as the trumpet blew. Again came the rush and the *whang* of metal. This time Satyrane had aimed more shrewdly. Blandamour popped out of his saddle, lit on the horse's rump, and slid to the ground amid a shout of applause. Before he could be pulled aside another knight had taken his place. Satyrane rode him down, too, but came back from the encounter with his visor up, calling "Givors!" and shaking his head as though to clear it.

A squire hurried past with a cup of wine. Britomart called at him: "Am I needed yet?"

"No, my lady," he replied. "Ferramont is to ride the next run." Shea saw a little dark man with a black triangle on gold across his shield climb aboard his horse and take Satyrane's place. The pace of the jousting began to quicken. After Ferramont's second trip down the lists, two knights appeared at the opposite end. A page pushed past Shea calling for someone whose name sounded like "Sir Partybore" to join Ferramont for the defenders.

This time there was a double crash from the lists, which were getting dusty. Sir Partybore, or whatever his name was, went down. But he got up, clanked over to his horse, and pulled a big broadsword from the saddle bow. He waved it at the knight who had overthrown him, shouting something muffled in his helmet. The other turned back and dropped his broken lance. He drew a sword of his own, and aimed from the stirrups a blow that would have decapitated an elephant. The defender turned

154

it easily with upraised shield. The man on foot and man on horseback circled each other, banging away with a frightful racket. Ferramont had downed another opponent in a cloud of dust, and new knights from either side were preparing to ride.

Shea turned to Britomart. "Aren't you going to get in?"

She smiled and shook her head. "Those are the lesser knights of either side," she said. "You must know, good squire, that it is the custom of these tourneys for one or two knights of good report to ride at the beginning, as Satyrane has done for us and Blandamour for them. After that, those younger men have their opportunity to gain reputation, while such as we of the Companions remain aside until needed."

Shea was about to ask who chose the sides. But Britomart gripped his arm. "Ha! Look! With the gyronny of black and silver."

At the other end of the lists Shea saw a big blond man ducking into a helmet. His shield bore a design of alternating black and silver triangles all running to the same point, which must be "gyronny." "That is Sir Cambell and none other," continued Britomart impressively.

As Britomart spoke, the big man came storming into the press. One of the lesser knights on foot, attempting to stop him, was knocked down like a ninepin, rolling over and over under the horse's hoofs. Shea hoped his skull had not been cracked.

Ferramont, who had secured another lance, was charging to meet Cambell. Just before black-and-gold and black-and-silver came together, Cambell dropped his own lance. With a single clean, flowing motion he ducked under the point of Ferramont's lance, snatched a mace from his side and dealt Ferramont's a terrific backhand blow on the back of the head. Ferramont clanged heavily from his saddle, out cold. The stands were in a bedlam, Britomart shouting, "Well struck! Oh, well!" and shifting from foot to foot.

Near by Shea saw Satyrane's face go grim and

heard his visor clang shut as Cambell turned back into the mêlée, laying furiously about him with his mace and upsetting a knight at every stroke. Shouts warned him of Satyrane's approach. He turned to meet the chief defender and swerved his horse quickly, striking with his mace at the lance head. But Satyrane knew the answer to that. As the arm went up, he changed aim from Cambell's shield to his right shoulder. The long spear took him right at the joint and burst in a hundred shivering fragments. Down went Cambell with the point sticking in his shoulder.

With a yell of delight the defenders threw themselves on Cambell to make him prisoner. The challengers, more numerous, ringed the fallen knight round and began to get him back. Those still mounted tilted against each other around the edges of the mêlée.

A trumpet blew sharply over the uproar. Shea saw a new contestant entering the arena on the side of the challengers. He was a big, burly man who had fantastically decked every joint in his armor with brass oak leaves and had a curled metal oak leaf for a crest. Without any other notice, he dropped a big lance into position and charged at Satyrane, who had just received a fresh weapon on his side of the lists. *Whang!* Satyrane's spear shivered, but the stranger's held. The chief defender was carried six feet beyond his horse's tail. He landed completely out. The stranger withdrew and then charged again. Down went another defender.

Britomart turned to Shea. "This is surely a man of much worship," she said, "and now I may enter. Do you watch me, good squire, and if I am unhorsed, you are to draw me from the press."

She was gone. The wounded Cambell, forgotten amid the tumult around this new champion, had been dragged to the security of the tents at the challengers' end of the lists. The press was now around Satyrane, who was trying groggily to get up.

A trumpet sounded behind Shea. He turned to see Britomart ready. Oakleaves heard it, too. He wheeled to meet her.

His lance shattered, but Britomart's held. Though

156

he slipped part of its force by twisting so it skidded over his shoulder, his horse staggered. Oakleaves swayed in the saddle. Unable to regain his co-ordination, he came down with a clatter.

The warrior girl turned at the end of the lists and came back, lifting a hand to acknowledge the hurricane of cheers. Another of the challengers had taken the place of the oakleaf knight. Britomart laid her lance in rest to meet him.

Then a knight—Shea recognized Blandamour by the three crossed arrows on his shield and surcoat—detached himself from the mob around Satyrane. In two bounds his horse carried him to Britomart's side, partly behind her. Too late she heard the warning shout from the stands as he swung his sword in a quick arc. The blow caught her at the base of the helmet. Down she went. Blandamour leaped down after her, sword in hand. Somebody shrieked: "Foully done!" Shea found himself running toward the spot, dragging at the big sword.

Blandamour had swung up his sword for another blow at Britomart. He turned at Shea's approach and swung at his new adversary. Shea parried awkwardly with the big, clumsy blade, noticing out the corner of his eye that Britomart had reached a knee and was yanking a mace from her belt.

Blandamour started another swing. Can't do much with this crowbar, thought Shea. He was trying to get it round, when he got a violent blow on the side of the head. He reeled, eyes watering with pain. More to gain balance than to hit anything, he swung his sword round like a hammer thrower about to let go.

It caught Blandamour on the shoulder.

Shea felt the armour give before the impact. The man toppled with a red spurt of blood. The world was filled with a terrific blast of trumpets. Men-at-arms with halberds were separating the contestants. Britomart snapped up her visor and pointed to the man in armor at her feet, jerking like a headless chicken.

"A favor for a favor," she remarked. "This faitour knave struck you from behind and was about to repeat the blow when my mace caught him." She noticed that the groveling man's surcoat bore the green bars of Sir Paridell. "Yet still I owe you thanks, good squire. Without your aid I might have been sped by that foul cowardly blow that Blandamour struck."

"Don't mention it," said Shea. "Are we taking time out for lunch?"

"Nay, the tournament is ended."

Shea looked up and was dumfounded to see how much of the day had gone. The herald who had opened the proceedings had ridden across to the booth where the judge of the tournament sat. Now he blew a couple of toots, and cried in his high voice:

"It is judged that the most honor of this tournament has been gained by that noble and puissant lady, the Princess Britomart." There was a shout of approval. "But it is also judged that the knight of the oak leaves has shown himself a very worthy lord and he also shall receive a chaplet of laurel."

But when Britomart stepped up to the judge's stand, the knight of the oak leaves was nowhere to be found.

The stands emptied slowly, like those at a football game. Some spectators hooted after Blandamour and Paridell as they were helped out. Shea caught a glimpse of Chalmers, hurrying after the veiled girl who had been his neighbor in the stands.

She moved slowly, with long, graceful strides, and he caught up to her at the entrance to the castle. Someone, hurrying past, bumped them into each other. A pair of intense eyes regarded Chalmers over the low face veil.

"It is the good palmer. Hail, reverend sir," she said in a toneless voice.

"Ahem," said Chalmers, struggling to find something to say. "Isn't it . . . uh . . . unusual for a woman to . . . uh . . . win a tournament?"

"Ywis, that it is." The voice was toneless still. Chalmers feared he had managed things badly. But she walked by his side down the great hall till a blast of warmth came from a fireplace where a serving man had just started a blaze.

"The heat!" she gasped. "Bear it I cannot! Get me to air, holy sir!"

She reeled against the psychologist's arm. He supported her to a casemented window, where she leaned back among the cushions, drawing in deep breaths. The features outlined against the thin veil were regular and fine; the eyes almost closed.

Twice Chalmers opened his mouth to speak to this singularly-abstracted girl. Twice he closed it again. He could think of nothing to say but: "Nice weather, isn't it?" or "What's your name?" Both remarks struck him as not only inadequate, but absurd. He looked at his knobby knuckles with the feeling of being attached to a set of hands and feet seven times too big for him. He felt an utter fool in his drab gown and phony air of piety.

Dr. Reed Chalmers, though he did not recognize the sensations, was falling in love.

The girl's eyelids fluttered. She turned her head and gave him a long, slow look. He squirmed again. Then his professional sense awoke under that intent gaze. *Something* was the matter with her.

Certainly she was not feebleminded. She must be acting under some sort of compulsion—posthypnotic suggestion, perhaps— Magic!

He leaned forward, and was nearly knocked from his seat by a violent clap on the back.

"Good fortune, palmer!" cried a raucous voice. The dark Blandamour stepped past him, one arm bound tightly to his side. "Gramercy for your care of my little rosebud!" With the undamaged arm, he swung the girl expertly from her place in the casement and kissed her with a vigor that left a damp spot on her veil.

Chalmers shuddered internally. The girl submitted with the same air of preoccupation. She sank back into the casement. Chalmers meditated on a suitably horrible end for this jolly roughneck. Something humorous and lingering, with either boiling oil or melted lead.

"Hi, Doc, how are we doing?" It was Shea. "Hi, Sir Blandamour. No hard feelings, I hope?"

The knight's black eyebrows came down like awnings. "Against you, you kern?" he roared. "Nay,

159

I'll give you a meeting beyond the castle gate and spank you with the flat o' my blade."

Shea looked down his long nose and pointed toward Blandamour's bandaged shoulder. "Be careful that iron arm of yours doesn't get rusty before you go that far," he remarked. He turned to Chalmers. "Come on, Doc, we got some reserved seats for the beauty parade. They're starting now."

As they left, Chalmers said: "Harold, I wish I could talk to that girl . . . uh . . . in private. I believe she's the . . . uh . . . key to what we're looking for."

Shea said: "Honest? She's Blandamour's lady, isn't she? I suppose if I fought him for her and beat him, she'd be mine."

"No, no, Harold, I implore you not to start any more fights. Our superiority over these people should be based on . . . uh . . . intellectual considerations."

"Okay. It's funny, though, the way they pass women around like bottles of liquor. And the women don't seem to mind."

"Custom," remarked Chalmers. "Beyond that, deep-rooted psychology. The rules are different from those we're accustomed to, but they're strict enough. A knight's lady is evidently expected to be faithful to him until he loses her."

"Still," Shea persisted, "if I had a lady, I'm not sure I'd want to enter her in this beauty contest, knowing she'd be turned over to the winner of the tournament."

"Custom again. It's not considered sporting to hold out on the other knights by refusing to risk an attractive lady."

They had been bowed into a kind of throne room with a raised dais at one end. At one side of the dais the bearish Satyrane sprawled in a comfortable chair. Six musicians with tootle-pipes and things like long-stemmed ukeleles were setting up a racket unlike any music Shea and Chalmers had ever heard. The knights and ladies appeared to find it charming, however. They listened with expressions of ecstasy till it squeaked and plunked to a close.

Satyrane stood up, the famous girdle dangling from his hand. "All ye folks know," he said, "that this is a tournament of love and beauty as well as a garboil. This here girdle goes to the winning lady. It used to be Florimel's, but she lost it and nobody knows where she is, so it's finders keepers."

He paused and looked around. "Now, what I want to say is that this here is a very useful little collop of jewelry, both for the lady and her knight. It has a double enchantment on it. For the lady, it makes her ten times fairer the minute she puts it on, and it hides her from anyone who would do her wrong. But, also, it won't stay around the waist of any wench who's not perfectly chaste and pure. That's for the benefit of the knight. The minute this lady can't keep her belt on he knows she's been up to tricks." He ended with a bellowing laugh. A few echoed it. Others murmured at his uncouthness.

Satyrane waved for quiet and went on. "Now, as to who wins, the honorable judges have eliminated the contestants down to four, but among the claims of these four they say they can't decide nohow. So they ask, lords and ladies, that you yourselves choose." Satyrane turned to the opposite side of the dais where four women sat, with veils over their heads, and called: "Duessa! Lady to Sir Paridell."

One of the girls rose and advanced to the front of the dais. Satyrane removed her veil. Her hair was red almost as bright as her heavily rouged lips. Eyebrows slanted low at the center. She looked a queenly, disdainful scorn at the audience. The company murmured its appreciation. Satyrane stepped back a pace and called: "Cambina! Lady and wife to Sir Cambell."

She came forward slowly—blond, almost as tall as Cambell himself, and of the mature, Junoesque beauty she dwarfed without outshining the fiery little redhead.

161

Shea whispered to Chalmers: "A little bit too well upholstered for me."

Just then there was a clang as an iron glove was thrown on the floor. Cambell's deep voice boomed, "My challenge to any one who tries to take her from me!"

There was no acceptance. Satyrane never turned a hair. He whipped off the next veil crying: "The Lady Amoret!" She stepped forward bravely, turning her head to show the perfect profile, but as Satyrane announced, "Lady and wife of Sir Scudamour," the delicate nostrils twitched. They gave an audible sniffle. Then, abandoning all efforts at self-control, she burst into a torrent of tears for the absent Scudamour. The Lady Duessa looked angry contempt. Cambina tried to comfort her as the sobs became louder and louder, mixed with words about, "—when I think of all I've been through for him—" Satyrane threw up his hands despairingly and stepped back to the fourth contestant. Shea saw one of the judges whisper to Satyrane. "What?" said the woodland knight in an incredulous stage-whisper. He shrugged and turned to the company.

"Sir Blandamour's lady, Florimel!" he announced, and drew the veil from the woman with whom Chalmers had been talking. Shea heard Chalmers gasp. The girl who advanced to the front of the dais with a sleep-walker's step and wide eyes was the most beautiful thing Shea had ever seen. Clapping and murmurs foretold who would win.

But there was a buzz of talk as well. Shea's ear caught Britomart's remark to Chalmers: "Good palmer! You who are skilled in magic and supersticerie, mark her well!"

"Why . . . why, Miss Britomart?"

"Because there's something here very strange. She's as like that Florimel of the Sea to whom the girdle really belongs as one pea to another. Yet I will swear it is not the same woman, and see!—all here are of the same mind."

In truth the hall was shouting for Florimel as the winner, but they were shouting for "Blandamour's Florimel," as though to distinguish her from the true owner of the girdle. Satyrane bowed and extended the jewelled trinket toward her.

With a word of thanks she took the belt. She clasped it around her middle. There seemed to be some difficulty about buckling it. She fumbled, worked at it a second, snapped it tight, lifted her hands— and the enchanted belt, still buckled, slid down her hips and thumped on the floor.

A low murmur of laughter ran around the room. Everyone looked at Blandamour who turned beet-color. Florimel stepped out of the circle of the belt and picked it up, a frown of puzzlement on her perfect features.

"Here, let *me* put it on," said the red-haired Duessa, and snatching it, suited the action to the word. As soon as she clasped it, the girdle popped open and slid down. She caught it and tried again. Same result. Shea noticed her lips were moving as though pronouncing a charm.

"At least, *I* can do it," said Cambina, and Duessa threw the belt at her angrily. But Cambina could not make the belt stay either. No more could the others, as they tried one after another. With each effort the knights' jokes grew louder and more barbed. Satyrane looked worried. Shea sympathized with him. This backwoods knight had tried so hard to give a polite tournament and party. Blandamour had ruined one with his back blow at Britomart, while the girdle was ruining the other.

But Satyrane was not done yet. "Ladies!" he shouted. "Cease, I pray you! The rules of the contest only provide that this girdle should go to the winner with nothing about her trying it on. That's Florimel, and she is now the lady of the winner of the tournament, who is—by the seven thousand virgins of Cologne, it's the Princess Britomart!"

The tall blonde stepped forward and said something to Satyrane, then turned to the company. "I do refuse this gift," she said, "since I am sworn to accompany Amoret till she finds her Scudamour."

Chalmers whispered: "Harold, I've simply got to

163

talk to that girl. For . . . uh . . . scientific reasons. Couldn't you persuade Britomart to accept her for—"

"I say to me!" Blandamour's shout drowned, every other sound. "If the winner won't have her, then she's mine again by right of reversion!" Satyrane, scratching his head, was the middle of a knot of knights.

"Assotishness!" shouted Sir Cambell. "If the winner won't have her, then she reverts to the champion of the other side and, marry, that am I!"

"I overthrew more knights than you today," cried Sir Ferramont. "If it comes to a question of the second best—"

Britomart cut in icily: "Good knights and gentles, I have changed my mind and will accept the charge of this lady."

"By my halidome, no!" bellowed Blandamour. "You refused her once, and she's mine!"

"Hey," Shea put in. "Didn't I knock you for a loop this morning? Then doesn't that—"

Blandamour spat. "That for you, springald! Pox on these legal points! I'm on my way!" He strode across the room, grabbed Florimel's wrist, and dragged her after him, snarling something inaudible through his mustache. Florimel whimpered with pain.

Shea bounded after them, spun Blandamour round and slapped his face. He jumped back and got the épée out just in time.

"Stop, fair sirs!" wailed Satyrane. The clash of steel answered him. His guests scattered, pushing furniture back. To them, stopping a good fight would be wicked waste of entertainment.

Shea remembered that in dealing with these broadsword men, you had to rely on footwork. If they got close enough for a good swing, you might get your blade snapped on a parry. He felt rather than saw the approach of a corner, and drove in a stop-thrust to keep from being backed into it. He heard a voice: "Nay, bid them cease. Blandamour uses but one arm."

"So does the other," came the answer, "and he has the lighter blade. Let them go."

Back and forth they went, *Swish, clang, tzing!* Shea

164

caught a ferocious backhand cut with a parry sixte, but his light blade was borne back by the force of the blow. The edge chopped through the sleeve of his jacket and barely nicked the skin. Blandamour laughed. Shea, thinking fast, grunted as if with pain, jumped back and dropped his épée. But he caught it with his left hand, and as Blandamour came hurling in, nailed him just above the knee. The knight's blade whistled round and clipped the tip off Shea's hat feather before Blandamour crashed to the floor on the stabbed leg.

"Enough!" shouted Satyrane, jumping between them. "Let there be an end of manslaying! Now I rule that Sir Blandamour has his just deserts for unknightly behavior, both here and at the tourney. Let any who challenge this prove it on me! Squire Harold, ye have won Florimel for your lawful paramour— Why, pest take it, where is she?"

Florimel, the fair bone of this knightly contention, had disappeared.

5

SHEA SAID: "I GET SICK OF THE FLATNESS OF THIS country. And doesn't it ever rain?" He sat on the white gelding he had purchased at Castle Caultrock, the armor that had been Sir Paridell's bundled up behind him. He had tried wearing it, but the heat made it unbearable.

Chalmers was just taking his bearings with a crude jackstave he and Shea had managed to patch together. He remarked: "Harold, you're an incorrigible varietist. If we had cliffs and a downpour you'd doubtless complain about that."

Shea grinned. "Touché, Doc. Only I get bored.

I'd even welcome a lion for the sake of excitement."

Chalmers climbed back onto the ass. "Giddap, Gustavus," he said, and then: "I daresay you'll have plenty of excitement if this wood harbors as many enchanters as they say. I rather wish you wouldn't challenge all the . . . uh . . . hard characters we encounter on the strength of your ability to fence."

"Well, what the hell, I've gotten away with it so far."

"Undoubtedly. At the same time it is just as well not to carry matters too far. I should hate to be left alone."

"A nasty, selfish point of view. Say, Doc, it's too bad the girls wouldn't come with us. That ebony spear of Britomart's gave me a feeling of solid comfort."

"You're not acquiring a . . . uh . . . sentimental fondness for that brawny lady?"

"Good Lord, no! She reminds me of Gert. I was just giving her practice in the theory and practice of feminine charm, for snaring her own boy friend. But, say, if anybody's loopy over a girl it's you! I saw the look on your face when Satyrane suggested Florimel had been carried off by enchantment."

"Why . . . ahem . . . nothing of the sort . . . that is, very well." Chalmers looked worried. "The trouble with traveling with a fellow psychologist is that concealments are impossible. However, I will say that Florimel's manner gave me to pause. When the girdle refused to stay on anyone, I became certain of the operation of magic. The laws of probability should have produced at least one faithful lady among so many." Chalmers gave a sigh. "I suppose Florimel was just an illusion. It was fortunate in a way. It gave us a good excuse to ask how to find an enchanter. Otherwise they might have suspected us of trying . . . uh . . . to make common cause with their enemies. The Faerie knights seem convinced that all enchanters are working against them. Perhaps they are right."

They rode in silence for a while. Then Shea said: "Looks like the woods begin about here." A little stream crossed the track in front of them, and beyond it the sparse timber gave place to dense forest. They dismounted, tying up Gustavus and the horse, which had been christened Adolphus, and produced their lunch.

Both munched in silence for a moment. Then Chalmers said: "Harold, I wish you'd promise not to get into any more fights if—"

"Hey!" said Shea, and leaped to his feet.

Out from among the trees loped a pair of naked, hairy, seven-foot ape men. They had huge ears with tufts of hair sprouting from them, and throat pouches like orangutans. In their hands were clubs. For a moment they stood at gaze, then came splashing through the stream at a gallop.

Chalmers ran to untie the animals, but they were leaping about, crazy with fear. In a glance Shea decided he could never reach Sir Paridell's sword. He would have to use the épée, feeble as that toothpick was against those huge clubs.

The first of the ape men ran at him, bellowing. Shea never knew whether he had gained his senses or lost his nerve, but the next instant he and Chalmers were running round and round the tethered animals, with the ape-men foaming through their tusks behind.

One of the creatures boomed something to the other. On the next circuit the fugitives were surprised to run head-on into one ape-man who had stopped and waited for them. Shea was in front. He saw the cub swing up in two hairy hands and did the only thing possible—extend the épée and fling himself forward in a terrific flèche.

His face was buried in fur and he was clutching at it for support. The hilt was wrenched from his hand, and the animal-man went screaming off, with the weapon sticking through him.

Shea himself was running; over his shoulder, he saw Chalmers was running, with the other ape-man gaining, twirling up his club for the blow. Shea had an instant of horror and revulsion—the poor old Doc, to pass out this way, when he couldn't help—

Twunk!

The feathered butt of an arrow appeared in the thing's side, as though it had just sprouted there. The club missed Chalmers as the creature staggered and turned. *Twunk!* The second arrow took it in the throat, and it collapsed in a clump of bracken, screeching and thrashing. Shea tried to stop; Chalmers careened into him and they went down together.

Shea sat up and wiped leaf mold from his face. Footsteps preceded a tallish, slim girl in a short-skirted tunic and soft leather boots. She had a bow in one hand and a light boar spear in the other, and she moved toward them at a springy trot as though it were her normal gait. A feathered hat like Shea's sat on her red-gold hair, which was trimmed in a long bob.

Shea got up. "Thanks, young lady. We owe you a life or two. I think the thing's about dead."

"I'll make certain. Those Losels are hard to kill," said the girl. She stepped to the bracken and jabbed. She seemed satisfied as she pulled the spear out, wiping its point on some moss. "Is the old man hurt?"

Chalmers gained breath enough to sit up. "Just . . . *puff* . . . winded. I am . . . uh . . . merely middle-aged. To whom do we owe our rescue?"

The girl's eyebrows went up, Shea noticing they were a delightful color. "You know me not? I hight Belphebe."

"Well," said Shea, "I . . . ah . . . hight Harold Shea, esquire, and my friend hight Reed Chalmers, the palmer, if that's how you say it."

"That would be your blade sticking in the other Losel?"

"Yes. What happened to it."

"I will even show you. The creature died when erst I saw it."

Losels. Shea recalled the table at Castle Caultrock, with Britomart telling Sir Erivan he would not find it easy to come to grips with Busyrane the enchanter, because Busyrane's castle was in "the wood where the Losels breed."

"We're on the right track, Doc," he said to Chalmers as he helped the latter up and followed Belphebe.

168

Chalmers merely gave him a sidelong glance and sang softly:

> "But when away his regiment ran,
>   His place was at the fore, oh,
> That celebrated, cultivated, underrated
>   nobleman,
>   The Duke of Plaza-Toro!"

Shea grinned. "Meaning me, I suppose? I was just setting a good pace for you. Here's our other Losel." He pulled the épée from the repellent corpse.

Belphebe gazed at the instrument with interest. "Marry, a strange weapon. May I try its balance?"

Shea showed her how to hold the épée and made a few lunges, enjoying to the full his first recent chance to show off before an attractive girl.

Belphebe tried. *"Ouch!* These poses of yours are as awkward as a Mussulman at Mass, Squire Harold." She laughed and tossed the épée back to him. "Will you show me more another day?"

"Glad to," replied Shea. He turned to Chalmers. "Say, Doc, it seems to me we were eating lunch when the fracas started. Maybe the young lady would like to help us finish it."

Chalmers gulped. "I had—this harrowing experience had quite driven the thought of food out of my mind, Harold. But if Miss Belphebe would like to—by all means—"

"If I may give that I may get," she said. "Hola, attend!" She pulled out an arrow and tiptoed slowly away from them, peering intently into the greenery. Shea tried to follow her gaze, but could see nothing but foliage.

Then Belphebe brought up the bow; aimed, drew, and released all in one movement. To Shea it looked as though she had loosed at random. He heard the arrow strike. Down from the trees fell a large green macaw-like bird. It struck the leaf mold with a thump, and a couple of green feathers gyrated down after.

Gustavus and Adolphus still trembled and tugged at their reins when the three approached them. Shea soothed them and took them down to the stream to drink while Chalmers started a fire and Belphebe stripped the feathers from the parrot. Presently she was toasting the bird on the end of a stick. She was so deft in rustling a meal in the open that Shea felt no desire to compete with her in scoutcraft.

Chalmers, he was surprised to observe, was holding his right forefinger against his left wrist. He asked: "What are you doing, Doc? Taking your pulse?"

"Yes," said Chalmers gloomily. "My heart seems to be—uh—holding up all right. But I'm afraid I wasn't cut out for this type of life, Harold. If it were not for pure scientific interest in the problems—"

"Aw, cheer up. Say, how's your magic coming along? A few good spells would help more than all the hardware put together."

Chalmers brightened. "Well, now—ahem—I think I may claim some progress. There was that business of the cat that flew away. I find I can levitate small objects without difficulty, and have had much success in conjuring up mice. In fact, I fear I left quite a plague of them at Satyrane's castle. But I took care to conjure up a similar number of cats, so perhaps conditions will not be too bad."

"Yeah, but what about the general principles?"

"Well, the laws of similarity and contagion hold. They appear to be the fundamental Newtonian principles, in the field of magic. Obviously the next step is to discover a system of mathematics arising from these fundamentals. I was afraid I should have to invent my own, as Einstein was forced to adapt tensor analysis to handle his relativity equations. But I think I have discovered such a system ready made, in the calculus of classes, which is a branch of symbolic logic. Here, I'll show you."

Chalmers fished through his garments for writing materials. "As you know, one of the fundamental equations of class calculus—which a naive academic acquaintance of mine once thought had something to do with Marxism—is this:

$$\vdash : a + \sim a = \mathbf{I}$$

"That is, the class *alpha* plus the class *non-alpha* equals the universe. But in magic the analogous equation appears to be:

$$\vdash_1 : \mathbf{I} \subset a + \sim a$$

"The class alpha plus the class non-alpha *includes* the universe. But it may or may not be limited thereto. The reason seems to be that in magic one deals with a plurality of universes. Magic thus does not violate the law of conservation of energy. It operates along the interuniversal vectors, perpendicular, in a sense, to the spatial and temporal dimensions. It can draw on the energy of another universe for its effects.

"Evidently, one may readily have the case of two magicians, each summoning energy from some universe external to the given one, for diametrically opposite purposes. Thus it must have been obvious to you that the charming Lady Duessa—somewhat of a vixen, I fear—was attempting to operate an enchantment of her own to overcome that of the girdle. That she was unable to do so——"

"The fowl is ready, gentlemen," said Belphebe.

"Want me to carve?" asked Shea.

"Certes, if you will, Master Harold."

Shea pulled some big leaves off a catalpa-like tree, spread them out, laid the parrot on them, and attacked the bird with his knife. As he hacked at the carcass he became more and more dubious of the wisdom of psittacophagy. He gave Belphebe most of the breast. Chalmers and he each took a leg.

Belphebe said: "What's this I hear anent the subject of magic? Are you practitioners of the art?"

Chalmers replied: "Well—uh—I would not go so far as to say——"

"We know a couple of little tricks," put in Shea.

"White or black?" said Belphebe sharply.

"White as the driven snow," said Shea.

Belphebe looked hard at them. She took a bite of parrot, and seemed to have no difficulty with it. Shea had found his piece of the consistency of a mouthful of bedsprings.

Belphebe said: "Few are the white magicians of Faerie, and all are entered. Had there been additions to the roster, my lord Artegall had so acquainted me when last I saw him." —

"Good lord," said Shea with sinking heart, "are you a policewoman too?"

"A—what?"

"One of the Companions."

"Nay, not a jot I. I rove where I will. But virtue is a good master. I am—but stay, you meet not my query by half."

"Which query?" asked Chalmers.

"How it is that you be unknown to me, though you claim to be sorcerers white?"

"Oh," said Shea modestly, "I guess we aren't good enough yet to be worth noticing."

"That may be," said Belphebe. "I, too, have what you call 'a couple of tricks,' yet 'twere immodesty in me to place myself beside Cambina."

Chalmers said: "Anyhow, my dear young lady, I —uh—am convinced, from my own studies of the subject, that the distinction between 'black' and 'white' magic is purely verbal; a spurious distinction that does not reflect any actual division in the fundamental laws that govern magic."

"Good palmer!" cried Belphebe. "What say you, no difference between 'black' and 'white'? 'Tis plainly heresy. . . ."

"Not at all," persisted Chalmers, unaware that Shea was trying to shush him. "The people of the country have agreed to call magic 'white' when practiced for lawful ends by duly authorized agents of the governing authority, and 'black' when practiced by unauthorized persons for criminal ends. That is not to say that the principles of the science—or art —are not the same in either event. You should confine such terms as 'black' and 'white' to the objects for which the magic is performed, and not apply

172

it to the science itself, which like all branches of knowledge is morally neutral—"

"But," protested Belphebe, "is't not that the spell used to, let us say, kidnap a worthy citizen be different from that used to trap a malefactor?"

"Verbally but not structurally," Chalmers went on. After some minutes of wrangling, Chalmers held up the bone of his drumstick. "I think I can, for instance, conjure the parrot back on this bone—or at least fetch another parrot in place of the one we ate. Will you concede, young lady, that that is a harmless manifestation of the art?"

"Aye, for the now," said the girl. "Though I know you schoolmen; say 'I admit this; I concede that,' are ere long one finds oneself conceded into a noose."

"Therefore it would be 'white' magic. But suppose I desired the parrot for some—uh—illegal purpose—"

"What manner of crime for ensample, good sir?" asked Belphebe.

"I—uh—can't think just now. Assume that I did. The spell would be the same in either case—"

"Ah, but would it?" cried Belphebe. "Let me see you conjure a brace of parrots, one fair, one foul; then truly I'll concede."

Chalmers frowned. "Harold, what would be a legal purpose for which to conjure a parrot?"

Shea shrugged. "If you really want an answer, no purpose would be as legal as any, unless there's something in the game-laws. Personally I think it's the silliest damned argument—"

"No purpose it shall be," said Chalmers. He got together a few props—the parrot's remains, some ferns, a pair of scissors from his kit, one of Belphebe's arrows. He stoked the fire, put grass on it to make it smoke, and began to walk back and forth pigeon-toed, holding his arms out and chanting:

"Oh bird that speaks
    With the words of men
Mocking their wisdom
    Of tongue and pen—"

173

Crash! A monster burst out of the forest and was upon them before they could get to their feet. With a frightful roar it knocked Chalmers down with one scaly forepaw. Shea got to his knees and pulled his épée halfway out of the scabbard before a paw knocked him down too. . . .

The pressure on Shea's back let up. He rolled over and sat up. Chalmers and Belphebe were doing the same. They were close to the monster's chest. Around them the thing's forelegs ran like a wall. It was sitting down with its prey between its paws like a cat. Shea stared up into a pair of huge slit-pupiled eyes. The creature arched its neck like a swan to get a better look at them.

"The Blatant Beast!" cried Belphebe. "Now surely are we lost!"

"What mean you?" roared the monster. "You called me, did you not? Then wherefore such surprise when I do you miserable mortals the boon of answering?"

Chalmers gibbered: "Really—I had no idea—I thought I asked for a *bird*—"

"Well?" bellowed the monster.

"B-but you're a reptile—"

"What is a bird but a reptile with feathers? Nay, you scaleless tadpole, reach not for your sorry sword!" it shouted at Shea. "Else I'll mortify you thus!" The monster spat, whock, *ptoo!* The green saliva sprayed over a weed, which turned black and shriveled rapidly. "Now then, an you ransom yourselves not, I'll do you die ere you can say 'William of Occam'!"

"What sort of ransom, fair monster?" asked Belphebe, her face white.

"Why, words! The only valuable thing your vile kind produces."

Belphebe turned to her companions. "Know, good sirs, that this monster, proud of his gift of speech, does collect all manner of literary expression, both prose and verse. I fear me unless we can satisfy his craving, he will truly slay us."

Shea said hesitantly: "I know a couple of jokes about Hitler—"

"Nay!" snarled the monster. "All jests are stale. I would an epic poem."

"An—epic poem?" quavered Chalmers.

"Aye," roared the Blatant Beast. "Ye know, like

> Herkeneth to me, gode men
> Wives, maydnes, and alle men,
> Of a tale ich you wil telle,
> Hwo-so-it wile here, and there-to dwelle.
> The tale of Havelok is i-maked;
> Hwil he was litel, he yede ful naked."

Shea asked Chalmers: "Can you do it, Doc? How about *Beowulf?*"

"Dear me," replied Chalmers. "I'm sure I couldn't repeat it from memory. . . ."

The monster sneered: "And 'twould do you no good; I know that one:

> Hwæt! we Gar-Thena   in gear-dagum
> theod cyninga   thrym gefrunon,
> hu tha æthelingas   ellen fremedon.

" 'Twill have to be something else. Come now; an epic or shrive yourselves!"

Shea said: "Give him some of your Gilbert and Sullvian, Doc."

"I—uh—I hardly think he—"

"Give it to him!"

Chalmers cleared his throat, and readily quavered:

> "Oh! My name is John Wellington Wells,
>   I'm a dealer in magic and spells,
>   In blessings and curses
>   And ever-filled purses,
>   And ever-filled purses,
>   And ever-filled—

175

"I can't! I can't remember a thing! Can't *you* recite something, Harold?"

"I don't know anything either."

"You must! How about *Barbara Frietchie?*"

"Don't know it."

"Or Chesterton's *Lepanto?*"

"I don't—hey, I do know one long poem. But—"

"Then say it!" cried Chalmers.

Shea looked at Belphebe. "Well, it's hardly suitable for mixed company. Monster, if you'll let the young lady go—"

"Nay!" roared the Blatant Beast. "To your verses, tadpole!"

Shea turned a stricken face to Chalmers. "It's *The Ballad of Eskimo Nell.* What'll I do?"

"Recite it, by all means."

"Oh, Lord!" Chalmers was right, of course. But Shea had begun to feel an affinity for the red-haired huntress. He drew a deep breath and began:

> "When Deadeye Dick and Mexican Pete
> Set forth in search of fun,
> 'Twas Deadeye Dick who . . ."

He wished he knew a bowdlerized version; he didn't dare try to change the wording extempore.

> "They hit the strand of the Rio Grande
> At the top of a burning moon,
> And to slake their thirst and do their worst
> They sought Black Mike's saloon."

On he went, getting redder and redder.

> "Soon Deadeye Dick was breathing quick
> With lecherous snorts and grunts . . ."

176

Out of the corner of his eye he saw Belphebe's face. It registered puzzlement.

> "Then entered into that hall of sin,
>   Into that Harlot's Hell,
> A lusty maid who was never afraid:
>   Her name was Eskimo Nell . . ."

Shea went faster and faster to get to the end of the awful epos. He finished with a sigh of relief, and looked up to see how the Blatant Beast was taking it.

The monster got slowly to its feet. Without a word to its late captives, it lumbered off into the woods, shaking its reptilian head.

Shea next looked at Belphebe. She said: "A life for a life. Truly we should be friends henceforth, and fain would I be such, did I but understand your craft of magic. That magic is white that draws such a monster nigh, you'll hardly assert. That poem—half the words I understood not, though meseems 'twas about a battle betwixt a warrior maid and a recreant knight."

"You might put it that way," said Shea.

"Riddle me those words, Squire Harold. For ensample—"

Shea interrupted hastily: "Some other time, Miss Belphebe, if you don't mind. Right now we want to get our bearings. Is this what they call 'the wood where the Losels breed?' "

"Aye. Some say the enchanters created that gruesome race of monsters to be their cattle."

Shea asked innocently: "Why, is the place infested with enchanters too?"

"Marry, a mort of 'em. Take care lest you fall into their snares."

Chalmers broke in: "Ahem . . . could you tell us where there are any—uh—magicians to be found?"

Shea scowled at his partner. Belphebe's face changed. "Now wherefore would you know such things?"

"We're trying to rescue somebody we think they

177

have, and we thought if we could—uh—gain the confidence of one—"

"Meseems that is a strange and not well-thought-on plan," said the girl coolly. "Yet, since you wish, straight on, and I warrant me you'll find enough of the naughty rogues." She waved her hand. "And now, good gentles, if you will even pardon me, I must trim the ears from the Losel I slew—"

"You must *what?*" demanded Shea.

"Trim the ears from the Losel. For trophies. Already I have pairs an hundred and twenty and two. Good morrow, gentles."

"That," said Shea when they were on their way, "is my idea of a real girl. And you had to put her off us by that crack about magicians!"

"Very fine girl, provided she doesn't put an arrow through you and cut off your ears for trophies. I confess my taste runs to a somewhat more sedentary type of female. I doubt whether I can stand much more excitement of this sort."

Shea said: "I know how you feel. Traveling through Faerie is just one damned encounter afte another." His two narrow escapes in one day had left Shea feeling like a damp washcloth.

Chalmers mused: "It is logical that it should be so. The *Faerie Queene* indicates that this is a world wherein an endless and largely planless concatenation of encounters are a part of the normal pattern of events— Merciful Heavens, another one! What's that?"

"That" was a big black leopard which leaped out suddenly into their path. It snarled with the sound of tearing sheet iron. The mounts bucked and started to whirl against the bits.

"Stop, Doc!" yelled Shea, manhandling Adolphus around and reaching behind him for the broadsword. "If you run, it'll jump you sure!"

He tumbled off, snubbed his reins around a convenient stump, and faced the leopard with the broadsword in one hand and the épée in the other. This was getting to be a worse bore than the Garaden Institute. If I stand my ground, he thought, it probably won't

178

attack, but if it does— There was a book he had read once—what was its name?—about a Lithuanian who hunted jaguars with a spear. If it springs, impale it with the épée; if it stands off and claws, chop with the broadsword—

The leopard snarled again. It seemed uncertain. Then, to Shea's astonishment, it swelled and changed into a huge lion. He felt a prick of fear. A man might handle a 150-pound leopard, but a 600-pound lion—not even a mortal stab would keep it from ripping him up, once it got to close quarters. He was in for it—

"Harold!" Chalmers' voice was not too near. "It's all right."

"The hell it's all right!" thought Shea, holding his ground for want of anything better to do.

The lion did not spring. Instead it grimaced. The fanged mouth became a beak, wings sprouted from its shoulders, and it was a griffin. That, Shea realized, was not kosher; griffins did not—

Chalmers called, closer. "It's the man we're looking for."

Shea relaxed. "Take off the false whiskers, Mr. Magician; we know you," he said. The griffin began to dwindle and dissolve. Shea turned to Chalmers, who was struggling with a patently balky Gustavus. "Didn't you say something about when away his regiment ran, his place was in the fore, oh—"

"I couldn't control this confounded beast. And it's 'at the fore, oh,' not in. How do you do, sir?" This was to the exgriffin, which had become a stout, dark, bald man, who stood glowering at them, fists on hips.

"I do right well," said the man. "What do you two here? Eh? Seek trouble? You've come to the right market."

Shea grinned. "In a way, I suppose we are, if you call yourself trouble."

"Ho, you seek my professional service! I warn you I handle no minor matters, like turning cows sour or the manufacture of love philters. That's witch-wife work. I'm a master magician."

"Then we're delighted—"

"Ahem," said Chalmers. "Excuse me, Harold. I

should like to explain to the gentleman that our interest is professional, looking to an exchange of information that might be mutually profitable."

"Ho!" cried the enchanter. "You two claim to be magicians? How do I know you speak sooth? Tell me that, eh?"

"Well . . . uh—"

"Work a spell for him, Doc," said Shea.

"Oh, dear me. I don't suppose he'd be satisfied with more mice—or cats. All I can think of now is one I prepared for conjuring up a dragon."

"What the hell, that's fine! Go ahead with your dragon!"

The magician's ears caught the last word. "Dragon? D'you think you can really produce a dragon? Let's see you do it!"

"But won't it be . . . uh . . . dangerous?" This was Chalmers.

"Have no fear. I'll get a counterspell ready. Dolon protects you. *The* Dolon." He strutted.

"Show him, Doc."

Chalmers, with a look of baffled and apprehensive resignation, began to make a list of the properties needed. A small red salamander was discovered under a stone. Most of the other things they had already, but a snapdragon plant was called for, and there was none in sight. "Conjure one up," said Shea, coolly. The harassed psychologist looked annoyed. But, with the aid of a roadside weed, he produced a snapdragon plant the size of a tree. *The* Dolon snorted.

Chalmers laid out his properties, lit a fire with flint and steel, and began an incantation:

"By Fafnir and Hydra,
　　Apophis and Yang:
With the length of Nidhöggr,
　　Tiámat's sharp fang,
The shape of the lizard,
　　The strength of the bear,
Thou, scaled like the serpent.
　　Emerge from your lair!

Steed of Triptolemus.
　　Beowulf's bane.
Symbol of Uther.
　　And bringer of rain—"

Shea prudently hitched the animals' reins around
a tree. If the dragon turned out to be winged and
hungry— He wished that his damned reckless impulsiveness had not made him force Chalmers' hand.
If *the* Dolon's counterspell didn't work—

The oyster-colored smoke of the fire thickened
and darkened. Chalmers bit off his chant in mid-stanza
and scrambled back. A reptilian head a yard long
was poking toward them out of the smoke.

The head had a scaly neck behind it. Then came
a foreleg and another. The dragon seemed to be crawling from nothingness through an orifice somewhere in
the smoke, ballooning out as it came. There it was,
complete to stinger-tipped tail, gazing at them with
yellow cat's eyes.

Shea breathed, not daring to attract its attention
by a movement: "If it starts for us, Doc, you get
on Gustavus and I'll let go the reins."

Dolon's face was twisting as though he had swallowed too big a mouthful. The dragon lurched a few
steps, not toward them but off at right angles, opened
its terrible mouth, gave a whistling *"beeep!"* and began to crop the grass contentedly.

"God bless my soul!" said Chalmers.

"He'd better," replied Shea. "Look!"

A second draconian head was pushed through the
smoke. This one was squirted out in a few seconds.
It looked at the three men, then wandered over to a
clump of bright-colored flowers, sniffed, and began to
eat them. Now a third and a fourth head were already
in sight. As fast as the dragons were extruded, more
followed them. The field down to the very confines of
the trees was crowded with them, new arrivals butting
the others to make room or scratching their sides
on trees. Shea was counting: "Thirty-three, thirty-

181

four—We better untie the animals and move or we'll get stepped on. Thirty-six, thirty-seven—"

"Dear me," remarked Chalmers, fingering his chin, as they backed among the trees. "I rather feared this. The same thing happened with the mice."

"Fifty-two, fifty-three—" Shea continued. "My God, the country will be overrun with them!"

Dragons had overflowed the field and were lurching through the trees with their ungainly gait, munching everything green in sight, and mooing at each other with the same plaintive beeping sound. "Ninety-eight, ninety-nine, one hundred. Oh, boy!"

The fire suddenly died, and the cascade of vegetarian dragons ceased. "My God!" said Shea in an awe-struck voice. "One hundred reptilian Ferdinands!"

Dolon's voice was that of a man shaken to the core. "Forsooth, you do things not by halves. Though I mind me I once succeeded with a bushel measure full of pearls." Dolon snapped his fingers. "By Ahriman's toe nails, are you not those who even now bested the Blatant Beast?"

"That's us," said Shea. "How did you hear about it?"

"The Beast passed me a few hours ago, and warned me of a prow company. He said he demanded a trifle of poesy, as is his custom, and you gave him a lay full of such—ah—spice that even he durst not repeat it for shame. The like had never before happened to him, and he seemed much downcast thereby. But was there not another of you? The Beast mentioned three."

Chalmers cleared his throat, but Shea quickly answered: "No; he's got us mixed up with another bunch."

" 'Tis a thing conceivable; the Beast is in sooth of the lower orders, and cannot count beyond two." Dolon shook a finger and said with a slight leer: "Now about these dragons: Tell me, fellow magicians, was't not by error you got eaters of grass? Eh? No secrets in the trade!"

"Ahem. No use taking unnecessary risks," said Chalmers, still looking a trifle wall-eyed.

"Doubtless," remarked Dolon with a glance that

Shea just barely saw, "you can exorcise them as rapidly."

"We could," said Shea, before his companion had a chance to answer. "For the dragon-disappearing spell, though, we need an aneroid comptometer, and we lost ours. Do you have one with you?"

"An . . . ah, certes, an ameroid combompeter. Nay, I fear me not so. Last spring came a black frost that killed all the plants on which ameroid combompeters grow." He spread his hands regretfully. "However, meseems these dragons will in the long run be a benefit, making rare good sport and food for our friends and servants, the Losels. And now, Sir Magicians whom I have not seen, explain your purpose in Loselwood."

Chalmers spoke. "Uh . . . we're looking for a lady named Florimel, and were advised we might find her here. Do you know the young person?"

Dolon chuckled. "The real Florimel or the false?"

"The real or— The one who was at Satyrane's tournament recently."

"That would be the false one, made by the Witch of Riphœa. A fair piece of work—though I will say I care not much for these witches. Duessa is the only one who has any standing in the Chapter— And that brings me to remark, magical sirs, are you members of one of the outland Chapters? My memory is practically infallible, and I do not recall having seen you at our meetings."

Chalmers stammered: "We . . . uh . . . that is . . . can you tell me a little more about this Florimel? The . . . uh . . . false one."

Dolon waved his hand. "A mere witch's thing— a creature made of snow, of no special value. You must let me show you the really fine chess player *I* made sometime, or the imps I conjured up to handle my torture work. Really an achievement. Busyrane, our archmagician, doubtless called this false Florimel in for inspection." He accented the last word and snickered. "But you haven't answered my question, magical sirs."

Shea spoke up boldly. "The point is, we'd like to join up with you."

"You mean you have been working independently and we know it not?" Dolon narrowed his eyes suspiciously. "Aye; Busyrane opened the Chapter but a twelvemonth ago and you may well have slipped his attention. I trust you have not refused his invitation. Our archimage is not soft or slow with unlicensed magicians. He has a spell that turns 'em into spiders. Witty, is he not, eh?"

"Good gracious!" said Chalmers. "But how does one acquire a license?"

"That falls somewhat upon the applicant. Our charter calls for a round twenty-one master magicians, the magic number. Naturally, you behold in me one of the leading masters, whether by ability or seniority. There is also a class of journeymen, who handle the ordinary work, and one of apprentices. Perhaps you have talent enough to be elected to mastership. There are three or four places unfilled, I believe. The next meeting comes in five days, and with my backing your election would be certain."

6

DOLON, IN THE FORM OF A HANDSOME STALLION, trotted in front. Shea leaned back in his saddle and, watching the stallion's ears carefully, murmured: "Doing all right, aren't we, Doc?"

"I suppose so, but I admit to being somewhat apprehensive as to what will happen if both the Companions and the Chapter of Magicians learn we've been cooperating with the other party. This . . . ah . . . playing both ends against the middle may get us in trouble."

"Maybe," said Shea. They rode on in silence.

Once a tiger glided out from between the trunks ahead. Gustavus and Adolphus, both rapidly approaching nervous breakdowns, tried to bolt from the trail. Dolon turned himself from a stallion into an immense buffalo. The tiger slunk off, snarling.

The sun was already low when the trail made a right-angled bend and dipped under a bank. A huge oak door was set into the earth. Dolon, again in his natural form, waved a hand, and the door flew open. "Fear not for the safety of your mounts," he said. "An invisible wall, which none may penetrate without my warrant, surrounds this place."

Shea, dismounting, said: "That ought to be nice for keeping the mosquitoes out."

Dolon laughed dutifully, then shook his head. "Ah, good 'prentice, how true! Is it not sad that a man of genius must concern himself with petty moils and worries?"

The air was stuffy inside. The first thing Shea saw was a huge pile of dirty dishes. Dolon was evidently not the neat type of bachelor. Beyond was an object that made his scalp prickle. It was the life-sized nude statue of a young man, stiff, at one side of the room, emitting a faint bluish glow. It held aloft a torch, which Dolon set alight.

The enchanter noticed Shea's glance of inquiry. "A former 'prentice of mine," he remarked. "I found he was a spy from Queen Gloriana's court, where a few of those high-born grandees practice a kind of magic they call 'white.' So there he stands, with all his sensations alive and the rest of him dead. Eh, Roger?" He pinched the statue playfully and laughed. "I'm really the best humorist in the Chapter when I'm in the mood. Let me show you my collection of Mallamies."

"What's a Mallamy?" inquired Chalmers.

Dolon looked at him hard, then decided it was a kind of joke and laughed. He began taking bottles off a shelf and holding them up to the light. Each contained a human figure about an inch tall. "Homunculi from the hand of great master, Mallamy himself," he explained. "He specialized in this art, and none other has been able to shrink folk to so small size. Even I, Dolon, cannot equal his art. This is the finest collection of his figures in existence.

185

It wants only a blond Saracen. Busyrane has one, but he will not yield it, though I have offered him a water fay, which his own collection lacks. He insists that water fays are not permanent, since any accident will bring water in contact with the bottle and they can work a spell of their own and so escape."

He sighed. "You see how things fall short of perfection even for the greatest of us. But come in, good sirs, and seat yourselves in my cabinet. Only 'ware the cockatrice as you go down this passage."

"A cockatrice?" said Shea.

"Aye. A rare, priceless idea of Busyrane's. All masters of the Chapter are supplied with them. They are just outside our inner cabinets and under an enchantment, so they may not look on any member of the Chapter—or his friends. But should any of Gloriana's people essay to enter, the cockatrice looks on them and they turn to stone."

Dolon threw open a door and led the way down a dimly lighted passage. Behind bars at one side the beast stalked to and fro with a clatter of its scaly tail. It turned its head this way and that. The stench made Shea want to vomit. Over his shoulder he saw Chalmers' lips moving. He hoped it was with a protective counterspell, not prayer. Dolon's voice floated back: "—had to get them after Cambina, one of those 'white magic' practitioners, got into Mallamy's cabinet and drowned him in a pool of alkahest. Thank Lucifer, she married that oaf, Sir Cambell, and marriage cost her some of her powers—"

The door banged behind them. Shea gasped for air as though he had swum up from the bottom of the ocean.

The table was ready and the food—thank Heaven, thought Shea—not too highly spiced. Whittling at a steak, he asked: "What's this meat? It's good!"

"Fried Losel," said the magician calmly.

Shea saw Chalmers halt a mouthful in midair. He felt himself gag momentarily; it was, after all, on the borderline of cannibalism, and after the cockatrice— He forced himself to go on eating. Squeamishness right now was a luxury.

Dolon poured out some wine, sat back and, rather to the travelers' astonishment, produced and lit a clay pipe.

"Aye," he pronounced, "competition is the curse of our business. One playing against another, and those curst companions of Gloriana making sad work of us all—that's how matters stood till Busyrane organized our Chapter. Why, I mind me, I had a very good thing once, very good. Found a man of property who wanted a love philter. I made it for him, and he refused to pay. As he was more ass than human, I promised him his ears should grow an inch a day, with the price doubled for each inch they grew till he got me to take the spell off." Dolon laughed and puffed. "I told you I was a good deal of a humorist.

"Well, what does he do but go to Malingo, who gives him a counterspell at half price! No more of that now."

Shea had a question: "Look here! If you magicians all cooperate so well, what went wrong at Satyrane's tournament? That girdle wouldn't stay on the false Florimel, or on Duessa either for that matter. I should've thought Busyrane would see to that."

Dolon chuckled. "Briskly questioned, springald! The trick with the girdle was doubtless Duessa's doing. It's in her style. She tried to remove the enchantment already on it, but when she found she couldn't do that, clapped another atop, so 'twould fit nobody. But Florimel's case was an error, I fear me much." He shook his head. "Especially if in good sooth Busyrane has sent for her. Nothing would gall those high knights and ladies of the court half so much as having one of their queens of beauty, approved chaste by the test of the girdle, to live with an enchanter. But now, alack, there's a doubt."

Shea saw Chalmers start and run his tongue around his lips at the mention of the connection between Busyrane and Florimel. He pressed questions about the Chapter to give Chalmers a chance to recover. But now Dolon shut up like a clam, with suspicious glances. Shea had uneasy memories of the cockatrice and the spy in the outer room.

The magician finally rose. " 'Tis time we retired, eh, magical sirs? 'Twere wise to set out for Busyrane's tomorrow. If we arrive ere the meeting be called, I'm sure that my connections and the skill in intrigue for which I'm known will enable me to secure your election."

A whisper: "Hey, Doc, you asleep?"

Another: "Merciful Heavens, no. Not in this place. Is *he?*"

"If he isn't, that's a damned good magical snore. Say, can't we do something about that poor guy he made into a statue?"

"It would be injudicious to attempt it, Harold. Moreover, I'm not certain I know how. It would jeopardize our whole plan of campaign."

"Didn't know we had one. Are we stringing along with him?"

"I suppose we must if we really intend to help Queen Gloriana and the Companions. I may also mention Florimel. Dolon remarked that she was made of snow—created. I find it difficult to credit and rather awful. I fear we must join this Chapter and ... uh ... bore from within, as if it were."

"I suppose," said Shea thoughtfully, "that the Chapter explains why the Land of Faerie is sort of running down."

"Yes. The enchanters had just discovered the—"

"Say, Doc!" Shea's whisper was almost loud. "If the Chapter was formed a year ago, *Faerie Queene* time, and it had already been started when Spenser wrote, which was four centuries ago, Earth time— Faerie time must be much slower than ours. If we go back, we'll land somewhere in the twenty-fifth century—along with Buck Rogers."

"*If* we go back. And also if the curvature of the spacetime vectors is uniform. There might be sine curves in the vectors, you know."

"Never thought of it. Say, how come your dragon spell was so extremely successful?"

188

Chalmers permitted himself an under-the-breath chuckle. "A property of the mathematics of magic. Since it's based on the calculus of classes, it is primarily qualitative, not quantitative. Hence the quantitative effects are indeterminate. You can't— at least, with my present skill I can't—locate the decimal point. Here the decimal point was too far rightward, and I got a hundred dragons instead of one. It might have been a thousand."

Shea lay still a moment digesting that thought. Then: "Can't you do something about that?"

"I don't know. Apparently the professionals learn by experience just how much force to put into their incantations. It's an art rather than a science. If I could solve the quantitative problem, I could put magic on a scientific basis. I wish, Harold, that to-morrow you could . . . uh . . . manage to distract Dolon for long enough to allow me to possess myself of one of his textbooks. His place is such a hurrah's nest that he's certain not to miss it."

The three riders—Dolon had conjured up a horse because, he said, taking the form of one for a long journey would be fatiguing—had been going for miles through Loselwood. They saw deer, but no other living creatures. Conversation was scarce till they came out on a road, once wide and well graded, now much overgrown. Shea reasoned that this was one more sign of how the enchanters were getting the best of the Faerie knights.

He pushed his mount alongside the magician. "With your superlative powers, Dolon, I wonder they didn't elect you head of the Chapter instead of Busyrane."

Dolon shrugged. "I could have had the post at good cheap, ho-ho! But I would not strive and moil for it. I'm really a very good judge of human nature, so I arranged Busyrane's election, knowing he would do it well."

"You must be just about perfect," said Shea.

" 'Just about,' my 'prentice friend, is a weak phrase. I *am* perfect. I've no doubt that people in ages to

189

come will date the history of true wizardry from my entry into the field."

"Modest, too," remarked Shea, drawing a quick glare from Chalmers.

Dolon dropped his eyes. "Too modest, I sometimes think. Yet do I guard against such affectation —hola! Here's an encounter!" An armored horseman had appeared at the far end of the defile through which they were riding. His lance came down and he trotted toward them.

Dolon cried: "Ten thousand devils, 'tis Artegall himself! Flee, or we are undone!" Looking a bit undone himself, the magician whirled his horse sharp round on its hind legs.

A woman's voice behind them called, "Stand, all of you!" Belphebe was perched on a rock at the side of the defile, covering them with bow bent full.

"To the air!" screeched Dolon, the last word going beyond human pitch as he changed to hawk and flapped slanting upward. There was the flat snap of the bow, the whistle of the arrow, and there was a puff of feathers. Down hurtled the hawk, changing to Dolon with an arrow through his arm as he fell. He landed, *plop,* in a soft spot. Shea observed that these people really knew something about swearing in the minute or two before Artegall's lance jabbed him.

"Dismount, runagates!" roared the knight. It seemed the best thing to do. The man was as big as Cambell, cased in steel, yet moved quickly. Besides, Belphebe had another arrow already nocked.

Artegall pushed up his visor to show a stern, swarthy face with a broken nose. He produced a couple of looped chains, which he slipped over the victims' heads, tightened, and locked. "You're in arrest," quoth he.

"What for?" asked Shea.

"For judgment by the high justice of the court of her majesty, Queen Gloriana."

Chalmers groaned. "The high justice," he explained in a low voice, "means the death penalty if we're found guilty."

"Then I'll take low," said Shea.

190

"You had better not ask it. He probably has the privilege of low justice himself, which means he can sentence you to about five years in prison right here. He probably would."

Belphebe had come down from her rock. "Dolon, by the splendor of Heaven!" she cried. "I bear witness, Sir Artegall, that when I met this pair in Losel-wood but yesterday, they were asking after magicians. Guard the young one well; he bears a blade of much power, which I doubt not has some enchantment on it."

"Say you so!" observed Artegall, with an un-pleasant expression. "By my halidome, we are well met, then. A pretty gift for the queen's justice! Let's see that little sword." He yanked Shea's baldric up over his head, nearly taking off an ear.

He climbed back on his horse, holding the end of the chains. The prisoners had no choice but to trot along behind him.

Chalmers managed to whisper: "Don't try to tell them we're on the right side. Britomart will clear us if necessary. We must . . . uh . . . retain Dolon's confidence."

They plodded on. The more Chalmers thought about it the less he liked the idea of being dragged off to the Faerie court for judgment. If they were released with Britomart's help, any enchanters they met afterward might reasonably ask them how they came to escape when Dolon was condemned. Of the master magician's condemnation there could be little doubt. Artegall looked at him with pure detestation. Belphebe, trotting along beside them, was amusing herself by catching the enchanter's eye, putting one hand around her neck, and making strangling sounds. The great Dolon did not seem to be enjoying it.

Shea? Shea was admiring Belphebe's springy stride. Anything Chalmers did would have to be on his own. Fortunately, Chalmers had succeeded in pur-loining and sneaking a look into one of Dolon's text-books that morning. There was a simple weakness spell in it; not much of a spell, lasting only a few hours and easily guarded against if one knew it were coming. But it required no apparatus beyond twelve blades of grass, a small piece of paper, and some water.

Chalmers stooped and pulled up the grass blades as he stumbled along, holding them in his mouth as though he merely wanted something to chew on. He slipped a hand inside his robe, ostensibly to scratch, really to tear a page corner from Dolon's book. This also went into his mouth; saliva ought to be a fairish substitute for water. He mumbled the incantation. If it worked, Artegall and Belphebe ought to be weakened enough to let the prisoners escape.

Shea decided that he liked the little spray of freckles across Belphebe's nose, but that it was difficult to admire a girl who had a bead drawn on one's right kidney with a longbow. He would like to see more of Belphebe. She had about everything, including an adventurous spirit not unlike his own—

Why the devil was he so tired? He could barely drag one foot after the other. He should be hardened to strenuous living by now. Belphebe was drooping, too; the spring had left her walk. Even the horse's head hung.

Artegall swayed in his saddle. He made one monstrous effort to balance himself, overcompensated, and slowly fell into the road with the dignity of a toppling factory chimney. The crash halted the procession. The horse sat down jerkily and sprawled beside its rider, its tongue lolling out. Chalmers and Dolon followed suit, their chains jangling.

Artegall heaved himself up on one elbow. "Sorcery!" he drawled languidly. "The rascals have tricked us! Skewer them, Belphebe!"

The girl fumbled with her bow. Chalmers rolled over and reached hands and knees. "Come on, Harold! Rouse Dolon!" he said. He smothered a yawn and started to crawl. "Dear me, I wish I could learn to keep these spells within bounds!"

Shea tried to leap over Dolon; lost his balance and fell across the magician. Dolon grunted as Shea's knees dug into him, but he, also, made his hands and knees. The three prisoners set off down the road in that fashion.

Shea looked back. Belphebe was still on her feet,

trying to draw the bow, but lacking strength to pull it more than a few inches. She aimed up and let fly at random. The recoil knocked her over backward. The arrow soared in a whispering parabola and thwunked into the seat of Dolon's pants with just enough force to stick. The magician yelped and increased his speed to almost a mile an hour.

"Hurry," said Shea. "They're coming after us." Belphebe was crawling along at a fair rate, regardless of the abrasion of her bare knees. Behind her, Artegall brought up the rear of the bizarre parade like some monstrous tailless lizard. In his armor he could barely move.

"Belphebe's gaining," remarked Shea, after a minute.

"That sorrows me not," said Dolon, with a nasty expression. He fished a knife from his boot.

"Hey," said Shea, "not that!"

"And wherefore not?"

While Shea was trying to think of a reasonable answer, a man in a kilt appeared at the side of the road. For a moment he stared in astonishment at the singular procession, then put a willow whistle in his mouth and blew.

"The Da Derga!" gasped Dolon. "Ah, woe are we, to be caught thus!"

A swarm of the wild men came trotting through the trunks. All wore tartan kilts. With them were a number of lean, rough-coated dogs. The five crawlers were efficiently bowled over and frisked for weapons. Shea found himself looking into the ugly, bearded face of a gigantic redhead, who moved a rusty broadsword back and forth an inch from the prisoner's throat as though he were sawing. The redhead seemed to think it very funny.

"Sure and is it not a strange thing to find them so?" remarked a benign-looking graybeard. "The folk would be taking poison to make them so weak."

"Do we be takin' them back entire," asked another, "or just their heads to put in the hall, now?"

"Shame on you, Shawn! 'Tis a month now since the gods have had a proper sacrifice. 'Tis a lack of proper reverence you show, I'm thinking."

193

Shea could have thought of one or two terms more appropriate than lack of reverence. But he was not consulted. He was tied up and suspended from a pole. For the next hour or so, as the carriers of the pole jounced along, the pain in his wrists and ankles was too exquisite for him to think coherently.

They followed deer trails, ultimately emerging into a clearing with tents around it. The Da Derga were evidently on a raiding expedition; there were no women or children to be seen. The captives were dumped in a row near a rough-hewn wooden altar with ominously dark stains down its sides.

Shea whispered: "Can't you work a spell, Dolon?"

"Aye, as soon as I recover from this curst weakness. Malediction on the bungling knave who clipped us in it!"

"I'm afraid I was . . . uh . . . responsible," said Chalmers humbly.

"May Beelzebub fly away with you then! After this, stick to your dragon-juggling tricks, and leave true magic to the great Dolon. Was it not the grass-and-paper spell?"

"Yes."

"I trow I recognized the symptoms. Haro! 'Twill not wear off for hours, and by that time we shall be dead as Judas Iscariot. Ah, 'tis foul that the greatest master of magic the world has seen should come to an end thus, like a netted herring! The tragedy of it makes me weep."

He lapsed into gloomy silence. Shea thought desperately—what could they do? If neither the wily Dolon nor the powerful Artegall could help, the case appeared hopeless. Another last-minute rescue from outside would be too much of a coincidence to hope for.

Three men in long white robes, absurdly garlanded with leaves, came out of a tent. One of them thoughtfully whetted a long knife. The sound it made on the stone was hard to bear.

The one with the knife came over and looked down at the captives. The amiable-looking chieftain remarked: "Sure, 'tis a likely lot they are, isn't it?"

"They'll do," replied the Druid. "For a chance-

194

met lot, they'll do. The two younger are the handsomest. We take them first. But if it's so weak they are, how shall we ever get them to walk to the altar?"

"A couple of the lads will support them. Oh, Murrahu! Would you be getting your pipes?"

The Da Derga had formed a circle around the clearing. One of the Druids stood with his arms out and face to the sky, chanting, while another gestured symbolically over the altar. A third marched round the clearing, followed by the bagpiper. The piper cut loose with a sound like a thousand angry beehives. It seemed to Shea that a procession of ghostly figures was following the two marchers, floating in some medium of faint iridescence that made their forms and even their existence uncertain. The Da Derga bowed low as priest and piper passed, and stayed bent over till that trail of misty things had gone by.

It was extremely interesting. Shea wished he were in a position to appreciate it without being dominated by the thought that these were probably his last sense impressions. He wondered if the gods of the Da Derga had something in common with the ancient Celtic deities— By the great horn spoon, he had an idea!

A barbarian was cutting his bonds. Two others heaved him and Belphebe to their feet and supported them by the arms. Their expressions were of rapt ecstasy. Shea muttered out of the side of his mouth: "Hey, Belphebe, if I get you out of this, will you call a truce till we can explain?"

The girl nodded. The Druid with the knife took his place at the altar. Another came over to the captives, faced about, and started to lead them. Summoning all his strength, Shea barked: "Hey, Mr. Priest!"

The Druid turned. He had a kindly expression. "Now, laddie," he said, "it's no good shouting! Sure, 'tis an honor to be the first to go to the gods."

"I know it. But you don't think the gods will be satisfied with a bunch of weak fish like us, do you?"

"True enough for you. But the gods do be giving

195

credit when a man offers the best he has, and faith, you are that."

"You could make us better, though. We're under a spell. You're a pretty good magician; why not take this weakness off us?"

The Druid's expression showed cunning. "I'm thinking you're saying that for your own benefit and not for ours, but 'tis rare good sense you speak, my boy." He looked at Shea, then at Belphebe and waved his hands toward them, mumbling. Shea felt the force flow back into his body. The old priest addressed the two with him: "Hold them tight, now, lads. It wouldn't do at all, at all, if they used their strength to get away."

The rough hands of the Da Derga clamped down on Shea's arms till he winced. He saw that Belphebe wasn't enjoying their grip either. He held himself relaxed, as though putty in their hands.

The procession approached the altar. The piper was red-faced, but seemed to be maintaining himself by that unique power all pipers have of keeping going long after ordinary people would collapse for lack of breath. Shea's feet dragged. The Druid with the knife awaited him with the supremely peaceful expression of a man who is rendering his own happiness sure by a great and noble act. The altar was only four paces away. He glanced toward Belphebe. Three. She was looking anxiously at him as though awaiting a signal. Two. He felt what he was waiting for—the relaxation of the tired, sweaty hands of the huskies. One. It was now or never.

Shea snapped his left heel up and back. It hit a hairy kneecap, and the barbarian went down with a yell of pain. He let go. Shea spun around on the other heel, driving his left knee into the other guard and at the same time punching him in the Adam's apple. The second guard, not expecting this demoniac burst of energy, let go and dropped, strangling in the agony of the throat punch.

What followed took seconds. The other two guards got their signals crossed, and instead of one of them holding Belphebe, both let her go to run at Shea. The woods girl pounced on the Druid with the knife and sank her teeth into his hand.

The guards were good rough-and-tumble fighters, but under the handicap of having to take their captives unharmed. Shea was under no such inhibition. He jabbed one in the eyes with his fingers and kicked the other in the belly. Somebody screeched. Belphebe ran past with a bloody knife in her hand, yanking Shea after her.

The other Da Derga were too dumfounded by the sacrilege to interfere. She and Belphebe raced through a hole in their circle just as the barbarians began reaching for their broadswords.

Then they were among trees, running madly. Belphebe glided ahead of Shea without even breathing hard. He guessed she could leave him behind if she wished. She seemed to know the woods by instinct. She swerved right, squeezed between a pair of trunks, down to a brook, splashed along its bed for fifty yards, then off into the woods again.

"Up!" cried Belphebe suddenly, and climbed a trunk with the agility of a small boy, lending a hand to help Shea. They crouched together in a crotch and listened.

Scattered sounds of pursuit came, now here, now there. The Da Derga had spread and were beating the woods. Shea and Belphebe held themselves still, almost breathless. There was a rustle of snapped twigs and a pair of the barbarians walked past a few yards from their tree, leading one of the huge dogs. "Sure, 'tis a terrible thing," said one of them. "Three men cut up, and one of them a holy man."

"A wicked, cruel thing. And poor Fion, with his lovely neck all broke in. It's inhuman monsters they are, those two."

The sounds died. They waited, and Shea explained his and Chalmers' plan to her in a whisper.

Belphebe gave Shea a level glance. Apparently satisfied with his sincerity, she asked: "Why said you not so sooner, good squire?"

"I couldn't in front of Dolon without giving the

197

whole show away. If you don't believe me, Britomart will give us good characters. Honest."

"You mean you plan still to go on with this witless scheme?"

"Of course, if we can rescue our people."

"You think Artegall would let Dolon go?"

Shea hesitated. "I don't know Artegall. But you're right; he's the kind that, once he gets an idea, won't change it for hell or high water."

Belphebe gave a gurgling little laugh. "You should be a court jester, Squire Harold. But your wit is well taken; that describes Artegall eractly."

"Well, we'll have to see to it that Artegall can't interfere till we've left."

"Nay. In honor I cannot take the side of that foul enchanter—"

"Look, Belphebe. Use your head. The knights of Faerie have been trying for years to catch up with these enchanters, haven't they?"

"That is good sooth."

"And they haven't made out very well, have they?"

"Gentle Squire, you argue like a doctor. But I fear me you are right."

"All right. This riding around in an iron shirt and knocking off an occasional enchanter isn't going to get you anywhere, either. Now, my boss and I have a plan for getting into their organization and rounding up the whole batch at once. Why not let us try?"

"But how shall I—"

"Oh, tell Artegall we made a private truce to escape the Da Derga, and one of the conditions was that we get a head start before—" He stopped, listening.

Faintly, the drone of bagpipes wafted to them.

Belphebe cried: "The ceremony has begun again. Haste, or our friends are sped!" She began to climb down, but as they went Shea asked: "What can we do?"

"I'm not without some knowledge of things in the woods and their secret ways." She dropped to the ground and started to whistle a strange little tune. When the whistle reached an ear-piercing pitch, a unicorn came trotting forward. It nuzzled up to her, pawing the ground, and she vaulted onto its back.

"How about me?" asked Shea.

Belphebe frowned. "Right glad would I be to have you ride with me, but I misdoubt this steed will bear the weight. And they are ever jealous beasts, not liking to go two and two. You could hold the tail."

That seemed unsatisfactory. But Shea thought, after all, I know some magic and ought to be able to conjure one up, and a conjured unicorn probably won't object to this one. "If you'll show me that brook, I'll see what I can do," he said.

He composed his incantation on the way to the stream. At its bank he made a model, as well as he could, of the animal's head in wet sand, and stuck a stick in it for a horn. Then he recited:

"Oh, steed that feeds on the lightning
   And drinks of the whirlwind's surge,
In the name of the horse of Heimdall,
   I conjure you now, emerge!

"Strong and docile and valiant,
   Decked with the single horn,
In the name of the horse of Mohammed,
   I conjure you to be born!"

The brook exploded outward with a *whoosh* of spray. Shea jumped up and rubbed the water from his eyes—then rubbed them again to make sure. Once more, the travelers' magic had been almost successful.

Standing in the creek was a fine big bull Indian rhinoceros.

7

SHEA HAD A MOMENT OF PANIC. THEN HE REMEM-
bered that the bad reputation of the rhinoceros tribe
is based on the cantankerousness of the two-horned
black rhino of Africa. Anyway, he couldn't fool
around conjuring up more animals. As he had asked
for a docile one, this was presumably it. He landed
astride the rhino's back.

The rhinoceros might be docile, but it was un-
accustomed to riders. When it recovered from the
shock of its arrival in an unfamiliar section of
spacetime, it scrambled out of the creek and galloped off through the trees in the wrong direction.
Shea dug his fingers into the folds of its armor and
hung on, yelling at Belphebe: "Hey! See if . . . ugh
. . . you can . . . ugh . . . herd this thing!"

The rhino, seeing the unicorn on its right, charged
snorting and baring its incisor tusks. The unicorn
whirled aside and poked the rhinoceros in the ribs
as it lumbered past. The rhinoceros, now thoroughly upset, tried to flee. Belphebe skillfully herded
it toward the camp of the Da Derga.

The bagpipes were louder. The rhinoceros, now
more afraid of the unicorn than of this noise, headed
straight for the sound. Shea clung to its back, hoping
it wouldn't ram a tree. The trees sprang apart in
front, and there was the camp of the Da Derga. A
couple of guards held Chalmers across the altar. The
Druids had found another knife.

Shea yelled: *"Yeeeeeow!"*

Heads turned toward him. The upraised knife hung
suspended. Shea had a blurred picture of the camp
streaming past, and everywhere the backs of the

Da Derga departing in a swirl of tartan. They screamed most gratifyingly.

Beyond the altar Shea tumbled off his mount and walked back. Belphebe had already cut the bonds from the others; but, stiff and weak as they were, they could not move.

"I trust," said Chalmers feebly, "that you are . . . uh . . . convinced of the inadvisability of visiting the world of Irish myth, Harold."

Shea grinned, "Well, yes, since you mention it." He turned to Dolon. "I can take this weakness off you. But I'm sure a master like you would have a much better method than anything I could use. If you'll give the spell to me, I'll use it instead of my own."

"Marry, that will I. Few youngsters are so polite as to appreciate the powers of the masters these days. Bend down—"

Artegall raised a feeble hand to Belphebe. "What ails you, girl? Fall on these caitiffs! Slay them "

"The squire and I have a truce."

"A truce!" he growled. "Make a truce with the devil, or the Da Derga, but not with these enemies, of human kind. The queen's majesty shall hear of this."

Shea was working the spell on Chalmers. As he got up he grunted: "Thank you, Harold. Really, do we have to go on—"

"Shut up, Doc," snapped Shea. He didn't intend to have his delicate bit of finagling gummed up at this stage. Then he turned to Dolon and worked the spell again.

The magician seemed annoyed that Chalmers should have preceded him, but it turned out to be a good idea. The moment Dolon was on his feet, he snatched up one of the discarded sacrificial knives and flung himself toward the helpless Artegall. Belphebe tripped him as he tried to go past. Before he could get up, Shea was on his back with one hand on his neck and the other on his wrist. "Drop that!" he yelled.

The magician's bulbous body heaved convulsively. Shea found himself gripping the neck of an enormous snake of the python type. With horror he felt the immense rubbery strength of the thing as it writhed a section from under him and tried to throw a coil around his body.

But, as the snakes have no hands, Dolon had perforce dropped the knife. Shea put the edge of it against the scaly throat. "Change back," he gritted, "or I'll saw your head right off!"

Dolon changed back. "Are you clean daft?" he sputtered. "There's a stinking fool 'prentice for you —ruining our chance to get rid of our greatest enemy."

"Not at all, master," said Shea, relaxing his grip a trifle. "You forget there's a truce on. Belphebe and I agreed not to have any scrapping until we've separated."

"You mean to keep your word with *them?* 'Tis against nature and therefore void."

Shea clamped down his grip again and turned to Artegall. "If I release you from the weakness spell, will you give me your word of honor to let us have a two-hour start?"

"Fool! Doltard!" shouted Dolon. But Artegall settled the question. "Covenant with an enchanter? Not I! Slay me if you will; you shall not rid yourselves of all Gloriana's knights so easily!"

Shea sighed at the unreasonableness of men. "Doc, watch Dolon for a minute, will you?" He got up and said to Belphebe: "Take care of him after we go." Then, more softly: "Say, how can I get in touch with you again?"

She thought. "If you go not beyond the confines of this great wood and know but how to call my unicorn of the forest—not that ungainly great beast of yours—"

"Can you whistle the tune for me—softly?" She did so, and he followed till he could do it. But she finished with a smile. "I misdoubt you could entice her close enough. These unicorns fear not maidens, but men they are greatly wary of."

Shea pondered, then drew Chalmers aside, leaving Belphebe to guard Artegall against Dolon. "Doc, can you conjure up sugar?"

"Harold, you are a continual source of astonishment

to me. I really feel quite worn out, though. I'm incapable of coherent effort—"

Shea shook him by the shoulders. "Listen, Doc!" he said fiercely. "I'm pretty close to the edge of collapse myself, but if you ever want to see Florimel again, you can't let me down! This is just a little applied psychology; to wit, setting up an androphiliac fixation in the libido of one female unicorn. Now, go to it!"

Water, charcoal from the remains of one of the Da Derga's cooking fires, and a spell produced a double handful of neat patty-shaped molds of maple sugar, which Shea rather dubiously guessed would do. The unicorn sniffed suspiciously from a distance, then under Belphebe's coaxing teetered close enough to taste. It munched meditatively, wiggling its ears, then reached out its muzzle for more. Shea fed it another piece, then ostentatiously put the remainder in his pocket.

"All right," he said, "we're off. Say, Belphebe, maybe you better hitch J. Edgar Hoover's feet to the unicorn and haul him off before the Da Derga come back to see what happened." He glanced at the glowering Dolon. "Two hours truce now, and you can thank Heaven they took her bow away."

The dark was beginning to close in. As they reached the road, Dolon worked a spell and produced a horse. He mounted.

"Hey!" said Shea. "What about us?"

"I say a pox on you, 'prentice, for a rebellious rogue. Wend afoot and learn what it is to flout the great Dolon."

Shea put on a sly grin. "You don't understand, master. Don't you think it pays for the Chapter to have someone that the opposition thinks is a real man of honor? I'm just building myself up for the job. When we get ready to put something really good over on that bunch and catch a lot of them at once, instead of just these two, I'll come in handy."

Dolon considered a moment, then a smile ran round his red, full lips. "Oho! Sits the wind so? You want that red-polled baggage, eh? Well, when we capture her, you shall have her before she goes to the torture chamber—if the Chapter chooses to admit you. For I tell you fairly I doubt you are skilled enough in the more practical forms of magic."

Chalmers spoke up. "Ahem. You confessed, Dolon, that you of the Chapter occasionally . . . uh . . . work at cross-purposes."

"Aye. 'Tis the nature of things. For look you, magic is an art disorderly."

"But it isn't! We can show you how to change all that."

"Here's strange doctrine! Do you jest?"

"Not at all. Didn't you notice the Druids' methods of doing magic?"

"Those priests of the Da Derga? Magic they have, aye, but so meager a sort any lout can outdo them."

"That's not the point. It's not what they do, but how they do it. One man invokes their gods; another changes the altar from wood to stone, and so on. One man per function, and all timed to work together. That's real organization. Now, if . . . uh . . . your Chapter were organized like that—"

Shea cut in: "You've been trying to break down Queen Gloriana's government and set up a council of magic to rule in its place, haven't you?" Nobody had told him that, but it seemed a reasonable guess.

"That we have; but the others worked singly, without any such leaders as myself to guide them."

"But even you, master, you're only one, and can't be everywhere at once. As it stands, your Chapter is a professional guild. It keeps you from cutting each other's throats by competition, but that's all. You won't get anywhere just bopping off an occasional knight. We can show you how to make a real organization out of it with all the parts working together as smoothly as the Faerie knights work together. The beauty of such an organization is that when it gets such a man of genius as yourself to guide it, everyone in the organization becomes a kind of extension of the leader's personality. It's just as though your Chapter were made into twenty-one Dolons. Gloriana's government could never stand against that."

"Ho-ho!" cried Dolon. "Now this proves once more that I am, as some are good enough to say, the great Dolon, and practically infallible in my judgment of men. I knew from the beginning that your minds held some noble and worthy plan for the advancement of the Chapter and the cause of magic. But I was forced to test you to bring it out. So—we are friends again, and I'll seal the bond by bringing forth your beasts and belongings."

He wheeled his own horse behind a tree. He worked a spell that sent a pillar of smoke towering through the branches to catch the last rays of the sun. From beneath it Adolphus and Gustavus trotted out to stand in the twilight beside their masters, the former with Shea's épée at the saddle. Dolon came back, grinning as though at some private joke.

"I shall present you to the Chapter as specialists in strange beasts," he remarked amiably. "That monster you rode to our rescue was as fearsome a hobgoblin as ever I saw, friend Harold. You see, I have the custom, not common among great men, of being affable to my juniors."

It was growing very dark under the trees, and the horses began to stumble on the ruinous road. Another hour of riding brought them to an opening. Midway along it and fairly close to the road, a thatched hut stood in the inadequate moonlight. One window was lighted.

"The castle of Busyrane," remarked Dolon.

"It seems somewhat . . . uh . . . exiguous," offered Chalmers timidly.

"Ho-ho! You know not our Archimage, who is a master of show and illusion, and sets such gulls to catch the unwary. Do but watch."

As Dolon spoke the moon was blotted out. Shea heard a flutter of wings. Something brushed past his face. There was a sensation of insectlike crawling on his left hand that made him snatch it from the bridle. A long, low ululating shriek rose from out of the dark. The horse quivered uncertainly beneath him. Its hoofs clacked on stone in the velvet black. Down at stirrup level a face appeared. It had huge, drooping ears and ragged teeth fixed in a permanent grin above the pendulous lower lip. There was no source of light for it to be seen by, nothing but that face floating by itself.

"The master makes you welcome and bids you dismount," mouthed the face indistinctly.

A clawlike hand reached up to help Shea from his mount. Though by now well inured to shocks, he could not help a shiver at the clammy cold touch. Dolon chuckled behind him. He shook off the horrors and followed the guidance of the corpselike fingers down a corridor of utter dark. Something rustled, and he caught the sickening odor of cockatrice. A door closed. He was standing in a big room, blinking in a flood of light, with the other two beside him.

An elderly man, wearing a palmer's robe like Chalmers', came forward to greet them. He smiled graciously. "Welcome, good Dolon! To what fortunate chance owe we your presence here before the meeting?"

"To the same chance that brings me here with these two stout fellows, whom I rescued but today from Artegall's curst clutches." This version was a trifle startling, but Shea had the sense to lay low as Dolon described his thrilling rescue of Shea and Chalmers. He went on: "Most noble Archimage, a plan has occurred to me. As you know, people are good enough to say that I have a talent for plans amounting almost to genius.

"Surely, noble Archimage, you are sib to the fact that you are but one and cannot be all places at once. As it stands, you head the Chapter well; but it is a professional guild. It prevents our cutting each other's throats by competition, but no more. What we need is an organization that will work together as the Faerie knights work together. It would be as though our mastership were composed of twenty-one Busyranes. Gloriana's government would have ill hap against it, eh?

"By the favor of fortune, I fell in with these two, desirous of admission to the Chapter. With that skill at judging character for which I am well known, I saw at once that they were experts in exactly the form of organization we need, I present you, therefore, Reed de Chalmers, magician, and Harold de

Shea, apprentice, as worthy members of our society. In magic, their art is the conjuration of singular and unheard of beasts. The Blatant One himself has fled before their spells."

"Enchanted, magical sirs," said Busyrane, with a polite bow. "Your application shall receive the most earnest attention. We presume, good Dolon, you have heard the sad news?"

"That have I not."

"Poor Malvigen is slain—spitted with an arrow by that she-devil Belphebe."

"The curst vile tripping wench!" Dolon turned to Shea and Chalmers. "Magical sirs, I ask you, is this not a hard thing? Here's a man who spent a lifetime in the study and practice of magic; Malvigen. Made himself a great specialist in erotic dreams, excelling even the great Dolon in that one art. Now he's snuffed out in a second, like a wild boar, and for why? Because his attainments violate what those at the court choose to call morality."

Shea woke from a dream of being shrunk to a statue of one inch and swallowed by a snake. His clothes lay over a chair. They had evidently been given a magical laundering and mending, since they looked as good as new, in contrast to their worn and dirty state of the previous evening.

Chalmers came in. His clothes also were clean, and he looked younger than Shea remembered having seen him. He burst out: "I've found Florimel!"

"Shhh! For Pete's sake not so loud. Tell me about it."

"She was walking on the battlements. Really, this place is quite large when seen by daylight. Busyrane was most affable. It appears he intends to use her for the object—perfectly legitimate from his point of view—of causing dissension—"

"Okay, Doc. Okay! I get it. You're all excited. What did you really find out? Who is this Florimel, anyhow?"

"She was . . . uh . . . manufactured out of snow by a person called the Witch of Riphœa, as a duplicate or double of the genuine Florimel, who seems to have disappeared. Busyrane tells me it is at least theoretically possible to find a magical spell that will endow her with a genuine human body. He was most kind, most kind. I am afraid we may have misjudged—"

"Yeah. He promised he'd help you fix her up, I suppose."

Chalmers was suddenly dignified. "As a matter of fact, he did. But I cannot see how this affects—"

Shea jumped up. "Oh, my God! Next thing you'll be selling out to the magicians and letting Gloriana's crowd go chase themselves—as long as you can make this snow girl."

"That's not fair, Harold! After all, you were the one who insisted that we go ahead with our campaign, when I was willing to—"

"Yeah? Who had the bright idea of getting pally with the magicians in the first place? Who got up this marvelous plan—"

"Young man, let me tell you that you're grossly unreasonable as well as grossly reckless. You've placed us in one predicament after another by getting into fights for no good reason. You force my hand by making me use spells before I've tried them out. Now, when I wish to embark on a really important scientific experiment—"

"I suppose it never occurred to you that Busyrane might be trying to suck you in to work for him by means of this girl. He controls her, and—"

"*Shh!* You needn't shout!"

"I'm not shouting!" roared Shea.

A knock on the door made them both go silent. "Uh . . . ahem . . . come in!" said Chalmers.

Busyrane stood on the threshold, rubbing his hands. "Good morrow, magical sirs. We heard your conversation and bethought us there might be something our humble household might supply or our feeble powers obtain for your use."

Chalmers made a good recovery. "We were wondering—You know, the job of providing organization requires a special . . . uh . . . methodology. The science of combinational magic . . . uh . . . uh—"

Shea took over. "What we mean is, could we have the loan of some laboratory facilities?"

"Oh, certes, that lies within our gift. We have a disused chamber that would admirably serve. A few prisoners, even, on which you may experiment. We shall be happy, also, to furnish you with a cockatrice. If your honors will have the goodness to follow our poor person—"

When the head enchanter had left them, Shea and Chalmers drew deep breaths. They had watched him for the least sign of suspicion, but he had displayed none—so far.

Chalmers said: "Let me offer my apologies for . . . uh . . . my hastiness."

"That's all right, Doc. I shouldn't have flown off the handle. And I'm sorry for running you ragged by being reckless."

They shook hands, like a pair of shame-faced small boys. "What's the program now?" asked Shea.

"Well . . . ahem . . . I'd like to restore Florimel —that is, to give her a human body. Also, she might not find a person of my years peculiarly congenial. I observe Busyrane is able to assume almost any age he wishes."

"Ha—" Shea had started to laugh, but stopped as Chalmers gave him a hurt look. "After all, Harold, what's so heinous about wishing to be young?"

"It isn't that, Doc. I just remembered something you said—about amorous adventure having few attractions for a person of your age."

Chalmers smiled in mild triumph. "You forget that if I succeed in the rejuvenating process, I shall no longer be a person of my age!"

8

"GOOD GRACIOUS," SAID CHALMERS. "THAT'S THE SEC-
ond time you've wandered off the incantation!
Whatever is on your mind, Harold?" Shea stared ab-
sently at the big steel cage filling half the laboratory.
Into it, with the aid of a pot containing a small
fire, they were trying to conjure a dragon—one
dragon. "Nothing much," he replied, "except I'm
wondering about his flock of bogymen that's due to
show up for the meeting tomorrow."

It was only half the truth. Shea had not given
up his idea of a grand assault on the place and the
capture of all the enchanters at once. The previous
evening, without telling Chalmers, he had been out
to look over the ground.

At the precise point where the gate began to
fade from view, with rocks and trees on the other
side of the building showing through it, he stopped
and took careful bearings on the nearby landmarks.
He chuckled internally over the thought that these
invisible castles wouldn't be practical if the people
of Faerie knew a little elementary surveying. Then
he wedged the gate open with a small stone and
slipped off among the trees.

There he cautiously whistled the tune Belphebe
had taught him. No result. He went through it a
second time and a third, wondering how long it
would be before his absence were noticed. He was
just about to give up when he saw a unicorn, ap-

parently the same one Belphebe had ridden, peering from behind a tree. It sniffed suspiciously before coming forward to mouth one of the maple-sugar lumps.

Shea wrote:

DEAREST BELPHEBE: We are at Busyrane's castle. It lies about two hours' ride along the road from the place where we got away from the Da Derga. Looks like a hut till you turn off the road east and follow a track till you get to a big oak tree, the biggest in the neighborhood, in line with a hill that has a round top. Then you can see the castle. Could you arrange to be in the neighborhood in about forty-eight hours? I'll call the unicorn at that time and if you're riding it, will see you. Be careful about the magicians, will you?

H. S.

He impaled the note on the unicorn's horn and shooed the animal away. Now, he thought, if I make a break from the castle, I'll have a guide. If I don't, at least I'll see her again—

That was last night. During the morning, he was more and more nervous and preoccupied, and now for the second time he had wandered from the incantation he and Chalmers were trying to work. "Nothing much," he had answered Chalmers' inquiry. Chalmers glanced at him shrewdly and hummed:

"Heighdy! Heighdy!
Misery me, lackadaydee!
He sipped no sup, and he craved no crumb,
As he sighed for the love of a layde!"

Shea looked at his partner sharply, but Chalmers' expression was bland. How much did he suspect?

But Chalmers was wrapped up in the task. "Now," he said, "let's try again. 'By Fafnir and Python, Midgardsormr and Yang—' " the incantation rolled out. The smoke from the fire in the cage thickened, and the amateur enchanters went on, ready to yell the counterspell Chalmers had worked out if the thing got out of hand.

It was a variant on the original dragon spell, with wording and preparations slightly changed. There was a shrill metallic hiss and a minor convulsion in the smoke. The incantation stopped. The incantators stood gauping.

They had produced a dragon all right. One dragon, not a hundred. But this dragon was ten inches long, with bat wings and a prominent sting on the end of its tail. It breathed fire.

The bars of the cage had been made strong enough to hold a dragon of conventional size. But this little horror fluttered up to them, squeezed through, and flew straight at the experimenters.

"Yeow!" yelled Shea, as a blast of flame from its jaws singed the hair off the back of his hand. *"Awk!"* shrieked Chalmers as the sting got him in the ankle. They tumbled over each other and dashed around the laboratory, Shea brandishing his épée and Chalmers swinging a pestle. The dragonlet dodged past them and flew through the door into the corridor. There was a rustle and a heavy clank.

Shea went down the corridor. He came back with his face a trifle white.

"The cockatrice looked at it," he said, and held out a perfect stone dragon, ten inches long.

"Put it down," said Chalmers gloomily. He hobbled around, looking for something to put on his stung ankle. "Damnation, Harold, if there were only some way to control these things quantitatively—"

"I thought that was it," replied Shea. "What went wrong to give us that animated blowtorch?"

"I don't know. The only . . . uh . . . certitude is that we got our decimal point off again. We got point oh oh oh one dragon instead of a hundred dragons. I confess, the solution eludes me. The calculus of classes contains no aspect of quantitative accuracy—"

The rest of the day gave them a sea horse three feet long and, after some effort, a cask to put it in; six stuffed owls with blue glass eyes; and finally a large and amiable tomcat with nine tails. The last experiment found a moon looking in the castle window, so they gave up and went to bed. Chalmers murmured sadly that if he tried to give Florimel a human body in the present state of his knowledge, he'd probably make her into a set of lovely but embarrassing Siamese triplets.

There were noises during the night. Neither slept well till toward morning. When they rose, someone was tapping at their door.

It proved to be a long-eared, potbellied imp, who handed them a sheet of parchment, grinned, and sped off down the corridor. Shea and Chalmers read:

Ye Enchaunters' Chapter

will meete in Council this daye
in ye greate Hall of Castle Busyrane

Archimage	Maistre Magitian Busyrane
Viceregente	M. M. Dolon
Archiviste	M. M. Courromont
Keeper of ye Moneys	M. M. Voulandoure

Ye Fyrst Daye

Addresse of ye Archimage	M. M. Busyrane
Reading of ye minutes	M. M. Courromont
Report on ye treasurie	M. M. Voulandoure

Here will neue members be Thought on
Now cometh ye professional meeting

I. 𝔐. 𝔐. Dolon—"Ye Poweres magickal of six selected Water Fay—Human Hybrids."

II. 𝔐. 𝔐. Sournoy—"A neue use for ye Bloud of unbaptized infants."

III. 𝔐. 𝔐. Nuisane—"Of ye Comparative efficacie of ye Essence of ye Spotted Frogge & ye Common Green Frogge in sleeping Enchauntments."

These all with Diverse experiments and shews by ye Maistres aforesaid.

Day ye Second

Ye Maistres will meete in Executive Council in ye P.M.

Banquet   at Vespers
Maistre of ye Toasts   𝔐. 𝔐. Nuisane
Ye Black Masse will be Celebrated after, followed by a Graund Ball, with various Comely Witches, Sprites, and Succubi.

"Sounds like a big occasion," observed Shea. "Let's go down to the great hall and see whom can we find."

They found their way to a huge room whose stained-glass windows bore pictures of mystical signs grouped round centerpieces of knights in magical torment. Already five people were gathered at one end, talking earnestly. Shea recognized Busyrane, Dolon, and Duessa. He caught a fragment of a story Dolon was telling:——"and I say he was no more than a bungling poursuivant, journeyman though he ranked. Imagine summoning up a devil, but leaving one corner of the pentagon open! He deserved no better than he got—ho-ho!—which was to have his head torn off by the demon's red-hot pincers! Ha, here come my pair! Busyrane, do 'em the honors!"

The Archimage bowed, first to Duessa and then

to the new arrivals. "We are highly favored," he said, "to present Master Reed de Chalmers, who has applied for elevation to the honorable state of mastership in our Chapter. He is most expert, in the production of singular monsters, also a man full of ideas for the benefit of our order. Also his apprentice, Harold de Shea."

Was there a slight change in the voice on that last sentence? Shea could not be sure, and Duessa was curtsying, pronouncing in a fine contralto: "Enchanted, good magical sirs." With that red hair she was certainly a beauty when she wanted to be gracious. If only—

Plop! A bare-necked vulture flopped through the window and lit beside them, then changed into a hook-nosed man in a long monk's outfit. "The good Fripon!" exclaimed Dolon. "How wags the world with you?"

"By your leave, not well," croaked the good Fripon, sadly. "I had all but trapped that wretch Belphebe when what does she do but get a counterspell from Cambina, then shoot an arrow through one of the best sprites I ever had. Curse her! She's killing off the Losels, too."

"I live for the day when I can tear her toenails out," said Duessa venomously. Shea's scalp tingled. A dust whirlwind that puffed in the window set everyone coughing, and dissolved into a short, fat man, who mopped his brow.

"Whew!" he said. "Fatiguing! Still it's better than walking for a man of my figure. Hope you have an ample lunch, Busyrane. Always thinking of my belly, that's me, Voulandoure, at your service. Ah, fair Duessa! And the good Fripon! Still cheating the grave-digger, my gloomy friend?" He poked Fripon's ribs.

Now magicians began to pour into the hall, by window and door, so many of them Shea could not keep up with their names. The trumpet for the midday meal found him vainly trying to catch up—

215

and also separated him from Chalmers, who was taken in tow to sit at the masters' table.

Shea found himself next to a fuzzy-haired youth who said shyly: "Pray, generous sir, may I see your enchanted blade?"

"Huh?" said Shea. "But it—" before it occurred to him that no useful purpose would be served by disillusioning these people about the épée. He produced it and handed it over. The fuzzy young man waved it over the table, making noises of approval.

"I feel no sudden access of strength," he remarked. "The spell must be very subtle. Or perhaps it is one you use on yourself—no, that could not be, for Cambina's magic prevented the use of such spells at the tournament. Hey, Grimbald!" He reached across and touched the blue-jowled man on Shea's other side. "He beat two of the most renowned knights of Faerie with this toothpick!"

"Aye," replied the other, looking up from his plate, "including one of ours." He addressed Shea directly. "Knew you not that Blandamour and Paridell, though they wear the Faerie livery, are in the service of this Chapter? Nay, you're not a member—how could you? But 'ware both in the future."

That explained a lot, thought Shea: the actions of the two knights, for one thing; and for another, why the magicians were so polite to him, though his rating was no more than that of an apprentice. There would be something practically supernatural about modern fencing technique to these people.

Busyrane had arranged his hair so that the light falling through the stained-glass window touched it to a halo. He might have been some kindly saint as he began:

"Magical sirs and ladies: Many are the pleasures that have fallen to our lot, but none equal to that of beholding you here assembled beneath our humble roof to carry on the good name and high purpose of magic. Ah, how much better and brighter a world it were if all in it could but know you all—could but see you all. My friends—"

216

The afternoon was warm, the lunch had been ample, and Shea had a feeling of having heard something like this before. His eyelids began to weigh on him. The smooth voice rolled on:

"—in the days of King Huon of glorious and blessed memory, my friends, when we lived a more abundant life—"

Shea felt himself itching, now here, now there, now all over. He made one more effort to keep awake, then lapsed into an unashamed doze.

He was aroused by a mild patter of applause. Busyrane's place was taken by the keeper of ye archives, Courromont, a thin-lipped, bloodless-looking man, who hardly moved his mouth as he read:

"At the council of the Enchanters' Chapter on August 1st following the address of our beloved archimage six members were advanced in grade from apprentice to journeyman and one journeyman member to wit the esteemed Sournoy was advanced to the full rank of master magician it was furthermore decided to raise the annual dues from seven and a half to ten elfars papers were read at the professional session by Master Magicians Malvigen and Denfero with various works of magical prowess in illustration it was furthermore resolved in the executive session to empower a special committee for drastic action against certain representatives of the Old Order whose activities have become threatening to wit the knight Sir Cambell and Belphebe of the Woods and the Princess Britomart the knights of the Chapter Blandamour and Paridell were accordingly—"

Shea came wide awake, but there were no details. Busyrane merely asked if it were moved and seconded that the minutes be accepted. They were.

Voulandoure's fat face shone greasily in the heat as he droned off figures and urged members to pay their dues on time. What could those plans for drastic action have been? Presumably the late Malvigen had tried one of them when he got Belphebe's arrow through him, but what else?

His attention was snapped back by Busyrane's use of his name: "—proposed that the magicians Reed de Chalmers and Harold de Shea be admitted with the ranks of master magician and apprentice. If these gentlemen will kindly leave the room—"

Outside, Shea said softly: "Did you hear what they said about Belphebe?"

"Dear me, yes. Duessa seems quite determined on that point. She used a most vulgar term in speaking of her—one normally employed in the . . . uh . . . propagation of dogs. When—"

"What are they going to *do?* Specifically?" Shea's voice was urgent.

"I—" The door opened and a voice called: "Master Reed de Chalmers."

Shea was left to fidget for five minutes before being summoned. Busyrane grasped him by the hand at the door and led him to the front of the hall. "We present to you the apprentice Harold de Shea as a member of this Chapter," he said. "A very worthy magical person, adept in the production of strange monsters, adroit in enchantments connected with the profession of arms. Apprentice Harold de Shea"—he turned toward the new member—"as members of a high intellectual calling we despise the silly ceremonies of admission such as the court uses for its orders of knighthood. Therefore, we will merely bid you welcome; but doubtless the other apprentices will have something to say to you tomorrow night after the Black Mass."

Voulandoure came over and squeezed Shea's hand in his own thick, moist ones. "My 'gratulations, also, magical sirs!" He lowered his voice. "May I point out the initiation fee—"

"Ahem," said Chalmers, who had joined the group. "How much?"

"Fifty elfars for yourself, Master Magician Reed, and twenty-five for 'Prentice Harold."

Chalmers looked slightly stricken. He fished out the money bag. His face showed some relief, but not much, when its contents proved adequate. "I should think," he remarked, "that with so many fine magicians about, you'd have no difficulty in conjuring up . . . uh . . . all necessary funds."

A shadow crossed the face of ye keeper of ye moneys. "Alas, magical sir, our great problem! 'Tis a department involving the use of the philosophers' stone and the blood of infants, this much we know. But our research in the question has been interrupted by the activities of that curst court and the Companions, and I fear me we shall never succeed till we rid ourselves of them."

"Aye," said Dolon. "The one who came nearest the solution was the enchantress Acrasia. She did make a conjured gold that was all but permanent; met every test, and would only turn to ashes when one pronounced a Pater Noster. But where's Acrasia now? Eh? Dead, down and drownded by one of Gloriana's Companions, a murrain on them all!"

"Good Master Dolon!" It was Busyrane. "The professional meeting is called, and I doubt not the other masters are as eager as we ourselves to hear your paper."

Shea found the fuzzy-haired youth at his elbow. "D'you play at checks? We 'prentices are left much to our own devisings when the masters gabble."

"Checks?"

"Aye, you know, king, queen, knight, fool, pawn, check and you're mate. I'm hand in glove with one of Busyrane's imps, who'll furnish us a mug or two of musty ale to pass the time while we play."

It sounded an attractive program. But Shea remembered that chess game afterward. The fuzz-haired apprentice was not naturally a good player. Shea beat him in the first two games easily, winning the small bets the youth insisted on "to make the sport more interesting." Then the musty ale or the youth's magic—too late Shea remembered what profession he was an apprentice in—rose up and bit him. The fuzzy one's pieces turned up in the most unexpected places, executing the most astonishing gambits and combinations. With every new defeat Shea grew more annoyed. Whether through annoyance or the musty ale, he began offering to double the bets for the next one.

When the doors at the end of the hall were flung open and the master magicians emerged, the fuzzy youth was remarking gaily: "That makes eighty-six elfars, sixteen you stand in my debt. Ha-ha, that reminds me. Did I ever tell you about the journeyman Sligon, who owed my master, Voulandoure, sixty elfars over a box of dice? He refused to pay—said he couldn't—even when Voulandoure sent him a plague of boils. Well, wasn't it funny, when Sligon was playing with his own cat one day, that he should turn into a fish? I say a good magician should never lack for money, when there are people who can be kidnaped and ransomed. Don't you agree?"

"That's right," said Shea with a heartiness which he hoped didn't sound too hollow. He got up to join Chalmers.

The elder psychologist was looking pleased with himself. "A trifle harrowing that session, but gratifyingly informative," he said as they went toward their rooms. "I really feel I've learned something about quantitative control. In fact, I'm confident that in a few months' research I can learn enough not only to transform Florimel and to rejuvenate myself, but also to . . . uh . . . revolutionize the entire practice of magic in Faerie, to make its benefits available to all."

"Yes, but"— Shea looked worried—"did you find out what they intend to do about Belphebe?"

"I gather that that is a matter for the . . . uh . . . executive session of tomorrow. But as I understand the outlines of the plan, it is not to direct the enchantments against her in person. She's protected against them. They intend rather to place spells on the two or three places where she sleeps, with the design of causing her to fall into so deep a slumber that she can be captured."

They paused on Chalmers' threshold. He added: "However, I wouldn't worry about the young woman's . . . uh . . . safety, Harold. As I understand it she is to be brought here, and I am sure that as a member of the Chapter I can persuade them not to harm her. In fact—"

"For the love of Mike, Doc, are you throwing in with these guys, or just plain daffy? Didn't you hear Duessa talking about pulling Belphebe's toenails out, come the Revolution, and Dolon mentioning the torture chamber? Wake up! You're being an old fool!"

"Harold, I must request you not to use such intemperate language. After all, I'm somewhat your senior, and I require the uninterrupted use of all facilities as well as your own cordial cooperation to put this matter on a scientific basis. In a few months I shall be in a position to effect an industrial revolution in magic—"

"Theory! Months! I might have known that's what you'd be after! Can't you realize somebody's in danger?"

"I shall certainly give my most earnest attention to persuading the other members of the Chapter that this young woman to whom you are so attached is innocuous, and—"

"Oh, for Pete's sake! Forget it! Good night." Shea stalked out, more angry with Chalmers than he had ever been before. He did not hear the velvety click of the Judas window in Chalmers' room. Nor could he overhear the two men in the secret passage that led to that window.

Busyrane's voice was bland. "We were good enough to warn you that the young man was a suspicious character and mingled somehow in the affairs of the court."

"Can it be that my judgment, usually so keen, was altogether thrown off?" asked Dolon.

"Oh, you were right about the older. He's a proper magician and devoted to the Chapter. But the younger—he'll bear more than watching. A friend of Belphebe, forsooth!"

9

SHEA LAY IN BED, STARING AT THE BLACK CEILING. No use trying to get the Doc to do anything. His heart was in the right place. But between his devotion to Florimel and his devotion to theory he could not be convinced that these enchanters, who talked so glibly of intellectual achievements, were bloody-minded racketeers who intended to put Belphebe, Britomart, and a lot of others to a slow and intricate death.

Shea shuddered as he thought of it. Whatever was done to save them, he would have to do, quickly. Yes, and to keep Chalmers from turning the products of his really fine scientific mind over to these rascals.

The castle was silent. He slipped out of bed, dressed, and buckled the faithful épée over his shoulder. It would not be much use against enchantments. But as long as the enchanters themselves believed it had magical power, it would help.

The door swung open noiselessly. There was no light in the corridor. The stone floor was cold under Shea's feet. His soft leather boots made soundless progress. If he kept one hand along the wall, he thought he could find the way to the great hall, and so out. Step—step—the hand that had been following the wall touched nothingness. An appalling odor of cockatrice assailed his nostrils. Evidently the door of somebody's laboratory. He went down to hands and knees and slithered past an inch at a time, hoping the creature would not wake up.

So. Here was the head of the stair. He took one step down, two—and felt something soft touch his ankles. Another step and the something soft was clear to his waist, catching at him. It felt ropy and vaguely slimy, a whole tangle of slime—cobwebs! For a moment Harold Shea felt unreasoning panic, as it seemed that going ahead and turning back would be equally fatal. Then he realized that this would be some of Busyrane's magic, part of the ordinary castle safeguards, and of no special significance.

Yet what would cut through or destroy cobwebs? Fire. He had no fire. But in his previous adventure in Scandinavian myth, Surt's giants had made use of flaming swords, and he had the épée. With an incantation to make use of the law of similarity it might become a flaming sword. On that narrow, stone-walled spiral staircase it was altogether unlikely that anyone would be able to see the light.

With the ghostly fingers of the cobwebs clutching at his legs, Shea stood on the stair and thought as he never had before of a spell:

Sword, sword, sword that is now my salvation,
　　Make me a light to cut through these cobwebs;
　　Be like Surt's sword to cut through this maze.

He could feel the hilt growing warm.

Help my escape to reach consummation;
　　In the name of Durandal, help me to be free.

It was not outrageously good poetry, but the hilt was so hot that he snatched it out. A smoky red flame ran down the blade and dropped from the point, revealing the whole stairwell from wall to wall and as high as Shea stood, filled with a solid mass of the hideous gray material. A man could smother in it easier than not. Busyrane left nothing to chance.

Shea slashed at the stuff with the flaming épée. It shriveled left and right before him, back against the wall with hissing, foul-smelling flames running along the strands. He advanced slowly, cutting one step

223

at a time. As he reached the bottom and the last cobwebs, the fire in the blade went out. He was in the great hall; but a few steps carried him through it, across the forecourt and to the gate.

A moon looked down out of a cloudless sky. Shea cursed it softly to himself, wondering whether he ought to take a chance on crossing the open stretch between gate and the shelter of the trees before it set. He decided to try it.

Bending low, he scuttled rapidly across the space, his cloak, flapping like a vampire's wings. He made it without stumbling and looked back. The castle had disappeared. There was nothing visible but stony ground with the hut in the middle.

Once among the trees, he began pacing the circuit of the clearing, whistling very softly to himself the unicorn tune and pausing to listen. A quarter of the way round he was halted by a tense whisper, "Stand, sir!"

"Belphebe!"

"Aye." She stepped from her place of concealment, arrow drawn to the head. "In good sooth you look like Harold de Shea. But show me how you hold that narrow sword."

Shea drew the still-warm épée and demonstrated.

"Certes, then you are indeed he. I feared lest the enchanters had sent a phantom forth to beguile me. Right glad I am to see you, Squire Harold."

Shea said: "Say, I'm glad to see you, too. I knew I could depend—"

"Save your fair speeches for another hour. Here is danger. What is toward?"

Shea explained. Belphebe said: "For myself I fear not, though I thank you for the warning. Yet it's somewhat otherwise with Britomart, who has not the protection of the woods so close as I. And sure it were shame to miss the chance of catching the entire Chapter at once. Let me think. I left Artegall at a woodcutter's cot on the far flank of Loselwood. His man Talus had gone to fetch Cambina, that she might heal his bruises and calm his mind."

"So Cambina's a psychologist too! Why does he need his mind calmed?"

"Why, sir, he's the chief justiciar of all Faerie. Without a calm mind, how shall he hold the balance even? Let us go thither and lay this matter before him. Certes, we two cannot lay so many rogues by the heels alone."

Two hours of walking brought Shea to the yawning stage. The moon had set. Under the black trees, even the sure-footed Belphebe found the going hard. She was ready to listen to suggestions for a nap.

"Sleep is still far from me now," she said. "If you wish, I will keep watch for the first hour—which should be till the stars of the Bear sink to the top of that tree." She pointed. Shea, too drowsy to notice, composed himself to rest.

The next thing he knew, he was being shaken awake in a brightening world.

"Hey, young lady," he said through his first yawn, "I thought you were going to wake me up after the first hour?"

"And so thought I. But you were so in comfort that I wanted the heart to rouse you. I need but little sleep."

"Naughty. What about my masculine pride?"

She made a face at him. "I forgot that. Men are such foolish carls about it. But come." She danced a step or two. "Tirra-lirra, a brave day! Let's forth and seek our breakfast."

As they walked along, Belphebe peering toward thickets for an edible target, and Shea a bit woozy from lack of sleep, he asked: "D'you suppose Cambina will have calmed Artegall down so he'll listen to my explanations before he starts carving?"

"A thing to think on! Will you hide whilst I speak him fair?"

"Guess I'll take a chance on his temper." Shea wasn't going to have his dream-girl suspect him of timidity at this stage. He was sure he could outrun the bulky justiciar if necessary.

"Marry, I would not have you answer otherwise!" She smiled at him, and he felt rewarded. She went on, scrutinizing him: "Many knights, squires, and yeomen have I kenned, Master Harold, but never a wight like you. You speak fair, yet half the time

225

with words I wot not of. You promised to explain the meanings of those wherewith you put the Blatant Beast to rout."

Shea replied: "Curiosity killed a cat."

"*Miauw!* Yet of this cat's allotted nine, I have several left to draw upon."

"I really can't, Belphebe. Magical reasons."

"Oh. Well then, tell me the meaning of the strange thing you called the Lady Cambina even now."

"Psychologist?"

"Aye."

Shea gave an account in words of one syllable of the science of psychology, and of his own experiences in its practice. Under the girl's admiring curiosity he expanded. Before he knew it he was practically telling her the story of his life. As soon as he realized this, he cut his autobiography off short, not wanting to leave her with nothing to be curious about.

Belphebe said: "A strange tale, Squire. Gin you speak truth, this homeland of yours were worth the seeing." She sighed a little. "The wilds of Faerie I know like my own palm. And since I will not tarry at Gloriana's tedious court, there's nothing left for me but to hunt the Losels and such vile— *Sst!*" She broke off, moved slowly a couple of steps, and loosed an arrow. It knocked over a rabbit.

While they dressed and cooked their breakfast, Shea thought. He finally ventured: "Look here, kid, some day Doc and I will be going back, I suppose. Why don't you plan to come with us?"

Belphebe raised her eyebrows. " 'Tis a thought audacious. But stay—could I live among the woodspaths as I do here?"

"Unh." Shea imagined the horrible complications that would ensue if Belphebe tried to lead her present life in Ohio's close-fenced farmland. "I'm afraid that wouldn't be practical. But there's plenty else to do."

"What then? How should I live in one of your great towns?"

That problem had not occurred to Shea. He revised his estimate of Belphebe. The girl might look like something out of a medieval romance, but she had a core of hard common sense. The only job he could think of for her was giving bow-and-arrow lessons, and he hardly supposed the demand for professional archers to be large.

He said vaguely: "Oh, we'll figure something out. Doc and I would see to it that you were—uh—uh . . ."

"Harold!" she said sharply. "What are you proposing? Think not that because I lead a free roving life, I—"

"No, no, I didn't mean—uh . . ."

"What then?"

He thought again. One obvious solution was staring him in the face; yet to bring it up so early might spoil everything. Still, nothing ventured . . .

He drew a deep breath and plunged: "You could marry me."

Belphebe's mouth fell open. It was some seconds before she answered: "You jest, good Squire!"

"Not at all. People do it in my country, you know, just like here."

"But—knew you not that I am affianced to Squire Timias?"

It was Shea's turn to stare blankly.

Belphebe said: "Nay, good friend, take it not so to heart. I had thought it known to the world, else I should have told you. The fault was mine."

"No . . . I mean . . . it wasn't . . . let's skip it."

"Skip it?" said Belphebe wonderingly. Shea bent over his rabbit-haunch, muttering something about the meat's being good.

Belphebe said: "Be not angry, Harold. Not willingly would I hurt you, for I like you well. And had I know you sooner . . . But my word is given."

"I suppose so," said Shea somberly. "What sort of man is your friend Timias?" He wondered whether the question had a useful purpose, or whether he was showing a slight touch of masochism in keeping the painful subject alive.

Belphebe's face softened. "A most sweet boy;

shrinking and sensitive, not like these brawling knightly ruffians."

"What are his positive qualities?" asked Shea.

"Why—ah—he can sing a madrigal better than most."

"Is that all?" said Shea with a touch of sarcasm.

Belphebe bridled. "I know not what you mean. 'Tis even the core of the matter that he's no bold confident venturer like yourself."

"Doesn't sound to me like much of a reason for marrying anybody. I came across a lot of cases like that in my psych work; usually the woman lived to regret it."

Belphebe jumped up angrily. "So, Squire, you inquire of my privy affairs that you may sting me with your adder's tongue? Fie on you! It regards not you whom I marry, or why."

Shea grinned offensively. "I was just making general remarks. If you want to take them personally, that's your lookout. I still say a woman is taking a lousy chance to marry a human rabbit in the hope of making a lion out of him."

"A murrain on your general remarks!" cried Belphebe passionately. "An you would company me, I'll thank you to keep your long tongue in its proper groove! Better rabbit than fox with pretense of marriage—"

"What do you mean, pretense?" barked Shea. "I meant that when I said it! Though now I see that maybe it wasn't such a good idea—"

"Oh, you do? You change your mind quickly! I'll warrant me you'd have done so in any case!"

Shea got himself under control, and said: "Let's not go any farther with this, Belphebe. I'm sorry I made those cracks about your boy-friend. I won't mention him again. Let's be friends."

Belphebe's anger wilted. "And right sorry am I that I threw your proposal in your face, Squire Harold; 'twas a sad discourtesy." Shea was surprised to see a trace of moisture in her eye. She blinked rapidly and smiled. "So, we are friends, and our breakfast done. Let us be on."

The new sun was a patch of flecks of orange fire through the foliage. They found a sluggish little stream and had to squeeze through the thickets on its banks.

They reached a stretch of drier ground where the glades expanded to continuous meadow and the forest shrank to clumps of trees. They left one of these clumps and were swishing through the long grass, when a leathery rustle made them look up.

Overhead swooped a nightmarish reptile the size of an observation plane. It had two legs and a pair of huge batwings. On its back rode Busyrane, all clad in armor but his face, which was smiling benignly. "Well met, dear friends!" he called down. "What a pleasing thought! Both at once!"

Twunk! went Belphebe's bow. The arrow soared through one wing membrane. The beast hissed a little and banked for a turn.

"Into the woods!" cried Belphebe, and set the example. "The wivern cannot fly among the trees."

"What did you call it? Looks like some kind of a long-tailed pterodactyl to me." Shea craned his neck as the sinister shadow wove to and fro above the leaves.

Belphebe led the way to the opposite side of the grove. When Busyrane circled above the segment away from them, they dashed across the open space and into the next clump. A shrill hiss behind and above warned them that they had been spotted.

They worked their way through this grove. From under the trees they could see Busyrane silhouetted against the sky, while he couldn't see them.

"Now!" said Belphebe, and ran like an antelope through the long grass. Shea pounded after. This was a longer run than the first, a hundred yards or more. Halfway across he heard the hiss of cloven air behind and drove himself for all his strained lungs were worth. The shadow of the monster unblurred in front of him. It was too far, too far—and then he was under the friendly trees. He caught a glimpse of the reptile, horribly close, pulling up in a stall to avoid the branches.

Shea leaned against a trunk, puffing. "How much more of this is there?"

Belphebe's face had a frown. "Woe's me; I fear this forest thins ere it thickens. But let's see."

They worked round the edges of the grove, but it was small, and the distance to all others, but the one they had come from, prohibitively great.

"Looks like we have to go back," said Shea.

"Aye. I like not that. Assuredly he will not have pursued us alone."

"True for you. I think I see something there." He pointed to a group of distant figures, pink in the rising sun.

Belphebe gave a little squeak of dismay. "Alack, now we are undone, for they are a numerous company. If we stay, they surround us. If we flee, Busyrane follows on that grim mount— What are you doing?"

Shea had gotten out his knife and was whittling the base of a tall sapling. He replied: "You'll see. This worked once and ought to again. You're good at tree climbing; see if you can find a bird's nest. I need a fistful of feathers."

She went, puzzled but obedient. When she returned with the feathers, Shea was rigging up a contraption of sapling trunk and twigs, tied together with ivy vine. He hoped it wasn't poison ivy. It bore some resemblance to an enormous broom. As Shea lashed a couple of crosspieces to the stick he explained: "The other one I made a single-seater. This'll have to carry tandem. Let's see the feathers, kid."

He tossed one aloft, repeating the dimly remembered spell he had used once before, and then shoved it in among the twigs.

"Now," he said, "I'm the pilot and you're the gunner. Get astride here. Think you can handle your bow while riding this thing?"

"What will it do?" she asked, looking at Shea with new respect.

"We're going up to tackle Busyrane in his own element. Say, look at that mob! We better get going!" As the pursuers came nearer, thrashing the brushes of the near-by groves in their hunt, Shea could see that they were a fine collection of monsters: men with animal heads, horrors with three or four arms, bodies and faces rearing from the legless bottoms of snakes.

They straddled the broom. Shea chanted:

"By oak, ash, and yew,
The high air through,
To slay this vile caitiff,
Fly swiftly and true!"

The broom started with a rush, up a long slant. As it shot out of the grove and over the heads of the nearest of the pursuit, they broke into a chorus of shouts, barks, roars, meows, screams, hisses, bellows, chirps, squawks, snarls, brays, growls and whinnies. The effect was astounding.

But Shea's mind was occupied. He was pleased to observe that this homemade broom seemed fairly steady though slower than the one he had hexed in the land of Scandinavian myth. He remembered vaguely that in aerial dogfighting the first step is to gain an advantage in altitude.

Up they went in a spiral. Busyrane came into view on his wivern, beating toward them. The enchanter had his sword out, but as the wivern climbed after them Shea was relieved to see that he was gaining.

A couple of hundred feet above the enemy he swung the broom around. Over his shoulder he said: "Get ready; we're going to dive on them." Then he noticed that Belphebe was gripping the stick with both hands, her knuckles white.

"Ever been off the ground before?" he asked.

"N-nay. Oh, Squire Harold, this is a new and very fearsome thing. When I look down—" She shuddered and blinked.

"Don't let a little acrophobia throw you. Look at your target, not the ground."

"I essay."

"Good girl!" Shea nosed the broom down. The wivern glared up and opened its fanged jaws. He aimed straight for the red-lined maw. At the last minute he swerved aside; heard the jaws *clomp* vainly and the bowstring snap.

"Missed," said Belphebe. She was looking positively green under her freckles. Shea, no roller-coaster addict, guessed how she felt.

"Steady," he said, nosing up and then dodging as the wivern flapped toward them with surprising speed. "We'll try a little shallower dive."

Shea came down again. The wivern turned, too. Shea didn't bank far enough, and he was almost swept into the jaws by the centrifugal force of his own turn. They went *clomp* a yard from the tail of the bottom. "Whew," said Shea on the climb. "Hit anything?"

"Busyrane, but it hurt him not. He bears armor of proof and belike some magic garment as well."

"Try to wing the wivern, then." They shot past the beast, well beyond reach of the scaly neck. *Twunk!* An arrow fixed itself among the plates behind the head. But the wivern, appearing unhurt, put on another burst of speed and Shea barely climbed over its rush, with Busyrane yelling beneath him.

Belphebe had her acrophobia under control now. She leaned over and let go three more arrows in rapid succession. One bounced off the reptile's back plates. One went through a wing membrane. The third stuck in its tail. None of them bothered it.

"I know," Shea. "We aren't penetrating its armor at this range. Hold on; I'm going to try something."

They climbed. When they had good altitude, Shea dove past the wivern. It snapped at them, missed, and dove in pursuit.

The wind whistled in Shea's ears and blurred his vision. Forest and glade opened out below; little dots expanded to the pursuers on foot. Shea glanced back; the wivern hung in space behind, its wings half furled. He leveled out, then jerked the broom's nose up sharply. The universe did a colossal somersault and they straightened away behind the wivern. In the seconds the loop had taken, the beast had lost sight of them. Shea nosed down and they glided in under the right wing, so close they could feel the air go *fuff* with the wing beat.

Shea got one glimpse of Busyrane's astonished face before the wing hid it. The scaly skin pulsed over the immense flying muscles for one beat. "Now!" he barked.

Twunk! Twunk! Belphebe had drawn the bow hard home, and the arrows tore into the beast's brisket.

There was a whistling scream, then catastrophe. The wide wing whammed down on the aviators, almost knocking Shea from his seat. They were no longer flying, but tumbling over and over, downward. The top of a tree slashed at Shea's face. Dazedly, he heard the wivern crash and tried to right the broom. It nosed up into a loop and hung. A cry from behind him, receding toward the earth, froze him. He saw Belphebe tumble into the grass, twenty feet down, and a wave of the monster men close over her.

Shea manhandled his broomstick around, fervently wishing he had a lighter one—a pursuit job. By the time he got it aimed at the place where he had last seen Belphebe, there was no sign of her or of Busyrane either. The wivern sprawled bloatedly in the grass with hundreds of the enchanter's allies swarming round it.

Shea drew his épée and dove at the thick of them. They screeched at him, some of them producing clumsy breast bows. He swooped toward a monster with a crocodile head as the strings began snapping. The arrows went far behind, but just as Shea stiffened his arm for the gliding thrust, Crocodilehead thinned to a puff of mist. The épée met no resistance. As Shea held his glide, parallel with the ground, he found the crowding monsters disappearing before him. He pulled up, looking back. They were materializing behind. More arrows buzzed past.

He circled, cutting another swath through them. No sign of Belphebe.

At the third charge an arrow caught in his cloak. The flint head of another drove through his boot and a quarter inch into his calf. The goblins were learning anti-aircraft fire. But of Belphebe there was still no sign, and now the ghost men were streaming toward him out of the woods on all sides. In every direction they were hopping, yelling, drawing their crude bows.

He climbed out of bowshot and circled, looking. No luck. It would have to be some other way. He felt slightly sick.

He went up higher, till the vast green expanse of Loselwood spread out before him. The sun was well up. Under it he fancied he could see the region where he had tangled with the Da Derga. Beyond should be the edge of the forest, where he and Chalmers had met their first Losels.

10

AN HOUR OF CRUISING SHOWED HIM A CLEARING with a little garden, a thatched cottage, and a circular palisade of pointed stakes around the whole. He helixed down slowly.

A man came out of the wood and entered the palisade through a gate. Shea caught a glimpse of red face and black beard as his own shadow, whisking across the grass, brought the man's eyes upward. The man dashed into the cottage as if all the fiends of Hell were after him. In a moment two armored men came out. The shield of one bore the striking black and silver gyronny of Sir Cambell.

> "By oak, ash and yew;
> My broomstick true,
> Like a dead leaf descending,
> So softly fall you!"

That was not quite the right way to put it, as Shea immediately learned. The broom settled slowly, but remorselessly literal, carried the imitation of a dead leaf to the point of a dizzying whirl. Cottage, forest, and waiting knights came to him in a spinning blur.

Shea felt ground under his feet. He staggered dizzily.

Artegall roared: "By'r Lady, 'tis the enchanter's varlet!" His sword came out, *Wheep!*

Shea said: "You're just the man I'm looking for—"

"That I warrant!" His laugh was a nasty bark. "But you'll accomplish no more magician's tricks on me. I have a protection, which is more than you have against this!" He shook the sword and swung it back.

"Wait a minute!" cried Shea. "I can explain, honest—"

"Explain to the devils of Hell, where you soon will be!"

At that moment Britomart and Cambina came out of the cabin. Shea wondered frantically whether to run toward them, try to start the broom, or— What was that? A set of little patterns was faintly visible on Artegall's breastplate as he turned in the morning sun. They were the type of pattern that would be left by soldering on brass oak leaves and then prying them off.

"Hey!" he said. "You're the guy who showed up in the oak leaves at Satyrane's tournament and won the second prize but didn't stop to collect it!"

"Huh? How knew you— What mean you, rogue?"

"Just what I say. You fought for the challengers, and Britomart knocked you off your pony, didn't she?"

" 'Tis to be said . . . ah—" Artegall turned his scowl on Britomart. She glared back.

"Come, good friends," said Cambina, "no variance. I proclaim it was Sir Artegall, for I penetrated his disguise. Come, Artegall, confess; you cannot hide the sun at the bottom of a bucket."

"I suppose I must," growled the knight. "I did

235

but wish to make proof whether I were as strong in the lists as I seemed, or whether certain of the knights would rather fall off their horses than oppose the queen's justiciar." He turned to Britomart. "You have a rude way toward an affianced husband, my lady!"

Shea caught Britomart's eye and winked violently. She turned on Artegall a look that would have melted granite. "Ah, my dear lord, had I but known! Yet surely you shall feel no shame at that one overthrow, for 'twas the combination of that enchanted ebony spear I bear and your own horse's stumbling, neither alone sufficient." She reached for his mailed arm. "When we are wed I shall leave these broils and tournaments to you."

Cambell and Cambina looked at Britomart, then at each other. The look implied they had never seen her act *that* way before. Shea repressed a grin. The brawny blonde learned fast.

Artegall smiled shamefacedly. "Why, dearest dame, that were a great sacrifice indeed. I knew not you cared so." His voice hardened. "But we have here a most villainous young rascal."

"No rascal," said Britomart, "but a true and loyal squire, whom I have sworn to my service and that of the queen."

"Then what of his soaring through the sky like a bug or witch? Nay, he's of the tribe of enchanters—"

"Not so," interrupted Cambina. "His magic is white, even as my own; and my art tells me that this Harold de Shea will speak the truth if you'll let him."

Artegall scowled, but asked: "Then what's the truth he would speak?"

Shea told his story quickly before a new argument could start. "That is good truth, I guarantee," said Cambina, when he had finished, "and Belphebe is in deadly danger."

"Then why stand we here at words?" snapped Artegall. "Ho, woodcutter! We start at once. Food and horses, as soon as they may be had, for all of us."

Shea disapproved of this cavalier treatment, but

didn't feel called upon to comment. He said: "Going to collect an army?"

"Nay, not I. Time presses us too close. Here we must count on our own good arms and Cambina's magic. Art afraid?"

"Try me."

"There's a stout younker." The frown in Artegall's brows cleared a bit. "I will be just and admit I held you wrong."

The moon in this world, Shea observed, set only twelve or thirteen minutes later each night, instead of the fifty minutes later of his own earth. He and his four companions were crouched at the edge of the opening that held Busyrane's unseen castle. They did not attempt it till the moon had disappeared.

As they crossed the open space Shea whispered: "I'm afraid I can't find the gate. Too dark to see my landmarks."

"Small loss," answered Cambina. Shea saw her dimly, doing things with her wand. Out of nothing grew a faint phosphorescence that resolved itself into a row of bars.

Cambina pointed the wand at it. The instrument elongated, flexing itself like some tame worm. The tip groped with the lock, inserting itself gently. There was a faint click.

The wand withdrew, then poked its end through the bars. Under the night song of the insects there came a faint grate as the bolt slid back. The gate was open.

As they tiptoed through, the infinitesimal jingle of the knight's armor sounded to Shea's ears like an earthquake in a kitchenware factory. Cambina pointed. Over their heads on the wall appeared a sentry, visible only as a cloak and hood, glowing with a phosphorescence almost too faint to be visible. The hood swung its black cavity toward them. Cambina pointed her wand, and the sentry froze in that position.

Light and music streamed from the windows of the great hall. Shea, leading because of his knowledge of the place and the fact that his tread was most nearly soundless, was heading for the door, when he tripped over a huge, hairy leg.

With simultaneous grunts a pair of Losels who had been stretched out on the steps rolled to their feet. While the one nearest was fumbling in the dark for his club, Shea drove the épée through the creature's throat. Behind him he heard the other's club swish up—

But the club failed to come down. He looked around and saw the Losel, club aloft, frozen to a statue like the sentry. The other Losel was expiring with quiet bubbling noises.

Cambina did things with her wand, and the door of the building swung open. There was light and noise within, but no one to see them. Across the corridor in which they stood was the entrance to the great hall, the door slightly ajar. Within, the revelers were too occupied with their grand ball to be watching the door.

Shea beckoned the four heads close to his and breathed: "This corridor runs around to the serving entrance."

"Are there other doors beside those two?" asked Artegall, and when Shea shook his head went on: "Then do you, Squire, with Cambell and Cambina, take that entrance. Here Britomart and I will take out stand; for this is the place where they will naturally come and we are, I think, the best men-at-arms."

Heads nodded. Shea and the other two stole down the corridor. Just before they reached the service entrance, an imp crossed the corridor from the kitchen with a tray in his hands.

He saw them. Cambell bounded forward and cut the imp in two. The bottom half of the imp ran back into the kitchen. There was an instant uproar.

The three ran a few steps to the service entrance and flung open the door.

Shea got one brief static picture of a roomful of magicians and red-lipped women looking at him. Some had their mouths open. Busyrane sat at one end of the horseshoe facing him, and he thought he recognized Chalmers. Before he could be certain, the photograph came to frenzied life.

He turned to face the noise behind. Out of the kitchen boiled a mass of imps and hobgoblins, bearing spits, knives, rolling pins. Shea neatly spitted the first on his épée, dodging the counter. The imp leaped backward off the blade and came on again. Behind him Shea heard the roar of the Chapter, Cambell's deep war cry, and the whack of swords against his shield.

"I can . . . handle these," panted Cambina. Her wand darted to and fro, freezing imp after imp. The rest started to run.

Shea turned back toward the hall, just in time to thrust through the throat a magician trying to roll under Cambell's legs with a knife, while others engaged the knight's attention.

The noise was ear-splitting. Cambell filled the door, and at the far end Britomart was doing equally well. Artegall had leaped into the hall and was swinging his great sword with both hands. His temper might be bad, but he was certainly a good man to have around in a roughhouse.

The lights dimmed to negligible red sparks. Cambina cried a spell and waved her wand; the magicians glowed with blue phosphorescence in the dark. The scene became that of a photographic negative—a wild one, with some of the enchanters turning themselves into winged things to flee, others hurling themselves upon the fighters, striking sparks.

A whole press at once bore down on Cambell. Shea saw a glowing head fly from its shoulders, and himself thrust past the knight's shield arm against something that gave before his blade. Then he was out in the room. A green mist whirled about him, plucking. A pink flash and it was gone.

Right in front of him a magician became a monstrous crab. Shea dodged it, clashed weapons with a still-human enchanter, thrust him through, and then went down as the falling man grabbed him by both ankles. He was stepped on four times before he kicked himself free. Colors, sparks, flashes of light danced about the room.

Just ahead a whole crowd were boiling around Artegall. Shea took one step and found himself confronting Busyrane in person. Busyrane's eyes were twice their normal size with slit pupils, like a cat's. For all his venerable appearance the enchanter was swinging a huge sword as though it were a foot-rule.

Shea gave back, almost slipping on a spot of blood. Busyrane came leaping nimbly after, slashing. The big sword, half seen, whirled in a continuous snaky blur. Shea parried, parried, backed, parried, and parried. The wall was against him.

There was no time even for ripostes against this demoniac attack. Shea took the last refuge of an outmatched fencer; leaped into a corps-a-corps and grabbed Busyrane around the waist with his free arm.

The magician seemed made of rubber and piano-wire. One hand clawed at Shea's face. Shea ducked and buried his face in Busyrane's cloak, trying to trip him. The magician fumbled for a dagger. Shea reflected that the weapon was probably poisoned.

But just at this moment Busyrane was jerked backward, dragging Shea to his knees after him. Shea threw himself back and up. Then he saw what was the matter with Busyrane. Around the archimage's neck was clasped a pair of large, knobby hands. Just that and nothing more. Around the room, above, flitted a dozen more pairs of those disembodied hands, swooping at the throats of the enchanters.

Shea lunged. But Busyrane was made of stern stuff. He got the hands loose, his own sword up, and came back with a low cut. Shea lunged again. The magician, groggy from that strangling grip, had strength enough left to beat off Shea's remises and one-twos. Shea tried a coupé and one-two and felt his point go home. He held his lunge, stabbing and stabbing.

Down went Busyrane. Shea looked around. The windows of the hall were jammed with the bats and owls and things into which the magicians had changed themselves. They were beaten. The knobby hands clustered around them, tearing off wings and wringing necks with fine impartiality.

The lights flared up again. It was all over. Dead and dying monsters about the great hall changed back into men. Cambell, Artegall, and Britomart picked themselves up from the floor, slowly and with effort. Cambina drooped against the service door, almost fainting.

Artegall's deep voice boomed: "Ha! Lives one yet?" Shea turned to see him kick over a table and swing back the big blood-dripping sword. He gave a leap and clutched the arm in time.

"Thank you, Harold," said Chalmers from the floor where the table had been. Florimel was beside him. He was squeezing the neck of a bottle in both hands. The large joints of those hands were familiar. Shea realized that the disembodied pairs that had wrought such havoc among the enchanters were out-size copies of his partner's.

"Nice work, Doc," remarked Shea. To Artegall he said: "Don't. He's on our team."

Chalmers gave a hand to Florimel. "You observe," he remarked. "the improvement in my technique, although, goodness gracious! I didn't expect the hands to be quite as efficacious as that!" He looked round the room, where nearly half the corpses showed marks of strangulation.

Cambell carried his wife to a seat and supported her. He said: " 'Twill pass. She is much fordone with the labor of defeating those enchanters' spells, and 'tis well she did so or we were all dead men."

Artegall growled: "Master Harold has slain this Busyrane, a good end for as bad a man as drew breath; and Master Reed has slain more than any two of us with his own magic."

"Said I not they were true and gallant gentlemen?" said Britomart.

"True, my sweet." He wiped the sword on the skirt of an enchanter's robe. "Kneel, sirs!"

Shea and Chalmers went to their knees, but Cambell plucked at their sleeves. "Nay, on one knee only."

Artegall tapped each on the shoulder. "I dub you knights. Be brave, honest, and true in the name of our gracious majesty. Rise, Sir Harold; rise, Sir Reed."

Shea's irrepressible grin broke out as he stood up. "How does it feel to be named official racket buster, Doc?"

"Quite . . . uh . . . normal, I assure you. The really important fact about this evening's work is that I've discovered the secret of quantitative control. Frege's definition of number solves the problem with relation to the calculus of classes."

" 'The number of things in a given class is the class of all classes that is similar to the given class'?"

"Precisely. By treating numbers as classes—that is, the number two as the class of all pairs, the number three as the class of all triples, we can—"

"Say!" cried Shea. "Where's Belphebe?"

"I don't recall having seen the young woman. As I was saying, once the problem of introducing a quantitative element—"

"But I've got to find Belphebe! Busyrane caught her this morning. He must have brought her here."

Nobody else had seen her. Florimel offered: "There be gruesome great dungeons below. Mayhap—"

"How do you get to them?"

Chalmers said: "Before you go searching, Harold, I have a spell against magicians that you really must learn."

"To hell with that! She may be down there now!"

"I know. But Duessa and Dolon certainly escaped this . . . uh . . . holocaust, and there may be others."

"Be warned," rumbled Artegall. "The rash falcon strikes no game, Sir Harold. We shall need all and more than all the protection we can get to prowl those passages."

Cambell spoke up: "Cambina, I greatly fear, can do no more for the present, gentle sirs."

"Okay, okay," groaned Shea. "Why didn't you use this spell before, Doc?"

"Why," said Chalmers, innocently, "it would have blown me back into my own universe! And I have too much to live for here." He exchanged beams with Florimel. "You see, Harold, the casting of a spell produces on both the caster and the . . . uh . . . castee an effect analogous to that of an electrostatic charge. Ordinarily this has no particular effect and the charge dissipates in time. But when a person or thing has passed from one space-time vector to another, he or it has broken a path in extradimensional space-time, creating a permanent . . . uh . . . line of weakness. Thereafter the path is easier for him—or it —to follow. If I accumulated too much magicostatic charge at one time, it would, since this charge is unbalanced by the fact that I am at one end of this space-time path . . . uh . . . it would by reaction propel—"

"Oh, for God's sake! Let's have the spell now and the lecture later."

"Very well." Chalmers showed Shea the spell, relatively simple in wording but calling for complex movements of the left hand. "Remember, you've been doing spells, so you probably have a considerable charge at present."

They left Florimel and Cambina with Cambell and divided into two parties. Artegall went with Shea.

Smooth stone changed to rough ashlar as they went down. Their torches smoked, throwing long shadows.

The passage turned and twisted until Shea had no idea where he was. Now and then they stopped to listen—to their own breathing. Once they thought they heard something, and cautiously crept to peer around a corner.

The sound was made by water dripping down a wall. They went on. Shea could not help glancing over his shoulder now and then. Artegall, his iron shoes echoing, paused to say: "I like this not. For half an hour we have followed this passage into nothing."

A side passage sprang away. Shea proposed: "Suppose you go a hundred steps ahead, and I'll go the same distance this way. Then we can both come back and report."

Artegall growled an assent and set off. Shea, gripping his épée, plunged into the side passage.

At a hundred paces the passage was the same, receding into blackness ahead of him.

He returned to the T. It seemed to him that he reached it in less than half the time it had taken him to leave it. There was no sign of Artegall, just black emptiness inclosed in rough stone.

"Artegall!" he called.

There was no answer.

He yelled: "Sir Artegall!" The tunnels hummed with the echo, then were silent.

Shea found himself sweating. He poked at the stone before him. It seemed solid enough. He was sure, now, that this T had appeared in the passage after he passed it, about halfway to where he had gone.

He set off to the right. If Artegall had gone this way, he should catch up with him. An impulse made him stop to look back. The leg of the T had already disappeared.

He ran back. There was nothing but solid stone on both sides.

His skin crawled as if a thousand spiders were scuttling over it. He ran till he began to puff. The passage bent slightly, one way, then another. There was no end to it.

When he rounded a corner and came on a human being, his nerves seemed to explode all at once.

The person shrieked. Shea recognized Belphebe.

"Harold!" she cried.

"Darling!" Shea spread his arms—torch, épée, and all. She threw herself into them.

But almost immediately she pulled loose. "Marry, I'm but a weak woman and forgot my pledged word! Nay, dear Harold, dispute me not. What's done is done." She backed away determinedly.

Shea sagged. He felt very tired. "Well," he said with a forced smile, "the main thing's getting out of this damned maze. How did you get down here?"

"I sprained my ankle in my fall this morning. And Busyrane's minions—"

"Hah, hah, hah!" Dolon, large as life, stepped

through the side of the wall. "The two mice who would kill cats!"

Shea crouched for a flèche. But Dolon made a pass toward him. Something wrapped around his legs, like an invisible octopus. He slashed with his épée, but met no resistance.

"Nay, there shall be a new Chapter," continued Dolon, "with my own peerless presence as archimage. First, I shall prove my powers on your bodies—a work worthy of my genius, doubt it not!"

Shea strained at the invisible bonds. They crept up his body. A tentacle brushed his swordarm.

He snatched his arm out of the way, reversed his grip on the hilt, and threw the weapon point-first at Dolon, his whole strength in the movement. But the épée slowed up in midair and dropped with a clang to the floor.

His hands were still free. If Belphebe was set on marrying this guy Timias, what did it matter if he got squirted back by the rocket effect of a magicostatic charge?

He dropped the torch and raced through the spell. Dolon, just opening his mouth for another pontifical pronouncement, abruptly looked horrified. He shrieked, a high womanish scream, and dissolved in a mass of tossing yellow flame. Shea caught Belphebe's wrist with his right hand to snatch her back from the blaze. . . .

Pfmp!

Walter Bayard and Gertrude Mugler jumped a foot. One minute they had been alone in Harold Shea's room, the former reading Harold Shea's notes and the latter watching him do it.

Then, with a gust of air, Shea was before them in a battered Robin Hood outfit, and beside him was a red-haired girl with freckles, wearing an equally incongruous costume.

"Wh-where's Doc?" asked Bayard.

"Stayed behind. He liked it there."

"And who . . ."

Shea grinned. "My dream-girl. Belphebe, **Dr.** Bayard. And Miss Mugler. Oh, damn!" He had happened to glance at his hands, which showed a lot of

245

little blisters. "I'm going to be sick for a few days, I guess."

Gertrude showed signs of finding her voice. She opened her mouth.

Shea forestalled her with: "No, Gert, I won't need a nurse. Just a quart of calamine lotion. You see, Belphebe and I are getting married the first chance we get."

Gertrude's face ran through a spectrum of expressions, ending with belligerent hostility. She said to Belphebe: "But—you—"

Belphebe said with a touch of blithe defiance: "He speak no more than truth. Find you aught amiss with that?" When Gertrude did not answer, she turned to Shea. "What said you about sickness, my love and leman?"

Shea drew a long breath of relief. "Nothing serious, darling. You see, it *was* poison ivy I tied the broom with."

Belphebe added: "Sweet Harold, now that I am utterly yours, will you do me no more than one service?"

"Anything," said Shea fondly.

"I lack still the explanation of those strange words in the poem wherewith you bested the Blatant Beast!"

BOOK THREE

The
Castle
of
Iron

1

"LISTEN, CHUM," SAID THE ONE WHO BREATHED through his mouth, "you don't hafta kid us. We're the law, see? We'll pertect you both all right, but we can't do nothing unless we got facts to go on. You sure they haven't sent you no ransom note?"

Harold Shea ran a hand desperately through his hair. "I assure you, officer, there isn't the least possiblity of a ransom note. Since it's a matter of paraphysics, she isn't even in this world."

The red-faced one said: "Now we're getting somewhere. Where'd you put her?"

"I didn't put her anywhere. Didn't have anything to do with it."

"You say she's dead but you don't know who done it, is that right?"

"No, I didn't say anything about her being dead. Matter of fact, she's probably much alive and having a fine time. She just isn't in this space-time continuum."

"That's just dandy," said the mouth-breather. "I think you better come down to the station house with us. The lieutenant wants to see you."

"Do you mean I'm under arrest?" asked Shea.

The one with the red face looked at his partner, who nodded. "Just holding you for investigation, that's all."

"You're about as logical as the Da Derga! After all, it's my wife that's missing, and I feel worse about it than you could. Will you talk to a colleague of mine before you take me down there?"

The one who breathed through his mouth looked back at his companion. "I guess that's right, at that. We might get something."

Shea stood up and at once was patted from breast to hip with a flowing motion. "Nothing," said the red-faced one disappointedly. "Who's this friend of yours, and where do we find him?"

"I'll get him," said Shea.

"You'll get a poke in the puss. You just sit quiet and Pete will get him for you." The one with the red face motioned Shea back to his chair and, unlimbering an unpleasant-looking automatic pistol from his hip, sat down himself.

"Oh, all right. Ask for Dr. Walter Bayard in the next office."

"Go ahead, Pete," said the red-faced one.

The door closed. Shea viewed his visitor with wary distaste. A mild schizoid of the suspicious variety; an analysis might turn up something interesting. However, Shea had too many worries of his own to be much interested in uncovering a policeman's suppressed desire to do ballet dancing.

The policeman regarded Shea stolidly for a while, then broke the silence. "Nice trophies you got there." He nodded towards a pair of Belphebe's arrows that hung on the wall. "Where'd you get 'em?"

"They're my wife's; she brought them from the land of Faerie. Matter of fact that's where she probably is."

"Okay; skip it." The cop shrugged. "I'd think you brain experts would start on yourselves . . ." His mouth gave a quirk at the strange disinclination of the prisoner to discuss things on a rational basis.

There were steps in the hall; the door opened to admit the one who breathed through his mouth, followed by big, blond, slow Walter Bayard and (of all the people Shea did not want to see) the junior psychologist of the Garaden Institute, Vaclav Polacek, otherwise known as "Votsy" or "the Rubber Czech."

"Walter!" cried Shea. "For God's sake will you—"

"Shut up, Shea," said the red-faced one. "We'll do the talking." He swung ponderously toward Bayard. "Do you know this man's wife?"

"Belphebe of Faerie? Certainly."

"Know where she is?"

250

Bayard considered gravely. "Of my own knowledge, no. I assure you, however—"

Votsy's eye brightened, and he grabbed the arm of the one who breathed through his mouth. "Say! I know who could tell you—Doc Chalmers!"

The policemen exchanged glances again. "Who's he?"

Bayard cast a vexed glance at the junior. "As a matter of fact, Dr. Chalmers left only day before yesterday on a rather extended sabbatical, so I'm afraid he cannot be of much help. May I ask the nature of the difficulty?"

The red-faced one, quick on the trigger, said: "Day before yesterday, eh? That makes two of 'em. Know where he's gone?"

"Uh—uh—"

"Couldn't have gone off with this Mrs. Shea, could he?"

In spite of the situation there rose a unanimous laugh from Shea, Bayard, and Polacek. "All right," said the red-faced one, "she didn't. Now I'll ask you another one. Do you know anything about a picnic day before yesterday to Seneca Grove?"

"If you're asking whether I was there, no. I know there was a picnic."

The one who breathed through his mouth said: "I think he's covering up too, Jake. He talks like Snide Andy."

The red-faced one said: "Leave me handle this. Dr. Bayard, you're a physicologist just like Dr. Shea, here. Now how would you explain it in your own language that at this picnic Dr. Shea and his wife goes off in the woods, but only one of 'em comes back, and that one ain't this wife of his, and besides he goes around saying 'She's gone!' "

"I can explain it perfectly well," said Bayard, "though I don't know whether you will understand my explanation."

"Okay, suppose you come along too and tell it to the lieutenant. I'm getting a bellyful of this runaround. Bring him along, Pete."

Pete, the mouth-breather, reached for Bayard's elbow. The effect, however, was like touching the button that set off a nuclear reaction. As far as Pete, Bayard, Polacek, and Shea were concerned, the lights in the room went into a whirl of motion that became a gray-gleaming circle. They heard Jake's voice cry thinly: "No you don't!" with the accent at the end rising to a squeal, and felt rather than saw the orange, dahlia-shaped flame of the unpleasant automatic, but the bullet never touched any of them, for—

Pmf!

The floor was cold beneath their feet.

Shea braced himself and looked around. Marble all right: there seemed to be miles of it in every direction stretching out in a tesselated pattern of black and white to where pillars leaped from it on every side, slender and graceful, supporting a series of horseshoe-shaped Moorish arches, and thence reaching back invisibly into the distance. The pillars were of some translucent substance that might be alabaster or even ice. Oriental, Shea thought.

"Listen," said Pete, "if you try to get away with this you'll go up for it all. This ain't like New York; they got a Lindbergh law in this state."

He had dropped Bayard's arm and was dragging out the twin of the red-faced cop's pistol. Shea said: "Don't bother shooting; it won't go off."

Bayard looked vexed. "Look here, Harold, have you been working some of your damned symbolic logic formulas on us?"

"Holy Saint Wenceslaus!" said Votsy, pointing. "Look there!"

From among the pillars that receded into the gloom a procession advanced. It was headed by four eunuchs—they must be that, loathsomely fat, grinning, wearing turbans on their heads and blue silk bloomers on their legs, each bearing a long curved sword. Behind came a file of Negroes, naked to the waist, with earrings, carrying a pile of cushions on their heads.

"You're under arrest!" said Pete, pointing the gun at Shea. He turned toward Polacek. "You want to preserve the law, don't you? Help me get him out of here."

The eunuchs went down on their knees and bumped their heads upon the pavement as the Negroes, in perfect step, broke left and right to dump piles of cushions behind the four. Pete turned his head uncertainly, then turned back quickly as Shea sat. The reflex tightened Pete's finger on the gun, which gave out a loud click.

"I told you it wouldn't go off," said Shea. "Make yourself at home." He was the only one who had done so thus far; Polacek was turning his head round and round until it looked as though it might come off; Bayard was staring at Shea with an expression of furious bewilderment, and the policeman was clicking his pistol and working the side in a futile manner between clicks. Behind the file of Negroes another procession of butter-faced men emerged from the shadows of the colonnades, bearing an assortment of zithers, brass gongs, and eccentric-looking stringed instruments, to group themselves at one side.

"Nothing you can do about it. Honest," said Shea; then, addressing himself to Bayard particularly: "You know about the theory of this, Walter. Sit down."

Bayard sank slowly into the pile of cushions. Polacek, bug-eyed, and Pete the cop, distrustfully, imitated him. One of the eunuchs pranced before the musicians, clapping his hands. Instantly they struck up an ear-wracking combination of shrieks, growls, groans, and howls, with a bearded vocalist, who seemed to have wildcats tearing at his entrails, raising his voice above all. Simultaneously, a door seemed to have opened somewhere among the darknesses behind the colonnades. A breeze fluttered the musicians' garments; underneath their squallings came the sound of distant, rushing waters.

"Cheer up," said Shea. "Here comes Room Service."

A dark-skinned dwarf, with a big aigrette held to his turban by an emerald clip, scuttled toward them, his arms filled with cushions. He flung them on the floor at the feet of the four, salaamed, and was gone. The caterwaulings of the music changed sharply, all the instruments together emitting seven high-pitched notes. Among the pillars, in the direction where the dwarf had disappeared, a flicker of motion appeared, grew, and developed into seven girls.

At least they appeared to be girls. They wore Oriental costumes, whose only resemblance to those pictured on calendars, however, lay in cut and color. Their long, loose pajamas were of the heaviest wool; so were the veils that covered all but seven pairs of black eyes and mops of black hair, while the bodices concealed everything above the waist. The howling of the musicians waxed as the girls cut a series of capers that could only by the remotest courtesy be called a dance.

"The vaudeville's corny," said Polacek, "but I'll take the one on the end."

"I'd hate to see him loose in a harem," said Bayard.

"I wouldn't," replied Polacek. "I wonder if she speaks English."

"You probably aren't speaking English yourself," said Shea. "Relax." Under those costumes it was hard to tell, but he was fairly certain that none of these was Belphebe.

The policeman, sitting bolt upright on a cushion, had stripped his gun in the space between his knees. Moreover he had gathered up the bullets that it had already disgorged, and with an expression of honest bewilderment was examining the firing-pin dents in their primers. Now he looked up.

"I don't know how you guys worked this," he said, "but I'm telling you to get us out of here or you're gonna do more time than Roosevelt was president."

"Wish I could," said Shea, "but Dr. Bayard will tell you it wasn't our doing that got you here."

"Then what *did* do it? Did you conk me on the head so now I'm dreaming? Or are we all dead? This sure don't look like the heaven they told me about at the First Presbyterian Church Sunday school."

"Not exactly," said Shea, "but you're getting warm. You know how sometimes when you're dreaming you wonder whether you're dreaming or not?"

"Yeah."

"And how sometimes when something unusual

happens to you when you're awake, you again wonder if you're awake? Well, we've discovered that the universe is something like that. There are a whole lot of different worlds, occupying the same space, and by mental operations you can change yourself from one to the other."

Pete shook his head as if to clear flies from it. "You mean you can go to Mars or somepin by just thinking about it?"

"Not quite. This isn't Mars; it's a world in a whole other universe, with different assumptions different from ours. What we do is fix our minds on those assumptions."

"Assump— Oh hell, if you say so I'll take your word. I'd think you was giving me a line, except . . ."

The seven had pranced off among the pillars. From the opposite direction another set of dancers emerged. They wore ankle-length trousers and loose embroidered coats with what might have been pairs of coffee-cups beneath. "Hi, Toots!" said Polacek tentatively. Scrambling to his feet he took two steps and grabbed for the nearest, who avoided him lightly without missing a step of her dance.

"Sit down, you damn fool!" barked Shea; the dancers swung past and began to retreat.

"How long d'you think this will keep up?" inquired Bayard.

Shea shrugged. "No idea. Honest."

As though in answer, the orchestra changed beat and tune, with a violent banging from the strings and drums. From behind the disappearing dancers another pair of eunuchs stepped forward, bowed to the four, then faced each other and bowed again. Between them emerged four girls, each with a small brass tray holding a fancy jar. Bayard gasped; Polacek whistled; the policeman ejaculated: "Mother of God!" The costumes of all were ample in cut but so thin they might better have not been there at all. The wearers were definitely mammals.

The girls sidled delicately towards their customers, bowed together with the precision of Rockettes, and flopped among the cushions at the feet of the four.

"You can't bribe me," growled Pete the cop. "This

only gets you smart guys another charge. Indecent theatrical performance."

Keeping time to the music, each of the girls whipped the lid from her jar, stuck her finger into it, withdrew it covered with something yellow and gooey, and thrust it into her customer's face. Shea opened his mouth and got a fingerful of honey. He heard Bayard gag and cry "No!" and turned in time to see him try to avoid the finger. Pete the cop was dabbing a honey-smeared face with his handkerchief, while his houri seemed determined to apply the stuff internally or externally.

"Better take it," advised Shea. "They're here to give it to us."

"You can't bribe me!" repeated Pete; and Walter said: "But I don't like sweets! I'd rather have beer and pretzels."

Out of the corner of his eye, Shea could see Polacek with one arm around his houri's neck, while with the other hand he conveyed finger-doses of honey to her mouth in exchange for those he received. He caught on fast.

Shea accepted another installment himself. "O moon of my delight," implored the policeman's girl, "is thy breast narrowed? Know that thou hast so infused my heart with love that I will rather drown in the ocean of mine own tears than see my lord dismayed. What shall his unworthy handmaiden do?"

"Ask her for something to drink," said Bayard, tentatively touching his tongue to the finger that was being offered him, and shuddering over the taste.

"Is this truly my lord's desire? To hear is to obey." She sat up and clapped her hands three times, then snuggled down again against the shrinking policeman's legs. He seemed past speech. The leader of the orchestra dropped his instrument and also clapped, and from among the pillars the dwarf who had brought the cushions came skipping forward again, this time with a big tray on which shone four elaborate silver flagons. Bayard raised himself to peer into the one set before him, then groaned.

"Milk! It needed just that to top off this mess. Who the hell wants to go to Heaven? Good Lord!"

Shea, glancing across the head of his own houri, saw that if the liquid in the flagon was indeed milk, it was milk of a most peculiar kind, with small congealed lumps floating in it. Before he could experiment, Polacek shouted: "Holy smoke, you guys try this stuff! Best cocktail I ever tasted!"

The resemblance to a cocktail might be incidental, but the flavor was delicious and the potency unlimited. As Shea took a long draft he could feel a wave of warmth running down his gullet. He handed the flagon to his girl. "What do you call this drink, little one?"

She kissed the edge of the flagon where his lips had touched it and glanced at him archly. "O beloved youth, this is none other than the veritable Milk of Paradise."

Bayard had heard, "Paradise?" he cried. "Harold! Votsy! I'll bet you anything I know where we've landed. Don't you remember—

> " '—For he on honey-dew hath fed
> And drunk the milk of Paradise.'?"

"What you giving us?" demanded Pete the cop. "This is Xanadu, Coleridge's Xanadu," explained Bayard.

> "In Xanadu did Kubla Khan
> A stately pleasure-dome decree,
> Where Alph, the sacred river, ran—' "

"Alph! Alph!" The girls scrambled to their feet and bowed in the direction of the sound of running water.

"There you are," said Bayard. "Alph, supposedly based upon the legends about the river Alpheios in Greece—"

"That's it, all right," said Shea. "Listen, officer, I'm not responsible for this, and I don't know how

257

we got here, but he's right. Wait a minute, though, Walter. This is a jam. Remember, the poem was unfinished; as far as I know we've landed in an incomplete spacetime continuum, one that's fixed in a certain set of actions, like a phonograph needle stuck in one groove. This show is apt to keep right on going."

Bayard put both hands to his head, the policeman gibbered thickly, but Polacek waved an empty flagon. "Suits me," he cried happily, reaching for his girl again. "We'll do all right, won't we, babe?"

Just then the orchestra struck a strident note. The girl at whom Polacek had snatched dodged his arm, whipped up her tray with a smooth motion, and ran. Another group of seven dancing girls emerged from the pillars. One of them, apparently a soloist, carried a pair of short curved swords, which she began to brandish.

"But look here, Harold," said Bayard, "can't you do something about this? You've been telling us how good you were at magic in cosmoi where it works. Can't you get us off this goddam vaudeville circuit?"

"Yeh," said Pete the cop. "I'll tell you, Shea, I'll make a deal with you. Know a feller in the D. A.'s office, and I'll get him to go eesh—easy with you on these here charges. Maybe, maybe, forget the indeshent performance one." The Milk of Paradise seemed to have warmed him a little.

"I can try," said Shea. "I don't know how it'll work with all this racket."

The cop heaved himself up unsteadily. "I can fix tha'," he said. In two bounds he was upon one of the astonished eunuchs, wrestling with him for his scimitar. The musicians stopped with a squeal and a murmur of voices; then one struck a gong, three times, ringingly. From among the pillars a whole parade of grim-looking janizaries advanced with long nasty spears in their hands, just as Shea wrested the scimitar from Pete. Bowing before the eunuch, Shea presented him his weapon, saying: "The humblest of your servants abases himself." Then he turned on Pete, whom Bayard was, with a little difficulty, restraining.

"You—utter—damned—jackass!" he said. "I don't care if you're the number one cop in Ohio; you can't get away with that here. How'd you like to see your head paraded around on the point of one of those pikes?"

Pete shook his head as if to clear it. "How—how could I see it if—"

"Or spend the rest of your life in a specially re-frigerated cell?" Shea addressed Bayard: "Remember the 'Beware, beware!' and 'caves of ice' part? This paradise has got thorns in it; you take it the way they dish it out to you, or you'll be sorry."

He led the way slowly back to the cushions. The janizaries had disappeared, and another file of dancers was coming out from among the pillars, this group specializing in bellybuttons. Pete the cop flung himself heavily into the cushions, and Walter Bayard sat down morosely.

"All right, you guys," said Shea, "try not to interrupt me while I give a whirl at a sorites. If there is something, *c,* such that the proposition *phi* concerning *x* is true when *x* is *c* but not otherwise, and *c* has the property *phi,* the term satisfying the proposition *phi* concerning—" His voice trailed off, and he sat with lips moving. Polacek watched him closely. Pete, head buried in his arms, murmured: "And me a married man!"

However, Shea's sorites was never completed. Through the domed building, far among the arches, rang the thunder of a cosmic voice—the kind of voice God might have used in telling the worshippers of the Golden Calf where to head in. It said: "Oh, goodness gracious, I do believe I've made a mistake!"

The voice was that of Dr. Reed Chalmers.

Shea and Polacek leaped to their feet. The musicians stopped; the dancers paused.

Then musicians, dancing girls, pillared hall began to go round, faster and faster, until they dissolved into a rioting whirl of color. The color faded to foggy gray. The gray threw up whorls that condensed

259

into other colors, and faded into the outlines of another room—a smaller room, bare and utilitarian.

Shea and Polacek were facing a table. Behind it sat a short man and a pale, lovely, dark-haired girl. The man was Dr. Reed Chalmers. There were touches of black in the unruly gray hair that flowed from beneath the edges of a gaudy turban and some of the lines were missing from his face.

He said: "I am glad to see you, Harold. I hoped —Oh, for goodness' sake, did I get Vaclav too?"

2

"YEAH, YOU GOT ME," SAID POLACEK. "RIGHT AWAY from a swell party. Walter, too."

Shea looked around. "But where is Walter? He was on those cushions—holy dewberries, Doc! He must be still back there in Xanadu with that cop, watching cootch dancers and eating honeydew. And he hates both of them!"

"Xanadu? Dear me, most unfortunate, most distressing." Chalmers fingered the papers before him. "I desired merely to establish contact with you, Harold, and I assure you the association of the others was quite accidental. I really don't know—"

Shea smiled crookedly. "I really don't know myself whether I ought to thank you or bawl you out, Doc. What have you done with Belphebe? You snatched her, too, didn't you? At least I hope so. She just disappeared while we were out on a picnic together, and they were going to arrest me for murdering her or kidnapping her or something."

"Yes—uh—there are certain difficulties." Chalmers' fingers moved nervously. "I am afraid there was rather a—uh—grave error on my part. I find the attitude of the police shocking. Though I do not think you need have worried about the legal complications. It would be well-nigh impossible to establish a *corpus delicti* under the circumstances."

"That's what you don't know, Doc. Gertrude Mugler was on the picnic, and she was the one who hollered copper when we went off on a walk together and I came back without her, nearly out of my mind because I didn't know whether some magician had hauled her back to Faerie. That woman could establish a *corpus delicti* or a society for boiling men in oil, and she would, too."

The pale girl made a small sound.

"Sorry," said Shea. "Lady Florimel, I present Vaclav Polacek, known in our country as the Rubber Czech."

"Hail, fair squire," said the girl. "The titles of your land are passing strange; yet not, methinks, stranger than that garb you bear."

Shea became conscious of a neat pin-stripe suit. "I might say the same thing about Sir Reed's headgear. What are you doing in that rig, what did you get me here for, and where are we?"

Chalmers said: "You display an unscientific tendency to confuse thought by the simultaneous consideration of different categories of information. Pray allow me to organize my thoughts and data. . . . Ahem. I presume it was you who employed the spell against magicians on Dolon, and in so doing projected yourself to our—er—point of departure? I confess I do not understand how you also projected the young lady. . . ."

"I had hold of her hand. We're married."

"My sincerest congratulations. I trust the union will prove happy and—er—fruitful. Your departure, you will remember, was attended by the destruction of the Chapter of Enchanters, and as a result I found myself faced by a problem rather beyond my powers. Namely, the transformation into a real person of a human simulacrum made of snow." He nodded in the direction of Florimel, who gazed at him adoringly. "I therefore—"

"Doctor, you got a chair?" asked Polacek.

"Vaclav, your interruptions are even more disturbing than Harold's. Kindly seat yourself on the floor and permit me to continue. Where was I? Ah, upon examination of available data, I was gratified to discover that there existed in Faerie the mental pattern of a universe whose spacetime vector arrangement made it possible of attainment from that place by the familiar methods of symbolic logic. To wit, that of Ariosto's *Orlando Furioso*."

"Why should that be easy to reach?" inquired Shea.

"Ahem. I was about to explan. Lodovico Ariosto was an Italian poet, who wrote the *Orlando Furioso* in what we should call the early sixteenth century. This work was considered the main source from which Spenser, a highly imitiative writer, secured the ideas whence he produced *The Faerie Queene*. Since each of these universes contains the same basic mental pattern, it is easy to perceive how transference from one to the other would be a relatively light task, and I felt confident that I would find here a number of experienced practitioners of magic. Vaclav, I perceive you are not following me."

"No," said Polacek from the floor, "and I don't believe Miss—Lady Florimel is either."

"It's not necessary that she should. For your benefit, however, I will explain that this similarity of basic mental pattern establishes, as it were, certain connective roads between the two universes, over which passage in our vehicle of symbolic logic can be achieved with a reasonable certainty of reaching the desired destination."

Polacek felt in his pockets. "Anybody got a cigarette? I believe you if you say so, Doctor, but I still don't get why you had to send for Harold, and why we had to land in that cabaret."

Chalmers fussed again with the papers, uneasily. "The process was attended by—uh—certain inconveniences. I can only describe them by—taking things in order, if you will permit me to do so. To localize the matter, we are in the castle of the leading magician of the *Furioso* Atlantès de Carena, in the Pyrennees, near the Franco-Spanish border. For your benefit, Vaclav, I should explain that these places are by no means the same as we should understand by the terms employed at—uh—let us say, the Garaden Institute."

"All right, but why jerk me back here?" asked Shea. "You might at least have asked me first."

"Surely, Harold, you realize that symbolic logic is not a thing that can be handled like a telephone. As a matter of fact, the inconveniences to which I referred had become so grave that there appeared to be no other course open to me. I may be mistaken. Working with Atlantès has been most interesting, most interesting. I have been granted the opportunity of correcting many of the principles of magic in view of the somewhat different laws that control it here.

"However, I feel that I owe this young lady here a certain duty." He indicated Florimel, and blushed as Polacek and Shea both snickered.

"Ah—Atlantès has been most coöperative, but I hope I am less easily impressed by an enchanter's affability than formerly. Not only has he been unable to accomplish anything for Florimel, but these people are also Muslims with somewhat—peculiar standards of morality. I have been led to the idea, amounting almost to an absolute conviction, that it would be necessary for me to provide additional protection for Florimel. As matters stand, or stood before I took the perhaps unwarranted liberty of—er—transporting you here, I was the only barrier between her and our, I fear, by no means well-disposed host."

"I don't get all of it," said Shea. "Why couldn't you just take her somewhere else?"

"But where, my dear Harold? That is the very nub of the difficulty. To return to our own universe would be to lose the young lady, since she is of magical origin, and there's no provision for magic in the mental pattern. It must be regarded as impossible, at least until she has attained complete humanity. It would be possible, of course, to attain the world of Dante, but I am not sure that the atmosphere of the *Inferno* would be conducive to the health of a person made of snow. Moreover, Atlantès is an extremely competent magician, quite capable of either following her to another place or of preventing her going."

"A most persistent, arrant lecher," said Florimel.

Chalmers patted her hand and beamed. "I feel I owe an apology to you, and to Vaclav. However, one of the functions of friendship is to permit occasional impositions in times of emergency. And I trust you will look upon me as a friend."

Polacek waved a hand. Shea said: "It's all right, Doc, and I'll be glad to help, especially since you brought Belphebe along, even if it did get me in trouble with the cops. Where is she, by the way?"

Chalmers became more embarrassed than ever. "That is—uh—the difficulty over which I owe you my sincere apologies. It was undoubtedly due to an error of selectivity. Er, I had not intended to transport her from our universe at all. If you are familiar with the *Furioso,* Harold, you will remember that among Spenser's imitations from it was a character called Belphegor, the cognate of Belphebe. . . . When the young lady arrived, there was a certain amount of—uh—confusion of identity, as it were, with the result, the unfortunate result, that she has no memory of another name or a previous existence. At the present moment I really cannot say where she is, except that she is undoubtedly in this universe."

"Do you mean to tell me that my own wife doesn't even know me?" yelped Shea.

"I fear not. I cannot express—"

"Don't try." Shea looked around the room gloomily. "I've got to find her. She may be in trouble."

"I don't think you need be apprehensive, Harold. The young lady is quite competent."

"Aye, marry, that she is," said Florimel. "She dealt Sir Roger such a buffet as will make his head spin for long when he would have let her from going without the castle but the now. Be comforted, Sir Harold."

"Who is this Sir Roger, anyway?" Shea glowered.

"I think I had better introduce you to my—uh—your associates," said Chalmers, and stepped around the desk to open the door behind Shea and Polacek. The air held an unmistakable faint odor of olive-oil, and as they stepped across the threshold, their feet gave back a metallic ring from the floor.

"Ah, yes," said Chalmers. "Perhaps I omitted to mention the fact that this castle is constructed of iron. That also is attended by certain—uh—inconveniences. Will you come this way, gentlemen?"

Another passage branched from that into which they had committed themselves, and led down a ramp towards a pair of double doors, with an oil lamp hanging from chains and throwing but little light. As they approached the doors, Shea heard the wailing sound of an instrument theoretically musical, like those in Xanadu. Polacek's eye brightened as he ran his tongue between his lips. "Babes?" he asked.

Without answering, Chalmers waved his hand at the doors, which swung open smoothly. They were looking at the backs of a pair of Arab-dressed musicians squatting on the floor, one blowing into a tootle-pipe, the other slowly tapping with his fingertips a drum about four inches in diameter. Beyond, a slinky dark girl in gauzy drapes revolved in the paces of a slow dance.

Beyond her again a dozen or more men were visible in the dim light of more oil lamps, dressed in bright Oriental costumes that seemed to have been specially spotted with grease for the occasion. Sprawled upon cushions, they gazed at the dancer with unsmiling, languid interest, exchanging a word from time to time, and looking toward the farther end of the room, as though to take their cue from the man who sat there. He was bigger than the biggest of them, with the figure of a wrestler. His young face bore strong lines, but just now it showed a sulky, petulant expression. A dapper little graybeard, like a brown mouse, was whispering something into his ear to the accompaniment of fierce gestures.

He glanced up at the sound of the visitors' feet on the floor and trotted toward them. He bowed low before Chalmers. "The peace of God be with you." He bowed again. "Who be these lords?" He bowed a third time.

Chalmers returned one of the bows. "Let no less peace be with you, most magical lord of Carena.

265

These are—uh—lords of my own country. Sir Harold de Shea, and the esquire Vaclav Polacek."

"Oh, day of good luck!" exclaimed Atlantès de Carena, bobbing up and down like a ship in a storm. "Oh, day of Allah's grace that has brought two mighty lords of the Franks for these poor eyes to feast upon!" Bow. "Doubtless it is by some error that you have come to so poor a hovel, but in that error I am honored." Bow. "Ho! Let the best rooms be swept out and new ceremonial garments be prepared for Sir Harold de Shea and the squire Vaclav, for these be veritably the bringers of benisons." Bow.

Shea and Polacek kept up with the first two or three bows, but gave it up as the pace threatened to make them dizzy. Apparently satisfied that he had achieved something, the little brown man took each by the hand and led them around the circle where introductions and bows were repeated as though each man they encountered could not have heard what was said to the rest. There were Lord Mosco, the Amir Thrasy, Sir Audibrad—this last one is medieval European doublet and hose, without turban—and two or three more. In the intervals Polacek kept twisting his head to watch the dancer, until, at about the third introduction, Atlantès noticed.

"You desire this handmaid, noble lord?" he said. "By Allah, she is worth not less than a hundred pieces of gold, but you shall have her to your concubine, provided only that our Roger, for whom all things are done, puts not his claim upon her. And you will find her a pearl unpierced, a filly unridden, a gem—"

Polacek's face was reddening. "Tell him *no!*" whispered Shea fiercely. "We can't afford to get mixed up in anything."

"But—"

"Tell him no."

Atlantès' eyes were fixed on them, and there seemed to be an expression of amusement behind the wispy beard. "Listen," said Polacek, "I'll talk to you about it later. Since I'm just new here I'd like to see more of your castle before—enjoying your—uh—hospitality. And—uh—thanks anyway, your lordship."

"Hearing is obedience." His lordship led the way to the cushion that supported the sulky youth. "And here in the light of the world, the arm of Islam, the perfect paladin and cavalier of Carena, Roger."

The perfect paladin gave a bored grunt. "More Franks?" he said to Atlantès. "Are they of better omen than that red-haired wench whom the Frankish enchanter lately brought?" Shea stiffened and his heart gave a thump. However, the light of the world was addressing him. "Are ye the new tumbling jugglers my uncle promised? Though my heart is straightened, yet may it find ease in witnessing your tricks."

Shea looked at him coldly down his long nose. "Listen, funny-face, I've been made a knight by a better man than you are, and I don't like the way you talk about the 'red-haired wench.' If you'll come outside, I'll show you a few tricks."

Roger, surprisingly, broke into a smile of pure amiability. "By the beard of the Prophet (whom God sustain)," he said, "I had not thought to find a Frank so generous. For months have I slain no man, and my muscles rot from lack of practice. Let us then to the hand-play!"

"Lords! Light of my eyes! Coolth of my heart!" Atlantès bubbled. "You have no need of another death and know well that a doom lies on it that there be none in this castle, and more, these be my noble lords and guests, fellow-magicians, for whose life I would give my own. Come, sirs, let me show you to your quarters, which, though they be but pallets in a corner, are yet as good as Carena can offer. 'Take what I have,' said the Hajji, 'though it be but half a barley-cake.'"

He clucked on ahead of them like a motherly hen. The "pallets in a corner" turned out to be rooms the size of auditoriums, elaborately hung with silks and furnished with inlaid wood. The rivetheads protruding from the iron plates of the walls and ceiling, however, reminded Shea of the interior of a warship.

Atlantès was soothing. "Coffee shall be brought you, and new garments. But in the name of Allah,

267

magical sirs, let the voice of friendship avert the hand of disputation, and be not angry with the kinsman of your friend. Ah, lovely youth!" he brushed a hand past his eyes, and Shea was surprised to see a drop of genuine moisture glistening on it. "The glory of Cordova. I sometimes wonder that the perfumed Hamman bath does not freeze in despair of emulating such beauty. Would you credit it that such a one could think more on blood than on the breasts of a maiden?"

He bowed half a dozen times in rapid succession and disappeared.

3

"FOR THE LOVE OF MIKE, HAROLD!" SAID POLACEK, eyeing the voluminous robes with distaste. "Are we supposed to wear these nightshirts?"

"Why not? When in Rome, eat spaghetti. Besides, if you want to give any of the damsels around here the eye, you'll have to be in fashion."

"I suppose . . . That little wizard's a smart guy. Say, what's this, a scarf?"

Shea picked up a long red strip of textile. "I think it's your turban," he said. "You have to wind it around your head, something like this."

"Sure I get it," replied Polacek. He whipped his own turban around with nonchalant speed. Naturally it came apart in festoons around his neck, and another try yielded no better result. Shea's own more careful procedure stayed on but settled itself firmly in concealment of one ear, and with a tail that tickled his chin. Polacek laughed and made a face. "Guess we'll have to call for a tailor or wait till they dish out some real hats."

Shea frowned. "Look here, Votsy, take it easy, will you? You'll simply have to be less cocky around a place like this if you don't want to get all our throats cut."

Polacek jagged up an eyebrow. "Hairbreadth Harold telling me not to be so cocky? Getting married has made a different man out of you, all right. Speaking of which, what are the rules around this joint? I'd like to take Atlantès up on his offer and pitch a little woo at that dancer. She's built like—"

The door was flung open with a clang by a man whose hairy, pendulous-eared head bore a startling identity to that of a Newfoundland dog. Without giving time for stares, he barked: "Lord Roger!" and stood aside to let the perfect paladin and cavalier stride in. Shea noticed he moved surprisingly light for so big a man. He would be a dangerous antagonist.

"Oh, hello," he greeted the visitor coolly.

Polacek added: "Say, I'm a stranger here myself, but do you always walk in doors without knocking?"

"The lord is lord of his own saloons," said Roger, as though his name were Hohenzollern. He turned toward Shea. "It has reached me, oh man, that you are of knightly order, and I may without shame or hindrance take on myself the shedding of your blood. Yet since I am a warrior experienced, a person of prowess, it would be no more than just did I not offer to handicap myself, as by bearing no armor while you go armored in this combat when the wizards have lifted the death-doom from the castle."

If he had had the épée which served him so well in Faerie Shea would have returned the offer. Instead, he bowed: "Thanks. Nice of you. Tell me— do I understand that Atlantès is your uncle?"

"There is no other way to it," Roger tapped delicate fingers over a yawn. "Though he is rather like a grandmother, an old nanny with one eye, who holds all here from high sports for unmannerly diversions. Yet even this may be overcome if there be one with a will to warlike valor, who yet knows something of the placing and lifting of spells."

Shea was conscious of being keenly watched from behind the mask of boredom, and began to understand the purpose of the big man's visit, but it would not do to commit oneself too soon. He said: "Uh—huh. Say, tell me what's going on, will you? Sir Reed says Atlantès is worried about something. Are you expecting an attack by the Christian knights?"

"Ha! Christian knights I fear not, though it be all twelve paladins together." He flexed his muscles. "But of ifrits and enchantments know I nothing, and there is little joy here for any since the Duke Astolph stole the Atlantès' hippogriff."

Shea stood still, his eyes boring into Roger. "By the way, what was it that you were saying about a red-headed girl?"

Roger failed to notice the elaborate casualness of the question. "There is no glory but in Allah: it was but a few days since, during the time when Lord Dardinell was with us, when Atlantès and the other wizard, your friend, colluded to effect some great spell, with burnings and groans of evil spirits. There was nothing for it but that they must fetch from some far place this wench of ill omen; well shaped, but unwomanly in garb, a huntress; and having red hair, which of all things more surely foretells some disaster, of which I fear the loss of the hippogriff is but the beginning. Have you met this unlucky one before?"

"My wife," said Shea.

"In the name of Allah! Are there no damsels of good augury in your land, that you must company with such a' one? Doubtless she brought you a great dowry."

Without arguing the point Shea rushed on: "Has anything been heard of her since she left the castle?"

"It has reached me that one of the hunters saw her afoot in the mountains with Duke Astolph, a conjunction which brings a dread like midnight on the heart of my uncle, though what it may mean he knows not."

"Who's Duke Astolph, by the way?"

"Allah forgive your ignorance! He is one of the

twelve whom the Christians (may they be accursed!) call paladins; yet a doughty fighter, to whom I look for the best of sport when I may measure blows with him, though he comes from an island far in the north, where it is so chill that men's faces turn blue, even though they be Franks."

Polacek asked: "Say, Roger, if you dislike Christians so much, how come you're wearing a Christian name?"

The perfect paladin went into such a grimace that for a moment Shea thought he was going to hit Votsy, but then Roger seemed to restrain himself with an effort. "Not for your question, which is the rudeness of a dog which lacks stripes," he said, "but to the good will of this knight who has offered me the sacrifice of his blood, will I answer. Learn, oh unguided one, that we of Carena are of too noble spirit to engage ourselves in the quarrels of princes, but seek honor under whatever banners may offer it, so that if the battle be hot, it matters not whose name it be fought in." Roger gave a snort, and looked at Polacek with unexpected keenness. "What said you but now of the slave-girl who danced for our entertainment?"

"Well," said Polacek, "Atlantès had—uh—made me an offer—very generous of him, I thought, and I was just saying that maybe for politeness I ought to take him up—"

"Enough, base-born," said Roger. "Learn that this castle and all in it were builded to my pleasure, and if it be my pleasure to take the damsel to concubine, there is no help for it but I must do so." He growled "Peace of God," and strolled out. The dog-headed man pulled the door to behind him.

Shea looked at the door. "You see, Votsy? Monkeying with guys like that is like telling Al Capone you don't like the color of his tie. Now let's get into those clothes and go see Doc. I noticed he solved the turban trouble, and maybe he can help us."

He led the way down to Chalmers' apartment. The doctor was puttering away, chanting cheerfully:

"We've a first-class assortment of magic;
    And for raising a posthumous shade
With effects that are comic or tragic,
    There's no cheaper house in the trade.
Love philter—we've quan—

What can I do for you, Harold?"

"These confounded cummerbunds." Shea watched as the doctor took Polacek's and adjusted it with quick, expert fingers, then began winding his own. "Look here, Roger says Belphebe's somewhere in the mountains around here. You've got to get me out of this place to look for her."

Chalmers frowned. "I fail to see the necessity for any immediate departure," he said. "The young woman impressed me as being admirably fitted to—uh—take care of herself. A perfect case of conjoined biological and psychological adaptation. And it would be most inopportune for you to leave at the present moment. We must look for the—uh—better manner of serving our united interests, and I am at present confronted with a serious problem—"

"Oh, Votsy can stay here and take care of her," said Shea.

"Vaclav is a bright young man, but I am afraid he is inclined toward irresponsibility," said Chalmers firmly, ignoring Polacek's squawk of protest. "Also, he has a—uh—deplorable weakness for the fair sex, not to mention that he lacks training in the most elementary details of magic. You, therefore, are the only person upon whom I can rely at present."

Shea grinned ruefully. "Okay," he said. "You knew you could get me with that argument. But you'll have to help me find Belphebe as soon as things are cleared up here."

"I shall be glad to help as far as I can, Harold, as soon as we have reasonable assurance of success in humanizing Florimel."

Shea turned his head to conceal the sparkle in his eye. Knowing how mulish Chalmers could get, he didn't attempt to argue. But he was a trained psychologist too, and he suspected it would transpire that he could best assist the transformation of Florimel at a distance from Castle Carena.

Polacek said: "Listen, you two. I might as well be some use around here. Why not show me how this magic works?"

"I had planned a series of talks on the subject," said Chalmers. "We will begin with the basic concepts, such as the distinction between sympathetic magic and sorcery. . . ."

"How about teaching me a couple of good stiff spells right now? Something I can use? You can get around to the heavy theory later, and I'll understand it better if I know the practical application."

"That would be unsound pedagogy," said Chalmers. "You should be aware that I am not one of those so-called progressivists who believes that the pupil absorbs best material presented in an unsystematic and confusing manner."

"But—but—I got a reason—"

"Yeah?" said Shea. "What's going on in that object you use for a brain, Votsy?"

"That's my business."

"No tell, no spell."

"Vaclav!" said Chalmers, in a monitory tone.

Polacek struggled with conflicting impulses for a few seconds. "It's that little dame," said he. "The dancer. Of course, ordinarily I wouldn't care—" (here Shea laughed raucously) "—not having really met her, but I won't stand for that big oaf telling me what to do. I thought if you gave me a couple of spells I could put on him—"

"No!" cried Shea and Chalmers together. The doctor said: "We are, I think, involved in—uh—sufficient difficulties already without further complicating our situation. I really do not know, for instance, how to avoid Atlantès' importunities with regard to the death-doom on the castle."

"The big guy mentioned something about that," said Polacek. "What is it?"

"It appears that at some time a spell was put upon this structure, I would conjecture when it was erected. The general effect is that if a killing should be performed within it, the building will collapse, though I will not weary you with the details, which are fantastically complicated. While I would normally be most willing to assist Atlantès, it now occurs to me that should this doom be lifted, our friend Roger will no longer be restrained from cutting you or Harold into fragments by way of sword-practice."

Shea muttered: "I'm not afraid of that stupid ox. I'll bet that all he knows is sabre-practice, if he knows that much."

"Perhaps not. Nevertheless, I should provide myself with a weapon. It would be most regrettable if our friendly association came to a sanguinary end. Moreover, permit me to remind you that as a married man you have incurred certain—uh—responsibilities."

Shea subsided, feeling guilty over having forgotten for some minutes that he was a married man.

"I still think you ought to teach me a couple of spells," said Polacek. "I won't turn Roger into a mud-turtle or anything like that, I promise, but I ought to have enough to protect myself."

"The amount of knowledge you could acquire so hastily would be of little value for self-protection," said Chalmers firmly. "The course will be imparted as I have outlined."

Polacek jumped up. "You two give me a pain. I'm going to see Atlantès. Maybe he knows a trick or two." He stormed out, banging the door metallically.

Shea looked at Chalmers with concern on his long face. "Say, Doc, maybe I better go sit on his head, don't you think? He almost got into a jam with Roger already."

Chalmers shook his head. "I doubt whether Atlantès will impart enough magical information to enable our hasty young friend to—uh—jeopardize our safety, or for that matter, whether Vaclav can cause any particular damage in that quarter. In fact, it might be just as well if our host were allowed to gather the somewhat unfavorable impression of your—uh—characters that he is bound to form from contact with our associate. Now if you will lend a hand with this athanor, I shall finish compounding this mixture and we can retire for the night."

The last words set up a train of thought in Shea's mind that caused him to look more sharply at Chalmers. "Been rejuvenating yourself, haven't you?" he asked.

Chalmers flushed. "It seemed expedient, in view of the demands of my—uh—more active recent life. I was, as you perceive, conservative in my application of the formula, not wishing to become an adolescent by inadvertent overdosage."

Shea grinned nastily as he bore a hand with the athanor. "The more fool you, Doc. Don't you know what the statistics show about adolescents?"

4

HAROLD SHEA DREAMED HE WAS DROWNING IN AN ocean of olive oil, too thick for swimming. Every time he reached the edge of an overhanging cliff and tried to pull himself out, a gigantic Roger with a cruel smile on his petulant face pushed him down with the butt of a lance.

He woke to see Vaclav Polacek on the edge of the other bed, holding a handkerchief to his nose. The whole place reeked with the stench of rancid oil. Shea reeled to the window, which was closed with some alabaster material. As he fumbled it open, a blast of chill but fresh air struck his face. He gulped. Beyond the castle battlements he could see the snowy crags of a range of mountains, pink in the early sun.

"What the hell?" said Shea, thoughts of some weird attempt at poisoning floating through his mind. Staying as near as he could to the open shutter, he struggled into the loose garments provided for him, and, without waiting to jockey the turban into position, made his way into the hall. There the odor was overpowering. As he turned the corner he bumped head-on into the Amir Thrasy, who was toddling along with a cut-open orange held under his nose.

"What the hell makes this stink, my noble friend?" asked Shea.

"Truly, sir, you are right and it comes from nowhere but the ultimate pits of the damned. But as the reason, it has been whispered to me that Atlantès (may flies nest in his ears!) has forgotten to renew his spell."

"What spell?"

"Verily, none other than that by which the smell of this oil is restrained within bonds, as the djann are bound by the seal of Solomon. It is certain that there is no spell against rusting, and, unless this castle be kept well oiled, there would be no help for it that it must be overthrown. Yet is the spell for the sweetness of oil more fugitive than a leaf in tempest, and must have renewal from time to time, as . . ."

He stopped as Atlantès himself came bustling around a corner of the corridor. "In the name of Allah, on whom be praise!" he greeted them. "Most noble lords, forbear your anger from your unworthy servant." He was bowing up and down like a metronome. "Give me but the kerchief of your pardon that my dread may be appeared, and my heart eased!" More bows. "I pray you, enlighten me with your graciousness so far as to break fast with me. See, even now the air grows purer than a spring of fresh water! And your squire as well, glorious sir. Is the youth well?"

Shea's appetite, whatever it might normally have been, had vanished under the shock of the olive oil stench. Nevertheless he called to Polacek, and the Amir Thrasy fortunately saved him the necessity of a reply.

"In sooth," said he, "our pains are borne lightly for the sake of the pleasures to come, as we bore with joy the smell of the corpses the day Lord Roger slew the two thousand serfs at the gate of Pampelona, forgetting in his warlike fury to leave any alive for the withdrawal of the bodies.''

Their host conducted them to a breakfast consisting mainly of stewed lamb with a sour, whitish liquid which Shea took to be milk, rather noticeably unpasteurized. Roger, reclining on cushions across the floor from the young psychologist, gobbled horribly. There was no sign of Dr. Chalmers. When the mirror of chivalry had finished his meal by sucking leftovers from between his teeth, he stood up and said meaningfully to Shea: "Will it please your honor to slash at the pells, since under my uncle's ordnance we may not slash at each other?"

"What's pells?" demanded Polacek.

Ignoring this question in a marked manner, Shea said: "Delighted. But somebody will have to lend me a sword. I came away so quickly I left mine home."

The pells of Castle Carena were a row of battered-looking wooden posts in the courtyard. Beyond them, a couple of men in castle-guards' livery were shooting at targets with short, double-curved bows. Oddly enough, they had the heads of baboons.

As Shea and Roger came out, Lord Mosco, a Saracen so pudgy that he waddled, was facing the nearest pell with a scimitar in one hand and a round shield on his other arm. He gave a blood-curdling whoop, leaped at the post light as a cat for all his bulk, and swung. Chips flew. Mosco went into a dance around the unoffending wood, slashing forehand with a drawing cut, and yelling at the top of his voice: "Allah-il-Allah! Mahound! Mahound!" He stopped suddenly and walked back to where the others stood in a little group. "My Lord Margéan, will you give me the balm of your word upon my performance?"

Margéan, in a kind of shapeless cap instead of a turban, and whose nose had once been well broken, said judicially: "I rate it but indifferent good. Twice you exposed your left side during the recovery, and the warcry did not ring. The foe is always the worse for a lusty shout in his ears."

Mosco sighed. "Blessed by the name of God," he said resignedly. "I fear I am a lost man unless protected by His angels or the arm of our champion. My lords, shall we not grace our eyes with the sight of these Frankish warriors?" There was a murmur of assent. "Now there is nothing for it but you must smite at these pells, squire."

"Better say you have a sprained wrist," muttered Shea.

But Polacek had his own ideas. "I'll get along. I've been watching him, haven't I? Where do I get one of these toad-choppers?"

The Amir Thrasy handed over his own somewhat battered and nicked scimitar. Polacek marched up to the pell, yelled: "Rar, rah, rah, Harvard!" and swung up in an underhand slash. However, he had misjudged the height of the pell; missed it completely, swung himself clear round the circle, tripped over his own feet, and had to clutch the post to keep from falling.

"That's my special attack," he explained with a shame-faced grin. "I make believe I'm gonna chop him, but instead I jump into a clinch and wrassle him down where I can really get at him."

Nobody seemed to feel the episode at all funny. Margéan's face expressed disdain, while the others looked away, all but Roger, who glanced at Shea to indicate that he was next.

Shea hefted Thrasy's weapon; aside from the nicks in the blade, it was altogether wrongly balanced for his type of work. "Has anybody got a straight sword I could borrow?" he asked.

Lord Margéan, who seemed to be some kind of coach, clapped his hands and called; a castle servant with the blubbering muzzle of a camel appeared with the desired weapon. Shea hefted it. The blade was straight enough, but the sword was as purely designed for cutting as the scimitars; no point whatever, the end rounded off, and the hilt made for a small-handed man. The balance was better, though, and if the weapon was too heavy for a proper parry, it might do for a little lunging practice. Shea addressed himself to the post without shouting, did a simple disengage lunge, a disengage lunge with an advance, a lunge-and-remise. In five minutes he had worked up a healthy sweat, and was pleased to hear a murmur from the spectators, partly puzzlement and partly appreciation.

Margéan said: "Marry, sir knight, here's strange bladeplay; yet methinks that with a Frankish sword you would even skewer one or two of your foes." And they began to argue about the merits of Shea's system: "Look you, lords, with a proper point like a spear you could even drive through the fine mail of Damascus. . . ." "Nay, I like not these newfangled tricks. . . ." "But see the reach it gives you. . . ." "Howsobeit, men will slash when excited. . . ." "Oho!" (to sir Audibrad, who was awkwardly trying to imitate Shea's lunge) "it is plainly to be seen that the noble Sir Harold's tricks are not to be picked up in an evening over the coffee cups. . . ."

Only Roger looked contemptuous. Without preliminary words he strode up to the nearest pell, filled the castleyard with a yell, and swung an enormous scimitar. *Chunk!* went the blade into the wood, and then quickly *chunk-chunk-chunk-chunk!* With the last blow, the upper half of the pell flew off, turning end over end. He swung round and grinned rather nastily at Shea.

Shea gulped. "Nice work, O Pearl of the Age."

Roger thrust his scimitar back into its scabbard and handed it to one of the servitors. "O Frank, this is but the tenth or the hundredth part of what would be seen if I stood in battle before a worthy antagonist. Not that you, son of an unfortunate, would be such; for you do but dance and foint like one of my uncle's entertainers."

While Shea and Polacek were giving themselves sketchy baths by standing in their washbowls and emptying the ewers over each other's heads, the latter asked: "What's the program for the rest of the day?"

"For most of them it'll be loafing all afternoon, I expect, and then Atlantès' floor show in the evening."

"I should think those guys would get too bored to live!"

"Roger does. He wants to bash somebody, and I

don't quite figure why Atlantès won't let him loose to do it. There's something funny going on besides just this business of the old guy making passes at Florimel. Wish I'd read the *Furioso;* I'd know better what we were up against. We have a date with Doc now, you know; some of that new theoretical stuff he's been working up. Ready?"

"Okay, let's go."

When they reached Chalmers' apartment there was more than a suspicion of the olive oil smell that had awakened them. Chalmers was frowning.

"I am inclined to believe that the failure to renew the spell on the oil was not altogether an accident," he replied to Shea's question. "You will note that the odor persists here to a certain extent. Atlantès is extremely astute, and I have no doubt that he has become fully aware of Florimel's—uh—sensitivity. It really made the young lady quite ill."

Shea said: "Wonder why? Maybe the guy's a sadist. According to all the correlations, abnormal sex patterns should be common in this Moslem society where they keep all respectable women locked up. Besides his personality reminds me of that sadist we used as a case study—you know the one I mean —that real-estate fellow the SPCA got after."

"You mean Van Gilder?" Chalmers shook his head. "In the first place those correlations you speak of are mostly guesswork. Besides, it would be unprecedented for any genuine sadist to seek his satisfactions by such indirect methods."

"You mean," said Polacek, "that a real sadist has gotta turn the thumbscrews himself?"

Chalmers nodded. "Or at least be present directing the operation. No, there are various explanations for elaborate bits of malevolent plotting of this type, but—uh—sadism is the last one to look for. An ulterior motive is inherently more probable."

"Such as?" said Shea.

"Such as—ah—if Atlantès hoped to force me to use a counter-spell, which he would then watch and adapt to lifting the death-doom which he says overhangs this castle. Harold, please for that reason do not commit yourself to indulging Roger's penchant for mortal combat. One never knows when this conflict will materialize."

"I'm not afraid of him," said Shea, but without lightness.

"Looks to me like an awful lot of guys around here are anxious to get somebody bumped off," said Polacek. "Why don't you do something about it?"

"It is merely a matter of conducting oneself with ordinary prudence," said Chalmers firmly. "In an unexpressed contention of the type wherein we are engaged with the—uh—gentleman, the winner will undoubtedly be the party who longest restrains himself from ill-judged or impulsive action. Now, gentlemen, shall we begin?"

Half an hour later: ". . . the elementary principles of similarity and contagion," he was saying, "we shall proceed to the more practical applications of magic. First, the composition of spells. The normal spell consists of two components, which may be termed the verbal and the somatic. In the verbal section the consideration is whether the spell is to be based upon command of the materials at hand, or upon the invocation of a higher authority."

"That's a little different from the way you had it worked out before," said Shea.

"This is a somewhat different space-time continuum. I am trying to relate matters to our current problems, so pray do not interrupt. Now—uh—prosody is of the utmost importance if the first is the case. The verse should conform to the poetic conventions of the environment, to which the materials in question have become responsive. For instance in—uh—Asgard the verse, for maximum effectiveness, should be alliterative, whereas in Faerie it should be metrical and rhyming. In the world of Japanese mythology, on the other hand, the verse should comprise a fixed number of syllables in a certain—"

"But wouldn't any verse we made for the purpose naturally have the proper form?" asked Shea.

"It is possible. What I was about to say was that a certain—uh—minimum skill in versification is inseparable from the optimum results. That is why you, Harold, who have what might be called the literary

281

or inspirational type of mind, often attain quite extraordinary effects—"

"Listen," said Polacek, "one of the troubles with this joint is that they're prohibitionists. You mean to say that if I made some passes and sang out:

> 'Beer, beer, beautiful beer,
> Fill me right up with it,
> Clear up to here!

I'd get a couple of seidels?"

"Vaclav!" said Chalmers sharply. "Pray give your attention to the matter in hand. If you were to perform so rash an act, you would almost certainly find yourself filled with the beverage in question, but I doubt whether your organs would retain it. The utmost precision of expression is necessary. Kindly observe that the doggerel you quoted demanded that you be filled with the liquid instead of having it to drink. Now, where was I? Ah—magic will thus, I fear, always remain to large extent an art, just as in my opinion psychiatry will as well. However, there is also the somatic element of the spell, subject to more precise regulation. There is some point in connection with this element that eludes me, and on which I shall be glad to have any light that observation of Atlantès by either of you gentlemen can throw. I refer to the very adroit manner in which he is able to employ spells as an instrumentality for teleportation of human beings or even those only quasi-human—"

Shea's mind wandered as Chalmers droned along. They had worked out most of this stuff in Faerie, with Belphebe—Belphebe! She must be the same as the Belphegor the doctor had mentioned. With the springy step and the freckles under her tan. The question of getting her back concerned the somatic element, of finding out how Atlantès . . .

An eruption from Polacek jerked Shea out of his daydream. The Rubber Czech was on his feet, exclaiming: "Sure, I get it, Doc. Let's take time out to do some lab work. Watch that cushion while I turn it into—"

"No!" shouted Shea and Chalmers together.

"Aw, listen; can't you ever believe a guy can learn anything?"

"I remember," said Shea, "when you blew up the lab and almost killed yourself in sophomore chem, trying to make cacodyl. You stick around for some more lectures before you try enchanting even a mouse."

"Yeah, I know, but you can check me on each step, and I'm—"

The argument was squelched by the arrival of Florimel with: "I am somewhat more myself, my lord." But so, it turned out, was the lecture on magic. Shea wandered off to orient himself, while Chalmers undertook the difficult task of restraining Polacek.

5

IT WAS CLEAR AND BRIGHT UPON THE BATTLE-ments, and the air had the fine tang of a mountain climate. Around a corner where a turret gave both shelter from the breeze and exposure to the sun, Shea came upon Atlantès, busy with a scroll among long cushions. The little enchanter scrambled to his feet.

"O knight of the age, you are welcome. Will the friend of my friend have sherbets?"

"No thanks, noble host. I was just looking around, trying to find where things were in this place. You certainly have a fine layout."

"Alas, my lord, that it is no better. All things shall be done for him who eases the heart and broadens the bosom of Lord Roger."

"I wasn't aware that I'd done anything remarkable in that line. Will you have something special for him tonight?"

Atlantès snapped his fingers and shrugged. "Truly, I have nothing to set before you but seven virgins of Sericane, with faces like moons. All can play at the lute and sing, or hold converse in the law of the Prophet equal to Kasis, and the dealer who sold them to me declares they are sisters of a single birth, which is a very strange thing. Yet you, O auspicious one, will have seen wonders that are to this as the sun to the crescent moon."

He had tipped his head to one side and was watching out of the corner of one eye. What was he fishing for this time? Shea said: "I, O doubly auspicious one, have never seen anything like it. But tell me——" he let his voice fall "——your nephew, Lord Roger, will he like it as well as I? He seems restless."

The little man lifted his face toward the clear blue sky. "I testify that there is no god but God and I testify that Mohammed is the Messenger of God! Of a truth Roger is no less than restless, and longs for battle as a strong horse for the race-course."

"Why not let him go fight one, then?"

Atlantès tapped himself once or twice on the sternum in a manner which Shea supposed was to entitle him to credit for having beaten his breast. "To you I will tell no less than the truth. Know, then, that there is a prophecy of which I have learned by my arts, that unless the wonder of the age and the son of my brother goes forth directly to battle and by the light of the full moon, he will be lost to Islam if he departs ten miles from Carena. Yet at present there is no war, nor is the moon full, and I must answer before Allah the just, the omnipotent, if he be condemned to Jehannum."

"Yeah, I see. You're in a tough spot all right."

The magician clawed at Shea's arm. "Yet it is well said: 'There is no door but a key may unlock it.' Verily, I have not seen my brother's son so content with his lot for many months as when he looked upon your exercises this morning. Doubtless you have a spell to preserve you from death by arms?"

It occurred to Shea that he had never in his life been more politely invited to let himself be killed. But he said: "What keeps Lord Roger here? If he's so keen on getting out and breaking somebody's head, why doesn't he just walk through the door?"

"In truth, that is a question asked with the answer already known, for it is not hidden from me that you are aware of the pentacles of opposition."

"I get it. This is a kind of gilded hoosegow. You don't think you can keep Sir Reed and me in that way, do you?"

This time Atlantès went through the formula of wringing his hands. "May dogs eat my flesh if I ever held such a thought! Nay, auspicious sir, should you wish to hunt in those mountains, where often I myself have had good sport when the sap of youth was in me, it would give pleasure to your slave to provide a hunter for company. And should you wish to sport with the light of Islam, the pentacles can be let down."

He certainly was persistent. "No thanks, not right now," said Shea.

The graybeard nudged him and chuckled lecherously. "Think well on it, my lord. It has reached my ears that there be maidens among the villages more dainty than gazelles, and not all hunting is done with the bow."

"No thanks, O fount of wisdom," said Shea again, wondering how much of his statement of the prophecy was true. "Right now I'm much more interested in Florimel's and Doc's—that is, Sir Reed's—project for her. Business before pleasure, you know. How are you coming along on that, by the way?"

Atlantès went through his breast-beating routine again. "There is no god but God! It has not been revealed to me how this knot may be unloosed, though I have summoned up legions of the jann."

"Maybe I could help a little," said Shea. "I know a fair amount of magic, and once in a while I can do things that even Sir Reed doesn't pull off."

"In sooth, it were a greater wonder than burning water were matters otherwise, O master of magic. With joy and goodwill will I sumon you when the hour comes that you can aid me. Yet for the present there is no aid that can be given so great as that of the contentment of my brother's son."

Again! Would this little schemer ever let up trying to get Shea shortened by a head? Shea chose to ignore the last part of the remark. "Along what lines are you working? We might check results against each other."

"If it could be so, it were the delight of my heart and the expansion of my bosom. But it is unlawful for one of our religion to initiate other than true Muslims in the magical rites; were I to do so, you would instantly be torn in pieces by an ifrit stronger than a lion and with tusks three feet in length." The little man seemed to have had enough. He started for the stairs, the motion of his feet beneath the long robe making him look oddly like a centipede.

At the head of the stairs he turned to bow another farewell. Then a thought seemed to occur to him, for he held up a hand. "O auspicious sir," he called, "take warning. These peaks be ominous; very pillars of mischance. Let the hand of friendship avert the stroke of calamity, and in the name of Allah, I pray you, do not let down the pentacles nor go forth without help from me and mine."

The afternoon light was already beginning to throw panels of shadow among the higher summits. Shea walked on around the battlements, thinking of where Belphebe might be in this world, and longing for her high spirits. Damn Doc Chalmers anyway for getting them into this jam! It was a jam, too. That farewell of Atlantès, though couched in a tone of appeal, came as close to a veiled threat as he had ever heard. Suppose he did lower the pentacles and walk out, what would the old goat do? Hardly let loose the wonder of the age on him. That would run against the prophecy—if there was a prophecy. Shea thought about the question as he picked his way past a clanging iron shot-tower, and reached the conclusion that the prophecy was probably quite real. Atlantès was clever enough to run a double bluff by mixing a piece of important truth with evasions and half-truths in order to steer an opponent away from the former.

The only thing he could count on, however, was that the magician was putting the heat on his guests in the matter of finding a cure for Roger's boredom. Shea considered the question for a moment. The big lug appeared to care for nothing but fighting; couldn't there be some way of meeting the wish vicariously? Back in Ohio, when children became problems along this line, the matter could be taken care of with books of adventure. That clearly wouldn't do here; or—and Shea mentally kicked himself for not thinking of it sooner—toy soldiers.

Certainly there ought to be somebody around Castle Carena with skill enough to carve passable small figures of fighting-men, and he and Chalmers between them should be able to animate them magically enough to enable them to serve as miniature armies. The thought of the perfect paladin ordering battalions of six-inch wooden knights about the courtyard struck him as so delightful that he slapped the edge of the battlement and laughed. At that moment someone plucked his sleeve.

It was one of the castle servants, this time with the head of a bird—a very large bird, with a great round head and a long bill like one of Tenniel's borogoves.

"What's the trouble?" asked Shea.

Although the creature seemed to understand, its only answer was to open the beak for a kind of whistling bark. It pulled at his arm insistently until he followed, looking over its shoulder from time to time and whistling encouragingly as it led him down the stairs, along one of the metal corridors, and left him face to face with Polacek.

"Hi, Harold," said the latter cheerfully, with the air of an inventor about to give birth to the atom-powered space ship. "Say, you guys need me around places like this. I got hold of one of those hobgoblins that will find all the stuff we want. The only trouble is I can't find her!"

"What stuff? Whom?"

"The little dark one that did the dance last night.

287

All I got is her name: Sumurrud, or something like that. And what kind of stuff do you think? Tonsil-oil, of course."

"You get around fast, don't you? Lead on to the liquor, but you're out of luck on the girl friend. If Roger hasn't got her in his room giving her the works just to spite you, Atlantès has probably sent her back where she came from by magic."

"For the love of St. Wenceslaus! I never thought of that." The Rubber Czech's face looked annoyed. "I'll cook up a spell on that guy that will make him—"

"No!"

"All right, how about this? Suppose I go to Atlantès right off the arm, and ask him can he send me that little number back to Ohio. With a build like hers—"

"No! We're in enough trouble now. You don't even know her, Votsy."

"But—"

Shea sighed. "For an educated man you've got the most proletarian sexual behavior pattern—"

" 'Smatter with you; all worn out already?" said Polacek nastily, leading the way down a circular staircase in one of the castle towers. As this point in the argument was reached, so was a scullery, where the goblin, a purple-skinned object with an oversized head and spinkly little legs, was at his job of dishwashing. In one corner lay a large gaunt hound with a dish between his forepaws. The goblin held up a dirty plate, repeated a formula, and whistled. Instantly the dog reacted by licking the dish before him. As he did so the detritus disappeared from the plate held by the goblin.

"Guk!" said Polacek. "How do you like your dinner?"

Shea grinned. "Don't be squeamish. The stuff gets from the outside of the plate to the inside of the dog without touching a thing."

The goblin waddled over to them with a crablike gait. "Got it, Odoro?" asked Polacek with a wink. "He wants some too."

"Can get," said Odoro. "You got money, uh? Me want."

They went to Chalmers' laboratory for the money. At their knock there was a rustling from within, and when they entered, Florimel was some distance from Chalmers with her dress slightly rumpled and both of them looking hangdog. The doctor tendered some odd-looking square coins without comment.

As they made their way back to their own room, Shea laughed. "To see those two, you'd think it was a crime to hold a girl on your lap here."

"He's probably never done it before," remarked Polacek. "Well, he can have that human snowball if he wants her; I'll take that little Sumurrud. Did you know she was giving me the eye?"

The goblin joined them almost at once, producing from under one arm a small leather bottle wrapped in a ragged piece of discarded turban.

Polacek gave him some of the odd-looking coins, each of which the being tested with fanglike teeth. As he turned to go, Shea said: "Just a minute, Odoro." He had taken hold of the bottle. "Your master is pretty tough about liquor, isn't he?"

"Oh, yes. awful! Law of Prophet." Odoro touched a hand to his forehead.

"What would happen if he found out you had a supply and were selling it to people?"

The goblin shuddered. "Anathema, second class. Redhot pincers inside." His grin vanished. "You no tell, no?"

"We'll see."

Odoro paled to lavender and made a shifting motion from one foot to the other that turned into a series of hops. "Oh, you no do! I do you boon! So do no nightly!" he squealed. "Here, you no want wine, you give me back."

He danced up to Shea, reaching. Shea held the bottle high over his head and did a snap-pass to Polacek, who caught it like a down-field end. "Easy, easy," said Shea. "Remember I'm a magician too, and I can turn you into a red ant if I want to. This is evidence. All I want is a little information, and

289

if you give it to us you needn't worry about our telling anything."

"No got information," said Odoro sullenly. His eyes ran round and round the room from a swivelling head.

"No? Votsy, you go find Atlantès and tell him we've got a bootlegger here, while I keep an eye on—Oh, you don't want him to go? Maybe you do know a thing or two? I thought likely. Now then, is there a prophecy about Roger?"

"Yes—yes. Nasty prophecy. If he go out before full moon he join infidels, fight true believers. *Il hamdu l'Allah!*"

"Now, isn't that nice! All right, why doesn't Atlantès let Roger out just a little way? He's a wizard and would know how to keep him from going too far."

"Afraid Duke Astolph. He magician too; stole hippogriff."

"That clears up one point anyway. But look here, if Roger's so anxious to get out, why doesn't he just make it hot for Atlantès? Cut off his head or something?"

"Not know. Swear beard of Prophet, no know. Think Atlantès do something with—you know—mind—" Odoro pointed to his head—"drive Roger like horse. But Roger no got much mind, so hard to—uh—drive."

Shea laughed. "That's about what I thought. Give him another nickel, Votsy. You see, Odoro, you stick with us and you'll be all right. Now, what's Atlantès up to with Florimel?"

"Prophecy. Find in magic book."

"I daresay. What prophecy?"

"He lose Roger by woman knight, come on hippogriff."

Belphebe was out there somewhere in the hills, and so was the hippogriff. "But what does Florimel have to do with that?"

"Not know. Think maybe he change her shape with woman knight, burn her up, poof!"

"A fine kettle of fish. What kind of spell will he use?"

"Not know."

"You know about magic, don't you?"

"Not know that. Atlantès, he very good magician."

"Okay. Votsy, suppose you ask the very good magician to come—"

"Not know! Not know! Me ignorant!" wailed Odoro, beginning to hop again.

"Maybe he really doesn't know," suggested Polacek.

"Maybe. And maybe he gets a break for that crack about Roger. Run along, Odoro. You say nothing and we'll say nothing."

"Whew!" whistled Polacek when the door had closed behind the purple shape. "You certainly have got a nerve, Harold. With your luck and my brains —we get a drink."

Shea rummaged a couple of pewter cups from a low cabinet in the corner, uncorked the bottle, sniffed, and poured some of its contents into each cup. The wine was sweet and dark, nearly black, with something the flavor of port, though he judged the proof would be lower.

Shea sipped his, remarking with the air of an experienced conspirator: "You don't want to ask questions among the hired help without getting a hold on them somehow first. They may lie to you, or they may be souped up to report anything you ask to the boss. I think we've got this bozo playing on our team for the time being—but I don't like what he said about the deal Atlantès is cooking up."

"He means Belphebe, doesn't he?" said Polacek, holding out his cup for another drink.

"I'm afraid so. No, Votsy, we've got to hang onto some of this to keep Odoro in line. Besides, Atlantès would smell it on your breath a block away and know something wasn't kosher. We have to watch our step."

6

IT WAS PLAIN THAT ROGER WAS NOT ENJOYING THE party, although the seven virgins of Sericane were giving him most of their attention. Harold Shea didn't know that he altogether blamed the big bruiser. It was good second-rate cabaret stuff, which might have been fairly enjoyable had there been a comfortable place to sit, something to smoke, and something to drink. Reed Chalmers had excused himself early and gone off to enjoy the company of Florimel.

The dance went on. In the middle of a figure Roger suddenly stood up. "In the name of Allah! Oh, uncle, this is not less than the vilest of your entertainments. My liver is constricted, and I would broaden it by hunting bears among the mountains."

Atlantès broke off his conversation with one of the lords and began fluttering his hands, not aimlessly, but in the passes of a magical formula. However, it had no visible effect upon Roger, who trod firmly toward the door.

From beside Shea, Polacek said: "Say, I got an idea!" and wriggled to his feet and followed. Nobody but the seven girls seemed to mind the departure very much, even Atlantès going on with his whispered conversation. But as the number drew to a close Shea felt uneasy; Polacek had too great a capacity for trouble to be left wandering around the castle for very long with an idea in his head. He too got up and strolled out into the corridor.

No sign of Roger or his friend. Shea ambled along the hall and around a bend without seeing anything significant. He was about to go back when his eye lighted on a side-passage with a door at its end where a smoky light showed the interlocked pentacles that protect magicians who deal with devils. Atlantès' own laboratory!

In a moment the direction of his attention changed. The wizard was certainly well-occupied, and if he did come looking for anybody it would be Roger. Shea stepped up to the marked door. No handle; and it did not move when he pushed it. Barred with a spell beyond doubt; but by this time he knew enough magic to deal with the situation. Reaching to his turban, he plucked from the brush that adorned its front a couple of stiff bristles, detached a thread from the hem of his aba, and tied the bristles together in the form of a cross. Holding this up to the door he whispered:

"Pentacles far and pentacles near,
I forthwith command you disappear!
Shemhamphorash!"

He paused, hoping there was no basilisk on guard. There was not. The room was long and lower than it seemed from the outside. A row of alembics and other magical apparatus lay ranged on a long table at one side, faintly reflecting the blue-white phosphorescent light thrown from the eyes of an owl and a crocodile which stood on a pair of shelves. The animals were quite immobile; evidently Atlantès' private system of lighting, though not one that would ever be popular with interior decorators. Along the shelf beneath them was a row of books, terminating in little compartments, each of which had a title on its attached tag.

The books had characters on their backs which Shea tried in vain to puzzle out until he realized that in this space-time continuum he would be unable to read English or any other language in which books were printed without special instruction. With the tags on the scrolls he fared better:

Ye Principalls of Magick with ye Conjuration of Daemons Superadded; Poisons Naturall; The Lawful Names of Allah; One Thousand Useful Curses; The Carpets of the Lesser Jann; Al Qa'sib's Manner of Magickal Transformations; . . .

Ah! This one might have what he was looking for. Shea pulled out the scroll and glanced at it in the eyelight of the animals. It seemed to be almost as strong on general theory as Chalmers himself, but little or nothing as to practical details. A glance showed him that, as might be expected, the scroll had neither table of contents nor index, and its style was so rambling that getting anything out of it would need a week's work.

Shea slipped the scroll back into its pigeonhole and turned to the rest of the room. If the enchanter were really trying to exchange Florimel's body for that of the menacing "woman knight," there ought to be traces of his labors about. However, the apparatus held no traces of filters, and the big scarred oak table beyond their bench lay bare. Atlantès was a neat sorcerer. Where would he keep his notebooks? Beyond the table was a stool and beyond that a low cabinet built into the wall. Like the outer door it had no handle, and as Shea bent closer he could see that its front was inscribed with pentacles. But at a touch it swung open, and Shea realized that his counter-spell must have let down barriers all over the castle. The thought that if there were any ifrits or demons abroad tonight they could get in and have themselves a hell of a fine time made him giggle under his breath.

The cabinet was deep, its shelves set back in, and in front of them a long straight sword hung in its scabbard from a hook. Probably an enchanted weapon, but the counter-spell would have taken care of that. Shea was about to reach past it toward the contents of the shelves when his ear caught the faint sound of a voice ordering the outer door to open.

In a flash Shea had snatched loose the sword

and was on hands and knees behind the big table, which luckily had a decoration of carved wood reaching nearly to the floor.

The door opened. Shea could not see through the screening, but light from the corridor momentarily threw the shadow of a baboon's head across the wall on the side away from the door. The newcomer was one of Atlantès' servants, and a specially unappetizing member of the gang.

It stood in the doorway a moment, hesitant, as Shea himself had done. Then with the door swinging behind it, it stepped confidently toward the bookshelves. But then it fell quiet—too quiet. Shea heard it sniff; sniff again, like the puffing of a toy engine. Of course it would posess a keener sense of smell than a man. The servant worked its way over to the table that held the alembics, tracing Shea's movements, just audible as its feet pressed the carpet. Shea could imagine the snouted head turning this way and that. . . . He gathered his muscles and shifted weight to bring his left hand free for the scabbarded weapon, planning in his mind how to snatch it out with the least lost motion.

The baboon-head reached the outer edge of the table, sniff, puff, sniff, puff, as loud as a locomotive in the oppressive silence.

Hell suddenly broke loose in the castle. A chorus of shouts and bangings echoed through the halls. The baboon-head paused for a moment, then ran to the door on almost soundless feet and out. Shea forced himself to count seven, then scrambled up and followed. The servitor had rounded the corner and the sound of its running still echoed metallically.

Shea turned toward the entertainment hall in the direction of the noise, pausing only in the side passage long enough to catch the sword on the belt beneath his flowing aba. It made him feel better.

As he approached the entertainment hall he realized that the noise was coming from beyond. He ran past to a big winding staircase, and from where it spread to a landing he could see Atlantès and his guests coming up with swords, maces, and even musical instruments, chasing a wolf the size of a heifer.

It came straight toward Shea, but with its tail between its legs and looking utterly miserable.

Shea tried to dodge, then remembered the sword, but before he could dig it out of its hiding-place the creature was upon him. However, instead of leaping for his throat the wolf threw itself on the landing and rolled over, scrubbing its back along the iron floor. It waved its paws in the air, letting out an unwolflike "Wah-wah! Wah-wah!" Then it rolled back again and, keeping its belly to the floor, licked at Shea's shoes.

"Hey, wait a minute," said Shea to the crowding pursuers, who were trying to take swipes at the beast. "This is a rummy kind of wolf. It wants to be a pet. Atlantès, would you mind taking a look at it?"

The sorcerer dropped one of the singers' lutes and came forward. "Verily this is a most unfortunate rare creature, a wonder of wonders. Now shall you grant me room, Sir Harold." He squatted down and peered closely into the animal's eyes; it moaned. "There is no god but Allah! This is surely a werewolf. Oh, my lords, an evil hour has brought such a shape to Carena!" He reached to the neck of his robe and made a little tear in it. "Now I must seek by my arts to find how such a creature has passed our defenses. There is no doubt but that this is the work of the Christian enchanter, the paladin Malagigi, son of a hog and a she-dog, though I had heard of him imprisoned in Albracca." He looked round the circle. "My lords, we must seek a silver weapon for one of you to slay this brute, for being myself an enchanter I cannot."

Apparently silver weapons were in short supply. "O greatest of enchanters," advised Margéan, "shall we not affix silver monies to a wooden club and beat it to death?"

The wolf howled piteously. Chalmers, who had popped out of his own room at the sound of the commotion, had arrived in time to hear the last remarks. Now he put in a word: "Ahem—wouldn't it be the part of—uh—wisdom to attempt disenchanting the animal first? If I am correct in my

296

understanding, it would then lose any previous invulnerability."

Atlantès bowed. "O fortunate hour that has brought your father's son among us, Sir Reed! This is nothing less than the truth. Yet I am but a stick set in the sand beside you in such matters. As your head lives, you shall now do this for us."

"Um—if we had some holy water, it would be a—uh—comparatively-uncomplicated matter, but I will try." Chalmers turned his back, put one hand to his chin, and meditated. "I am not sure the versification will prove adequate, but we shall see:

"Wolf, wolf, wolf of the windy mountain,
   Wolf of fear;
   I conjure you by the bitter fountain;
   Disappear!"

His fingers moved rapidly. The wolf shuddered and turned into Vaclav Polacek rolling on the floor, clothes and all.

"Holy Saint Wenceslaus!" he cried, getting up. "Might as well shoot a man as scare him to death. Why didn't you lay off when I told you who I was?"

"You didn't tell us," said Shea.

"I did so. I kept saying, 'For the love of Mike, Harold, it's me, Votsy,' as clear as anything."

"Maybe it would have sounded like that to another wolf, but it didn't to us," replied Shea. "How did you get into that mess anyway? Did you run into this Malagigi that Atlantès is talking about?" There was a murmur of agreement through the group, as Atlantès' eyes darted back and forth.

"Well," said Polacek. He cleared his throat once or twice before he could get going. "It's like this, see? Roger isn't such a bad guy when you get to know him. He wanted to go hunting or something, and we were talking about it, but he said as how there was some kind of spell so he couldn't get out the door, and I said I'd been studying some magic, and so we went down there together, and he had the

297

right dope; the door wouldn't open. Well, you see, I remembered those somatic passes Doc was talking about and made a few of them, and boy, the door flew open just like that!" He paused. Shea started a little, then hoped Atlantès hadn't noticed.

"Go on, Vaclav," said Chalmers severely.

"Well, then I figured I knew enough about magic to maybe—uh—get that babe back—you know, the one you were going to introduce me to." He appealed to Atlantès. "So I worked a little spell, just like you said, but it turned me into a wolf instead. I'm sorry I made so much trouble."

"Must be your Slavonic ancestry," said Shea. "The Czechs are full of werewolf stories, and—"

He had not noticed the gathering clouds on Atlantès' forehead. Now the storm burst. "Son of a dog!" he shouted at Polacek. "Where is the pride of chivalry, the noblest of his race, who is worth ten thousand such as you?"

"Why, he went out to do a little hunting, like I said," said Polacek. "He said he'd be back before morning with something good."

This time Atlantès really did beat his chest. "Ah, woe to me! The doom has stricken!" Then he swung around to the three Americans. "But as for you, Nazarene dogs, who have plotted against me by the hand of your servant while partaking of my bread and salt, you deserve nothing more than to be flayed alive and to have your bodies buried in a pit with the excrement of hogs!"

"Hey!" said Shea, reaching forward to take Atlantès by the arm. "Those are fighting words where we come from. If you want to get tough about it—"

"Harold!" said Chalmers. "Let me handle this. We don't want—"

"We don't want anything to do with this thrip except to hand him a sock in the puss. D'you know what he's up to?"

Chalmers said: "Never mind, Harold. You have already informed me sufficiently. I'll defend—uh—myself and the young lady to any extent necessary."

Atlantès' fury had burned down to a glower. "O ill-omened sorcerers! Know that this castle was wholly established by the arts of which I am master, and within its walls I have such power that I could turn you to beetlegrubs in less time than the snapping of the fingers. Yet in the name of Allah, the omnipotent, the merciful, will I spare your lives to the undoing of the harm you have done, for it is written that once in his lifetime may the just man prefer mercy to justice without endangering his hope of paradise."

He extended both arms, closed his eyes, and cried in a high voice: *"Beshem hormots vahariman tesovev ha-esh, asher anena esh, et metzudat habsitell!"*

There was a whoosh and a buzz, like an electric fan in the adjoining room. Atlantès' permanent smile came back: so did his bow. "Behold, fellow practitioners of the noblest of the arts, if you will look beyond the walls of this castle, you will see it circled by an outer barbican of flame, sufficient to roast a sheep in less than a minute. For the hardiest of men to try to pass it the punishment would be no less than death. Yet if the Lady Florimel attempt it, who is a woman and yet no woman, she would leave no more memory than steam from the coffee cup. My gracious mercy extends so far that the fire shall instantly be removed when by your arts you bring Lord Roger back; and I will add to that bags of jewels so great that three men can hardly carry them. The peace of the one true God be with you in your meditations."

He bowed again and turned his back. The lords looked sullenly at the three (except Audibrad, whose sympathies, judging from the fact that he was trying not to smirk, were evidently in the other direction) and Chalmers began to dither. "I—uh—am unsure whether I am sufficiently advanced in the science of apportation, which I had presumed something of a specialty—"

"S-st!" said Shea. "If magic doesn't work, I'll take a running jump through and go hunt Roger myself. I don't mind having my eyebrows singed a little."

Atlantès, who seemed to have sharper ears than a cat, turned back. "Learn, rash youth," he said, "that

the very marrow of your bones would be inciner-
ated; and yet, of a truth, you say a thing I had
not thought on; for it will be far easier to remove
the Pearl of the Orient from thence to hither if he be
found by human eyes than only by arts magical; and
it will greatly pleasure my brother's son to cut your
throat from ear to ear beyond these walls. Go then;
I undertake to pass you unharmed through the flame."

"I'd like to go, too," said Polacek. His expression
showed that he did not look forward to a pleasant
time at the castle after his venture into wolfishness.

"Go, then, and Allah give you neither peace
nor a long life unless you bring my nephew home
again." He turned away again, this time for keeps.

Shea found Chalmers looking at him keenly. The
doctor said: "I wonder, Harold, if helping me and
Florimel was your most important motive in offering
to find Roger?"

Shea grinned. "It's the only one you know about
officially, Doc."

7

THE WHOLE CASTLE TURNED OUT TO SEE SHEA
and Polacek off on their Roger-hunt the following
morning. During the evening, Chalmers had tried to establish thought-contact with the peerless chevalier
as a preliminary to getting back by magical means,
but he had been forced to give up with the remark
that Roger had about as few thoughts as the human
brain could hold. In any case there seemed to be
interference, either from Atlantès himself or from
the curtain of flame he had thrown around the castle,
so the job clearly devolved upon Chalmers' two
juniors.

He did not believe that the threat of Atlantès'

plan to exchange the shapes of Florimel and the prophesied woman knight represented an immediate danger. Perhaps later; "But let us take first things first, Harold," he said cheerfully. "I think I can profitably employ my time in study and in attempting to establish communication with this Christian sorcerer Malagigi. It was—uh—remiss of me not to have thought of him before coming to Carena. I presume it would be superfluous to express a wish for your good fortune?"

Beyond the gate and a drawbridge over a dry ditch, the flames rose in a wavering wall, obscuring the nearby peaks. Shea could feel their heat on his face as he stood at the break of the drawbridge while Atlantès dipped a finger in a small bottle of oil and drew an isosceles triangle on his forehead and then a right triangle over the first, muttering a small spell as he did so. He repeated the process with Polacek and with the chief huntsman of the castle, a broad-shouldered swarthy man named Echegaray. Atlantès was all smiles as though they had had no hard words the previous evening, although Shea overheard the other lords making up a small pool as to who would find Roger and when.

Echegaray strode beside them towards the flame, a crossbow over his shoulder. When he came to the magic barrier, however, he stopped and looked inquiringly at Shea. The flames streaked soundlessly far over their heads; the light was so intense that it hurt their eyes and looked altogether real and terrifying, though the grass from which the flames sprang seemed unharmed. Shea felt like stopping too, but with Echegaray watching and the eyes of the whole castle boring into his back—he threw out his chest and marched straight through. Two steps did it, and the fire only tingled.

For a moment his companions did not appear. Then there was a half-choked yell and Echegaray came through, dragging Polacek behind him. The hunter looked at Shea, spat, and jerked a thumb at Polacek, who was swelling with indignation that had not yet quite reached the stage of words. "Tried to change his mind," said the hunter. "This way."

The road was no more than a track down the mountain whose peak the castle occupied, a track so steep moreover that one had to walk with care, watching the skirts of one's jelab. They were already below timberline and had to duck under the branches of tall trees along their way. A cool mountain breeze hissed through the pines and ruffled the brushes on Shea's and Polacek's turbans.

Shea unhooked the sword he had taken from Atlantès' cabinet, drew it out, and looked it over before fastening it to his outside sash. Like the one he had used in the courtyard, this sword had a rounded point and a thick, heavy blade—useless for thrusting and awkward on the parry, altogether better suited to a slashing fantatic on horseback than to a methodical épée fencer.

"Think we're gonna run into anything?" asked Polacek with wide eyes. "I ought to have something like that if we are." He turned to Echegaray and pointed to the huge broad knife in the latter's belt. "Hey, how about lending me that thing for a while? If we have any trouble it would be better to have all of us armed."

"No. Mine," said the hunter shortly, and took up the way again. Three hours brought them to the foot of the main peak. There the path began climbing and dipping across a series of spurs reaching down from another crest which thrust in from their right. The forest grew thicker here. Echegaray led them into the throat of a valley where a stream dropped past in a series of waterfalls and the ten a.m. sun failed to reach the bottom. The gorge widened to a valley which held a patch of swamp, where they had to squish almost ankle-deep along the edge of a pond. Shea jumped and Polacek stopped at a glimpse of white skin and gauzy wings as the water-fays, or whatever they were, ducked out of sight. Echegaray pushed ahead without looking back and they had to follow.

Beyond, the valley narrowed again. The mountain wall closed in so sharply on their side of the stream that they had to cross on a bridge which was formed of a single log. Echegaray simply walked across as if the log had been level land. Shea followed with difficulty, waving his arms for balance, and just barely making it with a leap at the end. Polacek stuck his thumbs into his sash and tried to imitate the hunter's jaunty step, but failed to watch his footing and fell in.

"Time to eat," said the hunter as Polacek climbed out of the shallow water, rubbing his shin and cursing with a verve to curl the leaves.

Echegaray abruptly perched himself on the edge of the bridge-log, unslung his pack, and brought out a piece of bread and a slab of dried meat, each of which he expertly divided into three portions with a slash of his knife, then waved a hand at the stream. "Water," he said.

As they munched and flexed tired muscles, Polacek said: "Say, Harold, how do you know where we're going and whether we'll find Roger there—not that I want to?"

"I don't," said Shea. He turned to the hunter. "How are you sure we'll find Roger in this direction?"

"Best place," said Echegaray with mouth full.

"Yes, but where are we?" He produced a piece of parchment on which Atlantès had drawn a sketch-map when the journey was decided upon. "We've twisted around so many times in this valley that I'm not quite sure which direction the castle lies in."

"Magic?" asked Echegaray, pointing to the map.

"No. Just a map."

"What?"

"A map. You know, a picture of the country with the roads and castles and things."

"Magic," said Echegaray flatly.

"Okay, it's magic if you like it that way. Now, if you'll show us just where we are on the map—"

"We aren't," said Echegaray.

"What do you mean, we aren't? We can't have walked far enough to get off the map."

"Never on map. We're on log." He patted it to make sure.

Shea sighed. "All I want is for you to show me the spot on the map corresponding to the place where we are now."

Echegaray shook his head. "Don't understand magic."

"Oh, to hell with magic. Look at this thing. Here's Castle Carena."

"No. Castle's a long way from here. We walk fast."

"No, no! This place on the map means Castle Carena. Now we want to know where we are, on the map."

Echegaray pushed back his leather cap and scratched his short black hair. Then his brows cleared. "Want us on map?"

"Yes. You're getting the idea."

The hunter took the map from Shea's hand, turned it around a couple of times, laid it on the ground, smoothed it out, and stood up—

"Hey!" yelped Shea. He caught Echegaray's shoulders and pushed him back just as the hunter's boot was coming down on the parchment. "What's the idea of stepping on my map?"

Echegaray sat down, a resigned expression on his face. "Said you wanted us on map. Magic carpet, no?"

"No. I didn't mean you were to be on the map physically." How the devil, wondered Shea, could you explain the principles of semantics to a one-groove mind like this?

"Whyn't you say so? First you want us on map. Then you don't. Can't make up your mind. Never saw such people."

Shea folded the map and put it back in his sash. "Let's forget it. What makes you think you're going to find Roger in this direction?"

"Best place."

"One-two-three-four-five-six-seven. Why is it the best place? What would he be doing in this direction rather than any other?"

"Crossroads. Knights always fight at crossroads." The hunter broke off a twig and whittled it to a toothpick. He used it with relish, pausing now and again to belch.

"Ready?" he said presently. Shea and Polacek nodded. Echegaray adjusted his pack, picked up his crossbow, and swung ahead.

The stream hung with them past another waterfall,

where an animal of some sort went crashing through the thicket and Echegaray with an instinctive motion whipped up his crossbow. Shea could not help thinking how Belphebe—if it were she—would be enjoying this country. Beyond, the path carried them across another high spur and through a screen of trees down to a three-pronged fork, the tracks in both directions broader and scarred by hoofmarks. Echegaray strode to the junction and looked along first one leg of the fork and then the other, his forehead contorted by thought.

"What's the matter?" said Shea. "I don't see our friend Roger here. Is that it?"

The hunter gave him a look that showed disesteem for those who waste words pointing out the obvious, and pointed in the direction that must be south by the sun's position. "Crossroads; village. Four miles." Then he pointed north. "Crossroads. Village. Twelve miles. Which?" He looked at Shea for orders.

"Say," said Polacek. "Why don't we split up and play the field? One of us would have more chance of talking that big lug into coming back than both together, and besides I know enough magic now to take care of myself—"

"No," said Shea firmly. "You try just one more spell and I'll have your neck and ears." He turned to Echegaray. "Which way is Lord Roger most likely to go?"

The hunter shrugged. "Both. You tell."

Shea thought: after all, why not let Polacek and Echegaray take one road while he took the other? Votsy couldn't get into too much trouble with this simple-minded but knowledgeable retainer holding his hand; and as for himself, he would just as soon not have the Bouncing Czech around if he should chance to meet Belphebe. The way to the north wound among trees.

"Look here," he said, "maybe that's a good idea of yours after all, Votsy. Suppose you and Echegaray take that road to the south and let me strike off on the other one. That way we'll be all right. Watch out for Belphebe, will you? She's supposed to be wandering around somewhere and I shouldn't want anyone taking pot-shots at her."

"Me neither," said Polacek. "Boy, could I use one of those cocktails she used to mix, right now! She's better than you since you taught her."

They shook hands, and Shea said: "Got any money? Good. Might be an idea to buy yourself some kind of weapon in the village if you can. Probably a mace; anybody can swing a club without practice. Start back in about four days whether you find him or not."

"Don't worry about me," said Polacek. "I figure I know how to get along with these types. Look how I contacted that purple guy with the booze in the castle when all you did was sit around on your duff."

Shea turned up the road, looking back once to wave as the other two disappeared down a slope behind trees. He wondered how long Polacek's short legs would stand the pace. It was in such a wood that he had first seen the girl, light-footed, with a feather in her hat, who announced her presence with an arrow that slew the Losel. Belphebe. His feet picked the way along without any conscious help from his mind, except that he was aware of going forward. And they'd been getting so beautifully adjusted, too. . . . No, not quite such a wood either. This one was more open; the trees were smaller and there was less brush. One could see—

One could see something moving among the trunks to the right, too large and too steady of progress to be an animal. Shea snapped to attention, whipped out the sword, and slipped into the cover of a tree. Then something answered his movement with a call of "Olé!" and stepped into plain view. Echegaray.

"What in the blue-belted blazes have you done with Polacek?" demanded Shea, gripping his sword firmly as the hunter trotted up.

"Left him. Talks too much. Go with you."

"Don't you know he's not fit to be allowed out without a keeper? Suppose you get right back there and keep an eye on him!"

For answer the hunter shrugged and gazed at the top of a tall tree with an elaborate lack of interest in anything else. Shea felt his temper rise, but there didn't seem to be much he could do about it, short of turning back along the road to overtake Polacek or going for Echegaray with the sword. He stuck his nose in the air and started along the path the way he had been going. Echegaray followed.

The trees began to crowd in from both sides, and from the bottom of a draw the way commenced to climb steeply. Shea found himself puffing, although he noted that the hunter in less hampering clothes was coming along like a machine. At the crest, the spur they had been climbing broadened out into a little plateau with colonnades of trees. Shea leaned against a big trunk, breathing deeply; Echegaray posted himself against another, the toothpick twirling in a corner of his mouth.

Twunk! Twunk! The tree jarred under the blows. Shea jumped—or tried to and found he couldn't. A long white-shafted arrow had pinned his sleeve to the tree, and another was affixed just beside his right leg. He caught a glimpse of Echegaray's astonished brown face as the hunter flung himself flat, then began to snake forward to the shelter of a fallen trunk, the crossbow dragging. He whipped a curved iron rod out of his boot and slipped one end of it over a stud in the side of the bow. A bolt dropped in; Echegaray's arm brought the piece of metal back and the bow was cocked.

There were no more arrows and the forest was silent. Echegaray's right hand scrubbed loose a pebble, which he tossed with a little noise into a bush at the far end of the log, at the same time peering cautiously around the near end.

"Drop!" he told Shea in a stage-whisper.

"Can't," said Shea. Thinking what a beautiful target he made for the unseen archer, he was trying to get the arrows out with his left hand. However, the position was awkward, and the deeply embedded shaft was made of some springy wood that would not break under his fingers' best efforts. His clothes were of a heavy, tweedy wool that would neither tear nor slide up the arrow. He gave a heave, then began trying to work his arm loose from the garment itself. Out of the corner of his eye he saw Echegaray watching the woods with bright-eyed attention, then bring the crossbow up slowly. . . .

Snap! The bolt flashed away among the trees with a beelike hum. Someone laughed and Echegaray snatched up his cocking-lever.

Before he could finish reloading a voice roared: "Yield thee, sirrah! Halloo, halloo, and a mort!" Out of nowhere an oversized man had appeared over the hunter, waving a two-handed, cross-hilted sword. He was ruddy-faced, with features so strikingly regular that they might have been copied from those of an imaginary Apollo. Around his neck was a scarf with diagonal stripes of red, blue, and brown, the ends of which were tucked into a leather jacket. A light steel cap allowed curling blond hair to escape round its edges, and a huge curled horn was strapped to his back.

Echegaray rolled over twice, whipping out his knife and coming up to one knee, but the point of the big sword was right in his face and he thought better of it. He sullenly dropped his weapon and spread his hands.

Down among the trees whither the crossbow bolt had flown, a hat with a feather came into view. The hat was bobbing on the end of a stick held by a girl in a knee-length tunic, a girl with freckles and reddish-gold hair cut in a long bob. She trotted toward them as though she were going to break into a dance step at any moment, and the other hand held a longbow with an arrow already nocked.

"Belphebe!" cried Harold Shea, his heart giving a great leap.

The girl, who had been looking at Echegaray, turned toward Shea with her eyebrows up. "What said you, Saracen? I hight Belphegor."

Shea looked blank. "Don't you remember? Harold Shea. Just an old husband of yours. The picnic."

She laughed. "Nor husband nor loveling have I, and had I such, 'twould be no son of black Mahound."

"You don't know anyone named Belphebe?"

There was a flicker between her brows. Shea remembered with sinking heart what Chalmers had told him about his wife's loss of memory. She turned to the big man: "Nay, my lord Astolph, methinks this rogue doth seek to cozen us."

"Rather. This other chappie is Atlantès' hunter again, right?"

"Aye. Small tiding shall we have from him, even though he be ware of all. Recall you not when erst we caught him? Your bolts, Master Echegaray!" She held out a hand, and the hunter, muttering something about "damned women . . . spinning-wheels" thrust forward a fistful of bolts.

"So? Have we them all?" The girl pulled the bandolier toward her and snatched out another bolt. "A clever rogue, is it not?"

Echegaray shrugged. "Worth trying," he said resignedly.

"Very well, my man, you may go," said the man who had been addressed as Astolph. "And I'll trouble you to keep on your own side of the line hereafter." Echegaray picked up his crossbow and silently disappeared among the trees.

The big man turned to Shea: "Now let's have a word with you, my fine Saracen fowl!" He stepped to the tree and wrenched out the arrows with a strength that made the task look easy. "I don't believe I've seen you before. Do you claim you know Belphegor?"

"Look here," said Shea. "I'm neither a Saracen nor a fowl, and I either married this girl or someone enough like her to be her twin sister. But she doesn't remember me."

"Daresay. It's a woman's privilege to forget, you know. They call it changing their minds, haw haw. But that's neither here nor there. We simply can't have you boffers from Carena running around and treating people the way Atlantès did this young lady. So you'd better stand and deliver an account of yourself if you want to keep that jolly head of yours."

Shea flared up. "Stand and deliver! Listen here, Dick Turpin, suppose *you* give *me*—"

"Dick Turpin? Wasn't he the highwayman chap from old England? Haw, haw, well said, oh. But I say, how would you know about him?"

"How would you?"

"We're asking the questions here, young fella. Belphegor, keep that arrow on him. Who—by Jove, don't tell me you're a wizard from my own universe, the one that's built around the British Isles?"

"I don't know how much of a wizard I'd rate, but I'm from there, all right. Only from the State of Ohio."

"American, as I live! Extrawdin'ry people, Americans—give me a million dollars or I'll cut your rug for a loop of houses, what? Isn't Ohio where the cinema colony is? Hollywood? No, that's in your province of Florida. Are you a gangster? I would say so, or you'd not be hand-in-glove with those paynims at Carena."

"I'm not a gangster and I keep telling you I'm not a Saracen. In fact if you'll step into the woods with me I'll prove it. These are only the clothes they gave me to put on," and Shea launched into a thumbnail sketch of his apportation.

"I say," said Astolph, "this chap Chalmers, your colleague, must be quite an adept. Don't know that I could do as well, though Malagigi could. Unfortunately they've laid him by the heels. Do you know my old friend Merlin?"

"You mean the famous one, the Welsh wizard? Is he still around?"

"Certainly. I meet him at the Sphinx Club in London. Do you know him?"

"I'm afraid I never met him personally."

Astolph's handsome face went a trifle grim. "That's unfortunate. Really, you know, with a war toward, we can't have strange wizards running around the borders of the Emperor Charles' dominions. Someone must vouch for you."

"There's Doc Chalmers."

"Another American. Doubtless another gangster."

"Echegaray."

"Atlantès' man. Come, you don't expect me to accept that, do you? Anything he said in your favor

310

would be a guarantee of bad faith, assuming you could get him to say anything."

"Well, there's Lord Roger. He won't say anything in my favor."

"A fool."

"I have a friend around here somewhere, who came with me—"

"Still another gangster! Really, old man, you're only making things worse. I can't let you go under the circumstances, and I can hardly use you as a prisoner for exchange, since there's no war as yet. So there's only one thing to do . . ."

Shea, perspiring at this reasoning, cried: "Belphebe!"

There was a frown of puzzlement on the girl's face, but she shook her head. "He has the proper figure of a man, but—my lord, I know him not."

"I have the high justice," said Astolph, as though that settled everything. "Kneel down."

"Damned if I do," said Shea, tugging at his sword and reckless of Belphebe's nocked shaft.

"Righto," said Astolph, making a restraining motion at the girl. "But half a tick. Are you base-born? Most Americans are."

"I'm not a duke or anything, but I've been made a knight, if that will do. By Sir Artegall of Faerie."

"Splendid. Ordeal of battle, and sound law, too. Only right to let a chap go out on his feet. Too bad you can't be shriven."

Shea got the sword out and shucked off his Muslim coats. As soon as he came within reach, Astolph took a stance, swung the big blade up, and struck down overhand with a wood-chopper's swing. Clang! Clang! Clang! Shea parried with the awkward blade, though the force of Astolph's stroke almost drove it from his hand. He took a backhand cut with it, which Astolph parried easily, then came back forehand, but his opponent jumped away with a lightness surprising in so big a man. His return was so rapid that he forced Shea to give ground.

The duke was good but not too good. After the third exchange Shea felt he could parry anything the big blade sent at him. However, the next clash brought a trickle of worry. Astolph's reach and length of blade were keeping him too far away for this clumsy weapon to be used as it was supposed to be used. If he could parry, he could not cut home, and in time the big man would wear him down.

Another whirl and he almost lost his sword. The handle was slippery in his grasp. He began to grow angry at the unfairness of this big lug, and with difficulty remembered that an angry fencer is a losing one.

Astolph drove him back again, almost into a tree, and lowered his blade for a second to get a better purchase. The sight of the exposed chest brought Shea's fencing reflexes to the surface. His right arm shot out, with the whole weight of his body behind it in a long lunge. The pounded point of the sword hit jacket and chest with a thump. Astolph, a little off balance and not expecting such a push, sat down.

"Yield thee yourself!" shouted Shea, standing over him and sighting on the Englishman's neck.

The duke's left arm came around like a jibing main boom and swept Shea's ankles from under him. Down went Shea. He was struggling in a bone-crushing wrestler's grip when he heard the girl cry: "Hold, enough! By the power of woods and water which is my domain, I bid you cease!"

Shea felt Astolph relax unwillingly and climbed to his own feet. A rill of blood trickled from the duke's nose where Shea had butted him, while Shea's turban was in his eyes, one of which was swelling, and the other end of the headdress was draped around him like one of Laocoön's serpents.

"I say, my dear," said Astolph, "you can't do this, you know. Ordeal of battle goes to a finish, and anything left of the loser has to be burned. I shall complain to the Emperor." He bent over, reaching for the big sword.

"Halt, sir! Would you try my bodkin?" She had drawn the tough shaft to the head and it pointed steadily at the big man's midriff. "I care not for the Emperor Charles of the Lord of Circassia in this domain. But I say this is a true man that has fought well, and that spared you when he might have slain, and be he Saracen or no, there shall henceforth be peace between you."

Astolph grinned and held out his hand to take Shea's in a hearty grip. "Needs must take the fortune of war. Jolly good thing you didn't make that hit with a pointed blade or I should have been properly skewered. I daresay you can show me a trick or two. Care to join forces?"

"I'm not sure," said Shea. "What kind of campaign do you have on?" He thought: if I can only get her to Chalmers, he can bring back her memory. In the meantime not all of Atlantès ifrits will pry me away from her.

"This bloody—excuse me, old girl—this Castle of Carena. Atlantès has Lord Roger in there, and there's a prophecy that our side can't win the war unless we convert him."

Shea snickered. "From what I've seen of that guy, I'd say you'd have a rough time converting him to anything he didn't want to do. He hasn't got enough mind to convert with."

Astolph waved a hand. "That's all right. He saw Bradamant, the lady warrior, you know, at the fountain of Love, and fell in love with her when he drank from it, so he can't do anything but what she wishes, at least until the spell is taken off. Atlantès was going to fly him to the Fountain of Forgetfulness, but I've bagged the mount."

A wave of relief swept over Shea. "You mean Bradamant is the lady warrior who is supposed to steal Roger from the Saracens? I was afraid—" and he gave a quick résumé of Chalmers' position with Florimel at Castle Carena, and why he had come hunting the big beef.

When he had finished, Belphebe said: "My lord duke, said I not it was a proper man? Sir, I thank you for your gentleness toward me; you may make me your devoirs." She whipped a knife like a steel sliver from her own belt and, taking down her cap, daintily split the feather in it along the middle, and handed Shea one half. "My favor."

313

Feeling awkward and a trifle confused, he tried to fix it in his breast. Silly, starting one of those formalized medieval courtships with its gambits and counters at this stage in their relationships . . .

Said Astolph: "So Roger's on the scram, as you fellas say? Very interesting; should have told me sooner. Stupid ass, Roger, though an awfully good fighter." He paused. "Do you know, this won't quite do, my friend. You and I are rivals in a sense. We both want Shaykh Roger, and for that matter so does the Lady Bradamant, though I really can't understand why. But I'll make you an armistice, matter to be decided by dicing, or whatever you say, but no magic. Are you genuinely a wizard, by the way?"

Shea looked down. "Not a very good one, I'm afraid."

"Come, young fella; no false modesty. Just cast me a little spell and demonstrate, so that we can have confidence in each other. Nothing like confidence, you know."

"Or leather either," said Shea. "It lasts." Belphegor-Belphebe was looking at him expectantly, and for his life he could not recall the passes of the somatic element that seemed so important in the magic of this space-time continuum. Wait a minute, though—there was the little spell Chalmers had used the other day to demonstrate that very point. The passes were simple and made a plant grow before the eyes; in Doc's case, a snapdragon. Grass would do to start with; it ought to make some kind of important-looking plant. Shea plucked a handful, laid it on the ground and knelt over it, closing his eyes in the effort of memory as he whispered:

"Though sore be my sowing,
    And more than ye know,
And the end of my growing
    Is only to grow;
Yet I cease not of growing for lightnings above
    me or death-worms below."

314

When he looked around again there was no sign of a plant. Nor any of the grass. He wondered what he had done wrong this time.

Astolph was looking straight at him. "By Jove! That's a neat bit, Sir Harold. Quite as good as Malagigi could have done. Apologies, old man."

"What is?" asked Shea. His voice sounded strangely muffled as though he were speaking through a blanket. Which, as he learned by putting his hand to his face, just what he was doing. His beard, sprouting at about an inch a second, had already spread down his chest and across his shoulders, the ends twisting and curling like the tips of thin and inquisitive worms. The beard passed his belt-line and engulfed his arms.

Frantically he tried to think of a counter-spell, and felt as though he were in Hell when the only thing he could remember was Chalmers' all-too-effective spell for raising dragons. Live dragons growing out of one's face, ugh! Or would it be snakes? The beard had passed his knees, his ankles, its questing points had reached the ground. Belphegor stared at him open-mouthed.

"Oh, bravo!" said Astolph.

The stuff was piling up on the ground in a little haycock. If it would only lay off a minute; give him a respite to think! He wondered desperately how long it would keep going if he failed to find the counter-spell. There was the mill that had ground the ocean full of salt. That might be legend, but in a universe where magic worked there was apparently nothing to stop such a process until coils of hair filled the forest and rose like a tide round the magic flames that now encircled the Castle of Carena. He stepped back, almost tripping over a root. If that pulsating hair got him down— But wait, maybe he could get Astolph to stop it. If the duke claimed Merlin as an acquaintance, he ought to know something of magic.

"Had enough?" he called over the growing mattress of wool to Astolph, whose head was now just visible.

"Thanks, yes."

"All right, fair's fair. Let's see you take the spell off."

"Righto." Astolph shifted his big sword to his left hand and swung it through the air, making a few expert passes with his right and mumbling a spell. The young mountain of first-rate upholstering-material vanished, and Shea tenderly felt his smooth cheeks. "You must meet Merlin some day," said the Duke. "Nobody likes a good joke like old Merlin. But I say, shall we get on with the business? Do you know, I believe the whole problem would become rather simple if we could get your friend out of Carena."

"I'm not sure he wants to get out," said Shea. "There's the question of Florimel."

"No trouble at all, old man. With a pair like you and your principal, we ought to be able to rescue Malagigi from Albracca, and it would be jolly odd if he couldn't do something for the lady. But I really don't see—" he went off into frowning concentration.

"What?" asked Shea.

"That wall of flame. Deuced awkward. That is, I know well enough how to deal with it, only we can't apply the solution."

"Sir Harold has been made immune to it," said Belphegor.

"Ah, but the problem is not smuggling him in, but getting this Lady—ah—Florimel out. It's this way, you see—" the big man turned to Shea with a wide gesture. "The Lady Bradamant owns a magical ring, very superior production, which protects one from any sort of enchantments, and also makes one invisible if taken into the mouth. If would be just the thing for your Florimel. Bradamant intended to use it to break into Carena for Roger, but she loaned it to Roland for no reason, and the silly beggar accidentally drank at the Fountain of Forgetfulness and lost his wits. Completely blotto. Can't remember where he put the ring or that there is a ring; can't even remember his name."

"I think I see," said Shea. "If we can get Roland to remember where the ring is, then one of us can extract Florimel from Carena and start all over again. But who's Roland? Is he important?"

"Really, old man! One of the twelve. The paladins. The companions of Emperor Charles. Best man of the lot in a fight."

"Oh," said Shea. The thought had occurred to him that this was not a problem in magic at all. Roland sounded like a fairly simple case of amnesia, and there was no reason why the techniques of the Garaden Institute should not work quite as well among these mountains as in Ohio. "I think I know a spell that will restore Roland's wits," he said. And if Roland's, he thought, why not Belphebe's? He must watch for a chance to try.

"Really? That would be wonderful. What do you say we go about it? Buttercup must be about somewhere." He put his forefingers in his mouth and whistled piercingly.

Something moved in the forest and a hippogriff trotted into view, wings folded neatly back against its flanks. The wings were mainly white with pulsations of rainbow hues flickering through them. The animal pricked up its ears as it came and poked at Astolph with its beak. He scratched among the roots of its feathers. "It answers me better than it ever did Atlantès," he said. "Those confounded Saracens don't know how to treat animals."

"What does it eat?" asked Shea practically. "I don't see how that eagle's head goes with a horse's digestive apparatus."

"Blooms from some of those African plants, I believe. Buttercup's not a heavy eater. Very well, everybody, all aboard! Bit crowded, what? What's that remark you Americans make when punching cattle? Brutal business that, by the bye; I never could see why you don't just herd the poor things instead of punching them. Oh, yes, yippee. *Yippee!*"

8

THE HIPPOGRIFF TROTTED SWAYINGLY UP A RISE.
Shea imagined that it would not be very fast on
the ground, thanks to the interference between the
magnified claws on the forefeet and the hooves behind. As they reached the granite hogback of the
crest, the claws clung securely enough to the rock, but
the hooves skidded alarmingly. Shea clutched
Belphebe-Belphegor around the midriff, and she
clutched Astolph, who did not seem at all perturbed.
The hippogriff spread its wings, blundered along the
ridge, flapping furiously, slipped again, teetered over a
fifty-foot drop, leaped into the air, swept down and
then up in a smooth curve that just missed the
treetops.

"Whew!" said Shea, the wind of the heights on his
face and a jellylike feeling in his center. "Sir Astolph,
I think your Buttercup should use a rocket-assisted
take-off."

"Wouldn't do, old man," said Astolph, over his
shoulder. "Laws of nature diff . . . frame of reference . . ." His words whirred away down the
wind of their passage as Shea reflected that according to the theory of dynamics, this beast wouldn't
even be able to get off the ground. The contact with
Belphebe sent tingles up his arms; he wanted to get
her away for a good long talk. She seemed unaware
of the emotion she was provoking.

The hippogriff apparently disliked the weight of
its triple load and at every clearing it sighted below,
tried to spiral in for a landing. Astolph had to bark
to keep it on course. After the third of these aborted
efforts, Shea saw a cleared area of some extent; the
details grew slowly to those of a small village with

thatched roofs, surrounded by a patchwork of planted fields, plowed ground and weedy meadow. The hippogriff, its horse end sweating, swooped eagerly down, skimmed the ground, pulled into a stall, and made a four-point landing that jarred Shea's teeth.

He climbed down and reached up a hand to help Belphebe, but she vaulted down without seeing him and he felt foolish. With the half-unconscious effort one makes to cover embarrassments, he swung toward the cottages, and as he did so, a chorus of screams burst from them. Men and women boiled out one after another, running for their lives. They were either deeply or suspiciously sunburned, and most wore nothing but long, dirty, ragged shirts. At the speed of their passage, they took no notice of hippogriff or riders.

After the spreading rout came two men. The shorter of the pair, a good-looking, youngish fellow with strong hands, seemed to be trying to pacify the other. The second individual wore the medieval-type garments with the hosen and the turned-up shoes that Shea had seen in Faerie, but with the laces of his jacket dangling. His face was unbarbered and his eyes roved. The fists waved in jerky motions; the voice growled.

"Upon my soul!" said Astolph. "Look here, you chaps, cheerio, and all that."

The shorter man gave a glance, waved a momentary hand, clamped a wrist-lock on the other and led him over to the newcomers. Shea perceived that the wild man would be handsome in a Latin sort of way if cleaned up.

"Greetings, most noble Astolph," said the short man, with as near an approach to a bow as he could manage with his grip on the other, "and to you, fair Belphegor, hail. The wrath is on our great companion once more; he had slain half the village, had I not let him. Yet in true gentilesse, the fault be not wholly his own."

"Indeed? Tell us about it, old man," said Astolph.

"Would you believe it, fair lady, and you, gentles? A hart of eight brought I home, as pricksome a bit of venison as ever a man saw before vespers. A

319

meal for the Emperor's own majesty, one might think; make it a pie, or what will you? Nay, these base varlets must even serve it up boiled, as though 'twere salt stockfish in Lent. I gagged, but our friend Roland put down the first two bites fairly enough. At the third, meseems he must have recovered a whit of the laws of cookery, for he gave a great howl like a lion and set upon the knaves, beating in their heads with his fists. But alas, to what purpose? Not even a crack will let savor into such skulls."

He looked round the group and his eye came to rest on Shea. "A paynim, ha! I thank you, Lord Astolph; a cut from his haunch will recompense me my venison." He gave a barking laugh to demonstrate that this was meant for humor. Shea smiled dutifully.

"Ah—er—" said Astolph. "Lord Reinald of Montalban, may I present to you Sir Harald de Shea? A johnny from England—that is, from one of our subject allies." He swung to Shea. "I'd be glad to present you to Count Roland d'Anglante, except that as you see, the poor lad wouldn't recognize you." The Count, who was apparently the wild man, was alternately sucking one finger and tapping the end of it in the palm of the hand on which Lord Reinald retained his grip. It seemed to provide him with deep satisfaction. "Sir Harold is also looking for Roger of Carena. Small world, isn't it?"

"The chase is like to be longer than that for Angelica," said Reinald, reaching his free hand inside his jacket and producing something which Shea did not quite make out to kiss before he went on. "We have it on the word of the kerns that Sir Roger passed through at spark of dawn, moving as though Saint Beelzebub were on his slot."

"Really, old man!" cried Astolph. "I must be losing my grip; to hear that he slipped past my watch is more startling than your canonization of Beelzebub."

Reinald shrugged and resisted a sudden jerk by his companion. "Let buy a candle for Lucifer, then. The thing's established—would you doubt my word?"

"No, but—look, here, old man, it's rather important for the Emperor. Whyn't you stop him?"

"Can a man live forever like a priest? Roland

slept; I tied him to a rafter and sought a damsel who had made certain signs by the fountain."

"How perfectly rotten of you!" cried Astolph. "What the devil did you funk the job for?"

Reinald grimaced. "Angelica lost, and fair Belphegor drives me to a distance with arrows sharper than Saint Cupid's own. What's left of life?"

There seemed not much more to say. They walked back toward the village, Astolph fingering his chin. He looked up to remark: "Do you know, I believe Sir Roger will head west, then double back to join Agramant's army. Sort of thing he would consider the height of cleverness." He turned to Shea. "Your gangster friend with the odd name won't find him. That direction would be the double bluff."

He paused and, pulling the hippogriff's head down to his lips, said something in its ear that sounded like a series of low-toned whistles. The animal cocked an intelligent eye at him and stood still.

Among the huts a table stood under a tree, and on it lay two large wooden plates heaped with boiled meat which gave off a powerful odor of garlic and was framed in congealing grease. There were no other plates in sight, nor anything to drink.

While the others waited politely Reinald went from door to door, shouting in each without result, then returned, shaking his head gloomily. "The rats have fled the larder," he said. "Beyond the mind of reasonable man to riddle out. Sir Harold, how wags it in your country? Would not men without number be glad and overglad to have lords of Charles' own court to hold them from harm?"

Shea raised his eyebrows. "It couldn't be that they're afraid of your friend's tempers?"

"Think you so, indeed?" Reinald's eye brightened and he nodded his head as though something new and important had come into his life. "They be base-born enough. Three or four has he slain, but no more; and even those without pretension to gentle blood. It might be, though; fear of death is ever dreadful to those who know it not for a mocker. A mystery."

The five made room on a couple of rough-hewn

benches and divided the meat with knives supplied by Reinald and Astolph, washing it down with water from the village well, drunk from the bucket. Shea hoped that the fauna of this continuum did not include typhoid germs, the back of his mind assuring him comfortingly that the deadliest disease present would probably be African fever induced by night air. All the same when he noticed a crawfish clinging to the moss inside the bucket, he and the crawfish pointedly ignored each other.

Reinald gnashed his teeth across a bone and addressed Astolph: "Start we tonight or attend the Lady Bradamant, the mirror of true valor?"

Said Astolph: "I don't really believe we gain anything by a night march, do you? After all, it will be hard going with Count Roland in such a state, and we shan't really lose anything, since I doubt if Roger is up to a night march. Up with the birds, then . . . but wait a tick. Our young friend here is a jolly good qualified magician, and says he knows a spell to bring Roland's wits back."

Reinald crossed himself. "Holy Saint Virgil, protect us! Those wits lost to black Mahound!"

"Would simplify—"

Count Roland, who had been slobbering over his meat, suddenly turned round to look at Shea and said in a loud, clear voice: "You Saracen! I slay you!" and leaped from his place, trotting around the table with dirty hands outstretched.

"Get him—" yelled Astolph, as the others scrambled to their feet, but the latter was upon Shea before he could more than get on his feet. He did the only thing he could think of at the moment to save his neck without bringing the others down upon him; viz, ducked, knocked the clutching right hand up with his own left and dug his own right with all his strength into the Count's belly. It was like punching a truck-tire, but Roland staggered two steps, almost upset the table, sat down with a fishlike expression spreading across his face, as he recovered his breath, began to cry.

Shea, shaking his hand to get the tingle out of his knuckles, almost laughed at the sight of Reinald's open

322

mouth. "By my halidome!" said the paladin. "A rude stroke was that."

"Oh, yes," said Astolph. "Quite good at the thrust, this young fella; nearly gutted me like a bird a bit back. If you ever fight him, Lord Reinald, guard against that straight lunge. Now look here, I think we can reach an agreement. Sir Harold, I take it, only wants Roger to exchange him for a brace of friends, now in durance in Castle Carena, where that blighter Atlantès is holding them in chancery. If he can restore Roland's wits for us, I say that with three paladins, we ought to be able to set him on the right track."

Reinald blinked once or twice in a way Shea found not altogether pleasing. "The Lady Bradamant would stand our certain aid, I doubt not," he said. "Is aught of philosophical apparatus required for your enchantment, Sir Harold?"

"No-o-o. Not that I know of; unless you have a nightlight."

"That wot I not of; but since there be no bar and our composition waits but on your action, speed on. It is good law that the vavassour render his service before he have his sustention."

Shea looked at Belphegor (whom he insisted upon calling Belphebe in his mind), but she was looking in the other direction, after a single glance. He was not at all sure that he understood what Reinald was saying and he would much rather have a tête-à-tête with his wife, but as near as he could make out, the two paladins were making a deal with him to get Doc and Florimel out of Castle Carena if he got Count Roland out of what seemed to be a case of simple throwback amnesia. He sighed and addressed himself to the task by turning toward the still softly sniffling paladin:

"There, there, that didn't really hurt much, did it? But when little boys are bad, they have to learn . . ." Belphegor's mouth fell open a little as he droned on, but the wild man looked at Shea interestedly, then suddenly seized him around the neck and implanted a greasy kiss on his cheek.

Reinald laughed openly; Astolph seemed to have

some difficulty in controlling his breath for a moment and announced that he was for bed. Shea turned toward the pale blue eyes now fixed on his in adoration.

"Want a story?" he asked. "If you'll come along I'll tell you one about three—dragons." The pattern seemed simple; age was suppressed beyond about a three-year-old level. He said rapidly over his shoulder to the others: "This is going to take some time, if the spell will work at all. You-all will have to get away from here and wait a while. I could use insulin shock, but that piece of philosophical apparatus isn't around, so I'll probably have to work half the night by my own method."

They went, willingly enough and yawning under the declining light. Roland listened with interest to the story of the three bears, translated into dragons, and demanded more. "No," said Shea. "You tell me a story instead, 'cause it's way past my bedtime. Then I'll tell you one."

Roland laughed delightedly. "They're all silly go-to-bed-earlies. What 'tory you want?"

"Well, tell me who you are."

"I'm me."

"Sure. You live in a cave, don't you?" Bits of the *Orlando Furioso* were floating through Shea's head; or was it the *Chanson de Roland*? He wished he could get them straight, but seemed to be doing all right so far, since his patient remained attentive. "And your mother's name is Madame Bertha. But what does she call you?"

"Gay-gay. That means 'snookums,' an' it's white and red."

Shea grunted internally. This mass of muscle, hair and dirt was about as far from a snookums as he could conceive. But at least the white and red was a tiny advance; those were Roland's colors. That was in the book. "What else do they call you?"

"Ruffy."

Not much there. "What's your father like?"

A pout. "Don't know. Gone to fight Saxons."

"Didn't he come back?"

The heavy face became woebegone. "Don't know."

"Yes, you do. No tell, no story."

Roland began to sniffle a little and Shea did not altogether blame him. It must have been pretty rough to move out of a castle into a cave where you didn't get enough to eat. But he was inexorable; Roland finally stopped sniffling and remarked: "Mama said he gained glory, and the syndics said we mustn't live there any more, and I was cold and had a fight and saw a fat man sitting in an inn and somebody blew a music and I don't like it here and I'm hungry."

The ice was beginning to crack. Shea felt a jump of joy in his heart and looked around for Belphegor, but she had vanished. With elaborately affected scorn, he said: "I know a better story than that."

"You do not, either! The fat man was a crowned king, and he was my mama's brother . . ."

A solemn moon came up and winked through the leaves, then settled slowly toward disappearance-point again as Shea desperately flogged his own memory and the paladin's on the details of the vanished career. Once he thought he was going to lose his man, when Roland mentioned the name of Angelica, put down his head and wept for quite five minutes; once he thought all would come clear at once, when Shea threw in the name of the giant Ferragus, and the paladin seized a bone from the table, leaping up and shouting "Montjoie!" But that one only collapsed into babbling. It must have been well past midnight, a poor hour for this country, when Roland once more got to his feet, and pressed the heels of both palms to his eyes.

"Sir," he said, "I know not your name aright nor true condition, and I am hindered from giving you the kiss of peace, since I perceive my own condition is less than that which knight and gentleman should hold. You have my favor; are you a necromancer?"

"I suppose I know something about magic," said Shea, suddenly feeling modest.

"I trust your penance will be small. There be others of our brotherhood about, an I mistake not?"

He looked toward where the moon was losing its struggle. "Let us seek them; I see it all, we must seek mount and away for time will press. Is the Lady Bradamant among them?"

9

THE LADY BRADAMANT WAS NOT IN THE HEADMAN'S house where Duke Astolph and Reinald were laid out with straw in their ears, the latter on his back and snoring like a Diesel engine. What was more important for Shea, neither was the Lady Belphegor. He felt defeated, but Count Roland was quite evidently not of the same mind.

"Ho!" cried that worthy paladin, in a voice that would have made the windowpanes shake if there had been any windowpanes. "Will you lie slugabed when there are deeds to do? Rouse out, I say!"

In the dimness of the hut, Shea saw Astolph roll over, swinging his arms. Reinald's snores checked for one moment, then began again in a higher key.

"Ha, rouse!" Roland shouted again, and somewhat unexpectedly, deposited a resounding kick on the recumbent form as Astolph came up, all standing. Reinald whipped up, light as a cat, one hand to his belt, and Shea caught a gleam of steel, but Roland laughed and extended both arms: "Nay, nay, my noble lord and brave friend, will you slit my weazand while still the paynim danger lies on France?"

Reinald relaxed with a growl. Astolph threw a branch on the dying fire, and as it blazed up, looked keenly into Roland's face. "I believe he's all right again," he remarked.

"Aye, my own man; grace to this young knight." Roland swung toward Shea. "Sir Harold, were I not sworn to poverty, the treasures of Babylon would be too small for your reward. Yet know that you have all my heart and true support in whatsoever shall not run counter to my knightly vow of fealty to the Emperor Charles. I have the ring. And now gentles, we must out and away." He cocked his head on one side. "Hark, I hear the shrill trumpet!"

"Then the trumpeter will have outwatched the bear," said Reinald, dryly. "Look you, good Roland, this quest of Roger gains naught by a night-march while we have Astolph, who can ride after him by day on the wings of the wind. Take then your rest; with the dawn we'll woo fortune."

"He's quite right, you know," said the Duke through a yawn. "Besides, I daresay you could do with a bath and some weapons before undertaking anything serious, and tonight there's precious little chance of your getting—"

He stopped, looking over Shea's shoulder, and the latter turned with a jump of the heart to see standing in the low doorway—Belphegor, arrow on string and the firelight throwing lovely shadows on her face.

She came a couple of paces into the room. "I heard the bruit, my lords, and thought—"

Said Reinald: "That there was something toward which might permit that after all you should take comfort in my arms?"

"Nay, my lord, I sleep lonely this night—and every other, where you're involved." She returned her arrow to its quiver and relaxed the string.

"Hey!" said Shea. "I want to see you." If that antiquated technique could work such wonders on Roland, there was better than a good chance that—

The girl inclined her head gravely. "Sir knight, you have made me your service. You may see me to my rest."

"Where is it?" he asked, as they reached the door.

"I have made my bed in the branches of an oak that overlooks these cots," she said. "My lonely bed."

Shea smiled a narrow little smile. "Mean to say you positively, positively don't remember being my wife?" and thinking that at best he'd probably have to break her of claustrophobia all over again. Being married to a girl who wouldn't sleep in a bed, he had found, was an experience that did not grow on one with repetition.

She drew away from him a little. "Now, sirrah, seek you to cozen me again? Certes, you'd be a more adroit seducer than yonder lord of Montalban, but I'll not be seduced."

Shea grinned. "I should hope not by that big lug, anyway. But say, don't you remember things?"

"Nay—that water of Forgetfulness whereof he drank have I never seen. I am free of the forests . . . and yet, and yet—there is a passage. I know not how I came to Castle Carena, save that I stood within beside a gray-haired wizard whom they called Sir Reed and his fair bride—ah, faugh!" She made a gesture of disgust.

"What's the matter with Sir Reed?"

"Not he, but that great loutish booby of a Roger. It had been insupportable but for the visit of Lord Dardinell and his squire Medoro."

"Huh?" said Shea in alarm. "What about this Medoro?"

"A most sweet lad. He took my part when all the others would have trapped me like a hare. Could I but count that he'd be more true to me than to a religion that bids him keep four wives—"

"My God, you can't do that!" cried Shea. "That's bigamy! Maybe I'd better—"

"Sir, you lose my favor when you still hold to the old tune like a musician who has only one note."

"Oh, all right, all right. Honest, darling, I'm only trying—well, skip it. How did you get out?"

"How—? Oh, one of the men there leaned on a staff, so I borrowed it from him, clouted a couple of pates, and it was ho!—and away."

"Didn't they chase you?"

"Marry, that they did, but I am somewhat lightfoot." (Shea could believe that. Looking at her hungrily as she paused under the big oak, he could remember her in a red bathing suit, easily outdistancing himself and a squad of friends along the beach of Lake Erie.)

"Okay. Now to go back a little. You don't remember meeting Reed Chalmers and me in Faerie by shooting a Losel that was after us? And you don't remember joining us in the campaign against the Enchanters' Chapter? Or that fight in the air with Busyrane on his dragon?"

"No. Should I? These names have a barbarous, outlandish sound to me."

"You certainly should remember, and you should remember some other things, too," he said, grimly.

"I think I can—"

"Put a spell upon me to work me to your will? Nay, I will assuredly contempt you from my grace, though I bade you accompany me that I might do you service."

"I'm sorry. Honest." (Shea wondered whether he ought to get down on one knee and kiss her hand, but decided he'd be damned first.)

She reached out one hand and touched his arm. "So. Well, the service is yours in any case—not for the pretty apology, but because we of the woods love not injustice."

"What injustice?"

"Think you you have a true composition with these lords? Then think again. Duke Astolph may be moderate well affected toward you, but not Lord Reinald, who holds it lawful to deceive and despoil all Saracens, among which he'd place yourself and all your friends."

Shea grinned. "I imagined they might be trying to clear out. But I'll be watching."

"Small service will that be. Astolph is to cast a spell of deep sleep on you tonight and they depart at dawn. He offered to take me and make me his leman, but I'd have none of him."

"The—excuse me for what I'm thinking. I thought Astolph was on the square."

"Oh, aye; a good wight, surely. But wrapped in law, like all the English, and when Lord Reinald spoke of his liege duty to the Emperor, and how with Roger beyond the castle, the victory of Christendom would be delayed by contention with you for his body— why then, Duke Astolph let himself be overborne."

Shea mused. "Will Roland let them get away with

329

it? He seemed grateful enough when I saw him, and he certainly owed me a favor."

Belphegor laughed tinklingly. "I give him not a fig's weight—oh, a most accomplished gentle knight that will swoon devotion like a rose, but will set duty to the Emperor and his war above all else, even more than Duke Astolph. Has he found the Lady Bradamant's ring?"

"He said so."

"Then even more. For look you, this Castle Carena is a haunt of paynim sorcery and nest of vipers, which being entered by the power of the ring, Roland would destroy and hold it for the day's best deed."

It was probably true. Shea remembered that the Count had made a reservation in favor of the Emperor in his promise of gratitude. "I guess I'm stuck with finding Roger on my own, then," he said, a little sadly. "What are you going to do?"

"I? In sooth, live my free life of the woods and fountains, sobeit Medoro . . . Since Roger's free of the castle, I hold myself free of my promise to help Duke Astolph hale him forth."

"Why not help me find Roger then?"

"Wherefore should I?"

Shea felt his throat dry up. "Oh, to help beat injustice, or just for the fun of the adventure . . . or something." He finished lamely, then went on again. "After all, you did promise to help Astolph."

"Ah, sir, but a debt lay there. It was Astolph and none other who turned the pursuit from Castle Carena when they would have taken me with horse and hound."

"What! You didn't tell me that." Shea felt a homicidal impulse toward Sir Reed Chalmers, who hadn't told him, either. Sir Reed, evidently felt that he'd put his foot into it about as far as he cared to.

"Aye; slew one of the Saracens and scattered the rest. But come, sir, you impose sleepless hours upon me to no purpose. You must find me an acuter reason, if I am to join your search for this Roger."

"Well—he'll head for the Saracen camp to get into the war, won't he. You might find—Medoro—there."

330

"Oh, fie, Sir Harold! Would you have me pursue a man like that great, buxom warrior-wench, the Lady Bradamant? You think but ill of those to whom you pay your devoirs. . . . Not that you are wrong as to the fact; poet though he be, Medoro will hardly neglect the summons of the trumpet at such an hour. Nay, your reason is against companioning with you for a search in that quarter. Now I must have a new one, doubly strong."

So, the dope's a poet, is he? thought Shea. "I don't know any more reasons," he said stoutly. "Except that just I want you to come along because I love you."

Belphegor-Belphebe caught her breath for one second, then extended her hand. "So you have found the key at last, and are my true knight. It is covenanted. I give you rendezvous at this spot, so soon as the paladins be again in slumber. Now go, ere stark suspicion o'er-spread their minds."

"What shall we do? Steal their horses?"

"Nay, the hippogriff? And Roland's steed is the great Bayard, who'd rouse his master on the instant."

"Oh, damn. I know a man named Bayard, but he'll never wake anybody up. What else—?"

"Go, sir, I said. Nay, no embraces."

"Good-night," said Shea, and made for the hut, feeling a tremulous half-hope such as he had not known since they were both prisoners of the Da Derga in Faerie.

He found the three squatting around the small fire on a hearth in the center of the floor. A hole in the ceiling above let out about a third of the smoke.

Astolph stretched, yawned, and with the air of a man preparing for a long sleep, began carefully unwinding his red-blue-brown scarf. Catching Shea's eye fixed on him, he remarked "School" briefly, then: "One can't exactly wear a tie in this country, you know. I had the colors made into a scarf instead."

"What school is it for?"

"Winchester," said the Duke, with just the right note of pride. "Oldest of 'em all, you know. Merlin's on the board of trustees. Wonderful thing, the public school system, though I don't know what will become of it with all this Socialism."

"I went to a public school in Cleveland myself."

"I daresay." Astolph regarded him with an air redolent of mistrust, and Shea perceived he had not taken the right way to influencing people. Before he could smooth matters out, Reinald lifted his head from where he was already down in the straw again: "Peace, you twain! A pox on your babble that keeps honest men from their rest."

"Righto. But first I fancy I'd better make certain Sir Harold here doesn't wipe us in the eye. Oh, you're a man of honor and a jolly good fellow, but this is merely a sensible precaution." Astolph had reached his feet as lightly as a cat while speaking and picked up the big sword, which he now pointed at Shea. "Lie quietly, old thing and take your medicine."

"You lie on a blanket of cloud, soft and white,
And you sleep, sleep, sleep through the murmur-
      ing night,
Your limbs are so heavy, your eyelids must close,
You're torpid, you're drowsy; you loll, drift, and
      doze—"

Shea, fully aware that this was a sleeping-spell, fought to keep his mind alert while casting about for a counter-spell. There was the one with the paper . . . no, that was a weakless spell . . . no . . . his thoughts were losing coherency.

"Come, ye spirits who generate pandiculation
And your brothers who revel in wide
      oscitation—"

The spell corresponded to something like hypnotism, and it was hard to keep his eyes from the tips of Astolph's fingers, moving in the passes. It was almost not worth the trouble of trying to beat it. After all . . .

"Come Morpheus hither, and Somnus and
        Coma—"

There was a story where you mustn't sleep. *King
of the Golden River?* No . . . *Kim*—and the boy
there had used the multiplication table. The memory
jerked him to effort. Three times three is nine . . .
if he could only keep on . . . this part was too
easy . . . six times seven is forty-two, six times eight
. . . The spell droned on, apparently without end . . .
eleven times thirteen is one hundred forty-three . . .

    "I by this authority conjure you, sleep!"

It was over. Shea lay with his eyes closed, but
his brain wide open, working on seven times fourteen. Reinald's voice came drowsily, as though the
paladin were talking through fur: "Will he sleep till
the morrow?"
    "Through several morrows, I should say," said As-
tolph. "I gave him a jolly good dose."
    "Almost put me to sleep myself," said Reinald.
He rolled over once, and in less than a minute was
back in the low-register snore that had preceded Roland's kick.
    Shea waited, wishing his nose would stop itching,
or that Astolph would quiet down next to him, so
he could scratch without being caught at it. His
eyebrow began to itch, too, then the rest of his face
in patches, so agonizingly that he wriggled it, trying
to throw off the feeling. Astolph turned over and
Shea froze into immobility, wondering whether a
snore would be convincing, decided against it and discovered that the itch had shifted to a point inside
his left ear. The Duke made another turn, loosed
a sigh of comfort and seemed to drift off. But it
was a good ten minutes—every one of which Shea
counted—before he dared to let his eyelids flicker
open.
    There was a small red glow at the center of the
room and an oblong of gray that was the door. Beyond, he judged it would be near the hour of false

dawn; the moon had long since disappeared. The three figures in the draw made darker blacks in the blackness of the hut, but lay perfectly still. Under the beat of Reinald's snores the rhythmic breathing of the other two was audible. Asleep all right, but he could not afford to take chances, therefore gave it another good ten minutes before stirring an experimental arm. The dark gray patch of the door turned abruptly bright blue, then dark gray again. Far away, thunder purred softly.

Shea thought a few unpleasant things about his luck and the weather. If the storm came this way, it would rain through that hole in the roof, certainly rousing Astolph and probably Roland. If he were to make a getaway, it would have to be right now.

He moved his hands slowly in the straw beside him, gathering up his turban, which had been serving as a pillow, and his sword. At the next rumble, he rolled to his feet, took two cautious steps and lifted his flowing outer garments from the peg where they had hung. The next two steps took him out.

A flash showed a huge pile of thunderheads nearby and the sound came long-continued, rolling closer. A little puff of wind whirled down the village street. The hippogriff was huddled where Astolph had left it, squatted head down and eyes closed. It trembled unhappily in the lightning flashes, its feathers stirring in the vagrant dashes of wind. When Shea touched it, the beast, bound by the Duke's magic, did not lift its head. To loose the spell on it would take fooling around, time, and maybe more skill than he had. The first drop struck his hand.

A brilliant flash and an avalanche of thunder. Shea, thinking he had heard a shout from the direction of the headman's house, whipped the jelab around him and ran just as the rain came pattering down, heading without equivocation along the street and toward Belphebe's tree. As he reached the edge of the forest shade, she stepped out before him, as wide-awake as an owl, unperturbed by the rushing rain.

"Did they—" she said; a crash of thunder drowned the rest.

334

"I think the storm woke them up," said Shea, shedding his outer cloak and hanging it around her. "How are we going to get out of here?"

"You an enchanter and know not this?" She laughed gaily, turned and whistled a low, lilting tune in a minor key, less than a third audible under the pattering leaves and whipping branches.

Shea strained his eyes toward the village and in the repeated lightning-glare, was sure he saw figures moving. "Hurry," he said. Then he heard a trampling behind and a voice shouted "Whee-he-he-he! Who calls?" Almost instantly it was answered by another and higher one: "Who calls?"

"Bel—Belphegor of the woods—a daughter of—" her voice seemed to check oddly.

"In whose name call you us?" bellowed the first voice."

"In the name of Sylvanus, Ceres, and the Fountain of Grace."

"What desire you?"

"To be carried faster and farther than man can run or beast gallop."

The trampling sounds closed in. Shea smelled damp horse, and the next flash showed that the voices belonged to centaurs, led by one with a grizzled beard. He said: "Belphegor of the mountains, we know you by all names, but who is this? Is it our mission to carry him as well?"

"Aye."

"Is he an initiate in the mysteries of wood, wold and fountain?"

"Nay, not that I wot on. But that am I, and he a friend in need."

"Whee-he-he-he! We are forbid by an oath more dreadful than death to take none but those who have reached the degree of the three great mysteries."

"Hey!" shouted Shea. Another flash had shown him the three paladins, leading their mounts more accurately in his direction than one would have believed possible. "What's this? Those lugs'll be here in a couple of minutes."

"There be rituals and vows through which all must

335

pass who seek to live by the forest ways, Sir Harold," said Belphegor. "A thing of many days."

"Okay, skip it. I'll shin up a tree and hide."

"Nay, not from Duke Astolph's magic. One blast of that great horn, and you'd come tumbling like a ripened nut. Will you stand, then? My bow is useless in this wet, but we have made compact, you and I, and will guard your bare side with my hunting knife."

"It won't work, kid," said Shea, "even though it is damn white of you." The pursuers were a bare two hundred yards away. Astolph had the big sword out, and the lightning-flash was reflected from it. Then inspiration reached him. "Wait a minute, I used to be a boy scout, and I had to pass an examination and take vows for that. Would that get me by?"

"What says he?" asked the bearded centaur. "I know not the chapter, yet—" Shea snapped out a brief account of the organization and the merit badge he had won in woodcraft, looking over his shoulder. Two or three centaur heads came together, and the bearded one returned. "It is believed, that we can lawfully take you, man, though this is the first we hear of such wonders, and your craft be that of the small things. Mount!"

Before he had finished the sentence, Belphegor had vaulted lightly onto his back. Shea scrambled somewhat less gracefully onto the back of the other centaur, finding it wet and slippery.

"Ayoi! Ready, brother?" asked Shea's mount, pawing with its front feet.

"Ready. Whee-hee-hee!"

"Whee-he-he-he!" The centaur began to bounce, and as Shea, unused to this kind of ride, wiggled on its back, turned around: "Put your arms around me and hold on," it said.

Shea nearly released his grip in surprise as the first long bound was taken and a shout came from behind. It was a female centaur.

He looked over his shoulder. The last flash showed the pursuing paladins before they were hidden among the trees. The hippogriff, its feathers bedraggled, looked more melancholy than ever, and its expression would remain with him all his days.

10

THE CENTAURS HALTED UPON A SMOOTH KNOLL. BE-
hind them rose the slopes of the western Pyrenees,
and before them the country rolled and flattened
away into the high plateau of Spain. The sun was just
pinking the crests.

"Here we rest," said Belphegor's centaur. "We
cannot take you further, for lo! the Amir's camp is
in sight, and our forests lie behind."

Shea slid off—legs stiff, eyes red, behind feeling as
though it had been paddled, and teeth as furry as
chows. Belphegor came down lightly on the balls of
her feet, increasing Shea's already vast admiration for
his wife. They thanked the centaurs, who waved farewell and galloped off as though their all-night run had
been merely a warm-up, sending their "Whee-he-he-
he!" after the travellers.

Shea turned in the other direction and shaded his
eyes. Through the early-morning haze he could just
see a village with white walls and flat roofs three
or four miles off. And away beyond it, a patch of
little tan humps would be the tents of Agramant,
Commander of the Faithful.

Shea gave Belphegor a long, searching look, not-
ing how fresh she seemed after an all-night ride.

"Is it the chivalry of your land to stare?" she
asked coolly.

"Sorry. I was just wondering what made you sort
of—hold up and change your mind about your name.
Last night, when the centaurs asked you."

A tiny frown appeared between her brows. "I
sooth, I know not. 'Twas as though a veil were drawn,
and I swam between worlds with my tongue framing
words spoken by another."

"I can clear that up so it won't happen again."

"Nay, no more of your spells, Sir Magician. I lay it upon you as a condition of this adventure we undertake, that you attempt no enchantments on me for whatever purpose." She looked at him earnestly, but her regard faded into a small yawn.

"Oh—all right," said Shea ruefully. "Wouldn't take much of an enchantment to put you to sleep though, now would it?"

"Marry, that shaft is not far from the clout. Could I but find a grove!" She looked around. "But this country is bare as a priest's poll."

"Shucks, why don't you try sleeping in a bed again?"

"Again? I have never—"

Shea suppressed a grin. "Sure, sure, I know. But lots of people do without dying of it, you know, and it even gets to be fun after a while." He looked towards the village. "There ought to be an inn in that town, and we'll have to go there anyway if we're going to stand any chance of finding Roger."

Amiably doubtful, she fell in beside him as he led the way down the slope to where a track took them toward the village. The matter still hung in abeyance when they reached the place, which did have an inn. This was a small house that differed from the private dwellings only by having a dry bush affixed over the door.

Shea banged with the hilt of his sword. Above, the shutters of a window swung outward. A villainous-looking head peered out to look in astonishment at the unshaven man in Saracen costume and the red-golden-haired girl with a longbow. Presently the proprietor appeared at the door, scratching himself under a leather jerkin whose laces were not yet tied. The request for breakfast and lodging seemed to depress him.

"O lord of the age," he said, "know that neither in this village nor for miles around is there so much food as would satisfy a sparrow, save in the camp of the Amir Agramant, on whose sword be blessings."

"Heigh-ho," said Belphegor, "then sleep we supless and dine our souls on dreams." She yawned again.

338

The innkeeper looked more lugubrious. "On my head and eyes, Allah preserve me from your displeasure, lady; but there is lacking in my poor house a place where such a moon of delight as yourself may companion with her lord. For behold, I have neither secluded alcoves nor a bath for the performance of the Wuzu ablution."

The girl's foot began to tap dangerously. However, Shea averted the storm by saying: "Don't let it worry you. We really want to sleep; and besides we're Christians, so the bath doesn't matter."

The landlord looked at him with an expression of cunning. "O man, if ye indeed be Christians, then there is nothing for it but you must pay ten dirhams before entering, for such is the regulation of the prince of the place, who is none other than that light of Islam, the Lord Dardinell."

Shea hearing the girl catch her breath slightly, remembered that Dardinell was the name of the man who had brought the poetic Medoro to her attention. It also occurred to him that the innkeeper was probably lying, or creating him, or both. To these peasant-village characters, a member of an out-group was fair game. . . . Shea, becoming annoyed, reached into the twist of the cloth belt where he had put the remainder of the coins Chalmers had given him. He pulled out a handful—a small handful.

"Listen, pickle-puss," he said menacingly, "I haven't got time to argue with you, and the lady is tired. You take these and give us a place to sleep, or you can take a piece of this." He indicated the sword.

"Hearing and obedience," mumbled the innkeeper, dropping back a couple of steps. "Enter, then, in the name of Allah the Omnipotent."

The entry was dark and somewhat smelly, with a set of stone steps going up to the right. The innkeeper clapped his hands twice. A door opened at the rear, and a very black Negro, so small as to be a dwarf, and naked to the waist, scuttled in. He grinned from ear to ear, and the speed with which he came suggested that he had overheard some of the conversation. The innkeeper did not seem to like his cheerfulness, for he fetched the dwarf a crack on

339

the ear that sent him spinning against the wall, and said: "O miserable buffoon, cease from mockery! You shall conduct these guests to the upper room and provide them with coffee of the night, as is the custom, for they have been long abroad and desire to sleep the day."

The dwarf got up, rubbing ear and cheek with one hand, and wordlessly motioned Belphegor and Shea up the stairs. The room at the top ran the whole width of the inn. It held ten beds like very low couches, only a few inches off the floor and covered with thin and moth-eaten Oriental rugs.

Belphebe looked at them with distaste. "Sir Harold, I know not how men can bear such shabby habitation, when they may live among clean trees."

She began to pace the floor, looking out of one window after another.

"It could be better," Shea admitted. "But anyway, we won't get rained on. Come on, kid, try it for once."

He yawned. The dwarf came trotting upstairs with a brass tray holding two little cups from which floated the appetizing smell of coffee. He set it on one of the beds, then bowed low. More out of the habit of tipping then anything else, Shea fumbled one of the odd-shaped coins and held it out. The little black man half-reached toward it, looking at Shea's face as though he suspected him of playing a joke in questionable taste.

"Go on, take it," said Shea. "It's for you. Honest."

With a snatch it was in the dwarf's hands, and he rolled over and over, holding the precious thing before his eyes and gurgling with delight. Shea picked up the coffee and took a long pull, then almost gagged. It was so cloyingly sweet as to be almost syrup. He asked Belphegor: "Is all the coffee like that around here?"

" 'Tis coffee. What else would you have?" she said, sipping her own.

"Why, you know how I like . . ." He checked himself; no use starting the same old argument with a real amnesiac, and it would only antagonize her. He amended: "I'd have a lot else. Hey, George!"

The dwarf, having ceased his antics, came trotting over to duck his head three times. Shea asked: "Have you got any of this stuff without sugar in it?"

The servitor seemed to be overtaken by some inner ill, for he put both hands to his belly and rocked from side to side, pointed to the cups and put both hands beneath one ear, then closed his eyes; jumped up, ran to the window and went through the motion of leaping out, then pointed to Shea.

"What's the matter?" asked Shea. "Can't you say anything?"

For answer the little man only opened his mouth and pointed again. He had no tongue.

"That's too bad, George." Shea turned to the girl. "What's he trying to put over?"

She gave a tired little laugh. "Meseems he would convey that this be a brew so potent another cup would make one leap from a height. Marry, the one will not affect me so." She set down her cup, raised a small hand over another yawn, picked out one of the less dirty beds, and stretched out on it.

"Me, either," said Shea. It was too much trouble to argue. He stretched out on another; it might be straw under the disintegrating rugs, but his weary muscles found it softer than down. "Sweet dreams, kid." At least the fact that there was a multitude of beds precluded any silly arguments about laying his sword down the middle, as in the medieval romances. Though if a man were too feeble to climb over. . . .

Just as he was whirling down into the pool of sleep it occurred to him that maybe the dwarf was trying to let them know that the coffee was doped, but he forgot before he could do anything about it. . . .

Somebody was shaking him, and the side of his face stung with the memory of a slap. That goddam innkeeper! "Lay off!" he growled, his head fuzzy, and wriggled from the grasp. Slap!

This was too much. Shea rolled to his feet and started to swing; or tried to, for his arms were instantly pinioned from behind. Clearing eyes showed that he was in the center of a circle of armed Saracens. In another and larger group, some of whom turned as he came erect, he caught the sheen of Belphegor's bright hair, now mussed. Two of them were holding her. One had a black eye; the other had lost his turban, and his face bore an interesting criss-cross pattern of scratches.

"O my lord," said the innkeeper's voice from well in the rear, "did I not warn you that these were indeed Franks, and violent?"

"Verily, you are a mountain of wisdom," said a commanding voice. "What shall be your reward for having at once provided a pearl beyond price for my couch and an arm of the best for my battle?"

"Lord, I ask no more than the sunlight of your favor, and the payment of my proper reckoning. This unlucky Frank keeps the gains he has doubtless made from the robbery of true believers in his belt."

The owner of the commanding voice turned: a tall man with an unpleasant, dish-shaped face. "Seek if this be so," he ordered one of the men holding Shea. The latter, seeing that it would do no good to struggle, refrained from doing so.

"Verily, Lord Dardinell," said the one who was robbing him, "he has fourteen dirhams and a half."

"Give them to the innkeeper," said Lord Dardinell, and, turning back to that worthy, added: "You shall surely wait upon me in my tent after the hour of the second prayer tomorrow, when I shall have made proof of this Frankish damsel. If she prove a filly, as you have declared, your reward shall be ten times this amount; but if not, then only the double."

"Hey!" shouted Shea. "You can't do that. She's my wife!"

One of Shea's holders hit him across the face as Dardinell, expression going glum, turned to the girl. "Is this indeed the truth?" he demanded.

Before she could answer, another voice, somewhat high-pitched, spoke up: "O Lord Dardinell, it cannot be. When lately we saw this damsel at Castle Carena, she was surely neither wife nor widow, but a free maid of the forest, the inspiration of poetry."

Dish-face ran a tongue around red lips. "There is but one resource," he said, "and that is to smite the head of this dog of a Frank from his body, so that if wived, the damsel shall be widowed."

"Yet it is written," said the other voice, which Shea noticed belonged to an olive-skinned young man with delicate features, "that one shall not deal unjustly even with unbelievers, lest it be held against you at the last day. It is also lawful that even if the damsel be widowed this very day, the three-day ceremony of purification is necessary before one shall go in unto her. Therefore I say, my lord, that we should hold them both in a secure place until a learned Kazi can find the line of truth among these thickets. Moreover, O Prince of warriors, was it not your own word but now that here was a good arm to the service of the Prophet, on whose name be peace? Yet of what avail the arm without a head to guide it?"

Lord Dardinell put a hand to his chin and bowed the spiked helmet surmounted by a crescent. "O Medoro," he said finally, with somewhat ill grace, "you argue more finely than a doctor of law, and in a manner to make one believe that your own eyes are set on the damsel. Yet I can find small flaw in your doctrine." Shea, who had been holding his breath, let it out in a long *whoosh,* and the other Saracens murmured approval.

Dardinell stepped over to Shea and felt his biceps. "How came you hither, Frank?" he asked.

Shea said: "I had a little run-in, you might say, with some of the Emperor's paladins." That ought to put him in the best light, and had the advantage of being true.

Dardinell nodded. "Are you a fighter of proved worth?"

"I've been in a few scraps. If you'd like a little demonstration, just turn me loose from this gent holding my right arm . . ."

"That will not be needed. Will you faithfully serve the Amir Agramant in this war?"

Why not? Shea felt he owed nothing to the paladins, while consenting would at least keep him alive long enough to figure out something. "Okay. Bring on your dotted line. I mean, I'll swear to uphold your just and merciful Amir and all that, et cetera, so help me Allah."

Dardinell nodded again, but added severely: "It is not to be thought that even if the Kazi decides that your marriage to this damsel be lawful, you shall retain ownership in her, for it is my wish that you pronounce upon her the formula of divorcement. Yet if you bear yourself well, I will give you sixteen others from the spoils, with faces like full moons. How are you named?"

"Sir Harold Shea."

"Sir Harr al-Shaykh. Hear a wonder: he bears both Nazarene and Muslim titles! How became you a chieftain?"

"I inherited it," said Shea ambiguously. "You know, border family," he added, remembering the Carenas. He felt easier as the grip on his arms relaxed. No, he decided looking around, there was no chance of getting the jump on the situation and releasing Belphegor. Too many of these guys had sharp-looking scimitars in their hands.

Lord Dardinell appeared to have lost interest in him. "Let the maiden be bound, but lightly, with silken cloths," he ordered. "O Medoro, you shall take this new warrior into your troop and see him armed; and your courage shall be responsible for his."

As the girl was led past, she looked toward Medoro instead of him, and Shea's heart ached. At the street a number of horses were tied, one of which was held for him to mount. It was a damn shame that there was no chance of going back for one crack at that innkeeper, but that would have to wait until more important things were cleaned up.

Shea winced as he climbed into the saddles, for his crotch muscles were as hard as cables after the long centaur ride. But they soon loosened under the rugged massage of the high saddle, and Shea was able to go along with only nominal discomfort.

As the cavalcade set off through a hot sun that had already passed noon, it occurred to Shea that it would take something more than magic to make his wife try sleeping in a bed again after this.

11

TENTS WERE PITCHED IN ALL DIRECTIONS WITH A maddening disregard of order. Over the whole brooded a smell suggesting that the sanitary arrangements were primitive. Muslims of every size and complexion wandered among the tents, though there was little about them to suggest that this was an army. In fact, it looked more like an imitation Oriental bazaar at a big fair. Little groups argued and haggled over bargains or just argued; men lay asleep, ignoring the flies that crawled over them; from somewhere came the banging that might mean a smith. As the cavalcade picked its way among the tents, the arguers stopped arguing and some of the sleepers sat up to watch.

They made audible and highly personal comments on Belphegor. Shea felt his own face burning and began to invent a long series of ingenious tortures for them. However, she held her head high, paying no attention as she was carried past sidesaddle on a led horse. She had not so much as spoken to Shea since their capture. He did not blame her, remembering how much his fault it had been for not being careful about that scoundrelly innkeeper and for failing to interpret the dwarf's warning aright. It was certainly a poor payoff for the way she had got him out of a jam to dump her into one like this. Still, the question was . . .

Medoro touched his arm: "We ride this way," and led off to the left, followed by three or four of the group. Presently they arrived before a large striped tent, before which stood a pole from which hung what looked like the tail of a horse. Medoro dismounted and flung open the flap. "Will you enter, O Harr?"

Inside it was at least cooler than on the road. Medoro motioned toward a pile of carpets near the cloth partition that divided this outer room from another, and sat down cross-legged on another pile adjoining. As far as Shea, no expert on Oriental ruggery, could judge, they were very expensive, specimens. The young man clapped his hands, and then said to the scraggly-bearded servitor who appeared from within: "Bring bread and salt. Also sherbets."

"To hear is to obey," said the man, and ducked out. Medoro stared moodily at the carpet in front of him for a minute, then said: "Will you have a barber? For I perceive that you follow the Frankish custom of shaving the face, even as I myself, and are long from the pleasure of this cleanliness."

"It might be a good idea," said Shea, feeling his rasplike chin. "Say, tell me, what are they going to do with her?"

"It is written that the tree of friendship may grow only beside the fountain of security," said Medoro, and lapsed into silence again until the servitor returned, followed by two more. The first carried a ewer of water and an empty basin. As Medoro extended his hands over the latter, the servitor poured water on them and then produced a towel. Then he performed the same service for Shea, who was glad to get off a little of the grime.

The second man had a tray on which stood something that looked like a flannel waffle, with a little dish of salt. Medoro broke off a piece of the waffle, sprinkled a pinch of salt on it, and thrust it toward Shea's face. The latter reached for it, but Medoro skillfully avoided his fingers and poked the morsel closer. Shea inferred that he was supposed to open his mouth; when he did so Medoro popped the object in and waited expectantly. It tasted fierce. As something more seemed to be expected, Shea in his turn broke off a piece of the flannel waffle, salted it, and returned the favor. The servitor disappeared. Medoro picked up his bowl of sherbet and sighed heartily.

"In the name of Allah, the Almighty, the Gracious," he said, "we have partaken of bread and salt together and have no harm towards each other. I have written a poem on that theme; would it broaden your bosom to hear it?"

The poem was long and, as far as Shea was concerned, did not make much sense. Medoro accompanied himself on a goose-necked lute he picked up from behind the rugs, caterwauling his refrain in a series of minors. Shea sat, sipping his sherbet (which turned out to be merely fresh orange juice) and waiting. In the midst of one of the refrains there came a squalling of many voices outside. Medoro flung down his lute, seized up one of the smaller rugs, and rushed outside for the afternoon prayer.

When he returned he flopped down on the rugs again. "O Harr, verily you shaykhs of the Franks know no more of the spirit of life in Allah, whose Prophet is the True and Indubitable, than a pig knows of the nuts whereon it feeds. Yet you shall now tell me nothing less than the truth: are you indeed an approved warrior?"

Shea thought that one over for a moment. "How the hell do I know?" he said finally. "I've done a little fighting when I had to, but I've never been in a regular formal battle, if that's what you mean."

"Aye. On bread and salt I cannot conceal it; I am myself as a stick in the sand. None dare love me but for my verses alone; yet I am of great family, and nothing less than the tradition of might will serve."

He picked up the lute again and struck a few melancholy chords. "May I be forgiven," he said languidly, "and let it not be borne overlong against me on the Day of Days. The Lord Dardinell said nothing less than that you were to be armed. Are you one of those Franks who will strike with the lance?" He brightened momentarily. "I have composed a poem on the subject of blood. Would your soul be soothed to hear it?"

"In a while, maybe," said Shea. "Don't you think we ought to get this arming business over with first, chum? Lord Dardinell will be coming around on a tour of inspection, and I don't think it would look good."

"Ah, Allah, deliver me from this life whose weight is irksome to me!" said Medoro, and without appearing to exert himself threw the lute across the tent, so that Shea heard it crack against some solid obstruction on the far side. Medoro, after a moment of silence, clapped his hands and ordered the thin-bearded servitor: "Summon my armorer."

The armorer was a squat, brawny man with black hair clipped close and black eyes. Shea judged he might be a Basque like Echegaray, but he spoke in the manner of the Muslims: "Will the wonder of the centuries deign to stand? Ha, hum; I have a suit of mail that may fit the Light of the East, but how will you be weaponed: A target, ha, hum. No doubt your magnificence will wish a scimitar also?"

"If you have a small straight sword with a point, it will do me swell," said Shea. Medoro appeared to have gone to sleep, with his mouth in a determined pout.

"O Shaykh Harr," said the armorer, "there may be such a weapon among the booty of Canfrano, but it is not to be hidden that these Frankish blades fail to hold the edge."

"Let's see one anyway. If it won't do, I'll take the longest and straightest scimitar you can find. With a point, too."

"May Allah strike me dead if you be not one of those who use the thrusting stroke! My father, who was smith before the Prince of Hind, has spoken of such in that land, but never have mine eyes been delighted by beholding such a one."

Medoro opened his eyes, clapped his hands, and told his valet: "Another lute, and tell the cook to set forth meats for the evening meal of my guest."

"Aren't you going to eat too?" asked Shea.

"My breast is straightened. I will dine on the food of thought." He took the new lute, struck it a couple of times, and gave vent to a long, howling note like that of a pin scratched across a windowpane.

The smith was still fussing and bowing. "It is revealed to me, O lord of the age," he said, "that there will be need for mail of unusual strength both on the shoulder and the upper arm—"

Medoro set down the lute. "Begone!" he shouted. "Master of noise, whose mother was mistress to a pig! Make your vile armor if you must, and send it here, but in silence."

As the smith scuttled out and the servitor began placing dishes before Shea, the young man relapsed into his playing and singing. It was not the ideal accompaniment to a meal. Shea managed as best he could the sticky mess before him without a fork; it was heavily spiced, but he was too ravenous to let that bother him. Coffee was brought, of the same appalling sweetness as that at the inn. Medoro laid aside his music to accept a cup. As he lifted it delicately to his lips, Shea said:

"What's eating you so, anyway? You act as though you'd lost your last friend."

"Nay," said Medoro, "I have found one, but—" he put down the cup, picked up the lute again, and sang:

"Ah, bittered is the heart
Which with all love must part;
The sun declines, and as it sinks
The tears from out my eyeballs start."

Although Shea was not overwhelmed by the pathos of the poetry, Medoro laid down the lute and began to sob.

"Pull yourself together, pal," said Shea. "Is it about our friend Belphebe—Belphegor, I mean?"

" 'Tis true. Spake you sooth when you said she was your wife? Or was that a ruse to balk my lord Dardinell?"

"Well," said Shea, "that's a long and complicated story . . ."

"Nay, fear not to open your soul to your comrade of bread and salt. True friendship is above the base weakness of jealousy, as says the philosopher Iflatun."

Shea calculated his reply with the care of a sharpshooter. "I've known the girl for some time. But as for the rest of it, her status now is exactly what it was when you met her at Castle Carena. Doesn't that make you feel better?" When Medoro only sighed gustily, Shea added: "I should think we could hire a lawyer or something—"

"Verily, Shaykh Harr," interrupted Medoro, "your understanding is darkened. Know that the Kazi will surely decide that it is lawful for the Lord Dardinell to go in unto the damsel; for if you pronounce not the formula of divorce, he will cause her to do so himself. Ah, what have I done that a mere woman should bring this sorrow upon me? It was clear that with hair of gold-red she would be of ill-omen. Woe's me! I have but delayed the inevitable hour for the three days of purification."

Shea said: "Anyway, I can tell you that anybody who tried to make proof of our girl-friend without her consent has got his work cut out for him."

But Medoro's tears were flowing again. Shea sat back, thinking furiously. This twerp was about as much use as a third leg, though Shea tried to be fair, balancing his natural jealousy of Medoro's libido towards Belphegor against the fact that the youth had, in a manner of speaking, saved Shea's life at the inn. However, Medoro knew the rules, and there was one resource which he had not yet exploited: his own knowledge of magic.

"Where have they got her?" he asked.

"Nowhere but in the harem-tent of Lord Dardinell."

Said Shea: "Do you know whether Roger—you know, the one from Carena—has joined the army?"

The Saracen's woebegone expression changed to one of fine contempt. "It has reached me that the misbegotten son of a whore is indeed among us."

"You don't like him, then?"

"By Allah, if a cup of water would save him from Hell, I would give him fire to drink. At Castle Carena but lately, when I was reciting my stanzas in lament of Farragus, which is the best and longest poem I have composed, he snatched the lute from my hands."

For the first time Shea felt a certain sympathy with Atlantès' bull-like nephew. However, he said: "Okay, then, I need Roger in my business. Specifically, I want to kidnap him and get him back to Carena. You help me do it, and I think I can show you how to get Belphegor out of hock."

The handsome face distorted into lines of fear. "O Harr, Roger is so potent that no ten could stand against him. In Allah alone is protection, but we two would be to him as mice before an eagle."

"Take it or leave it," said Shea coolly. What he really wanted was to get Belphegor out of there and never mind the small change, but the chances of restoring his wife's Belphebe memory were not too good unless he could get her to Chalmers, with the latter's superior knowledge both of psychiatry and of magic. If Medoro just wouldn't play, however, he could back down at the last moment.

Someone howled at the door of the tent. The servant scampered through, and returned presently with a package that proved to contain the arms. Shea examined them while Medoro remained sunk in gloomy thought. The sword, while still a curved saber with most of the weight toward the point, was straighter than most, and the smith had ground a fine needle point to it. There was also a spiked steel cap with a little skirt of chainmail to protect the neck, a dagger, a small round shield of brass hammered thin, and a mail shirt.

Shea laid them down and turned to Medoro. "Well?"

The young Saracen looked at him craftily. "O Lord Harr, how lies it in your power to perform things for which half this army were not enough?"

"You just leave that to me." Shea grinned. "I'll give you a hint, though; I know something about magic."

Medoro touched both sets of finger tips to his temples, and said: "There is no God but God, and it is written that none shall die before the appointed hour. Speak, and I will obey as though I were your Mameluke."

"Will Roger come here if you ask for him?"

"Nay, he would rather whip my slave from his door."

"Then we'll have to go to him. Do you know where he hangs out?"

"It is even so."

"Okay. But we won't do it just yet. I'm merely laying out the program. How much authority do you have around here?"

"O Shaykh, under Lord Dardinell I am captain of fourscore men."

Shea thought it would go hard with a Saracen army if it had to rely on captains like this languishing lady-killer to lead it, but just now he was too busy to pursue that question. "Can you bring them here, three or four at a time?"

"Hearing and obedience," said Medoro, who salaamed and began to get up.

Shea, who did not altogether like the scared look that persisted in Medoro's eyes, said: "Hold it; let's have just one to start with. We can try out the magic on him to make sure it works."

Medoro re-seated himself and clapped his hands. "Bid Tarico al-Marik enter and stay not, on the value of his head," he told the servant. Picking up the lute, he began to strum chords, the jewels in his bracelets flashing in the light of the Greek lamp that had been brought in with dinner.

"Lend me one of those bracelets, will you?" asked Shea. When the guardsman came in, Shea had Medoro order him to sit down and relax, then placed the lamp before the soldier. As the young Saracen continued to pick the lute, Shea dangled the bracelet before the soldier's eyes, twirling it this way and that, meanwhile repeating in a low voice as much as he could remember of the sleeping-spell Astolph had used on him.

Either as magic or as hypnotism the method was a little unorthodox; it seemed to work nevertheless. The man's eyes went blank, and he would have tumbled over if he had not been leaning against the wall of the tent.

Presently Shea said: "Can you hear me?"

"Aye."

"You will obey my commands."

"As the commands of a father."

"The Amir wants to surprise the camp. Discipline needs tightening up. Do you understand?"

"It is as my lord says."

"As soon as the evening prayer is over, you will draw your sword and run through the camp, cutting tent-ropes."

"To hear is to obey."

"You will cut all the tent-ropes you can, no matter what anyone says to you."

"To hear is to obey," repeated the soldier.

"You will forget all about this order till the time for action comes."

"To hear is to obey."

"And you will forget who gave you this order."

"To hear is to obey."

"Wake up!"

The man blinked and came out of it, wiggling as though his foot had gone to sleep. As he stood up, Shea asked: "What were your orders?"

"To watch well the door of Lord Dardinell's tent tonight. But as my head lives, Lord Medoro has given me none others."

"He forgot. You were to send in four more men. Isn't that right, Medoro?"

"It is as has been spoken," said Medoro languidly.

The man shifted his feet. "There was—"

"Nothing else," said Shea firmly. He looked at Medoro, who laid down his lute and stared back.

"Verily, Shaykh Harr," said the latter, "this is as though the prophets were again on earth. Will he assuredly cut the tent-ropes as you commanded?"

"If he doesn't, I'll put a spell on him to make him eat his own head," said Shea, who had decided that he could count on all the cooperation the twerp was capable of giving. "Listen, when those others come in, keep it up with that oriental swing, will you? I think it has something to do with putting them under."

12

WHEN THE LAST OF THE FOURSCORE GUARDS HAD been given his orders, Shea felt tired. Medoro, placing a delicately-formed hand over his mouth, said: "Surely we have now done so much that the darkness of Eblis must fall on the camp, and we can easily seize the damsel and make off with her. I am wearied, though somewhat comforted by the excellence of your plan. Let us sleep and await the deliverance of Allah."

"Nothing doing," said Shea. "In my country we have a proverb about Allah's helping those who help themselves, and there's one thing we've got to help ourselves to right now. That's Roger. Remember, you promised." He stood up, put on the steel cap, buckled on the sword and stuck the sheath of the dagger through the sword-belt. The mail-shirt, he decided, would have to stay behind, since for the kind of work he envisaged it was important to keep down weight. Medoro sulkily imitated him.

Outside the shadows were already stretching across the valley below the slope that held the encampment. Although Shea did not know when the hour of evening prayer was, he guessed it would be soon. That meant they must hurry if they wanted to catch Roger as part of the combined operation. Once the bruiser got loose with an uproar going on there would be no finding him.

But Medoro only sauntered along, possessed of a perfect demon of slowness. Every now and then he stopped to give or acknowledge a greeting, and those to whom he spoke seemed all to want to start an interminable discussion of nothing.

Shea thought these must be the most garrulous

354

people on earth. "Listen," he said finally, "if you don't come along, I'll put a spell on you that will make you challenge Roger to a duel."

Shea had heard of people's teeth chattering, and not from cold, but this was the first time he had actually heard it. Medoro mended his pace.

Roger, it appeared, lived in a tent of Spartan simplicity as to outline, but as big as Medoro's. Two fierce-looking bearded men were pacing back and forth in front of it with naked scimitars.

"We want to see Roger of Carena," said Shea to the nearest. The other paused and joined his companion, who was examining the callers.

The first guard said: "There are many tents in the camp. Let the lords seek another, since all are friends under Allah." He held his sword about waist-high, just in case.

Shea glanced over his shoulder to see the sun sinking fast. "But we've got to see him before the evening prayer," he insisted, shaking off the fingers Medoro was plucking at his sleeve with. "He's a friend of ours. We knew him in Carena."

"O Lord, the Prince Roger's withers will be wrung. Yet it is written that it is better that one man should have an unhappiness, which endures only the appointed hour of God, than that two should lose their lives. Learn that if Lord Roger should be roused before the hour of evening prayer, we two should lose nothing less than our heads, for so he has sworn it by the hair of his beard."

"He hasn't got one," said Shea. Medoro, however, plucked insistently and whispered: "Now there is no help for it but we must leave this project for the other, since we are evidently not to be admitted by these two good men. Would you try steel against them and so provoke the shame of Islam?"

"No, but there's something else I'd try," said Shea, whipping round on his heel. Medoro followed him dubiously until they reached the side of the tent next door. With his dagger Shea cut eight long slivers of wood from one of the tent pegs. Two of these he stuck under the brim of his helmet, so that they projected like horns, and two more he inserted under his upper lip, hanging down like tusks. Then he decorated Medoro's wondering face likewise with the remaining four.

That ought to do for what Doc Chalmers called the "somatic" part of the spell. As for the verbal part, how could he do better than Shakespeare, slightly modified for the occasion? Shea turned round and round on his heel, moving his hands in Chalmers' passes and chanting in a low voice:

"Black spirits and white, red spirits and gray,
Mingle, mingle, mingle, you that mingle may;
Fair is foul and foul is fair;
Change, O change the form we bear!"

"Okay," he said to Medoro; "come along."

They swung round the corner of the tent. The guard who had been talking to them was just facing their way. He took one look at them, gasped: "The Jann!", dropped his sword, and ran for his life. The other guard looked also, turned a curious mottled color, screamed: "The Jann!" Falling on the ground he tried to bury his face in the grass.

Shea lifted the flap and led the way boldly in. There was no light in the outer compartment, and it was already dim with exterior twilight, but there was no mistaking the mountain of flesh piled among the rugs. Shea started toward it, but in the darkness tripped over some small object. He pitched forward and, unable to stop himself, struck the mass of Roger in the midriff in the position of a man kneading a vast vat of dough.

Roger awoke at once, rolling to his feet with incredible speed. "La-Allah-il-Allah!" he cried, snatching a huge scimitar from the wall of the tent. "Ha, Jann! I have not fought Jann!" The sword curved back for a blow as Medoro cowered away.

"Wait!" yelled Shea.

The scimitar checked. "Hold it a minute, will you?" said Shea. "We're really friends. I'll show you." He stepped over to Medoro, pronouncing the counter-spell and pulling at the chin-length tusks into which the slivers beneath Medoro's lips had turned.

Nothing happened. The tusks did not give. Between them Medoro still wore his foolish, frightened grin, and above, a pair of bull-like horns continued to project from neat holes in the young man's helmet.

Shea repeated the counter-spell again, louder, feeling of his own face and head, and discovering that he was likewise festooned with horns and tusks. Again, however, nothing happened.

Far away somewhere a voice rose in a banshee howl. That would be an imam whose alarm clock, or whatever he used for the purpose, was a little fast, calling the faithful to prayer. The others would soon follow.

Shea faced Roger and said: "Listen, let's talk this over. We're Jann, all right, sent here by the big boss to fight with the best mortal fighter in the world. But we have some pretty terrible powers, you know, and we want to arrange things so you don't have to put on a scrap at odds of more than two to one."

It sounded phony as hell in Shea's own ears, but Roger let the scimitar droop and grinned beefily. "By Allah the Omnipotent! The hour of good fortune has come upon me. Surely there would be no greater pleasure than to be with two of the jann in battle bound."

Roger flung himself among the rugs, half-turning his back toward Shea, who motioned frantically to Medoro to sit beside the colossus. Shea hoped Medoro would keep doing what he did best, namely talking. The twerp was probably too scared to do anything else, for he flopped beside Roger, saying: "Among our people we have a poem of the combats of the jann. Would your lordship care to hear it? If you have a lute—"

"O Jinn I would hear it not much more than a poem about dogs pissing in the street. Learn that at Castle Carena I acquired the taste for the despisal of poetry, since the worst of all poets came among us to visit: Medoro by name."

Shea caught the glance of appeal and indignation which Medoro flashed over his shoulder through his jinn makeup, but continued to stroll about the tent, out of the conversation. A large dagger with an ornate gold-hilted handle hung on the wall; he hefted it by the scabbard blade and looked at the back of Roger's head.

"Know, O Lord Roger," said the poet rapidly, "that by poetry and song alone is the world advanced. For it is the rule of the Prophet, on whose name be blessings . . ."

A steel spike stuck up through the center of Roger's turban, meaning that he had on some kind of helmet beneath the cloth. If Shea hit him while he wore that, the dagger-hilt would merely go bong, and Roger would turn and grapple.

Medoro was talking a perfect flood of words that made little sense.

Shea reached down, gripped the spike firmly, and switched it forward, tumbling helmet and turban both over the big man's face.

"Ho!" cried Roger's muffled voice as he reached upward.

Thump! The dagger-hilt hit his shaven poll in the medular region. Shea was left with the helmet-and-turban combination in his left hand as the ox rolled over and down. From outside came the united squalling of the call to prayer.

A thread of spittle ran down Medoro's chin beside the left tusk, and his hands fluttered wildly. "There—there is no gug-grace or goodness but in Allah," he babbled. "What thought is now to be taken for preservation?"

"Suppose you just leave that to me while you get busy and find some extra turbans. I haven't steered you wrong yet, have I?"

Medoro, familiar with camp life, quickly found the turbans in the inner compartment, and they tied Roger firmly, winding him round and round with them and knotting them until he looked like a cocoon. He seemed to be breathing all right; Shea hoped his skull were not fractured. Time was getting shorter and shorter, with the show outside about to begin.

Medoro said: "O Lord Harr, surely we shall never be able to move him hence, and what of the fearsome appearance you have put upon us?"

"Shut up," said Shea. "I'm thinking."

"If we had but the magic carpet of Baghdad—"

Shea snapped his fingers. "Right on the button! I knew I'd forgotten something. Here, find stuff that'll make a small fire with a lot of smoke. Is there a feather anywhere around here? Don't argue with me, damn it. This is important if you want to see Belphegor again."

When Medoro returned from the inner compartment of the tent with a few twigs and the aigrette of an ornamental turban, he found Shea already busily at work. The journeyman magician had caught a couple of the big blue flies that buzzed about in vast numbers, and looped a silken thread from Roger's wrappings about them, attaching one end of it to the fringe of Roger's main carpet. The flies tried to take off as he released them.

"Put those twigs in a little pile here and light them," Shea directed, rolling back the carpet to leave a bare space on the ground.

While Medoro made the light with flint and steel and a tinder-box, Shea pulled the aigrette apart and began weaving it into the carpet, knotting it into the fringe. Outside something seemed to be going on. As the flame caught, shouts and the sound of running became audible.

The twigs, aromatics, filled the tent with a pungent smoke as Shea recited the spell he had been composing:

"Be light—*cough!*—carpet, as the leaves you
    bear;
Be light as the clouds that fly with thee.
Soar through the skies and let us now but share
The impulse of the strength. Let us be free
From—*cough! cough! cough!* If even
The Roc and all the Jann could fly like we

Then were they—*cough!* right aërial indeed.
To you the spirits of the sky are given
That they may help us in our sorest need.
Cough-cough-cough!"

The smoke died. The carpet was beginning to wiggle, parts of it rising from the ground and settling down again with a slight *whump,* while the tumult outside increased. The jinn that was Medoro rubbed smarting eyes.

"O Shaykh Harr," he said, "this is not the worst of poetry, though it must be admitted that you failed to accompany it with the lute. Moreover there was a foot missing from the fifth line, and the end is somewhat weak."

"Never mind the higher criticism, but help me get this elephant onto the carpet, will you?" said Shea.

They rolled Roger over and wrapped him in one of the sitting carpets before depositing him on the—Shea hoped—flying one. His eyes had come open and regarded them balefully. Where the gag allowed, the muscles of his face moved in something like prayer.

Shea flung back the tent door and looked out. There was certainly something happening in the gathering dusk; people running in all directions with manifold shoutings. As Shea watched, a big square tent with a pennon on top, farther along the hillside, corkscrewed down into collapse.

"Sit down and hold on," Shea told Medoro. He himself climbed on the carpet, which seemed to be showing signs of restlessness even under Roger's weight. Reaching to his full height, Shea swung his sword at the roof, which split to show an indigo sky from which one solemn star winked back at him. He squatted and declaimed:

"By warp and by woof,
High over the roof—"

Chop! went a sword into one of the tent-ropes outside. Chop! went another. "Stand, in the name of Allah!" shouted a voice.

Shea finished:

> "Fly swiftly and surely
> To serve our behoof!"

The tent collapsed, and the carpet swooshed up and out through the gap, its fringes flapping.

13

A BAREHEADED MAN AND ONE OF SHEA'S ROPE-cutters were arguing so violently that neither noticed the carpet as it soared over their heads. Agramant's camp was in pandemonium beneath; everywhere tents were wobbling and collapsing. Some were as large as circus-tents, and great was the fall thereof. Lumpy objects moved under the enshrouding canvas, and here and there men fought. Out on one of the spurs of the hillside a tent had gone down into a fire which blazed brightly in the gathering gloom, while people ran around it, trying to beat out the flames or douse them with futile small buckets of water.

The carpet heaved and bucked, swirling this way and that. A little experiment showed Shea that he could direct its movements by pulling left, right, up, or down at the fringe of its leading edge. However, further experiment added the information that it was so very sensitive on the controls that he must be careful lest he throw them into a loop. Roger almost rolled off as the vehicle took a vicious down-curve. Medoro, though he had not eaten, seemed to be having trouble keeping whatever was in his stomach.

"Where is it?" shouted Shea.

Medoro pointed to one of the largest tents of all, well up on the slope, with a swarm of pennons floating from its multiple peaks. Dardinell's pavilion. Shea jerked at the fringe, and the carpet did a sweeping bank towards it.

The pavilion was a young city in itself. Besides the main tent, a score of lesser, outlying structures were connected to it by canopies. Among them the powerful figure of Dardinell himself could be seen among a group of officers on horseback who were trying to bring order into those on foot.

"Where's the harem?" demanded Shea. Medoro put one hand to his tusks to hold back a gulp, and with the other pointed toward an elongated tent that sprang from one side of the main structure.

As the carpet swooped, the sound of Shea's voice brought a face in their direction. There was a yell, the whole group flowered with faces, and a flung javelin went past. Before more could follow they were over the tangle of lordly tents and out of range. They sailed in toward the roof of the harem tent. As they did so, Shea, controlling the carpet with his left hand and some difficulty, whipped out his sword and made a twenty-foot gash in the fabric.

He then took the carpet around in a curve and back to the hole he had made. "Duck!" he said to Medoro. Aiming carefully, he drove for the hole, which had been widened by the tension of the ropes. One of Shea's horns caught the edge for a moment, then ripped through. They were inside.

They were in a room full of women, so little below that Shea could have joined hands with them by leaning over the edge. The women, however, did not seem in a mood to join hands; instead, they ran in all directions, screaming: "The Jann! The Jann!" Shea encouraged them by leaning over and gibbering a little.

The carpet moved smoothly to the nearest partitions and then stopped, its leading edge curling where it met the cloth, and its side edges flapping like some lowly marine organism. Shea reached out and slit the camel's hair across. The next room was a kitchen, empty save for the furniture of the trade. The next compartment held nothing but a pair of eunuchs throwing dice. These screamed in high voices, and one of them tried to crawl away under the outer edge of the tent, as Shea slit his way through the next wall.

"Damn maze," said Shea. The outer tumult of the camp had been dampened to a whisper by the many thicknesses of cloth. Two more partitions, both yielding empty rooms, and the coolness of the evening was once more on their faces. Shea could see a couple of soldiers afoot and a horseman running past, silhouetted against a fire further down the hill. He hastily manoeuvered the carpet around another curve and cut his way into the wall of the tent again. It was only the kitchen once more, and the whole structure of the tent seemed to be growing ricketty from the repeated slashings.

Nevertheless Shea warped his craft up to the kitchen's one unslit wall. A gash—and they had found their goal.

The room Lord Dardinell used for his more personal pleasures was full of precious things. Over against the wall, under a hanging out of which eddied a slow smoke of incense, priceless cushions had been piled on priceless carpets to make one of the most elaborate beds Shea had ever seen. In the midst of these cushions a bound figure writhed.

Shea tried to bring the carpet to a halt by pulling up on his leading edge, but that only took him to the ceiling; by pulling down, but that only brought him to the floor. He considered trying to snatch the girl on the way past as a broncho-buster picks a handkerchief from the ground, but rejected the idea as too risky. One hand would be needed for the carpet, and Medoro was no help at all.

He came around the room in another curve and recited:

> "By warp and by woof,
> In the midst of the roof,
> To save the fair lady
> Stand still and aloof."

The carpet halted. It was a long way to the ground, and this would be no time to sprain an ankle. However, Shea, swung over the side, let himself down to his full length by gripping the yielding fringe, and dropped. He landed in the midst of the cushions on all fours, and got to his knees.

The figure on the bed rolled over and glared at him with furious eyes from under a disordered mop of graying hair, grunting through its gag.

"Eeek!" shrieked Medoro from above. " 'Tis the Amir himself! We are surely at the last hour. There is no God but God."

And in fact it was indeed the Amir Agramant, Commander of the Faithful, Protector of the Poor, just and merciful Lord of Hispania, trussed, bound, and gagged with his own turban.

"By the mass! More magic!" said Belphegor's voice. Shea turned and saw her poised to spring at him, dagger in hand.

"Stop!" he said. "I'm Harold. Don't you know me?"

"A hornèd demon the lord of Shea? Nay but— and yet the voice—"

"Come on, you know me. This is just a gag; a magical gag. The other spook, up there on the rug, is your boyfriend Medoro. Now do you get it? We're here to save you."

"Nay, 'tis assuredly some trick. Come not nigh, or man or monster, your weasand will be slit."

"Medoro," called Shea. "She won't believe we're us. Make a poem for her, will you, chum?"

To judge by Medoro's expression, his muse was not in the best of fettle, but he valiantly cleared his throat and began in a whining voice:

"We are not lost to prudence, but indeed
Stand here bewildered. What shall be our rede?
Since none will aid us from this tent to flee,
By spells of great Lord Harr must we be free;
But ah! my heart is lost and passion-spent;
To none but Allah can we trust in need."

"Nay, I begin to trow," said Belphegor, her mouth
losing its hard line. "This is Medoro's veritable voice
which comes from the shaping. But what is now your
counsel, friends?"

"We're going out of here on that flying carpet, the
way we came in," said Shea.

The girl stood on tiptoe and reached. "But how
to attain it?"

"More turbans needed," said Shea, practically.
"Where would they be?"

Belphegor leaped across the tent. "This chest—"
and flung it open. Sure enough, it was filled with
fine silk turban-cloths, neatly folded. He linked three
of them together with solid square-knots and tossed
one end up to Medoro, who caught it on the second
try, and braced himself while Belphegor swarmed up
it, light as a squirrel. Then Shea took a firm grip on
the lowest knot and began to climb, but he had
barely cleared the ground when the turban-rope
went slack and he came down on his behind, the
rope on his head.

"Hey!" cried Shea, stepping on the Amir and he
stumbled to his feet. He saw Medoro, his jinn-eyes
shifting as he crouched at the edge of the carpet
and muttered. The edge of the carpet fluttered and
it shifted position a little.

Shea would have said something else and more
vigorous, but before he could get the words out,
Belphegor leaned over the edge, with: "Throw up
your end!" She caught it neatly, took a turn round
her waist and called: "Mount, Sir Harold!"

Shea hesitated, afraid of pulling the girl off, for
though he did not doubt her strength, he weighed
a hundred and sixty. But just at this moment a troop
of eunuchs flung aside the curtain and came wad-

dling into the room, pointing, yelling and waving
scimitars at least a foot wide. He swarmed up the
turban-rope clumsily but effectively as a thrown
dagger tumbled past him.

"Get over and let a man run this thing!" he said
to Medoro. He spoke to the carpet and they slid
through the gap in the tent-wall, out into the rapidly
descending twilight. The fire at one side of the camp
was still burning; figures appeared to be dancing before
it.

Shea jockeyed the carpet up to what he judged
was an altitude safe from arrow-shot and turned to
Medoro. "Well, what's the alibi? You better make it
damn good."

"I—I—but friend Harr, let the shield of our bread
and salt turn aside the sword of your anger. Truly is it
said by Al Qa'sun that he who sees into the hearts of
many can seldom see into his own. Ah, most miserable
of men!" He bent his head and the jewelled bracelets
flashed as he beat his breast. "Your servant had no
other thought but that when the end of the bond was
lost, so much was lost that I should regret it to the end
of days. But there is no might save in Allah, who has
preserved you to be the delight of our eyes."

"You damn twerp," said Shea, through his teeth. "So
you thought you'd sneak off and leave me and then
make a poem about it. That's the idea, isn't it?"

"Nay, I am but a reed in the wind of your displeasure, and my breast is straitened, my brother," said
Medoro, and reaching to the hem of his robe at the
chest, gave it a little rip. (Shea noticed that it appeared
to have been re-sewn several times; it was evidently a
habit with the young man.) "Now there is no help for
it but I must die." Two big tears rolled down his
cheeks and stood gleaming on the tusks.

Belphegor put her arm around his shoulders. "Ah,
unhappy wight, grieve not! Sir Harold, I charge you
straitly that you shall not overbear him, for he is a
troubadour, and I hold it somewhat less than knightly
to treat him as less than one who has sustained you
throughout this deed."

"Okay, okay," said Shea. "He's a hero and a pet. I

just don't know why we bothered rescuing you at all. You were doing all right when we came in."

It was Belphegor's turn to be hurt, as Shea observed with a touch of vindictive relish. "Fie, for shame!" she said. "If you'll magic me with your enchantments into the most ungrateful of wenches, I'll have my favor back."

Her nostrils moved and Shea, feeling suddenly wretched, turned to the business of navigation. It had been a splendid exploit, and they should all have been elated. Instead of which . . .

After a moment he got a grip on himself, realizing that he was being pretty immature in getting sore at Medoro, who was merely one of those schizoid types who can no more help disintegrating under stress than he, Shea, could help pulling himself together under similar circumstances. Aloud he said: "All right, folks, I think we've done enough quarrelling for one night." (He realized that he had done most of the quarrelling, but he was also captain, and an apologetic attitude would undermine the position.) "Are we for Castle Carena?"

"My bow," said Belphegor. "I am undone without it. Perchance 'twill be at the inn where we were taken. Will you do me the grace to see, Sir Harold?" The voice was still chilly.

"Good idea," said Shea, trimming the carpet a trifle in the direction of the town. "I'd like to take a poke at that innkeeper myself, and now I have the equipment." He stroked his tusks appreciatively.

Behind him he felt the girl shift herself gingerly on the yielding surface to a sitting position on the rolled-up rug that was Roger. A sound somewhere between a groan and a growl emerged; Belphegor leaped to her feet, making the carpet tip perilously. "What's here! Do carpets speak as well as move in your enchantments?"

Shea grinned over his shoulder. "That's your old boyfriend, Roger of Carena. We're taking him back to uncle."

"Verily?" She pulled back an edge of the rug and stared in the fading light, then gave a peal of silvery laughter. "Nay, this joys me much, and for this joy you are restored to favor as my true knight, Sir Harold. But I'd have one of the great bear's ears as a trophy." She whipped out her small hunting knife and the carpet heaved as Roger strove to wriggle in his bonds. Medoro's jinn-face took on a greenish cast. Shea said: "Cut it out, will you, girl-friend? We're getting there."

The town was below them, lemon-colored gleams picking out the windows of the inn. Shea circled the carpet round the structure and carefully manoeuvred it up to one of the windows that lighted the upstairs dormitory, peering in. There seemed to be no sleepers, only a feeble oil-lamp on a low table.

"I don't see it," he said. "Where did you leave it?"

"I deemed I had laid it upon the bed next to my own, with my quiver," she said.

"Not there now. Medoro, you and I will have to do a little searching. Beautiful, you stay here and see that the carpet doesn't drift away from the window, because we may come back running and dive through. You can move it by pulling gently on the fringe here, but don't do it if you don't have to. If Roger makes a fuss, you can have *both* his ears."

Medoro said: "Oh, my lord and brother, is it not more meet that I should wait, both as one who can defend this carpet from attack, and because I know not one bow from another?"

"No!" said Shea. "Come along."

He let himself carefully through the window, reaching up a hand to help Medoro. They scoured the dormitory from end to end, peering under carpets and in corners, but not a trace of archery-tackle.

"Inshallah!" said Medoro. "It was ordained from the beginning of the world that we should not . . ."

He broke off at the sound of approaching horses, and then of voices downstairs. Shea tiptoed to the head of the stairs. A voice was just saying: "Uncle, are there within your caravanserai certain fugitives from the justice of the Commander of the Faithful?"

"My head be your sacrifice!" came the voice of the innkeeper. "Were there such, I had long since delivered them to the servants of the Prince, straitly bound. But are there not other inns than mine?"

The owner of the other voice replied: "By Allah,

368

our breasts are narrowed, and an enchantment lies upon this expedition for the abatement of the Nazarenes! For behold, Lord Dardinell must bring home to the camp a damsel with hair of ill-omen, a very Frank, who indeed aroused the jealousy of the sons of Satan the stoned. For with the setting of the sun what should befall but there came unto the camp an army of furious Jann, each taller than a tree and pinioned with four wings of brass, who spurned over our tents as though they had been toys. By the grace of Allah, few were slain, though many ran in panic, and we have come to recall those who fled, lest they be taken later and fire be applied to their feet so they may see no more."

The innkeeper apparently turned around to show them into the lower rooms, for his voice became inaudible and there was a sound of feet. But a moment later he picked up again ". . . the apartments for sleeping, which be untenanted."

Medoro jerked at Shea's arm and cast an imploring glance toward the window. Shea got out his sword and putting his lips close to his fellow-jinn's ear, murmured: "Draw, and we'll scare the living bejesus out of them after that story he told. When I jump and yell, you do the same." He waved the weapon; Medoro produced and waved his own though with somewhat uncertain gestures. The footsteps started up the stair; Shea leaped with a whoop, in time to see three soldiers, with the innkeeper behind them.

He must have looked a hundred feet tall, coming down from above, and behind him Medoro emitted a shrill yell that was even more blood-curdling than his own. An answering scream came from the men below, mingled with a clatter of dropped weapons and the sound of heavy bodies hurling themselves any old way toward escape. For a few seconds the bottom of the stair was a confused mass of trunks and limbs; then the soldiers fought their way loose and raced out the door.

The last one to get to his feet was the innkeeper, who as low man had been trampled by all three others. He was a little too slow on the getaway as hoofbeats diminished into the distance. Shea noted that he had both hands up for the formal tearing of his garments and his mouth open for a scream, but that both his motor nerves and his vocal seemed paralyzed.

He was not quite up to cutting the fellow down in cold blood, so he gave him a stiff left to the nose. The innkeeper dropped like an English heavyweight and rolled over, burying his face in his arms and awaiting the end.

"Look for that bow while I play footsie with this guy," said Shea, digging his toe into the innkeeper's ribs.

Medoro sidled past, his eyes rolling as though he expected Shea to begin carving steaks off the unfortunate man at any moment, but the latter contented himself with goosing the fellow tentatively with the point of the sword, until the young Saracen returned, waving the bow and saying: "By the omnipotence of Allah, it is indeed found!"

"Uncle, or whatever your name is," said Shea, "if you want to stay alive a little longer, lie where you are till you count slowly up to one hundred. Then you may get up and tell anybody you like about how the Jann spared your life. Okay, Medoro."

As the carpet resumed its slightly undulating flight, Medoro inched forward and patted one of Shea's feet. "Know, O auspicious Lord Harr," he said, "that this is a deed worthy to be written in the most divine verse on tablets of silver with letters of gold. It is given to poets, in the name of the Prophet, on whose name be blessings, to know all that passes in the minds of men, and had I but a lute, I would compose verses—"

"Too bad you haven't got the lute," said Shea. "But right now I'm more interested in figuring out the shortest way to the Castle of Carena."

Belphegor pointed. "Sir Harold, it lies almost under the star of the Lion, thitherward. Behold that triad of bright stars; the lowest lies under the pole. And for your help in aiding Medoro to find my weapon, much thanks. It was knightly done to accompany him."

Shea, looking down at the broken ground where the shadows were now deep, guessed that they were making twenty to thirty miles an hour. As the rolling highlands gave way to swollen, solid peaks of mountain, he had to put his vehicle into a climb to avoid the crests. All three began to shiver in their light clothes, and Medoro's teeth rattled. Shea envied Roger the rug.

That gave him an idea. They must be far enough from Agramant's camp so that over those stony mountains it would take days for the Amir's men to catch up. Why not rest comfortably through the remainder of the night? He put the carpet into a glide toward a low rounded peak and set it down, murmuring (under his breath so that Medoro would not hear) a spell to keep it there.

The Roger-rug grunted again as the rear end of the carpet touched a stone. It occurred to Shea that there was no particular reason why the big man should be comfortable while Belphebe-Belphegor was cold that night, so the prisoner was unrolled from his rug; and then it occurred to him that it would be interesting to hear what Roger had to say, so he removed the gag.

The perfect chevalier had plenty to say, beginning by calling them offspring of Marids and one-eyed sows, then running up and down the chain of their ancestry and remarking that his uncle would have them pickled in brass bottles under the seal of Solomon. With academic interest Shea noted that the invective had a certain weakness toward the end. The slow brain of the big lummox had evidently not quite been able to resolve the contradiction of Jann who spoke with the voices of Shea and Medoro.

The poet plucked at Shea's sleeve. "O brother," he said, "shall we not rather release him for the night; for it is contrary to the law of the Prophet that a man shall not be allowed to take his relievements. As is said by Abu Nowas—"

"As is said by myself, nothing doing," replied Shea. "I don't want to sit up guarding this big lug all night, and if Bradamant gets hold of him, he'll forget all about the law of the Prophet, anyway."

He was astounded to hear the big lug groan, and see a glistening tear on his eyelids in the star-shine; and even more astounded when Roger shut up completely.

Belphegor and Medoro moved a little apart and sat on a rock, talking softly and looking at the bright, near stars. Shea saw his arm go round the girl's waist and guessed he didn't dare try anything at this stage, and

371

under the circumstances, there didn't seem to be much point in building a campfire. He pulled a twig from the top of a scrubby bush and bit down on it, trying to pretend that it was a pipe and recalling the ad for some brand of tobacco—"A gentleman's solace."

Solace! That was what he needed. What was the use, anyway, of this running across a parade of universes not even real and having nothing to show for it? What he ought to do was go back to Garaden, finish getting his doctor's degree, become a big-shot psychiatrist, consulted by alcoholics and the affluent screwy and make money. With money you could have everything—even affection. He recalled a statistic that Garaden had itself gathered, to the effect that something over sixty per cent of women could be happy and affectionate with any really good provider.

It wasn't really as simple as that, though. That redhaired spearshaft of a girl over there was his wife, none genuine without this signature, and just any girl who wanted a good provider wouldn't take her place. Anyway, he had a responsibility. He had married her and promised to keep her safe—particularly from such things as the Medoro menace. He had seen the thing so often in case-histories: women of her forceful type, thoroughly competent as long as sex was left out, falling for good-looking weaklings whom they felt the impulse to mother, and unhappy because of it. They usually ended up by despising the men in question.

Well, what? He couldn't very well murder Medoro, that was not in the limits of his own *ethos,* and it would probably have the contrary effect on the girl than the one he wanted. It would fix the love-image in her memory forever as something desirable and lost. Moreover, he had no desire to bump off Medoro. The guy was perfectly frank about his own weakness as a fighter or man of action of any kind, no sham about him. He was only miscast as a Saracen warrior, like one of the Marx brothers trying to play Hamlet. With the right kind of stage-manager . . .

The whole problem was one to pass on to Chalmers, that very well-integrated personality, who didn't mind tearing other people's lives apart to mend the details of his own.

Meanwhile, it would be a good idea to get some sleep. Medoro was supposed to watch Roger during the early part of the night. He hoped the idiot would not do anything stupid, like turning the perfect cavalier loose, but consoled himself with the thought that if Medoro did that, Roger would probably fall on the poet first and make enough racket to wake the other two up.

A wolf howled in the distance. Everybody moved, rustlingly at the sound. Another howl answered it. The howlers set up a duet, the howls became shorter and closer together, then they ceased. About that time Medoro began to croon in a minor key, presumably a poem of his own.

Lucky stiff, thought Shea, meaning the wolf.

14

"NOW WHERE THE HELL ARE WE?" DEMANDED HAROLD Shea.

Below the edge of the carpet nothing was visible but rocky peaks, pine-clad slopes and steep gorges, with now and then a metallic flash of water in them. "We've been flying for hours, and all we get is more of the same. I think we ought to stop at a gas station and ask."

A little frown came between Belphegor-Belphebe's lined brows. "As oft erst, Sir Harold, I wot not—right well—what you would say."

"It's like this; we seem to be a long time getting nowhere, and I could do with something to eat."

She looked at him, then glanced quickly sidewise and down. "I marvel that you are so eager to end this, our adventure; yet since you will have it so, there lies a road now below us which, an I mistake not, will lead us to Carena."

"You have the damndest eyes, kid. Where?"

She pointed. It was a mountain track like two or three they had glimpsed already, snaking down one side of a gorge, across a stream by stepping-stones, and up the opposite slope.

Shea banked and spiralled down toward the track. Belphegor indicated four dots ahead on the road which, as they approached, resolved into a man leading three laden asses. Shea slid in toward him, and just above head level, called: "Hi, there!"

The man looked up, his whole face seemed to dissolve, he gave a squawk of terror and began to run, the asses rocking behind him. The carpet zipped past a hairpin turn and came round in a long curve as Shea brought it back, crying to the girl: "You talk to him!"

"Nay, hold rather," she said. "He is so sore affrighted with your grim aspect that an you clip him close, he'll but leap a cliff and take the known death rather than the terror unknown."

"Allah upon you if you do!" said Medoro. "This is most excellent sport to see a merchant so buffooned."

"No, she's right," said Shea, slanting the carpet upward and away. "But it leaves us with a problem. How are we going to get close enough to anybody to ask questions, looking the way we do?"

"What need of question?" asked Belphegor. "I have given you the direction general; you have but to wait for night, then put this strange steed of yours aloft and to its pace, seeking for that ring of flame around the castle."

Shea glanced down to be sure he was following the road. "It isn't just finding the place," he said. "We've got to consider tactics, too. Duke Astolph is somewhere around with that damn hippogriff, and this thing's slow freight by comparison. I don't want to be enchanted down in flames, especially with you aboard, kid."

"Grammercy for your thought of me, fair sir," said the girl: "but I charge you that while we keep this quest, you shall no longer treat me as a woman *par amours,* but as a full companion."

The words were sharp enough, but did he imagine it, or had she said them in a tone anything but sharp?

There was not time to make a decision, for peering over the carpet's leading edge, Shea caught sight of a little fan of detritus at the side of a mountain which might be a mine entrance. "I'm going to land there," he told the others. "Belphebe—that is, Belphegor, suppose you go first and smooth out anyone inside."

The carpet slanted smoothly down to a landing in front of the mineshaft, which did not appear to be a mineshaft after all when one got close to it. As Shea stood up to stretch cramped muscles a man appeared at the low entrance. He was old, he was whiskery, and a dirty brown robe was gathered around his waist by a piece of cord.

For a moment he looked at the visitors with widening eyes, then took a step backward, and planting his feet firmly, lifted his right hand with two fingers upraised: "In the name of St. Anthony and the Virgin Mary," he said in a high voice, "depart, cursèd enchantments!"

Shea felt the muscles of his face relax into different patterns and reached a hand up to find that his tusks were gone. He looked at Medoro; the poet had lost his, too.

"Nothing to worry about, Father," he said to the old man. "We're really not enchantments ourselves, just had some put on us, and we're looking for directions."

The old man beamed. "Surely, surely, my son. There be many great and good men of your race, some of whom draw nigh unto God, though in strange wise. And all respect the hermit who has nought but his poverty. Whither wish you to go?"

"Castle Carena," said Shea, the thought flashing through his mind that even if this were the holiest hermit in Spain, his protestation of poverty was laid on with a trowel.

"By the road before you, my children. Over the next pass lies the valley of Pau; beyond it, the village of the same name, wherein stands the church of St. Mary of Egypt, whose vicar is an Austin friar. Beyond that again, a fork in the route—"

"Uh-huh," said Shea. He turned to Belphegor. "That must be the valley where my partner went hunting for

Roger just before I met you and Duke Astolph." He turned back to the hermit. "Have you seen any Christian knights going in that direction?"

The old man's face took on a troubled expression. "Nay, children," he said. "I know naught of warlike men or their contentions. These be vanities, even as gold."

Medoro plucked Shea's sleeve. "Of a truth," he said, "there is no truth in this man, and he has evidently seen more than he has told. Let us question him more nearly," He fondled the hilt of his dagger.

Out of the corner of his eye Shea saw Belphegor's fine features take on a look of distaste. He said: "Nothing doing. You don't know Christian hermits, Medoro. Roughing them up only makes them more obstinate, and besides, it wouldn't look good. Anyway, now we're rid of those Jann disguises, we can find out what we want to know anywhere. So long."

He flipped a hand at the hermit, who lifted his two fingers again and said: "The blessing of God on you, my son."

The three took their places on the carpet and Shea recited:

"By warp and by woof,
   High over the roof
Of mountain and tower
You shall fly in this hour."

Nothing happened.

Shea repeated the verse, and then tried several variations in wording. Still no result. The hermit smiled benignly.

The girl said: "Methinks I can unriddle this, Sir Harold. This religious has not only blessed us, but pronounced an exorcism against enchantments, so that whatever virtue the carpet possessed by your magic is departed, nor may return in his presence. 'Tis not the first such wonder of holy men, nor the last, belike."

"Are you a holy man?" asked Shea.

The hermit folded his arms complacently. "In my

humble way, my son, I strive to lead the sinless life."

"Oh, Lord!" said Shea. "Now I suppose we'll have to walk."

Said the hermit: "It were better for your soul to mortify the flesh by walking a thousand miles with bleeding feet than to travel at ease for one."

"No doubt," said Shea, "but right now there are a couple of things more important to me than my soul, and one of them is getting a good friend of mine out of a jam." He was talking over his shoulder as he unbound Roger's legs and made a loop in the knotted turbans to serve as a halter.

Something made a gruesome noise in the cave. Shea cocked his head. "You got an ass, Father?"

The old man's complacency gave way to a look of apprehension. "You would not rob me of my stay and sole companion, my son?"

"No. I told you we were on the square. I just wondered if you'd be interested in selling him."

With surprising alacrity the hermit disappeared into the shaft, to return presently with the ass; a big, tough-looking animal that would help them a good deal in the marching that evidently lay ahead. Shea asked how much; the hermit replied that the service of God could hardly be accomplished on less than five bezants, a figure at which Belphegor made a little round O of her mouth.

Shea felt at his belt, then remembered that the innkeeper had picked him clean and he had forgotten to repossess the money. "Damn," he said. "You got any money, Medoro?"

The Moor spread his hands. "Oh, my lord and brother, had I but a piece of copper, it were at your service. But it was ordained that my monies should be left in my casket, which is in the camp fo the Commander of the Faithful, the blessed."

"Hm," said Shea. "Okay, then, let's have one of those bangles," indicating Medoro's jewelled bracelets.

Medoro looked sour. "It is not to be concealed, O friend Harr, that such a jewel is worth a dozen such vile, scrawny beasts as that which stands before us. Has not your Nazarene imam pronounced that gold is vanity to him?"

"That's his risk," said Shea, folding the carpet into a saddle-pad and slinging it on the back of the animal.

"It will be devoted to the increase of holiness," said the hermit, unbinding the rope around his waist and helpfully installing it as a cinch. Shea turned to Roger, who had not said a word: "Okay, big boy, you get the ride."

The direct address seemed to touch off a spring within whatever nest of complexes served the big man for a brain. "Vile cozener!" he shouted. "May Allah descend on me if I separate your bones not one from another. Yet since you do me at least the honor to give me the better place, I will accord it in my mercy that you die before these others, Alhamodillah!"

"Nice of you," said Shea, firmly, tying Roger's feet together under the animal's belly. "But that's not quite the idea. It's just that you're less likely to get loose and massacre us while you're in this position."

They set out. The track had never been intended for wheeled traffic. It was so narrow that no more than two could go abreast, a distinctly less comfortable method of travel than the flying carpet. Shea took the lead, one hand on the ass' rope. It was an hour later when he held up a hand to halt the others. "People ahead," he said.

Belphegor came up to join him, bow bent and arrow nocked. The people turned out to be three asses, biting the tops off weeds at the cliff-side and a stout, weather-beaten man, sitting in the shade and resting. The man scrambled up at their approach, hand to knife, then relaxed as Shea said: "Good morning, mister. How's business?"

"Peace and good luck to you, friend," said the man. "Business have I none at the moment, but count that at sundown I shall have much; for look you, I am bound for Pau, where they are holding an auto-de-fé on a paynim sorcerer the day beyond tomorrow. Now that is thirsty work; and I have the wine to slake it." He gestured toward the asses, and Shea perceived that they were laden with skin bags that gurgled liquidly.

Shea thought of Votsy and Dr. Chalmers and didn't quite like the sound of that "paynim sorcerer." But before he could question further, Belphegor burst out:

"No more on this. Behold, Medoro, why I still love the free wildwood, when men will still do such things to one another. Have you other tidings, sirrah?"

"Why, not such as you would name tidings, now that you ask," said the man, unabashed. "A small thing only, that will serve as a tale when tales are told. If I were a timorous man, the tale would doubtless be longer and have an unhappy ending, but—"

Belphegor's foot tapped.

"To make a long matter short, as I was taking the short route over the mountain from Doredano, I was set upon by flying demons with horns and great tusks —doubtless a sending of that same sorcerer who will be so finely cooked tomorrow. Had I not fought my way through the press with this single blade, you would not see me here and I should have lost my profit. Ware them on the way. To what lord do you take your prisoner?"

"We're taking him to a lady," said Shea, firmly. "He has four black children and won't pay alimony. But she'll probably need a bodyguard who isn't afraid of anything, and we'll tell her you applied for the job. So long."

Heedless of Roger's howls of anger, he set out again.

It took them all day to reach the pass. The rests at Medoro's request became more and more frequent, and he finally developed a blister, which had to be ex-aimed by Belphegor, to Shea's intense disgust. She pronounced the infliction so bad that he would have to ride, and this time there was nearly a quarrel, Shea insisted on the danger from the big man's strength and skill with weapons, the girl equally insistent that Medoro was a third of their fighting strength and they would be in poor shape against any attack if he were eliminated.

She won, of course. Medoro mounted the ass, while Roger's feet were unbound and Shea made a slip-noose of turban for his neck, so that any sudden jerk would cut off the big man's wind. They declared a kind of tacit truce; Shea began to talk to him, and for a time wished he hadn't, since the only thing Roger wanted to discuss was broken heads and spilled guts. In desperation he turned to the subject of Bradamant,

379

which had previously produced so strange an effect on the big bruiser. The effect was all that could be asked. Roger looked at the ground and tittered.

"What's she like?" asked Shea. "I've never seen her."

Roger appeared to be undergoing an internal revolution. Finally, with a masterful effort, he produced: "There is no blessedness but in Allah and his Prophet. Her arms are like ash-trees and her buttocks like full moons. Should chance bring union between us, I will contest with you in arms in celebration. But it is to be remarked that your death will not make me master of your Frankish slave-girl with the ill-omened hair; for I would liefer consort with the uttermost daughters of Eblis."

The tables were neatly turned, decided Shea, and let well enough alone till they had crossed the pass and a mile or two down found a camping spot beside a stream. It was not yet twilight, but Belphegor declared that there would be little chance of game later, so she and Medoro went off hunting, while Shea built a fire.

Half an hour later they came back laughing, with four rabbits. She displayed her well-remembered skill at skinning and cooking them; Shea thought he had never tasted anything better, nor for that matter seen anything more pleasant than the spectacle of Medoro inserting morsel after morsel of meat into Roger's mouth, which the latter gulped with a rapidity that suggested he was trying to snap the fingers off.

After the meal, all felt better; Roger almost genial in spite of the fact that he had to be led behind a bush, and Medoro positively brilliant. He improvised comic rhymes; he effectively parodied Dardinell's parade-ground manner; he did a superb imitation of Atlantès working a complicated spell, including his dismay when the spell produced the wrong results. It came close enough so Shea laughed loud and carefree—whereupon Medoro suddenly went serious.

"Lord Harr," he said, "now that your breast is broadened, I would seek unto your advice, as that of an uncle or a learned man in the law. According to the most excellent book of the Prophet of God, on whose name be grace, which is the Book of the Cow, it is lawful for a Muslim to take unto wife what woman he desires. Yet it is written also that one wife is insufficient, whereas two quarrel with each other, and if there be three, the two will combine against the third, so that there is no safety but in a fourth. Yet this woman whom I would wed will have me as single wife only."

Shea smiled wryly. A delicious question to ask him! However, he thought, let's roll with the punch. He said: "It's a tough case. If you marry her that way, you violate your religion, and if she marries you any other way, she violates whatever religion she has, if any. I suggest you both become Zoroastrans. That can't be far from either one."

Belphegor said: "Who be these Zo-ro-astrans?" She tumbled over the word.

"Oh, they seem to have a pretty sound theology, for my money. They hold the existence of equal and opposed powers of good and evil, Ormazd and Ahriman. Gets around the difficulty of the doctors of theology. If God is omnipotent, how come there's evil?"

Said the girl: " 'Tis not far—" and stopped at the gasp of horror from Medoro.

His mouth was flapping open and shut, rather like that of a carp in a pool. When he found words, it was to say: "The Ghebers! To be a fire-worshipping alchemist! Why, they are filthy cannibals, who dance naked and eat the limbs of human beings. Why, I'd not union with the Queen of the Diamond Isles, had she all wisdom and the bed-arts of the Ethiopians, were she a Gheber! Nay, were she the most beauteous of mortal women to outward seeming, I would know her for the foulest of harlots by such token, who dined only on broiled rats' bones and hired Negro slaves to do her service."

Belphegor drew in a long breath. "My Lord Medoro," she said, "that is somewhat ungentle of you. I would pray you to think more deeply on't while we make our couches." She was on her feet, all one graceful movement. "I'm for a tree."

Next morning they breakfasted on the proceeds of the girl's hunting, Medoro slightly querulous over the lack of salt and Roger grumbling that there was no

Imam to call the proper hour of prayer. Shea said: "The way I figure it out, I doubt whether we can make the castle today, unless we get some animals to carry us in Pau."

Medoro looked at the girl. "By Allah, if we reach that castle never, it were soon enough for me, unless there be a good Kazi with witnesses there to marry us at once."

Shea opened his mouth, but the girl beat him to it. "Nay, fair Medoro," she said, "let us think not so fast on marriage. For behold, I am as bound by my plighted word as ever knight was, to stand by Sir Harold till this quest be fully accomplished. Whatever faith holds, one must keep faith."

The dampening of Medoro's spirits was only temporary. By the time they were ready to start, he was gay and cheerful again. When Shea led Roger to the ass with the intention of repeating the previous day's arrangement, the poet darted ahead and mounted it at once.

"Hey!" said Shea. "You had your turn yesterday. Now look here—"

Medoro looked down from his seat. "Now Allah burn my liver if I ride not this ass today," he said. "O, son of shame—"

Smack! It was a long reach but Shea landed right on the side of the jaw and Medoro landed with a plunk on the ground. He heaved himself up on one elbow as Shea looked at his own tingling knuckles, wondering what had made his own temper depart to the region where the woodbine twineth.

When he raised his eyes Belphegor was between them, hand on her little belt-knife. "De Shea," she said, in a grating voice, "this passes bearing; a most vile peasantish discourtesy. You are no more my knight, nor I your lady, till you make full apology, nor will I hold communion with you else."

Medoro rode the ass. Shea, trudging along in the dirt and stones, with his hand on Roger's halter, wondered whether the light of his life were exactly bright.

Proceeding grumpily under the pillar of disagreement that kept them all silent, they were still well short of Pau when afternoon drew in and Belphegor announced shortly that if they were to sup, she would have to hunt. This time Medoro did not accompany her, but as he got down from the ass, he suddenly shaded his eyes against the sun and pointed:

"Inshallah!" he said. "Lord Harr, look on a marvel. That tree is surely of peach, such as they have in the land of Circassia, and as the Prophet is the Witness, we shall have fruit to our repast." He skipped off with no sign of blister or limp and in a few moments was back with his arms full of ripe peaches.

It was at that moment that inspiration descended on Harold Shea. "Sit down and take care of Roger while I prepare them for eating," he said. Medoro wrinkled his eyes round a glance that might have been one of suspicion. "Listen, take it easy," said Shea. "I'm sorry I got sore at you this morning."

The poet's face broke out in a beatific smile. "Of a truth, Lord Harr, it is said that the Franks are in fury uncontrollable; but if one bear with them, in friendship generous." He took the slip-knot turban and led Roger to one side.

Shea took off his helmet, stuck it in the ground on its spike; it made a magnificent punchbowl. Four of the peaches went into it. Shea scratched the letters C, H and O with his knife-point on the remaining peaches and arranged them as Doc Chalmers had done which he so unexpectedly produced the Scotch whiskey in Faerie. Accident that time, Shea told himself, but this time whatever happened would be on purpose. He leaned over the helmet and with one eye cocked in the direction where Medoro was rather languidly holding to Roger's noose as the latter recounted one of his tales of assault and battery, repeated softly what he could remember of Doc's spell:

"So frequently as I with present time
  The earlier image of our joy compare,
So frequently I find our less than prime,
  And little joy than that we once did share:
Thus do I ask those things that once we had
  To make an evening run its magic course,

And banish from this company the sad
   Thoughts that in prohibition have their source:
Changes, peaches! From the better to the worse."

For a moment he had the dreadful fear that this
would give him a mess of rotten peaches, but when
he opened his eyes, the helmet was brimmed to over-
flowing with a golden liquid in which peach-pits and
deflated peachskins floated. Shea fished one of the
latter out and tasted the surplus. It was peach brandy
all right, of a magnificent flavor, and now that he caught
it at the back of his palate, a potency rarely equalled
in his own cosmos—about 120 proof, he would judge.

"Hey!" he called. "Bring him over here, Medoro. I've
made some peach sherbet for you."

The poet got to his feet, jerking the prisoner along.
He leaned over the helmet and sniffed. "By Allah, it
has a noble perfume, Lord Harr. You are the best of
the shah-bands; but it should be cooled with snow
for fair sherbet."

"I'll trot right over to one of the mountains and
get some," said Shea.

Medoro knelt and thrusting his face down to the
edge of the helmet, took a long pull. "Allah!" he said.
"Of a truth, snow is sorely needed, for this sherbet
burns like fire. If this be poison—" he glared at Shea.

"Then I'll be poisoned, too," and Shea took a drink
for himself. It certainly did warm the gullet going
down.

"Give me some of this sherbet, I pray, in the name
of Allah," begged Roger. Shea cautiously disengaged
the spike of the helmet from the ground and held it
for him, as he took a sip, then a drink.

When he lifted his face from the cup, Medoro said:
"O lord and brother blest and to profit increased, I
would have more of your Frankish sherbet; for the eve
is chill, and it does provide a warmth interior."

The helmet went round, and then again, Shea not
stinting when it came his turn. Belphegor's anger with
him began to fade a little into the background. She'd
get over it as soon as she realized her real identity,
and he could think of a dozen, twenty, thirty schemes

to produce that desirable result, only requiring slight details to be filled in. He could take care of that any time; in the meanwhile, Medoro was one of the most fascinating conversationalists he had ever met, and even Roger was not so bad a guy when you got to know him. The Saracen paladin was telling a tale of his adventures in Cathay, which Medoro was weaving into a ballad of immensely complicated rhythm-scheme, but he kept missing the rhyme at the third line of each stanza, and Shea was correcting him when Belphegor suddenly stood in the center of the little group, a brace of black-plumed birds in her hand.

Medoro looked up, and his mouth fell open. "Now may Ifrits remove me to the outermost depths of the sea an I futter not this damsel," he shouted, and lurched half way to his feet, then sat down. His brows contorted with effort; he tried to get up again and made it. Belphegor dropped the birds.

"I love you for your exceeding loveliness and surpassing beauty," said Medoro, "and you shall grant me the desire of the body, as Ali bin-Hayat says:

"Men craving pardon will uplift their hands;
Women pray pardon with their legs on high:
Out on it for a pious, prayerful work!
The Lord shall raise it in the depths to lie."

He giggled at the girl's horror-filled face, hiccupped, spread his arms and ran at her.

Smack! Medoro sat down abruptly. Shea cried triumphantly: "A most vile peasantish discourtesy!"

The young Moor heaved himself up again, his handsome features contorted. "By Allah!" he said. "You foulest of tribades and filthiest of harlots, that would reject the love of one of the house of Hassan for base-born Negroes! Farewell! I seek the camp where there are boys a thousand times lovelier and more faithful." Before any of them could guess his intention, he took three staggering steps to the ass, was on its back and belaboring it to a gallop in the direction whence they had come with his scabbarded scimitar.

385

Belphegor stood at gaze a second, then snatched up her bow and sent an arrow after him—too late.

"Shurr Harol'," said Roger with owlish gravity, "ish even as I have shaid. Thish red Frankish hair ish ill-omened. You had better be drowned in the shee if you sell not that slave."

Shea ignored him to take the helmet over to Belphegor. "Here, take a drink of this," he said.

She gave him a long, slow glance and accepted the offer with slightly trembling hands. The shaking quieted. "My thanks and good grace to you, Sir Harold," she said, "for I perceive that it is to you I owe this. It is like—like—" She seemed to flounder for a lost memory.

Shea said: "In Latin they would say *In vino veritas*."

"Oh, aye. Taunt me not; I should have seen him with clear eyes when he would have left you in the tent or put the hermit to the torture. A niggling and wittold does not make himself a true man with a lute and fair words."

She sat down and pressed the palms of both hands to her eyes. Shea sat beside her and put an arm round her shoulders, but she shook him off. From the background Roger croaked: "Flee away from thish ill-omened wench."

Shea could not be sure whether she was crying or not, and his heart turned flip-flops as he tried to think of something to do. He wished he had not drunk so much of the peach brandy; there seemed to be a haze between him and what he was trying to think.

The hands came down and Belphegor turned a woe-begone face toward him. "Nay, the fault's my own," she said, in a flat voice, "and you have been my true knight that would have saved me from a villain. Heigh-ho!" She sighed and stood up. "It falls dusk and we must sup soon if we're to take the road of our quest tomorrow. Nay, no hand-kissing; I'll not have these empty courtesies."

15

THEY CAME DOWN A HILL TOWARD PAU THROUGH
the morning light. "I suppose we could get some horses
there," remarked Shea, gazing at the range of thatched
roofs. "Has nobody any money? I'm broke, and we
haven't got Medoro with his gold bracelets."

Belphegor laughed. "Not a groat, I. To those of the
woodland seed 'tis the forbidden thing."

Shea looked at Roger. "O man," said the paladin,
"know that the hardest of riding is better than the
easiest footgoing, as says al-Qa'saf. But as for money,
what need? You have a sword to take or magics to
make as does my uncle Atlantès when he would have
money."

Shea gazed at Roger in astonishment. It was about
the first time he had ever heard the big man express
an idea, and for a wonder, it seemed a fairly good
one. The only trouble was that he had a little less than
no idea what type of spell would produce money. The
passes, yes—one could manage those—but the psycho-
somatic element?

Well, one could only try. A hundred yards or so
back a bank had caved in on a deposit of fine golden
sand. He scooped up a double handful of this, laid
it on a handkerchief and tied the corners together. Then
he laid the improvised pouch on the ground and traced
out a pair of interlacing pentacles, like those on the
doors of Atlantès' room in Castle Carena. Belphegor
was watching him, and it disturbed him slightly.

"Take this guy a little way off and cover him, will
you?" he asked. "Don't let him watch."

The spell—ah, yes, of course, good old Kipling. He
chanted:

"Iron's for the soldier, silver for the maid,
Copper's for the craftsman, working at his trade.
Sand is but silly stuff, sifting to a fall;
But gold, red gold! is the master of them all."

The handkerchief sagged and looked lumpy. Shea picked it up and heard a gratifying clink within. "All right," he called. "I guess we're set now."

The approaches to Pau seemed curiously deserted, the brown and green fields vacant of working men, no women and children at the doorways. Shea puzzled over it until he recalled what the wine-merchant had said about the auto-da-fé, and felt a sudden need for haste. But just at that moment a clanging sound came to his ears, and across the street he perceived a village smith, hammering away at an open-air anvil.

Shea led his prisoner over, and greetings were exchanged. "Where is everybody today?" he asked.

The smith jerked a thumb. "Down the road. Saint's shrine," he said shortly. "Auto-da-fé for the monster. Can't waste time myself." He hefted his hammer, in evident desire for them to be gone so he could carry on with his job. Shea thought these Basques a singularly uncommunicative lot. Nevertheless, he tried again:

"Monster? What monster?"

"Devil. Looks like a wolf. Caught in a wolf-net."

That would be Votsy, all right. The need for hurry was becoming acute, but horses would help. "We'd like to buy horses." He jingled the handkerchief of money.

The lines round the smith's eyes wrinkled craftily. "Have some," he said. "Come, see."

"I don't think I need to. You see, we're rather in a hurry with this prisoner, and we can get any money we spend back from the baron where we're taking him."

Suspicion mingled with the craft. The smith was clearly not used to dealing with customers who bought without asking the price. "Ten bezants," he said, flatly.

"Okay," said Shea. "Lead them out." He opened up his handkerchief-purse and produced a handful of bright gold pieces. As they touched the anvil, however, they instantly changed to little pinches of sand. The smith looked at them and then at Shea. "What's this?" he demanded.

Shea could feel a flush creeping up his face. "Ha, ha, just a joke," he said hollowly, and reaching into the pile, selected another handful to hand them to the smith. But suspicion had now completely gained the upper hand in the man. He rang each piece on the anvil, or tried to, for as soon as metal touched metal, these too dissolved into little cones of sand.

"Scoundrel! Cheat! Magician!" bellowed the man, gripping his hammer in both hands. "Out! Out! Ha, priest!"

Fortunately, he did not offer to pursue as the three beat a hasty retreat. Too late, on the road again, Shea remembered that Kipling's original poem had made iron, not gold, the master of them all, so that of course the spell had gone sour. It did not help matters any that even with the halter around his neck Roger was snickering.

Shea turned toward the girl. "Look," he said. "This hasn't anything to do with the job we're working on—" he glanced at Roger "—but I think a friend of mine is in trouble. Would it put you out too much to speed up the works?"

For answer she actually smiled at him. "Lead on," she said, and taking one of the arrows from her quiver, prepared to urge Roger to speed; but then: "Hold. Here's one that weeps and may not, for chivalry, be neglected."

Shea turned. With her back toward him and feet in the ditch that bordered the road, there was indeed one that wept. Her back hair was neatly ordered and her figure was young, which lent a certain predisposition toward relieving her distress. As the three halted beside her, she turned a face definitely pretty, though tear-streaked and somewhat dirty, toward them. "They —they—they seek to slay my sweetheart," she got out, before dissolving in another torrent of sobbing.

Belphegor said: "Sir Harold, whatever else you be chargèd with, here is a quest that turns all quests aside; a woman unjustly in trouble, to wit."

"I don't know about the unjustice," said Shea. "But

let's see." He addressed the weeping girl. "Who's they? You mean the people who are holding the auto-da-fé on the monster?"

"Aye. No more monster than me. Am I a monster?" She spread her arms and Shea noticed that her dress was low cut in front.

"Marry, tears mend no torn bodices," said Belphegor, just a trifle acidly.

"The—the priest t-t-took him down to the Saint's cross for burning. Save him!"

Shea hesitated, then looked at Belphegor. The girl was frowning, but she said strictly: "Sir Harold, meseems that her plaint would be of that friend you bespeak."

"I'm afraid so," he said. "You take—no, you'll need both hands for the bow, and I only need one for the sword. Giddy-ap, Roger." He unsheathed the blade; the girl who had been doing the weeping tagged along behind.

The road turned a shoulder and slanted up a hillside from which figures were visible, moving against the skyline. One or two people turned round, but nobody seemed in the least curious about the spectacle of a Saracen and a red-headed bow-girl leading a monstrous warrior by a noose. As he topped the rise and pressed forward, Shea saw why. The road here ran along the outer edge of a wide terrace on the side of the mountain. On the innermost edge of the terrace, against the cliff, something had been carved which looked rather like a phallic symbol with a halo round its head. In front of this singular erection a huge pyre of wood was erected, and around it a hundred or so peasants were crowding.

The wood was burning vigorously, and in its center, bound to a stake by neck and all four legs, was a huge gray wolf. The logs on which it sat were already a bed of hot coals, the flames around it were consuming its bonds, but except for the fact that the wolf had its tongue out and was panting, it seemed utterly unconcerned with the proceedings.

Shea suddenly recalled the spell under which Atlantès had let Polacek and himself out of the castle's flaming border, and wanted to laugh. Instead he said: "Hello, folks."

Talk died in a circle like ripples spreading from a thrown stone in a pool. A man in a patched black robe, who had been throwing sticks toward the center of the fire, turned and came toward him, blinking with near-sightedness.

"What goes on, Father?" asked Shea.

The priest produced a cross and began to mumble. "Oh, that's all right," said Shea. "I'm not a Saracen, and anyway I'm a friend of the hermit of the mountain." He indicated his prisoner. "See? We've captured Roger of Carena."

The priest studied the prisoner's face, pressing his own close. Roger hawked and spat, but only succeeded in adding another spot on the patched gown. The priest came toddling back toward Shea. "Worshipful sir," he said, "I perceive you are a very mighty man, and I trow, a good Christian. Sir, in your might, perchance you can aid us. Here have we a very demon from the uttermost depths of hell, in monster form, but his master Beelzebub, who is the Lord of Fire, will not permit him to burn."

Shea said: "I'm not sure he's as bad as you think. Had it occurred to you that he might be just a good man under an enchantment?" He stepped forward and raising his voice, addressed the wolf: "Are you Vaclav Polacek?"

The wolf barked twice and nodded vigorously, then raising one paw to emphasize the point, tore away the burned rope that held it. There was a universal "Ooooh" and backward movement in the crowd.

"I thought Doc Chalmers told you to lay off that stuff," said Shea, disgustedly. "Can you get loose?"

"Oow! Ououw! Ouououw!" said the wolf.

"Well, lay off it for a minute, for the love of Mike, till I get you off the hook." He turned toward the priest. "It's like I said. He's a Christian squire under an enchantment. I am Sir Harold de Shea." He did his best to strike an attitude. The priest looked at him with near-sighted skepticism.

"Votsy!" said Shea. "This guy don't believe you're

391

the goods. If those ropes are burned through enough, come over here and lick one of his feet."

"Wrrrower!" howled the wolf, and leaped against his ropes. They gave; there was a universal scream of terror from the assembled peasants and they scattered as the animal came leaping through the flames, throwing burning coals in all directions. The priest stood his ground, but his face was set in tight lines and he was vigorously fingering his rosary as the wolf that was Votsy sat down and licked at his feet. After a moment or two the priest put one hand down and gingerly patted his head, but removed the hand instantly as up the valley, in the direction they were going, a bugle sounded "Rump-te-umpte-um-tum." At least it sounded like a bugle. All the notes were flat.

Everybody gazed. Up the rise came a column of horsemen, headed by three who bore slender spears with dirty pennons of colored wool too heavy for the slow motion of their progress to lift and make clear. Behind them came the bugler, and behind them again, three knights in full plate armor with their helmets banging at their knees. Shea recognized Count Roland d'Anglante and Reinald of Montalban; the third had slightly more delicate features and a surcoat over his mail divided red and white across the middle, with a huge gold buckle occupying the center. They were followed by a score or more of mounted men-at-arms in iron hats with brims and mail-shirts of overlapping metal scales. His eyes were torn from the sight by an inarticulate burp from Roger, who suddenly seemed to have difficulty with his breathing, though the halter had not been pulled tight.

There was no point in trying to conceal anything, Shea stepped boldly to the center of the road and, holding his hand up like a traffic cop, said: "Hey!"

The bugle gave a toot, and the riders pulled up. Reinald cried: " 'Tis the turban-knight! How hight he—Sir Harold de—du Chaille? No matter. Hail, fair Belphegor!"

"Regard!" said the knight in the surcoat, in a high voice. "Roger of Carena, and in bonds. This may not be borne!" The knight vaulted down and Shea realized that "he" was a handsome, brown-haired woman of

392

show-girl size. She whipped a dagger from her belt. Roger was apparently trying to use one of his feet to dig a hole to fall into, his gaze fixed on the ground. Shea thrust himself between the two. "Listen," he said, "this guy's my prisoner."

Count Roland looked down from his horse benignly. "My lady and fair cousin Bradamant, peace; for this is good law. This young sir is a dubbed knight, Sir Harold de Shea, to wit, and if he holds Lord Roger bound it is by right of fair conquest."

"Then I challenge him!" said Bradamant, picking at her belt for a pair of gloves. "For this is my very soul and love and I will assay all desperately upon the body of any who holds him. Lord Reinald, be my aid."

"Cut them down!" said Reinald harshly.

Roland leaped down from his own horse, clanging like an earthquake in a kitchen. "Then must I even stand his, to make the balance fair; for this is a very gentle knight that has done me much service. Ho, Durandal!" He lifted up a great cross-hilted sword, and Belphegor drew back a couple of steps, snatching an arrow from her quiver and bending her bow—not at Bradamant but at Roger. Shea admired his wife's presence of mind, even if the mind was not entirely her own. Reinald looked black, but Bradamant checked her rush, and gave a little laugh.

"Nay, gentles," she said, "let us not fall on contention when Saracen banners be over the next crest, but dissolve this in amical agreement. Sir Harold, my hand." She put the dagger back and extended it.

Shea reached out and took it. "Okay, lady," he said. "My story is that I need this guy in my business. A friend of mine is in Castle Carena and can't get out, because Atlantès has built a wall of fire around it, and unless I deliver Roger there it's no dice."

"Ah, but—" said the lady warrior "—this is my more than friend and most dear love." She waved a hand at Roger, who said "Allah!" under his breath. "Surely, it is less than knightly to keep us one from the other."

"Yet even more so," said Belphegor, putting her arrow back and stepping forward in evident enjoyment of the prospect of a legal argument, "—were he to fail his duty to his vavassour and liege lord who is held prisoner."

"Ah, but the greater wipes out the less," said Bradamant. "In making deliverance of Lord Roger to this Saracen, Sir Harold would fail in duty to the Emperor Charles, who is liege lord to us all."

"Not to me," said Shea.

The three knights gasped, and Roland's face went a trifle grim. "Sir knight," he said, "a truce to profitless discourse. You know me for your friend; you will hear my judgment in this cause?"

Shea looked at the surrounding men-at-arms. Might as well put a good face on it, especially as Roland didn't seem to be a bad guy. "Sure," he said, "anything you say is all right with me."

"And you, my lady Bradamant?"

"That will I."

"Then hark." Roland unslung his big sword from his belt and kissed the hilt. "This is my judgment, given in honor, as the holy St. Michael stands my aid: that Sir Harold de Shea release the Lord Roger to the Lady Bradamant. But since she has the ring that daunts all enchantments, she shall forthwith take oath to rescue Sir Harold's lord from durance in Castle Carena. This deed I lay on her; and none other shall be accomplished till it be done."

Belphegor clapped her hands. "Oh, well thought on!" she said. Bradamant's face also expressed pleasure. She stepped to her horse, produced a sword almost as large as Roland's and held it out to him. He lifted the hilt up before her; she kissed it and extended one hand: "I swear it," she said, and turned to Shea. "Now handsell me your prisoner."

"What do I do?" he asked.

"Place his hand in mine."

"I can't. He's tied up."

"Loose him, want-wit!" She stamped her foot.

Shea was not sure this was a good idea, but nobody else seemed to have any objections, so he stepped around behind the big man, and untied some of the knots, then as Roger gave an explosive sigh of relief, took one of his hands and laid it in Bradamant's.

"Do you assign me all rights of war and ransom in this man?" she asked.

"Sure."

"Then I receive him." She dropped Roger's hand, and with a roundhouse swing, hit him a terrific slap on the side of his face. "Come, varlet!" Roger slowly lifted a numbed arm, and then, instead of hitting her back, surprisingly began to titter. "You accompany us to Carena."

Roger's face straightened out. "O my lady, I pray you, take me not back thither, where mine uncle will coop me up like a chicken."

"Tish! have I not the ring, which is proof against all that he can do? Sir Harold, will you ride with us?"

"Sure," said Shea. He looked around.

The wolf that was Vaclav Polacek was nowhere to be seen.

16

SHEA THOUGHT RAPIDLY. BRADAMANT COULD PROBably be trusted to keep her word, and even if she couldn't, there was no particular immediate danger to Doc and Florimel. But the danger to Vaclav was both immediate and particular. If they captured him again, someone was almost certain to think of strangling or using a silver weapon instead of the fire that failed. Very likely they would get him, too. He turned to the others:

"I think you could operate better at Castle Carena without us," he said. "There's a friend of mine in trouble, and I'm afraid I've got to do something about it. Bel—Belphegor, it's the sweetheart of that girl. Will you come along?"

She put two fingers to her lips. " 'Tis not in our compact. But—aye, that will I. Whither go we?"

395

"My guess would be that he'd be looking for that girl. Maybe we ought to go back to about where we found her."

"Think you he would return by the village where so late they'd have burned him?"

"You have something there, kid. Votsy is as nutty as a fruit-cake, but I think he'd be bright enough to cut around the back way."

"Come, then," said the girl. "I know some little of woodland trails." She turned to the paladins. "Gentles, I salute you farewell till a happier meeting."

The armored men raised their hands, the bugle blew again and the group broke up. A horse had been brought for Roger; Shea noticed that as he and Bradamant rode off in the direction of Castle Carena they were holding hands and not giving any particular attention to their route. In their condition, he wondered how good they would be at the business of getting Doc out of Castle Carena.

Behind the shrine the ground dipped sharply, then rose up a bank set with low bushes to the veritable forest beyond. Belphegor's eyes swept it from side to side: "Thither lies his slot," she said, pointing.

Shea could see nothing that looked like a trail, but when he plunged across the declivity at the girl's heels and up the other side, there was a broken branch on one of the bushes, and beyond, where she waved a hand, the mark of a wolf's pad, deeply impressed on the soft ground.

"Hey," he said, "wouldn't we save time by short-cutting along the road?"

She turned a laughing face. "Nay, who'd go road-wise when they could walk the free way of the forest? And more—it is the nature of the wolfish kind to be somewhat scatterwit in purpose. Trust me, we shall come on him the sooner by following direct. See, there turned he to the left."

She went more rapidly than Shea would have believed possible. The sun slanted down through the leaves in speckled patterns and occasionally a bird chirped or dipped and swooped away before him. His Saracen costume was not exactly what he would have chosen for the occasion, but he found himself suddenly happy.

Belphegor hummed a little air to herself as she examined some markings at the side of another little clump of bushes. "Here he turned aside to strike at some small game," she announced. "A rabbit, belike. And here he lay to rest after the pursuit. We gain; press on."

She was tireless; it was he who had to ask for the first halt, and later, for another. Toward what he judged to be noon they made the third pause by the side of a little stream from which they drank and shared half one of the birds left from the previous night's supper. The girl frowned suddenly.

"Sir Harold," she said, "it is passing strange, but meseems there is in this something familiar and not unsweet, as though all this were a twice-told tale. Yet sure am I that we have never wandered the wildwood together before."

"Oh, yes we—" began Shea and then stopped. No use giving her a jar that might set up a resistance to her redeveloping memory. "Do you think we'll find him?" he said instead, changing the subject rapidly.

"Oh, aye, and that soon. Come, let us be afoot again."

She was on her feet in a single graceful motion and they were off. The wolf had certainly done a good deal of circling, either because he couldn't make up his own mind, or perhaps because he had lost his way. Twice more they found places where he had rested, and then, as they passed another brook, the girl pointed suddenly. Shea saw a footprint into which the water was just oozing. He stopped, filling his lungs, and shouting: "Vaclav!"

There was a sound in the underbrush, and the wolf came trotting from behind a tree with his tongue out, shaking his head and bouncing in delight.

Shea said: "What was the matter? Get lost?"

"Arf!" said the wolf.

"Okay, now you're found. Listen here, you prize idiot. You've nearly gummed the works for all of us. Now you stick by us and don't get out of sight. I can handle some magic all right, but I don't understand the higher sorcery well enough to disenchant you, so we'll have to wait till we find Doc. As it is it's damned lucky Atlantès fire-proofed you before you turned into a werewolf again."

The wolf put its tail between its legs and emitted a moan of contrition. Shea turned his back and said to Belphegor: "Can you get us on the road to Castle Carena again?"

"Assuredly. It lies that way." She pointed. "But do you find the woods that are my joy so comfortless?"

"It's not that, kid. We got business. Afterward, we can come back here, if you like, and—oh, what the hell, let's go."

The approach of dusk found them still among trees. While Shea made a fire the wolf, under strict instructions, went to help Belphegor with her hunting, flushing game for her arrow and retrieving it afterward. She came back with five rabbits, two quail and a larger bird of some kind, remarking: "If we keep this adventure, I must even find some means of gaining new arrows. Two were lost on that bout, and though I have some skill as a fletcher, both tools and seasoned wood are wanting."

The evening's bag looked like a lot for three people, but the wolf ate everything they left and looked hungrily for more. Shea was glad that they didn't have much farther to go at this rate. It would wear both of them out to feed the confounded animal.

The sun was already high in the morning when they came out on the track, a few hundred yards short of the fork where he had separated from Polacek on the outward journey. Now they were on the last lap. The wolf, which had been alternately trotting on ahead and dropping back as though it found their pace unbearably slow, suddenly came tearing up, whining and emitting little sharp howls.

"What's the matter, old man?" asked Shea.

The wolf bounded, stiff-legged, nuzzling Shea's legs and running a few steps back in the direction of Pau.

"Wants us to go back and find that girl, I guess," said Shea. The wolf howled some more, then nipped Shea by the bagginess of his trousers and tried to lead him in the desired direction.

"Listen, I'm not—" began Shea, and then saw what the wolf had been trying to tell him. A column of dust was rising along the track, with heads moving beneath it. Belphegor shaded her eyes, then gave a little squeal. "The Saracens! By the foul fiend, how slipped they past Count Roland? And see—Medoro among them."

"He must have gone over the pass and picked up a party looking for us—or else that damned smith put him on our track," said Shea.

The heads jerked forward in more rapid movement. "They have spied us!" cried Belphegor. "Up yon hill-shoulder! They cannot reach us mounted there, and mayhap we shall gain the shelter of the trees."

The horsemen were coming on fast, about twenty of them. High-pitched yells announced that they had seen their quarry.

Shea and his companion reached the round of the shoulder and pelted through a clump of scrubby oaks. Beyond, a slope of crumbled shale towered over them. They sank in the loose stuff halfway to their knees, every effort to go higher loosening a minor landslide that carried them staggering back. It was like a tread-mill.

Below, a couple of horsemen were picking their way through the rocks at the base of the shoulder; others were spreading left and right. An arrow zipped into shale above Shea's head. He wished he knew some kind of magic that would work quick.

"No use," he said bitterly. "We'll have to stand and try to fight it out." He gripped the girl's hand and ran the few steps back down toward the trees.

The Saracens were skirmishing around the base of the shoulder, stopping now and then to yell. A few of them had double-curved bows and were letting off arrows.

Belphegor crouched behind a rock and let off one of her own shafts at a dodging shape. The shot missed, splintering on a stone behind. The next hit a horse, which reared and threw its rider. Belphegor dodged as half a dozen arrows clattered around her in return.

Medoro was on a fine white horse, well out of range. His voice floated up thinly. "Cease from shooting lest you do her a harm! She shall be taken alive, but I will give five thousand dirhams for the head of the man!"

A man threw up one arm and rolled out of his saddle, an arrow right through his body and tipped with a spurt of blood. The rest drew back, dismounted, and leaving one or two to hold horses, ran at the base of the shoulder with swords and spears.

Out from behind a rock slipped a big gray hairy shape which lit on the back of a Saracen with a long bound. Good old Vaclav! The man went down, screaming, in a voice that was suddenly choked, and Belphegor's bowstring snapped like a harp.

Thump! Down went one of the attackers, clutching his stomach and chewing at the grass. An arrow glanced up and away from the helmet of another. Thump! The leader of the rush was down, with an arrow right through the eye.

"Allahu Akhbar!" screamed Medoro from below. "Ten thousand dirhams!"

A Saracen stopped with an arrow through his forearm. The others set up a discordant yell and came rushing and stumbling up from all sides, clambering over those who had taken the girl's arrows. The wolf got the hindmost by the leg, wolf and man rolling down the hill, the latter squealing with terror as his weapon failed to bite. Belphegor nailed the man with the helmet neatly through the throat.

"My last shaft, Harold," she cried.

Smart girl, he thought, to plant it where it did the most good, and drove his arm forward in a long lunge. The scimitar-like blade was unhandy, but it went right through the open mouth of the man before him. Shea parried a cut with his dagger and swung, but the man had a helmet, which took the blow with a clang, and Shea's blade snapped off at the hilt. However, the blow had force enough to knock the man over backward, and he carried the legs from under a couple of others.

Someone hurled a barb-headed javelin just as Shea recovered from the stroke. The weapon missed and hung quivering in a tree. Shea and Belphegor grabbed for it together. He reached it first, jerked it loose, snapped it over his knee, and gripped the pointed end like a rapier. "Get into a tree," he called to the girl. The Saracens were closing in fast; Shea had just time to turn around, feint at the nearest, dodge his swinging cut, and lunge. The point got him right below the chin.

The next man gave ground, so that Shea's lunge fell short. He leaped back, barely parrying a cut from the side with his inadequate blade. They were ringing him, he couldn't face three ways at once, and was too busy parrying even for a quick thrust. A blow on the side of the head made his senses spin; only his helmet kept the edge out.

Then a sound drowned the shouts of the Saracens; a blast on a horn, deep, full and resonant. It sounded like the horn of Heimdall that had made the glaciers shake; but this one had a wild discordant edge that made Shea's skin crawl and his teeth ache. A dreadful feeling of fear and horror seized him; he wanted to burst into tears, to get down on his knees. The horn sounded again, and all at once the Saracens were bounding down the shoulder, their shouts changed to cries of panic. Shea almost ran after them.

A shadow floated across the shoulder and he looked up to see Duke Astolph soaring past through the air on his hippogriff. He was outlined against the sky as he raised the horn to his lips once more and blew the Saracens along the valley.

But not all of them. Shea looked down in time to see a short, bearded character—who must have been deaf, for he showed no sign of being affected by the horn—on one knee, not twenty yards away, drawing a curved bow. As the man released, Shea ducked almost instinctively and the arrow went over his head.

A cry made him turn round. Belphegor had reached for a dropped scimitar, and now she was sinking to her knees, the arrow sticking in her side.

Shea hurled himself at the Muslim archer, who dropped his bow and whipped out a short yataghan. For three seconds their weapons flickered like sunbeams. Shea parried and drove the javelin-point into the fellow's forearm, where it stuck between the bones.

The man dropped his weapon and pulled back, tearing the javelin from Shea's grasp.

Shea snatched up the yataghan. His antagonist fell on his knees and lifted the one good arm. "In the name of Allah! Would you strike a man unarmed?"

"Damn right I would," snarled Shea and did so. The head came off, bounced, bounced again and rolled down the hill.

Shea went back to where Belphegor lay among the rocks, her face pale and her eyes half closed. He took her in his arms.

"Harold," she said.

"Yes, dearest."

"All is crystal clear. I am Belphebe of the woods, daughter of Chrysogonë, and you are my dearest dear."

Shock was often a good cure in amnesia cases. But what the hell good did it do either of them now? He gulped.

"I would have borne your sons," she said faintly. " 'Twas a brave match and a joyous."

"It's not as bad as that."

"Aye, I fear me. I go to Ceres and Sylvanus. Kiss me before I go."

He kissed her. The lips smiled wanly and he placed his hand over her heart. It was beating, but slowly and weakly.

She sighed a little. "A brave match . . ."

"What ho!" said a familiar deep voice. Astolph stood over them, the horn in one hand, the hippogriff's bridle in the other. "Oh, I say, is the young lady hurt? That's a bit of too bad. Let me have a look at her."

He glanced at the projecting arrow. "Let's see the pulse. Ha, still going, but not for long. Internal bleeding, that's the devil. Quick, young fellow, get me some twigs and grass and start a fire. I believe I can handle this, but we'll have to work fast."

Shea scrambled around, cursing the slow inefficiency of flint and steel, but getting the fire going. Astolph had drawn an enormous pentacle around them with a stick and had whipped together a tiny simulacrum of an arrow out of a twig, with a bunch of grass representing the feathers. He tossed this in the fire, muttering a spell. The smoke billowed around chokingly, much more than so small a fire had any right to make. Belphebe was invisible.

Shea jumped violently as he observed, beyond the border of the pentacle, a pair of eyes hanging unsupported in the air on a level with his own. Just eyes, with black pupils. Then there were more pairs, sometimes at angles or moving a bit, as though their invisible owners were walking about.

"Stay where you are," said Astolph between spells. His arms were outspread and Shea could see him waving them through the smoke as he chanted in several languages at once.

Something deep inside Shea's head kept saying: Come on out; come out, come out; it's wonderful; we'll make you a great man; come out; just step this way; this will be the greatest thing you've ever known; come with us . . . and something stirred his muscles in a movement toward the eyes. He had taken a full staggering step toward the eyes before he got a grip on himself, and sweat stood on his forehead with the effort of trying to keep from another step.

Suddenly the fire went out, the smoke died as though it had been sucked into the ground and the eyes disappeared. Astolph stood by the ashes, big beads of perspiration on his handsome face. The lines around his mouth were drawn. "Bit of warm work that," he said. "Lucky you didn't put your head outside the pentacle."

Belphebe sat up and smiled. The arrow was gone and there was no trace of where it had pierced the tunic save a big bloodstain down the side.

"I'd jolly well like to fix that for you," said Astolph, "but I'm not exactly a magic laundryman, you know."

"My lord, you have done enough and more than enough," said the girl, getting a little unsteadily to her feet. "I—"

"Bye the bye," interrupted Astolph, "you could do with a bit of leaching yourself, Sir Harold."

Shea realized that he had been wounded. There was blood on his face from the blow the helmet had stopped, a cut on one arm and another on the thigh. All responded readily enough to Astolph's magic, by no means so drastic this time. As the Duke finished his passes, Belphebe reached for Shea's hand:

"So low we are whole and united. Will you forgive the seeming churlishness of one who knew not her own mind?"

"Listen, kid, do I have to answer that?" said Shea, and took her in his arms. Astolph looked down the slope.

17

AFTER A FEW MINUTES ASTOLPH SAID: "IF YOU TWO don't mind, you know, I'd like a word of explanation. I thought it a bit odd when you toddled off together, but——"

Belphebe swung round, with her gay laugh. "Duke Astolph, wit you well that this is my very true and beloved husband; yet save for the wound of which you leached me in such marvellous wise, I had not known it, for I was magicked here in a strange manner by Sir Reed."

"Really? Glad to hear it. Wonderful thing, marriage —increases the population. You might have done worse; he's been a stout fellow." He began counting "——six, seven, eight. You'll want your arrows back, won't you, old girl? Those Saracens have certainly had it. Shouldn't care to take that many on at once myself. Must be something to that sword-play of yours."

"Oh, we had them at a disadvantage," said Shea. "And while you're about accepting our thanks for saving our lives, will you tell us how you happened along so opportunely?"

"Simple matter, really," said Astolph. "I was out scouting. Agramant's on the move, and I daresay we shall have a battle. Too bad we haven't Roger on our side; bad man in a brawl, only Roland can stand up to him. I hear he reached the Mussulman camp."

Shea grinned. "He got out of it, too. I ought to know.

I brought him. The last I saw of him, he and Bradamant were on their way to get my friend Sir Reed out
of hock."

Astolph's eyebrows wiggled. "Indeed! Jolly good of
you, and tit for tat, what? I daresay the Emperor will
give you a title. Hello, what's this?"

This was Vaclav Polacek, in the form of a werewolf,
who had disentangled himself from one of the bodies
on the slope and was coming slowly up the hill. "A
werewolf, as I live! Extraordinary! Doesn't belong in
this time-stream at all."

Shea explained, and with a few expert passes, Astolph changed the wolf back into Vaclav Polacek. The
Rubber Czech felt his throat. "That last guy nearly
strangled me," he complained, "but I got him. And I'm
still sore all over from the pounding those peasants
gave me with their clubs. Boy, when they let me have
it I sure was glad I was the kind of wolf it takes silver
to kill."

"But how'd you get into that shape?" asked Astolph.
"I know enough magic to be sure lycanthropy isn't exactly a habit with you."

Polacek smiled with embarrassment. "I—uh—I got
fed up with walking and I tried to turn myself into an
eagle so I could look for Roger better, but I came out
a werewolf instead. I guess I made a mistake."

"Rather," said Astolph. "Now look here, young man.
I shouldn't try that again, if I were you. It's quite on
the cards that you'd make the transformation permanent, and you'd find it deuced embarrassing."

Polacek said: "It nearly was this time. I kept getting
the most awful craving for human flesh. Belphebe was
in a tree and I couldn't reach her, but you'll never
know how close you came to being eaten last night."

Shea gulped. Astolph laughed and said: "I really
must buzz off, you chaps. Now that we're well rid of
that scouting party, the Emperor will very likely want
to use this valley for his main advance. Cheerio! Come,
Buttercup." He was off.

"If we're going to run into any more armies, I want
some equipment," said Shea. "Come on, Votsy, let's
see what we can pick up."

They made their way slowly down the slope, trying

various weapons while Belphebe retrieved her arrows and tried, but rejected, some of those the Moors had used in their short bows. At the foot of the slope, the girl put her hand to her mouth.

"My love and lord," she said. "I am much foredone with weariness, and I doubt not it is the same with you. Shall we not rest a space?"

"Yes, let's, but not here, where there are so many stiffs lying around," said Shea.

They moved along the valley, slowly picking their way across stones, till they reached a spot where a grassy slope slanted down past trees from the left, and stretched out. Polacek said: "The only thing I could want now would be a three-decker sandwich on rye and a cup of coffee. How about it, Harold, could you conjure one up?"

"Might, but it probably wouldn't have any nourishment in it," said Shea with a yawn. "I don't know all about this magic business yet. I wish I knew what made that spell about the Jann go wrong. . . ." His voice trailed off. Belphebe's head was nestled in the hollow of his arm.

He thought he had only closed his eyes a minute, but when he opened them Polacek was snoring and the sun was already dropping toward the mountain rim.

"Hey," he said, "wake up, everybody. Company's coming."

It was indeed the sound of hoofbeats that had roused him. Up the valley four riders were visible. As they drew nearer, he recognized Bradamant, Roger, Chalmers and Florimel, the last riding side-saddle. They pulled up before the three at the roadside; there was a general shaking of hands and making of salutations.

Shea said: "I wasn't sure you could make it without help. How did you manage it?"

Said Bradamant: "Sir knight, if knight you be, know that the power of this ring against all enchantments whatsoever is very great. Therefore holding the ring in my mouth and Lord Roger by the hand, it was a light matter to cross so feeble a wizardry as the wall of flame, and thus to draw your companions forth with me. Do I stand acquit of my oath to you?"

"Yep," said Shea. "We're square."

"Then I'm for the north and the Emperor's army with this, my prisoner and new aid."

She motioned at Roger, who tittered again, and wriggled in his saddle so much that he almost fell off.

"Okay," said Shea. "Thanks and so long." He reached up to shake her hand but before the contact was made, there was a flash of light that seemed to split the evening sky and a violent explosion which sent a tall tree by the roadside spraying round the travellers in a fine rain of burned chips.

They turned with a simultaneous gasp to see Atlantès of Carena standing on the stump, outlined in shimmering light and with a wand in his hand.

"Link hands everybody!" said Chalmers, quickly. "He can't hurt us under the protection of Bradamant's ring."

"Vile traitors!" squealed the little magician. "Know that you had already been a thousand times worse than dead but that there stood among you the peerless paladin, the pearl of the age, my nephew. But now that I am near enough to direct my vengeance, you shall no longer escape." He pointed the wand at Chalmers and began muttering a spell. Blue lights flashed around the tip, but nothing happened.

"Better try the other barrel," said Shea. "That one missed fire."

Atlantès stamped and grimaced. "Allah upon me that I should forget the ring of enchantment!" He clapped a hand to his head. "Yet it is said: no victory without some pain of defeat." He began to trace patterns in the air. "Stir you from this spot and you shall receive the reward of your betrayals."

"Hold my hand carefully, Harold," said Chalmers, squatting and reaching with his other hand to trace a circle on the ground round the party. He added other geometrical elements to make a full-grown pentacle, reciting his own spells as he did so.

"There," he said, letting go Shea's hand. "We're safe from him for the time being, though we seem to be besieged. Dear me!"

Atlantès had pointed his wand again, the group felt

something rush past them in the air, and a rock on the other side of the road split in a blaze of light. Belphebe placed an arrow on her string.

"I do not believe that will be of any service, young lady," said Chalmers. "I am afraid, Harold, that this gentleman is a much better magician than I, and the most that can be accomplished at present is to accord a certain amount of protection—"

"Maybe I could do something," said Polacek.

"No!" said Chalmers and Shea together. Then the former went on. "However, Harold, you do possess a rather extraordinary skill with the poetic elements in magic. If we were to work together, we might be able to accomplish something."

"I dunno, Doc," said Shea. "We can try, but my spells haven't been going too well in this cosmos." He described what had happened with the growing of the hair on his face and the jinn disguises. Beyond the pentacle the sun was behind the peaks. In the long shadows Atlantès was incanting busily and under his wand a swarm of misshapen hobgoblins began to appear among the rocks. Apparently he meant to make a real siege of it.

"Goodness gracious, I am somewhat at a loss," said Chalmers. "You're certain you made the passes correctly, Harold? Hmmm—what was your poetic element?"

Shea described how he had used elements from Shakespeare and Swinburne.

"Oh, I am relieved. The explanation is quite simple. Like all semi-Mohammedan universes, this one is extremely poetic, and since you employed highly inspired poetry, the effect was somewhat beyond your original calculations. This also suggests a means of relief from our present situation. Do you happen to recall any lines from the major poets having to do with motion or progress?"

"How would Shelley do?" asked Shea.

"Quite well, I believe. Are you ready? Very well, suit the rhythm of your recitation to my movements." He began to make the passes with his hands as Shea recited:

"My coursers are fed on the lightning,
  They drink at the whirlwind's stream,
And when the red morning is brightening
  They have strength for the swiftness I deem:
Then ascend with me, children of ocean!"

The result was somewhat unexpected. The four
horses on which the party from Carena had come
bounded straight into the air as though on springs and
before anyone could stop them, leaped at Atlantès' collection of monsters, who scattered in all directions, but
not rapidly enough to keep themselves from squashing
under the flying hooves like so many tomatoes. Roger
whooped with laughter; Chalmers looked a trifle dismayed. "I confess——" he began, and then stopped,
looking up.

Against the fading evening sky Duke Astolph on
his hippogriff was soaring in to a four-point landing.

He addressed Shea: "Did you summon me, old man?
I hope it's important; that children of ocean spell is
deuced wracking, but being English I couldn't well re-
sist. Oh, I see; a spot of trouble with our old friend
Atlantès."

The proprietor of Carena sneered unpleasantly from
outside the pentacle. "O noble and puissant lords, now
there is no help for it but that you release to me my
beloved nephew, the pearl of Islam. For know that I
am of greater power than all magicians of the Franks,
save Malagigi alone, and he lies still in durance."

Astolph cocked his head on one side. "Indeed," he
said. "Do you want to be released, Roger?"

The pearl of Islam seemed to be having difficulty
with his breathing. He looked at the ground, then at
Bradamant, then quickly away. "By Allah, nay," he
finally managed to get out.

Astolph turned to the enchanter. "Tell you what I'll
do, old thing; I'll make you a sporting proposition. I
believe Sir Harold's friend here wants his lady to receive human form. I'll take you on in a contest to see
who can do it, winner take all, including Roger."

"By Allah, 'tis some Frankish trick," said Atlantès.

"Suit yourself, old man. I can transport them all

away from you on Buttercup, you know." He scratched the hippogriff behind the ears.

The magician lifted his hands to heaven. "I am afflicted by the sons of Satan," he wailed. "Nevertheless I will even accept this offer."

Both he and Astolph began making rapid passes. The Duke suddenly vanished, and a mist condensed out of the air around the pentacles, growing and growing until the spectators could no longer see one another. The air was filled with rustlings.

Then the mist thinned and vanished. Florimel had vanished from her own pentacle and stood in that of Atlantès. The latter said: "Behold—" and stopped as Astolph reappeared with a man as tall as himself; a man with a long white beard, neatly combed, and a mane of white hair. He was dressed with formidable correctness in cutaway, pin-striped trousers and spats, with a top-hat at a rakish angle on his head and a pink carnation in his buttonhole.

"Permit me," said Astolph, "to present the Honorable Ambrose Sylvester Merlin, C.M.G., C.S.I., D.M.D., F.C.C., F.R.G.S., F.R.S., F.S.A., and two or three etceteras."

Merlin said in a deep bell-like voice: "That girl's a sham of some sort. Just a trick, and I'll fetch the right one back." He whipped a wand out of an interior pocket, traced his own pentacle and began incanting. Again the mists thickened, this time shot with little lights.

Five minutes later they cleared and there were two Florimels, identical in dress, pose and appearance.

Merlin calmly slipped his wand in his pocket and stepped to the nearest girl. "This one's the real one, mine. Are you not, my dear?" He lifted his plug hat courteously.

"Aye, good sir." She gave a little squeal of pleasure. "And I do feel that blood, not snow flows in my veins."

Merlin held out a finger. A yellow flame appeared at the tip, bright in the dusk. He held up Florimel's arm and ran the flame quickly along it. "Observe. No more reaction than any normal person." He blew the flame out. "Must be off, Astolph. That numismatic exhibition at the Phidias Club."

410

"Many thanks, old man," said Astolph. Merlin vanished.

"Spawn of the accursed!" shouted Atlantès. "Here stands the veritable Florimel."

Shea noted that Chalmers was making passes. The other Florimel, the one in Atlantès' pentacle, blinked once or twice as though just awakened, and turned into the peasant girl Shea had seen weeping at the roadside near Pau. Polacek gave a gurk. "Hey, Cassie!" he called.

The girl gave one glance, and leaped for him, crying: "Oh, my wolfie!"

"I should say that settled the matter," said Astolph. "Come along, Roger."

"Nay!" said Atlantès. "May my hair turn to scorpions if I permit this!"

"Ah, but you can hardly prevent it, you know," said the Duke imperturbably. "Your spells won't hold these people any more. Laws of magic, you know; you made an agreement, and spells to keep from fulfilling it will fail."

"By the seven imps of Satan, Sir Duke, there was no agreement that I should not have your head," said Atlantès and raising his wand, began to incant again. So did Astolph.

Shea touched Chalmers on the shoulder. "Let's get out of here," he said. "I think there's going to be fireworks."

The three psychologists and their ladies turned their backs on the disputants and through the lulling dark started toward Pau. They had not gone fifty paces when there was a crack like a cannon-shot and the landscape flashed with electric blue. One of the magicians had thrown a thunderbolt at the other.

"Hurry!" said Chalmers. They ran. Crack followed crack, merging into a frightful thunder. The earth began to quiver beneath them. A boulder came loose from the hillside and lolloped down past.

As they ran they glanced back over their shoulders. The side of the hill was hidden by a huge, boiling thundercloud, lit from beneath with flashes, and a forest fire was already spreading from its base. A piece of the mountainside came loose and slid. Through the

411

repeated thunderclaps they heard the piercing sound of Astolph's horn.

"My word," said Chalmers, slowing down. "I—ah—perceive . . . that some further steps in rejuvenation will be necessary before I can indulge in much more athletics. I should mention, Harold, the reason why Atlantès was so very anxious to detain us. Apparently he has not yet learned the secret of interuniversal apportation, however adept he may be in other respects."

"I bet he never does learn it now," said Shea, a little grimly, looking back to where the battle between the two magicians had now settled down to a mere tornado.

"It would be just as well," said Chalmers.

"Say, you two," remarked Polacek, "while you're speaking about that, what about Walter?"

"Holy smoke!" said Shea. "He's been back there in Xanadu eating honey for a week and he doesn't like it."

A grin spread slowly over the face of the Rubber Czech. "That isn't all," he remarked. "Remember how long we were in Xanadu? It was hours, though it couldn't have taken Doc more than a few minutes to find out that he'd made a mistake."

"Goodness gracious!" said Chalmers. "Then Walter has been there a month or more. I must certainly address myself to the problem."

"What I want to know," said Shea, "is how we're going to get that cop back to Ohio. But I'm not going to lose any sleep over it."

He squeezed Belphebe's hand.

AFTERWORD:
FLETCHER AND I

My late friend and collaborator Fletcher Pratt (1897–1956) was a connoisseur of heroic fantasy before that term was ever invented. He read Norse sagas in the original and extravagantly admired E. R. Eddison's *The Worm Ourobouros*. Curiously, he despised Robert E. Howard's Conan stories—next to Tolkien's *Lord of the Rings* three-decker, the most successful books in the genre—because their occasional crudities and lapses of logic exasperated him. He had no use for heroes who merely battered their way out of traps by their bulging thews, without using their brains.

(Murray) Fletcher Pratt, the son of an upstate New York farmer, was born on the Indian reservation near Buffalo. He claimed that this gave him the right to hunt and fish in New York State without a license, but he never availed himself of the privilege.

As a youth, five foot three but wiry and muscular, Pratt undertook two careers in Buffalo. One was that of librarian; the other, that of prizefighter in the flyweight (112-pound) class. He fought several times, lost a couple of teeth, and knocked one opponent cold. When the story appeared in the Buffalo papers, the head librarian told him that it simply would not do to have one of their employees knocking people arsyversy. Forced to choose between the two careers, Pratt chose the library.

Soon afterward, Pratt entered Hobart College at Geneva, New York, on Lake Seneca. When the coach learned that Pratt had been in the ring, he tapped him for an assistant in his boxing class. Word got around that this funny-looking little freshman who was showing the boys in the gym how to do rights over lefts was

413

the real thing. Hence, somewhat to his disappointment, Pratt was never hazed.

At the end of Pratt's freshman year, his father fell on hard times. Pratt had to leave college. In the early 1920's, he worked as a reporter on the Buffalo *Courier-Express* and on a Staten Island paper. Later, he settled in New York with his second wife, the artist Inga Stephens Pratt.

For several years, Pratt held a succession of fringe literary jobs, such as editing a "mug book" (a biographical encyclopedia), in which people of small importance were persuaded to pay money to have their pictures and biographies included. He also worked for one of those writers' institutes that promise to turn every would-be scribbler into a Tolstoy and that keep the money coming in by fulsome flattery of the veriest bilge submitted to them. Later, as an established author, Pratt drew on these experiences in lecturing to writers' groups on literary rackets.

In the late 1920's, Pratt got a foothold as a free-lance writer. From 1929 to 1935 he sold a number of science-fiction stories to *Amazing, Wonder,* and other science-fiction pulps of the time. He also worked for Hugo Gernsback, then publishing *Wonder Stories*. Pratt translated European science-fiction novels from the French and the German. Gernsback had a habit of not paying his authors what he had promised, but Pratt got around him. He would translate the first installment or two of a European novel and then, when the material was already in print, say:

"I'm sorry, Mr. Gernsback, but if you don't pay me what you owe, I don't see how I can complete this translation."

He had Gernsback over a barrel. He also took off more than a year to live in Paris on the insurance money that he collected after a fire gutted the Pratts' apartment. He studied at the Sorbonne and did research for his book on codes and ciphers, *Secret and Urgent*.

Pratt learned Danish among other languages, spoke French with a terrible accent, and became friends with the curator of arms and armor at the Louvre, who once let him try on the armor of King François I. In his day, the king had been deemed a large, stout man. The flyweight Pratt found all the armor too small except the shoulder pieces; François had tremendous shoulders from working out with sword and battle-ax in the tilt yard.

Back in New York, Pratt—now a self-made scholar of respectable attainments—attacked more serious writing. After an abortive history of Alexander's successors, he hit his stride with books like *The Heroic Years,* about the war of 1812, and *Ordeal by Fire,* a popular history of the American Civil War.

The Pratt menage in New York attracted a wide circle of friends, drawn by Pratt's lavish hospitality and extraordinary sense of fun. One room of the apartment was cluttered with cages full of squeaking marmosets, which Pratt successfully raised by feeding them on vitamin tablets and squirming yellow larvae.

As a history, military, and naval buff, Pratt devised a naval war game, to which his friends were invited once a month. In odd moments, he had whittled out scale models (55 feet = 1 inch) of the world's warships, using balsa wood, wires, and pins, until there were hundreds of models crowding his shelves. The game called for the players to crawl around on the floor, moving their models the distances allowed on scales marked in knots; estimating ranges in inches to the ships on which they were firing; and writing down these estimates. Then the referees chased the players off and measured the actual ranges, penalizing ships hit so many points, according to the size of the shells, and depriving them of so many knots of speed, so many guns, and so on. When a ship had lost all its points, it was taken from the floor. There were special provisions for merchant ships, shore batteries, submarines, torpedoes, and airplanes.

For several years, the war gamers met in the Pratts' apartment. When this became too crowded, with fifty or more players at once, the games moved to a hall on East Fifty-ninth Street. After World War II, interest declined.

Pratt's interests also included the reading of sagas and gourmet cookery. He wrote a cookbook, *A Man and His Meals.* He taught at the Bread Loaf Writers'

Conference, was a Baker Street Irregular, and served for seven years as president of the New York Authors' Club. In 1944, he founded a stag eating, drinking, and arguing society, the Trap Door Spiders, which still meets periodically in New York.

In 1939, my old friend and college roommate, John D. Clark, introduced me to Pratt. A naval buff of long standing myself, I was soon an enthusiastic war gamer and a regular attendant at the Pratts' evenings, along with such colleagues as Laurence Manning, Malcolm Jameson, Ted Sturgeon, George O. Smith, and L. Ron Hubbard, who had not yet manifested himself as the pontiff of Scientology.

I had been free-lancing for a year and a half, having been fired as an economy measure from an editorial job on a trade journal. I was also in the midst of getting married. With the appearance of John W. Campbell's fantasy magazine *Unknown,* Pratt conceived the idea of a series of novellas, in collaboration with me, about a hero who projects himself into the parallel worlds described in our world in myths and legends. We made our protagonist a brash, self-conceited young psychologist named Harold Shea.

First we sent Harold to the world of Scandinavian myth, in *The Roaring Trumpet* (*Unknown,* May 1940). Pratt furnished most of the background for this story, since at that time my knowledge of Norse myth was limited to popular digests and retellings. I had not yet read such splendid sources as the *Heimskringla* and the *Prose Edda.*

For the second episode, we transferred Harold to the world of Spenser's *Faerie Queene* in *The Mathematics of Magic* (August 1940). I was never so enthusiastic about the *Faerie Queene* as Pratt was, finding it tedious for long stretches. Years later, however, when I took to writing verse, I composed a poem, *The Dragon-Kings,* using the Spenserian nine-line stanza, which is a most exacting verse form. Having sweated through three such stanzas, I was awed by the feat of Edmund Spenser, whose *Faerie Queene* comprises over four thousand.

The first two novellas were followed by *The Castle*

of Iron (April 1941), which took Harold to the world of Ariosto's *Orlando Furioso.* Also in that year, Holt brought out the first two novellas as the clothbound book *The Incomplete Enchanter,* which has since been through a number of editions. While Pratt proposed the basic themes for the first two stories, those for the later ones were worked out by discussion between us.

After World War II, Pratt and I rewrote and expanded *The Castle of Iron* to full-novel length, in which form it appeared in 1950. We also wrote two more novellas of the saga, placing Harold first in the world of the Finnish *Kalevala (The Wall of Serpents)* and then in the world of Irish myth *(The Green Magician).* After magazine publication, these two stories were combined in a cloth-bound volume, *Wall of Serpents.* It was not possible to include them in the present volume, first because of considerations of space and second because of contractual complications.

For obvious reasons, I cannot assess the virtues and faults of these works. I will say only that they were certainly heroic fantasy, or swordplay-and-sorcery fiction, long before these terms were invented. While Robert E. Howard is justly hailed as the major American pioneer in this subgenre, neither Pratt nor I, when we started the Shea stories, had even read a Conan story or ever heard enough about Howard to recognize his name.

Our method of collaboration was to meet in Pratt's apartment and hammer out the plot by long discussions during which I took shorthand notes. Observing the utility of Pratt's knowledge of shorthand from his journalistic days, I soon taught myself Gregg and have found it valuable ever since. I took the notes home and wrote a rough draft. Pratt then wrote the final draft, which I edited. In a few cases—our later stories of Gavagan's Bar, for example—we reversed the procedure, Pratt doing the rough draft and I the second. This did not work out so well. In such collaborations, it is generally better for the junior member to do the rough draft, since the senior member, as a result of experience, is likely to have more skill at polishing and condensation.

A fan magazine once asserted that in the Harold

Shea stories de Camp furnished the imaginative element and Pratt the controlling logic. Actually, it was the other way around. Pratt had a livelier and more creative imagination than I, but I had a keener sense of critical logic. In any case, I learned much of what I think I know about the writer's craft in the course of these collaborations. Pratt's influence on me in this matter was second only to Campbell's.

In 1941, L. Ron Hubbard wrote one of his several hilarious fantasy novels for *Unknown: The Case of the Friendly Corpse* (August 1941). This tale had some of Hubbard's funniest passages but let the reader down badly at the end. The hero, Jules Riley, had swapped souls with an apprentice magician on another plane, who up to then has been a student at the College of the Unholy Names. Another student tells Jules (now on this other plane) that Harold Shea appeared before him, claiming to be a magician from another world. The student challenged Harold to a sporting contest: the student would turn his wand into a super-serpent, and Harold could summon up his own monster, and they would see which creature won. But ". . . the snake just grew up and then grabbed him and ate him up before I could do anything about it."

Some fans were indignant at Hubbard's so brusquely bumping off a colleague's hero. Pratt and I thought of writing a story to rescue Harold from the serpent's maw and turn the tables, but after some floundering we gave up. Another writer's *mise en scène,* we found, so severely cramps the imagination that fancy plods when it should soar. In the end, we ignored Hubbard and sent Harold on to other milieux.

During 1941–42, Pratt and I wrote two fantasy novels, *The Land of Unreason* and *The Carnelian Cube.* Pearl Harbor came just as I was finishing my part of *The Carnelian Cube.* I volunteered for the Naval Reserve, was commissioned, and spent the war navigating a desk at the Philadelphia Naval Base. I did engineering on naval aircraft along with Heinlein and Asimov.

Pratt, a strong patriot and nationalist, described himself as a political conservative—although, when one discussed actual current issues with him, one found in him a surprisingly objective, pragmatic, almost liberal attitude. Kept out of the armed forces by his physical limitations and age, he wrote a war column for the New York *Post.* This ended when his editor forced him to guess on the outcome of the battle of the Coral Sea, and he guessed wrong. He also wrote a number of books on the war, especially the part played in it by the U. S. Navy.

Then Pratt became a naval war correspondent assigned to Latin America. An old Brazilophile who spoke fluent Portuguese, Pratt visited Brazil. He had long worn a mustache and, in the early 1930's for a while, a goatee. Now he grew a straggly full beard, graying reddish in color and of Babylonian cut. He hated razors, and the Navy forbade him to use his electric shaver on shipboard in the Caribbean. This was long before the revival of beards in the 1950's and '60's. His small size, whiskers, thick, tinted glasses, and loud shirts made an ensemble not easily forgotten.

After the war, Pratt resumed living in New York, while my family and I stayed on in the suburbs of Philadelphia. We continued our collaborations with the two later Harold Shea novellas and the Gavagan's Bar stories—a series of barroom tall tales, comparable to (though conceived independently of) Arthur C. Clarke's *Tales of the White Hart.* Pratt also wrote two first-class heroic-fantasy novels of his own: *The Well of the Unicorn* and *The Blue Star.*

When he had finished *The Blue Star,* Pratt told his friends that he planned a third fantasy novel, about a modern woman who finds herself in the body of another woman of 1,800 years ago. With the approach of the Civil War centenary, however, Pratt became so busy with better-paying nonfiction that, during his last few years, he gave up fiction altogether. He had written over fifty books, including many science-fiction stories, books on Napoleon, biographies of Edwin M. Stanton and King Valdemar IV of Denmark, and a history of the U. S. Navy.

He and I had discussed possible future works of fiction, such as another Harold Shea story laid in the world of Persian myth, or a Gavagan's Bar story about a vampire with a sweet tooth who attacked only diabetics. But they were never written. For, in 1956, when he was fifty-nine and had just begun to hit the best-seller lists, Pratt suddenly fell ill of cancer of the liver and soon died.

I have not tried to carry on any of our series alone, because I think that the combination of Pratt and de Camp produced a result visibly different from either of us alone. Besides, I have always had more ideas waiting to be actualized in writing than I could find time to get down. But some of those who have not read the tales of Harold Shea's adventures may still, I trust, get some entertainment out of them.

—L. Sprague de Camp
June, 1975

420

Enchanting fantasies from